SUMMER AT WILLOW LAKE

Susan Wiggs

CHIVERS

British Library Cataloguing in Publication Data available

This Large Print edition published by AudioGO Ltd, Bath, 2011.
Published by arrangement with Harlequin Enterprises II B.V.

| U.K. | Hardcover | ISBN | 978 1 4458 6027 5 |
| U.K. | Softcover | ISBN | 978 1 4458 6028 2 |

Copyright © 2006 by Susan Wiggs

Printed and bound in Great Britain by
MPG Books Group Limited

To the real-life golden anniversary couple,

Nick and Lou Klist.

ACKNOWLEDGMENTS

Deepest appreciation to Elsa Watson,
Suzanne Selfors, Sheila Rabe and
Anjali Banerjee; also to
Kysteen Seelen, Susan Plunkett,
Rose Marie Harris, Lois Faye Dyer
and Kate Breslin
for their enormous stamina and patience
in reading early drafts.

Thanks to Dale Berg and Mike Sack for
sharing their reminiscences of Catskills camps.

Special thanks to Meg Ruley and Annelise
Robey of the Jane Rotrosen Agency, and to
my terrific editor,
Margaret O'Neill Marbury.

WELCOME TO CAMP KIOGA

Franklin Delano Roosevelt once said, 'America's greatest contribution to the world is the summer camp.' Anyone who visits Camp Kioga discovers this for himself. Camp Kioga is a place where dreams still live and breathe, where you can dive into the crystalline waters of a pristine lake, hike to a mountaintop and lift your eyes to heaven, gaze into the brightly glowing embers of a campfire at night, and imagine all that life has in store for you.

CAMP KIOGA RULES

Camp Kioga flies three flags—the official camp flag, and the flags of the state of New York and the United States—which are raised each morning at sunrise and saluted by all campers at reveille. When flags are flown on the same halyard with the flag of the United States, the latter should always be at the peak. When the flags are flown from adjacent staffs, the flag of the United States should be hoisted first and lowered last. No flag or pennant may be placed above the flag of the United States or to the right of the flag of the United States. When the flag is half masted, both flags are half masted, with the U.S. flag at the midpoint and the other flags below.

1

Prologue

Olivia Bellamy tried to decide what was worse. Being trapped at the top of a flagpole with no help in sight, or having help arrive in the form of a Hells Angel.

Her plan to raise the flags over Camp Kioga for the first time in ten years had seemed so simple. Then the cable and pulley snagged, but Olivia was undaunted. She had set up an old aluminum ladder and climbed to the top, only to discover she still couldn't reach the snag. Shinnying up the pole was no big deal, she told herself—until she accidentally kicked over the ladder.

You idiot, she thought, hugging the pole for dear life. It was a long way down, and this was not exactly the Batpole. The galvanized steel was old and corroded, and if she slid down, she'd rip the skin from her hands and inner thighs.

She had just begun to inch toward the ground when a loud snort of unmuffled exhaust sounded from the road. She was so startled that she nearly let go of the pole. Instinctively, she clung tighter and shut her eyes. Go away, she thought. I can't deal with whoever you are right now.

The blast of the engine grew louder, and she opened her eyes. The intruder turned out to be a biker clad in black leather, his face concealed by a menacing black helmet and shades. Behind the black-and-chrome motorcycle, a rooster tail of dust rose in a tall plume.

Just my luck, she thought. Here I am in the middle of nowhere, and Easy Rider comes to my rescue.

Her arms and shoulders were starting to tremble. So much for all those hours of strength training at the gym.

At the base of the flagpole, the biker stopped, dismounted and engaged the kickstand. Then he leaned back to look straight up at her.

Despite the circumstances, Olivia found herself wondering what her butt looked like from his perspective. Growing up as she had, comforting herself with food until she'd earned any number of unflattering childhood nicknames, she'd never quite gotten over feeling self-conscious about her figure.

Play it cool, she decided. 'Hey,' she said.

'Hey. What's up?' Though she couldn't see his face, Olivia thought she detected a grin in his voice. She became sure of it when he added, 'Okay, sorry. Couldn't help myself.'

Great. Just her luck. A wise guy.

To his credit, he didn't make her suffer. He picked up the ladder and leaned it against the flagpole. 'Take it slow,' he coached her. 'I'll hold this steady.'

4

Olivia was sweating now, having reached the limit of her endurance. She scooted downward inch by inch, while her denim shorts rode upward. She hoped he wouldn't notice they were giving her an enormous wedgie.

'You're almost there,' called the stranger. 'Just a little more.'

The lower she shinnied, the less he sounded like a stranger. By the time her foot touched the top rung of the ladder, she was having seriously bad premonitions about this guy. She hadn't been anywhere near this place in years, this camp where she'd found both her wildest dreams and her worst nightmares. These days, she didn't know a soul in the remote mountain wilderness...did she?

In true neurotic fashion, she couldn't stop thinking about the fact that she hadn't done anything to her hair that morning. She wasn't wearing a smidge of makeup. She couldn't even recall whether or not she'd brushed her teeth. And the denim cutoffs she was wearing were too short. The tank top, too clingy.

Climbing down the ladder, she knew with each step that what awaited her at the bottom would be, at best, awkward humiliation. In order to reach solid ground, she was forced to descend into his waiting arms, which were braced on either side of the ladder to hold it steady. He smelled of leather and something else. The wind, maybe.

5

Her muscles, which had been screaming in protest a moment ago, now threatened to go slack with exhaustion. She used the last of her strength to give his arm a push so she wasn't trapped. He let go of the ladder and held up his cyborg hands, palms out, as if to show he came in peace. They were huge, in their black gloves. Darth Vader hands. Terminator hands.

'Okay,' he said. 'You're safe now.'

She leaned back against the ladder. When she looked up at him, the ground beneath her feet didn't feel so safe. Nothing felt safe.

He was huge, his bulk enhanced by all that leather, including chaps. A biker in chaps over faded Levi's, the leather worn to softness in all the most interesting places. She eyed the ripped T-shirt visible through the half-open jacket. His battered boots appeared as though they belonged to a man who actually worked in them. Except for the chains. She could see no earthly purpose for that bit of bling, except that it was sexy. Oh, God. It was.

'Thanks,' she said, quickly stepping out from between the guy and the ladder. 'I don't know what I would have done if you hadn't come along.' In his mirrored glasses, she could see her own reflection—flushed cheeks, wind-tossed hair. She wiped her hands on her shorts. 'What, um…' She fumbled. Maybe it *wasn't* him. Maybe all this fresh air and sunshine had muddled her brain. She adopted a neutral tone and decided to play it cool.

6

'Can I help you?'

'I think it's the other way around. You left a message on my voice mail. Something about a construction project?' With that, he peeled away the sunglasses, then unstrapped the helmet and took it off.

Oh, God, Olivia thought. I wanted it to be anyone but you.

He removed the gloves, keeping his eyes on her as he tugged them off, finger by finger. He squinted. 'Do I…have we met?'

Was he kidding? she wondered. Did he really not know?

When she didn't respond, he turned away and expertly raised the flag. Immediately, the wind filled it like a sail.

Watching him, Olivia forgot to move. To breathe. To think. With one look at those heartbreaker eyes, she was hurled back in time, the years peeling away like pages from a calendar. She wasn't looking at Easy Rider. She was looking into the face of a man, but in those ice-blue eyes, she could see the boy he was so long ago.

And not just any boy. *The* boy. The one who owned all the firsts, every significant milestone of her troubled and painful adolescence—the first boy she'd ever loved. The first she'd ever kissed. The first she'd ever— The first to break her heart.

Her whole body flared to life with a fiery blush. Maybe that was why the term 'old

7

flame' had been invented. Somebody always got burned.

'Connor Davis,' she said, speaking his name aloud for the first time in nine years. 'Fancy meeting you here.' Inside, she was thinking, I want to die. Let me die right here, right now, and I'll never ask for another thing as long as I live.

'That's me,' he said unnecessarily.

As if she could forget. The promise of the boy he had been was fulfilled in the man standing before her. He would be twenty-eight now, to her twenty-seven. Lanky height had filled out with solid breadth. His cocky grin and twinkling eyes were still the same, though the GI Joe jawline had been softened by a day's growth of beard. And he still—Olivia blinked, making sure she wasn't seeing things—yes, he still wore a tiny silver hoop in one ear. She herself had done the piercing, thirteen years ago, it must have been.

'So you're...' He studied the back of his left hand, where it appeared that he had scrawled something in purple ink. 'You're Olive Bellamy?'

. 'Olivia.' She prayed for him to recognize her the way she had recognized him, as someone from the past, someone important, someone who'd had a life-changing impact on his future. God, someone who'd risked getting sent home from camp for piercing his ear.

'Yeah, sorry. Olivia.' He studied her with

8

blatant male appreciation. He clearly misinterpreted her look of outrage. 'Didn't have a piece of paper handy when I checked my messages,' he explained, indicating the purple ink with which he'd scrawled a message on his hand. Then he frowned. 'Have we met before?'

She gave a short, harsh laugh. 'You're kidding, right? This is a joke.' Had she really changed that much? Well, okay, yes. Nearly a decade had passed. She'd lost a ton of weight. Gone from nut brown to honey blond. Traded her glasses for contacts. But still...

He just stared at her. Clueless. 'Should I know you?'

She folded her arms, glared at him and summoned a phrase he'd probably remember, because it was one of the first lies they'd ever old each other. 'I'm your new best friend,' she said, and watched the color drain from his tanned, handsome face.

His gorgeous blue eyes narrowed and then widened in dawning wonder. His Adam's apple rippled as he swallowed, then quickly cleared his throat.

'Holy shit,' he said in a low murmur. His hand went up in an unconscious gesture and touched the little sliver hoop. *Lolly?*

CAMP KIOGA CODE OF CONDUCT

Everyone is expected to participate in all planned activities as defined by the camp schedule and to be in regulation dress. Counselors are responsible for ensuring that campers participate in all sessions of the planned program activities, unless excused by the camp nurse or the director.

One

'Lolly.' The tall, lanky boy hiking up the trail behind her spoke for the first time since they left base camp. 'What the hell kind of name is Lolly?'

'The kind that's stenciled on the back of my shirt,' she said, flipping a brown pigtail over one shoulder. To her dismay, she felt herself blushing. Cripes, he was just a dumb boy, and all he'd done was ask her a simple question.

Wrong, she thought, hearing a game-show buzz in her head. He was pretty much the cutest boy in Eagle Lodge, the twelve-to-fourteens. And it hadn't been a question so much as a smart remark designed to rattle her. Plus, he said *hell.* Lolly would never admit it, but she didn't like swearing. Whenever she tried saying a swearword herself, she always stammered and blushed, and everyone could instantly see how uncool she was.

'Got it,' the kid muttered, and as soon as the trail curved around a bend, he passed her with a rude muttering that was probably meant to be an 'Excuse me.' He trudged on, whistling an old Talking Heads tune without missing a note.

11

They were doing a pairs hike, the first activity of the season. It was designed to familiarize them with the camp layout, and with another camper. They had been paired up as they'd gotten off the bus, while their duffel bags and belongings were being sorted and taken to their cabins. She had wound up with the lanky boy because they had both been last to disembark. She had folded her arms across her chest and sniffed, 'I'm your new best friend.'

He'd taken one look at her and shrugged, saying with an air of false nobility, "'Barkis is willing."'

The show-off. Lolly had pretended not to be impressed to hear him quoting from *David Copperfield.* She had also pretended not to see the way some of the other boys snickered and elbowed him, ribbing him for getting stuck with Lolly Bellamy.

He wasn't the typical Kioga camper, and as someone who had been coming here since she was eight years old, she would know. This boy, a first-timer, was rough around the edges, his hair too long, his cargo shorts too low-slung. Maybe he even looked a little dangerous, with his pale blue eyes and dark hair, a combination that was both cool and disconcerting.

Through gaps in the trees, she could see people walking in pairs or foursomes, chattering away. It was only the first day of

12

camp, yet already, kids were figuring out who they were going to be friends with this year. Lolly already knew they had ruled her out, of course. They always did. If it wasn't for her cousins, she'd be up a tree, for sure.

She pushed her glasses up the bridge of her nose, and felt a dull thud of envy in her gut as she looked at the other campers, who already seemed totally at ease around one another. Even the new ones, like the lanky boy, seemed to fit in. Fresh off the camp bus, they strolled side by side, yakking away and laughing. Some of the girls wore their camp hoodies slung nonchalantly over their shoulders, their innate fashion sense evident even with the regulation clothes. Most of the boys had their Kioga bandannas tied around their foreheads, Rambo style. Everybody strutted about as though they owned the place.

And of course, that was kind of funny. None of these kids owned Kioga. But Lolly did.

Well, in a way. The summer camp belonged to her nana and granddad. Back when she was in the Fledglings, the eight-to-elevens, she used to lord her status over the other kids, but it never really worked. Most kids didn't give a hoot about that.

The tall boy found a hickory stick and used it to beat at the underbrush or to lean on as he walked. His gaze darted around watchfully, as though he expected something to jump out at him.

'So I guess your name is Ronnoc,' she said at last.

He scowled and shot a glance over his shoulder at her. 'Huh?'

'Says so on the back of your shirt.'

'It's inside out, genius.'

'It was just a joke.'

'Ha, ha.' He stabbed the hickory stick into the ground.

Their destination was the summit of Saddle Mountain, which wasn't exactly a mountain, more like a big hill. Once they finally reached the top, they'd find a fire pit with log benches arranged in a circle around it. This was the site of many camp traditions. Nana once said that in the days of the first settlers, travelers would make signal fires at high points like this one in order to communicate long-distance. It was on the tip of Lolly's tongue to share the bit of trivia with her partner, but she clamped her mouth shut.

She had already made up her mind not to like this kid. Truth be told, she had made up her mind not to like anybody this summer. Her two favorite cousins, Frankie—short for Francine—and Dare, usually came with her, and they always made Lolly feel as if she had actual friends. But this year, they were driving to California with their parents, Aunt Peg and Uncle Clyde. Lolly's own parents didn't do

14

that kind of traveling. They only did the kind you could brag about afterward. Her parents pretty much liked anything they could brag about—trips, real estate, antiques, artwork. They even bragged about Lolly, but that was a stretch. Especially now, after sixth grade, the year her marks went down and her weight went up. The year of the divorce.

Now, *there's* something to brag about, she thought.

'We're supposed to learn three things about each other,' said the boy who had no sense of humor, the boy she didn't want to befriend. 'Then when we get to the top, we have to introduce each other to the group.'

'I don't want to know three things about you,' she said airily.

'Yeah, well. Ditto.'

The getting-to-know-you fireside chat was always tedious, which was a shame, because it didn't have to be. The little kids were best at it because they didn't know which things to keep to themselves, and which to share. Lolly was a perfect example of that. A year ago, she'd blurted out, 'My parents are getting a divorce' and had dissolved into tears, and her life had been a nightmare ever since. But at least back then, her admission had been genuine. In this age group, she already knew the introductions would be totally boring or phony or both.

'I wish we could skip it,' she said. 'It's going to be a complete drag. The younger kids

15

are more interesting because at least they'll say anything.'

'What do you mean, anything?'

'Like if their uncle is being investigated by the SEC or their brother has a third nipple.'

'A what?'

Lolly probably shouldn't have brought it up, but she knew he'd bug her until she explained. 'You heard me,' she said.

'A third nipple. That's total BS. Nobody has that.'

'Huh. Bebe Blackmun once told the whole group that her brother has three.'

'Did you see it?' he challenged.

'Like I would even want to.' She shuddered. 'Ew.'

'It's bullshit.'

She sniffed, determined to appear unimpressed by his swearing. 'I bet you have an extra one.' She didn't know why she said it. She knew the chances of him having three nipples were zip.

'Yeah, right,' he said, stopping on the trail and turning. In one graceful motion, he peeled off his T-shirt right there in the woods, in front of her face, so fast she didn't have time to react.

'You want to count 'em?' he demanded.

Her face lit with a blush and she marched past him, staring straight ahead. Idiot, she thought. I am such an idiot. What was I thinking?

'Maybe *you* have three nipples,' he said with mocking laughter in his voice. 'Maybe I should count yours.'

'You're crazy.' She kept marching.

'You're the one who brought it up.'

'I was just trying to make conversation because you're totally, one hundred percent b*ooo*ring.'

'Uh-huh,' he said. 'That's me. B*ooo*ring.' He sashayed around her, mimicking her walk. He hadn't put his shirt back on but had tucked it in the back waistband of his cargo shorts. With the *First-Blood* headband and the shirt hanging down like the back half of a loincloth, he looked like a savage. Very *Lord of the Flies.*

He was a total show-off. He—

She stumbled over a tree root, and had to grab for a nearby branch to steady herself. He turned, and she could have sworn she'd seen his arm flash out to keep her from falling, but he quickly resumed walking without touching her. She stared at him, not to be rude or nosy but this time out of concern.

'What's that on your back?' she asked bluntly.

'What?' Mr. Lord of the Flies scowled unpleasantly at her.

'At first I thought you forgot to bathe, but I think you have a really huge bruise.' She pointed to the back of his rib cage.

He stopped and twisted around, his face almost comically contorted. 'I don't have any stinking bruise. Man, you're kind of creepy. Extra nipples and now phantom bruises.'

'I'm looking right at it.' In spite of her annoyance at him, she felt a small twinge of compassion. The bruise was healing. She could tell by the way the color bloomed in the middle and faded at the edges. But it must've really hurt when it happened.

His eyes narrowed and his face turned hard, and for a second, he looked menacing. 'It's nothing,' he stated. 'I fell off my bike. Big deal.' He whipped around and kept going, hurrying so that Lolly had to rush to keep up.

'Look, I didn't mean to make you mad.'

'I'm not mad at you,' he barked at her, and walked even faster.

That was quick, she thought. Her first enemy of the summer. There were sure to be many more to follow. She had a knack for bringing out dislike in people.

Even though Connor said he wasn't mad at her, he was mad about something. There was fury in his taut muscles, his sharp movements. Big deal, so he hurt himself riding a bike. Usually when you fell off a bike, though, the casualties were elbows and knees, maybe the head. Not the back, unless you went tumbling down a hill and slammed into something really hard. Unless you were lying about what really happened.

She was both intrigued by and disappointed in this boy. Disappointed

18

because she desperately wanted to dislike him and not have to think about him again, all summer long. And intrigued because he was more interesting than he had a right to be. He was kind of edgy, too, with that too-long hair, low-slung pants, high-tops repaired with duct tape. And there was something in his eyes besides the usual stupid boy stuff. Those same ice-cube eyes that had read *David Copperfield* had probably seen things a girl like Lolly couldn't even imagine.

They hiked around a hairpin bend in the path, and a loud, steady rush of water greeted them.

'Whoa,' Connor said, tilting back his head to look at the hundred-foot waterfall. It gushed from some unseen source high above, tumbling over rocks, droplets turning to mist on impact. Everywhere the sunlight shone through, rainbows glowed. 'That's awesome,' he said, his cranky mood apparently forgotten.

'Meerskill Falls,' she said, raising her voice over the roar of the falling water. 'One of the tallest in the state. Come on, you can get a good view of it from the bridge.'

Meerskill Bridge had been constructed in the 1930s by a government work crew. Dizzyingly tall, the arched concrete structure spanned the gorge, with the falls crashing wildly below. 'The locals call this Suicide Bridge because people have killed themselves jumping from it.'

'Yeah, sure.' He seemed drawn to the cascade, which misted the trail on either side, cultivating a carpet of moss and lush ferns.

'I'm serious. That's why there's a chainlink fence over the top of the bridge.' She scrambled to keep up with him. 'It was supposedly put up, like, fifty years ago, after two teenagers jumped off it.'

'How do you know they jumped?' he asked. The mist clung to his dark hair and his eyelashes, making him look even cuter.

Lolly wondered if the mist made her look cute, too. Probably not. It only fogged her glasses. 'I guess they just know,' she said. They reached the bridge deck and passed under the arch formed by the safety fence.

'Maybe they fell by accident. Maybe they were pushed. Maybe they never existed in the first place.'

'Are you always such a skeptic?' she asked.

'Only when somebody's telling me some bullshit story.'

'It's not bull. You can ask anybody.' She stuck her nose in the air and marched to the end of the bridge and around the bend without waiting to see if he followed. They hiked along in silence for a while. By now, they were seriously lagging behind the rest of the group but he didn't seem to care, and Lolly decided that she didn't, either. Today's hike wasn't a race, anyway.

She kept stealing sideways glances at him.

Maybe she would experiment with liking this guy, just a little. 'Hey, check it out.' She lowered her voice to a whisper as the path skirted a sloping meadow dotted with wildflowers and fringed by birch trees. 'Two fawns and a doe.'

'Where?' He craned his neck around the woods.

'Shh. Be really quiet.' She beckoned, leading him off the path. Deer were not exactly rare in these parts, but it was always amazing to see the fawns in their soft-looking spotted coats and their big, shy eyes. The deer were in an open glade, the little ones sticking close to their mother while she browsed on grass and leaves. Lolly and Connor stopped at the edge of the glade and watched.

Lolly motioned for Connor to sit next to her on a fallen log. She took a pair of field glasses from her fanny pack and handed them to him.

'That's awesome,' he said, peering through the glasses. 'I've never seen a deer in the wild before.'

She wondered where he was from. It wasn't like deer were rare or anything. 'A fawn eats the equivalent of its body weight every twenty-four hours.'

'How do you know that?'

'Read it in a book. I read sixty books last year.'

'Geez,' he said. 'Why?'

21

' 'Cause there wasn't time to read more,' she said with a superior sniff. 'Hard to believe people hunt deer, huh? I think they're so beautiful.' She took a drink from her canteen. The whole scene before them was like an old-fashioned painting—the new grass tender and green, the bluestars and wild columbine nodding their heads in the breeze, the deer grazing.

'I can see clear down to the lake,' Connor said. 'These are good binoculars.'

'My dad gave them to me. A guilt gift.'

He lowered the glasses. 'What's a guilt gift?'

'It's when your dad can't make it to your piano recital, and he feels guilty, so he buys you a really expensive gift.'

'Huh. There are worse things than your dad missing a piano recital.' Connor peered through the binoculars again. 'Is that an island in the middle of the lake?'

'Yep. It's called Spruce Island. That's where they'll have the fireworks on the Fourth of July. I tried swimming out to it last year but I didn't make it.'

'What happened?'

'Halfway across, I had to call for help. When they dragged me to shore, I acted like I was almost drowned so they wouldn't accuse me of doing it to get attention. They called my parents.' This, of course, was what Lolly had wanted all along. Now she wished she hadn't

22

mentioned the incident, but once she started talking, she couldn't stop. 'My parents got a divorce last year and I figured they'd both have to come and get me.' The admission hurt her throat.

'Did it work?' he asked.

'No way. The idea of doing anything as a family is finished, kaput, out of the question. They sent me to this therapist who said I have to 'redefine my concept of family and my role.' So now it's my job to be well-adjusted. My parents act like a divorce is all fine and not such a big deal in this day and age.' She hugged her knees up to her chest and watched the deer until her eyes blurred. 'But to me, it's huge. It's like being swept out to sea, but nobody will believe you're drowning.'

At first, she thought he'd stopped listening, because he didn't say anything. He stayed quiet, the way Dr. Schneider did during their therapy sessions. Then Connor said, 'If you're drowning for real, and nobody believes you, then you sure as hell better figure out how to swim.'

She snorted. 'Yeah, I'll keep that in mind.'

He didn't look at her, as if somehow he knew she needed to get herself together. He kept peering through the binoculars and whistling between his teeth. Lolly thought she recognized the tune— 'Stop Making Sense' by Talking Heads—and for some reason, she felt fragile and vulnerable, the way she had when

23

they'd dragged her from the lake last year. And worse, she was crying now. She didn't recall the precise moment she had started, and it took all her strength to force herself to quit.

'We should keep going,' she said, feeling like an idiot as she crushed her bandanna to her face. Why had she said all those things to this boy she didn't even like?

'Okay.' He handed back the field glasses and hiked to the path. If things were awkward before with this kid, her breaking down and crying ensured that being his friend was impossible now.

Desperate to change the subject, she said, 'Did you know that every single counselor on the staff is a former camper?'

'Nope.'

She was going to have to do a lot better in the gossip department if she wanted to impress this kid. 'Counselors have secret lives,' she said. 'Not everybody knows, but they have these wild parties at night. Lots of drinking and making out, stuff like that.'

'Big deal. Tell me something I don't know.'

'Well, how about the fact that the head cook, Gertie Romano, was going to compete in the Miss New York State pageant, but she got pregnant and had to drop out. And Gina Palumbo—she's in my bunkhouse—told me her dad is an actual mafia boss. And Terry

Davis, the caretaker—he's, like, this huge drunk.'

Connor whipped around to glare at her. His shirt fell to the ground with the abrupt movement. She picked it up. 'Hey, you dropped this.' There was a smear of ketchup on the front of it, and a small label sewn in the back that read, Connor Davis.

'Davis,' she said, realization prickling over her like a rash. 'Is that your last name?'

'Nosy, aren't you?' he remarked, grabbing the shirt and yanking it on over his head. 'Of course it's my last name, genius, or I wouldn't have a tag that says so on my shirt.'

Lolly forgot to breathe. Oh, cripes. *Davis.* As in Terry Davis. Oh, cripes on a crutch. 'So, is he,' she fumbled, 'is Mr. Davis, the caretaker, any relation?'

Connor strode away from her. His ears were a bright, furious red. 'Yeah, that's him. My father. The "huge drunk." '

She bolted into action, following him. 'Hey, wait,' she said. 'Hey, I'm sorry. I didn't know...didn't realize...oh, man. I never should have said that. It's just some gossip I heard.'

'Yeah, you're a real comedian.'

'I'm not. I'm horrible. I feel horrible.' She had to run to keep up. She was covered in guilt, like slimy sweat. Worse. You didn't say stuff about people's parents. She ought to know. Her parents were pretty awful, too, but

25

she'd be offended if anyone other than her said so, and that was a fact.

But how could she have known? What were the chances? Everyone said Terry Davis didn't have a family, that no one ever came to see him, so the last thing she was expecting was that he had a son. Still, she should have kept her big fat mouth shut.

Terry Davis had a son. Amazing. In all the years the quiet, melancholy man had worked at the camp, she had never known. All she knew about him was that his father and her granddad had been in the Korean War together. Granddad said they'd met while bombing something called the Han River, and that Mr. Davis had been a hero, and for that reason, he would always have a place at Camp Kioga, no matter what. Even if he was, as she'd so stupidly said, a huge drunk. He'd been a fixture around the place, living alone in one of the staff cottages at the edge of the property. Those cottages provided housing for the cooks, caretakers, groundskeepers, drivers and maintenance crews, all the invisible people who worked around the clock to keep the place looking like a pristine wilderness.

Mr. Davis was a loner. He drove an old work Jeep, and often looked tired, prone to having what she'd heard her grandfather call an 'off' day.

'I'm really, really sorry,' she said to Connor.

'Don't feel sorry for me.'

'I don't. I'm sorry I said that about your dad. There's a difference.'

Connor jerked his head, tossing a wave of dark hair out of his eyes. 'Good to know.'

'He never said he had a kid.' The minute the words were out, she realized her mistake was getting bigger and bigger, every time she opened her mouth. Her jaw was a backhoe, digging deeper with each movement. 'I mean, I never—'

'He didn't want me coming here for the summer, but my mom got married again and her husband didn't want a kid around,' Connor said. 'Said three's a crowd in a double-wide.'

Lolly thought about the bruise she'd seen. This time, she remembered to keep her mouth shut.

'A double-wide trailer doesn't have much space for three people, but I guess you wouldn't know about that,' he added. 'You probably live in a mansion somewhere.'

Two mansions, she thought. One for each parent. Which just proved you could be miserable whether you lived in the 800 block of Fifth Avenue or in a Dumpster. 'My parents have been sending me away every summer since I was eight,' she told Connor. 'Maybe it was to get me out of the way so they could fight. I never heard them fight.' Perhaps if she had, Lolly reflected, the divorce might

27

not have been such a shock.

'When my mom figured out I could come here for free on account of my dad working here,' Connor explained, 'my fate was sealed.'

In her mind, Lolly put together the facts, like a detective. If he was coming here for free, that meant he was a scholarship camper. Each year, under a program her grandparents had founded, needy children were brought to the camp for free. They were kids who had rough family lives and were 'at risk' although she wasn't quite sure what 'at risk' meant.

At camp, everybody dressed the same, lived and ate and slept the same. You weren't supposed to know if the kid beside you was a crack baby or a Saudi prince. Sometimes it was kind of obvious, though. The scholarship kids talked differently and often looked different. Sometimes their bad teeth gave them away. Or their bad attitude. Or sometimes, like with Connor, a kid had this hard, dangerous look about him that warned people he didn't need a handout. There was nothing needy about him at all, no hint that he was 'at risk.' Except the hurt in his eyes when she had called his father a drunk.

'I feel completely cruddy,' she reiterated. 'And horrible. I shouldn't have said anything.'

'You're right. You shouldn't have. Crazy-ass girl, no wonder you go to a shrink.' He stabbed his stick into the ground and sped up. It looked as though he wasn't going to say

28

another word to her. Ever.

Fine, she thought. She'd blown it, the way she always did with other kids. And he was probably going to make sure the whole world knew it. He'd probably tell everyone she was all freaked out about her parents, in therapy. He would probably say he'd seen her cry. She had made an enemy for life.

She trudged onward, feeling more sweaty and cranky with every step she took. *You're an idiot, Lolly Bellamy,* she told herself. Each year, she came to Camp Kioga with ridiculously high expectations. *This summer will be different. This summer, I'll make new friends, learn a sport, live my own life, just for one single season.*

But once things got under way, reality set in. Simply leaving the city didn't mean leaving discontent behind. It came along with her, like a shadow, expanding and contracting with the light.

She and Connor Davis were the last to reach the summit. Everyone else was gathered around the fire pit. There was no fire because it was plenty hot and sunny. The campers sat on huge old logs. Some of the logs had been there so long they had seats worn into them.

The head counselors of Eagle Lodge this year were Rourke McKnight and Gabby Spaulding, who fit the Kioga mold perfectly. They were cute and perky. Each had attended Kioga as a camper. Now in college, they

29

embodied what Nana and Granddad called the Kioga 'esprit de corps.' They knew the camp rules, CPR, several key Algonquin words and the tunes of every campfire song known to man. They understood how to talk a camper out of feeling homesick. Among the Fledglings especially, homesickness was a dreaded epidemic.

In the olden days, homesickness wasn't a problem because the cabins had been rented by families. That was how camp used to work. As soon as the school year ended, the moms and kids would move into the bungalows, and each weekend, the dads would come to join them, taking the train up from the city. That was where the term 'bungalow colony' came from. A colony was a group of bungalows set close together. Often, Nana had told her, the same families returned year after year. They became close friends with the other camp families, even though they never got to see each other except in the summer, and they looked forward to camp all year.

Nana had pictures of the olden days, and they looked like happy times, frozen in black-and-white photographs with deckled edges, preserved in the black-paged camp albums that went back to the Beginning of Time. The dads smoked pipes and drank highballs and leaned on their tennis racquets. Nearby were the moms in their kerchiefs and middy blouses, sunning themselves in bent-willow lawn chairs while the kids all played together.

Lolly wished life could really be like that. Nowadays, of course, it couldn't. Women had careers and a bunch of them didn't have husbands.

So now the bungalows housed the counselors—scrubbed, enthusiastic college kids by day, party animals by night. Last summer, Lolly and three of her cousins, Ceci, Frankie and Dare, had sneaked off after lights-out and spied on the counselors. First there was the drinking. Then the dancing. A bunch of couples started making out, all over the place—on the porches, in the lawn chairs, even right in the middle of the dance floor. Ceci, who was the eldest of the cousins, had let loose with a fluttery sigh and whispered, 'I can't wait until I'm old enough to be a counselor.'

'Yuck,' Lolly and the younger cousins had said in unison, and averted their eyes.

Now it was a year later, and Lolly seemed to understand that fluttery sigh a little better. A kind of electricity danced in the air between Rourke and Gabby. It was hard to explain to herself but easy to recognize. She could totally picture them together in the staff area, dancing and flirting and making out.

As soon as a head count verified all were present, Rourke took out a guitar (there was always a guitar) and they sang songs. Lolly was amazed by Connor's voice. Most of the boys

31

mumbled the words and sang off-key, but not Connor. He belted out 'We Are the World,' not really showing off, but singing with the matter-of-fact self-confidence of a pop star. When some of the kids stared at him, he would just shrug and keep singing.

A few of the girls gaped openly, slack-jawed. Okay, so it wasn't Lolly's imagination. He was as cute as she thought he was. Too bad he was such a jerk. Too bad she'd blown it with him.

Then it was time for the introductions, which were as boring as she'd feared. Each partner was supposed to stand up and offer three facts about the person with whom they hiked up the mountain, the idea being that strangers who shared an adventure could wind up friends.

Cripes, she thought, she and Connor hadn't bothered to learn anything about each other except that they were enemies. She didn't know where he lived except in something he called a double-wide, if he had any brothers and sisters, what his favorite flavor of ice cream was.

There were no surprises in this group. Everybody went to the most exclusive schools on the planet: Exeter, Sidwell Friends, the Dalton School, TASIS in Lugano, Switzerland. Everybody had a horse or a yacht or a house in the Hamptons.

Big fat hairy deal, she thought. If the most

interesting thing about a kid was what school he went to, then he must be a pretty boring person. It was slightly interesting that the kid named Tarik attended a Muslim school and that a girl called Stormy was homeschooled by her parents, who were circus performers, but other than that, totally yawnworthy.

Nearly all of the other factoids were equally tedious or boastful, sometimes both. One kid's father was a publicist who had A-list celebrities on speed dial. Another girl had her diving certification. People came from families that won prizes—Pulitzer, Oscar, Clio. The kids flashed these credentials as if they were scouting badges, undoubtedly making stuff up in order to top each other.

Listening to everyone, Lolly came to a conclusion—a lie worked better than the truth.

Then it was her turn. She stood up, and she and Connor glared at each other through narrowed eyes, silent warnings leaping between them. He had more than enough information to humiliate her if he wanted. That was the thing about telling somebody something private and true. It was like handing him a gun and waiting to see if he'd pull the trigger. She had no idea what he would tell the group. All she knew was that she'd given him plenty of ammo to use against her.

She went first. She took a deep breath and

started speaking even before she knew what she was going to say.

'This is Connor, and it's his first time at Camp Kioga. He...' She thought about what she knew. He was here on scholarship and his father drank. His mother had just remarried and his stepfather was mean, which was why he had to go away for the summer. Lolly knew that with a few words, she could turn the gun on him. She could probably turn him into a kid nobody would want to be friends with.

She caught his eye and knew he was thinking the same thing about her.

'He puts ketchup on everything he eats, even at breakfast,' she said. 'His favorite group is Talking Heads. And he always wins at one-on-one.' She was guessing at that last bit, based on the fact that he was so tall, and he wore Chuck Taylor high-tops. And he seemed fast and had big hands. She was guessing at everything, as a matter of fact, but he didn't contradict her.

Then it was Connor's turn. 'This is Lolly,' he said, her name curling from his lips like an insult.

Moment of truth, she thought, adjusting her glasses. He could ruin her. She'd shown too much of herself on the way up the mountain. He cleared his throat, tossed his hair out of his eyes, assumed a defiant slouch. His gaze slid over her—knowing, contemptuous—and he cleared his throat.

The other campers, who had been restless through most of the exercise, settled down. There was no denying that the kid had presence, commanding attention like a scary teacher, or an actor in a play.

I hate camp, she thought with a fierce passion that made her face burn. *I hate it, and I hate this boy, and he's about to destroy me.*

Connor cleared his throat again, his gaze sweeping the group of kids.

'She likes to read books, she's really good at playing piano and she wants to get better at swimming.'

They sat back down and didn't look at each other again—except once. And when their eyes met, she was surprised to see that they were both almost smiling.

All right, she conceded, so he hadn't decided to make her a human sacrifice this time, or use her for target practice. She was torn between liking this kid and resenting him. One thing Lolly was sure of. She *did* hate summer camp, and she didn't even care if it belonged to her grandparents. She was never coming back here again for as long as she lived. Ever.

INVITATION

THE HONOR OF YOUR
PRESENCE IS REQUESTED
BY JANE AND CHARLES
BELLAMY
ON THE OCCASION OF OUR
50TH WEDDING
ANNIVERSARY.

YOU'VE SHARED IN OUR
LIVES WITH YOUR
FRIENDSHIP AND LOVE.
NOW WE INVITE YOU TO
JOIN US IN CELEBRATING
OUR GOLDEN
ANNIVERSARY.

SATURDAY, THE 26TH OF
AUGUST, 2006.
CAMP KIOGA, RR #47,
AVALON,
ULSTER COUNTY, NEW
YORK.

RUSTIC ACCOMMODATIONS
PROVIDED.

Two

Olivia Bellamy set down the engraved invitation and smiled across the table at her grandmother. 'What a lovely idea,' she said. 'Congratulations to you and Granddad.'

Nana slowly rotated the tiered array of tiny sandwiches and cakes. Once a month no matter what else was going on in their lives, grandmother and granddaughter met for tea at Astor Court in the Saint Regis Hotel in midtown. They had been doing it for years, ever since Olivia was a pudgy, sullen twelve-year-old in need of attention. Even now, there was something soothing about stepping into the Beaux Arts luxury of elegant furnishings, potted palms and the discreet murmur of harp music.

Nana settled on a cucumber slice garnished with a floret of salmon mousse. 'Thank you. The anniversary is three months away, but I'm already getting excited.'

'Why Camp Kioga?' Olivia asked, fiddling with the tea strainer. She hadn't been there since her last summer before college. By choice, she had put all the drama and angst behind her.

'Camp Kioga is a special place to me and Charles.' Next, Nana sampled a tiny finger sandwich spread with truffle butter. 'It's the place where we first met, and we were married there, under the gazebo, on Spruce Island in the middle of Willow Lake.'

'You're kidding. I never knew that. Why didn't I know that?'

'Trust me, what you don't know about this family could fill volumes. Charles and I were a regular Romeo and Juliet.'

'You never told me this story. Nana, what's up?'

'Nothing's up. Most young people don't give a fig about how their grandparents met and married. Nor should they.'

'I'm giving a fig right now,' Olivia said. 'Spill.'

'It was all so long ago, and seems so trivial now. You see, my parents—the Gordons—and the Bellamys came from two different worlds. I grew up in Avalon, never even saw the city until after I was married. Your granddad's parents even threatened to boycott the wedding. They were determined that their only son would marry well. In those days, that meant somebody with social status. Not some Catskills girl from a mountain camp.'

Olivia was startled by the flicker of hurt she recognized in her grandmother's eyes. Some wounds, it seemed, never quite healed. 'I'm sorry,' she said.

Nana made a visible effort to shake off her mood. 'There was a lot of class consciousness back then.'

'Still is,' Olivia said softly.

Nana's eyebrows shot up, and Olivia knew she'd better change the subject, or she'd be trapped into explaining what she meant by that. She looked expectantly at the teapot. 'Is it ready?'

They always split a large pot of Lady Grey, which carried a whisper of lavender along with the bergamot. Olivia's grandmother nodded and poured. 'Anyway,' Nana said, 'you have more important things than my ancient history to think about.' Behind her chic black-and-pink glasses, her eyes sparkled and for a moment she looked decades younger. 'It's a grand story, though. I'm sure you'll hear it this summer. We hope everyone will come for a nice long stay. Charles and I are going to renew our vows at the gazebo, in the exact spot where we first spoke them. We're going to reenact the wedding as much as we're able.'

'Oh, Nana. That's a...wonderful notion.' Deep down, Olivia was cringing. She was sure the idyllic picture in her grandmother's mind was a far cry from the reality. The camp had ceased operating nine years before and had lain fallow ever since, with minimal maintenance performed by a skeleton crew that mowed the grounds and made sure the buildings were still standing. Some of the Bellamy cousins and other relatives used the place for reunions or vacations, but Olivia suspected the camp had gone to ruin. Her grandparents were sure to be disappointed in the setting for their golden anniversary.

'You know,' Olivia said, determined to be diplomatic, 'some of your friends are getting on in years. As I recall, the camp is not wheelchair accessible. People would be more likely to attend if you had the affair at the Waldorf-Astoria or maybe right here at the Saint Regis.'

Jane sipped her tea. 'Charles and I discussed it, and decided to do this for us. Much as we love all our friends and family, our golden anniversary is going to be the affair we want. That's what our wedding was, and that's what we'll do fifty years later. We've chosen Camp Kioga. It's a way to celebrate what we've been in the past and what we hope to be for the rest of our lives—a happy couple.' Her cup rattled, just slightly, as she set it down in its saucer. 'It will be our farewell to the camp.'

'What do you mean by that?'

'The golden anniversary celebration will be our last event at Camp Kioga. Afterward, we'll need to decide what to do about the property.'

Olivia frowned. 'Nana? Did I just hear that right?'

'You did. It's time. We've got to come up with a plan for the property. It's a hundred acres of prime real estate, and it has been privately owned by my family since 1932. Our

40

hope is that we can keep it in the family for our children.' She looked pointedly at Olivia. 'Or our grandchildren. Nothing's sure in this life, but we hope the property won't be sold to a developer who will put up roads and parking lots and rows of those dreadful tract mansions.'

Olivia didn't know why the prospect of her grandparents letting go of the property made her feel wistful. She didn't even like the place. She liked the *idea* of the camp. Nana's father had received the property during the Great Depression as payment for a debt, and had built the compound himself, naming it Kioga, which he thought was an Algonquin word for 'tranquillity,' but which he later learned was meaningless. After the camp closed in 1997, none of the Bellamy offspring was inclined to take it on.

Her grandmother helped herself to a cornet filled with chocolate ganache. 'We'll discuss it after the anniversary celebration. Best to get everything settled so no one will have to make a decision about that after we're gone.'

'I hate it when you talk like that. You're sixty-eight years old, and you just did a senior triathlon—'

'Which I never would have finished if you hadn't trained with me.' Jane patted her hand, then looked pensive. 'So many important moments of my life took place there. The camp floated my family through the Great Depression, just barely. After Charles and I married and took over, the place became a part of who we are.'

So typical of Nana, Olivia reflected. She always looked for ways to hold on to things, even when she would be better off letting go.

'That's all in the future.' Nana's manner turned brisk as she took out some pages she'd obviously printed off from Olivia's Web site. 'We have business to discuss. I want you to prepare the property for our gala celebration.'

Olivia let out a short laugh. 'I can't do that, Nana.'

'Nonsense. It says right here you provide expert research, design and services to stage and enhance real estate for optimum market presence.'

'All that means is that I'm a house fluffer,' Olivia said. Some of the designers in her field objected to the expression, which definitely lacked a certain gravitas. They preferred house stager or property enhancer. Fluffer sounded…well, fluffy.

The expression was fairly descriptive of what the job entailed. In the service of people seeking to display their property at its best, Olivia was a master of illusion. An artist of deception. Making a property look irresistible was usually a simple, low-cost process, incorporating elements the seller already owned, but combining them in different ways.

42

She loved her job and did it well, and her reputation was growing accordingly. In some parts of Manhattan, agents would not even consider listing a property until it had been fluffed by Olivia Bellamy of Transformations. The job was not without its challenges, though. Since she'd launched her own firm, Olivia had learned that there was a lot more to property staging than weeding the flower beds, painting everything white and turning on the bread-making machine.

Still, a project the size of Kioga was not in the realm of her expertise.

'You're talking about a hundred acres of wilderness, a hundred fifty miles from here. I wouldn't know where to begin.'

'I would.' Jane pushed an old-fashioned, leather-bound photo album across the table to her. 'Everyone has a notion of summer camp in their mind, whether or not they even went to camp. All you have to do is create that illusion once again. Here are some pictures taken through the years to get you started.'

The photos were, for the most part, classic views of rustic cabins clustered on the shores of a lake in a pristine forest. Olivia had to admit that there was something both peaceful and evocative about the place. Nana was right about the illusion—or maybe it was a *de*lusion. Olivia had had a terrible time at summer camp. Yet somewhere in the back of her mind, there lived an idealized summer place, free of taunting children, sunburns and mosquitoes.

Her imagination kicked in, as it always did when she viewed a property. Despite her reluctance, she almost immediately started seeing ways to dress it up.

Stop it, she told herself.

'I don't exactly have the best memories of my summers there,' she reminded her grandmother.

'I know, dear. But this summer could be your opportunity to exorcize those demons. Create new memories.'

Interesting. Olivia hadn't realized her grandmother had known about her suffering. *Why didn't you stop it?* she wanted to ask.

'This project could take the entire summer. I'm not sure I want to be away that long.'

Nana lifted an eyebrow, high over the rim of her glasses. 'Why?'

Olivia couldn't keep it in any longer. Her excitement spilled out, along with her next words. 'Because I think I have a reason to stay.'

'That reason being a Brad Pitt look-alike with a Harvard law degree?'

Deep breath, Olivia, she cautioned herself. *You've been here before, and you've been disappointed. Take it easy.* She couldn't, of course. She nearly came out of her seat as she said, 'I think Rand Whitney is going to ask me to marry him.'

Nana took off her glasses and set them on the table. 'Oh, my dear, darling Olivia.' She used her napkin to dab her eyes.

Olivia was glad she had decided to tell Nana. There were some in her family who would react with more skepticism. Some—her mother being one of these—would be quick to remind her that at the ripe old age of twenty-seven, Olivia already had two failed engagements under her belt.

As if she could ever forget.

She pushed aside the thought and added, 'He's selling his apartment downtown. It's my latest project, in fact. I need to check on the finishing touches this afternoon because it's going on the market tomorrow. When he gets home from the airport, I'll be there, waiting for him. He's been in L.A. all week at the West Coast office of his firm. He said when he gets back, he's going to ask me.'

'To marry him.'

'I assume so.' Olivia felt the slightest flicker of unease. He hadn't actually said *that*.

'So selling his place is a good thing.'

Olivia felt herself smiling all over. 'He's looking at properties on Long Island.'

'Oh, my. The man is ready to settle down.'

Olivia's grin widened. 'So you'll understand...I need to think about your offer.'

'Certainly, dear.' She signaled for the check with a familiar, regal gesture that never failed to bring a white-gloved waiter scurrying.

'I hope it all turns out perfectly for you.'

*   *   *

As she hurried up the stairs to Rand's apartment near Gramercy Park, Olivia felt like the luckiest girl in the world. Here she was, enjoying the rare privilege of setting the scene for her own engagement, right down to the last detail. When Randall Whitney asked her to marry him, he would do so in a place created by her own imagination and hard work. So often in these situations, it was the job of the gentleman to create the proper ambience, and so often, he failed.

Not this time, Olivia thought, enjoying a delicious tingle of excitement. This time, everything would be just right.

Unlike the other times. With Pierce, the engagement had been doomed from the start by something Olivia refused to acknowledge until she discovered him taking a shower with another girl. With Richard, the moment of humiliation had come when she'd caught him using her ATM card to steal from her. Two strikes had left her doubting her own judgment...until Rand. This time, she wouldn't get it wrong.

She opened the front door, turned and pictured the way the apartment would look through Rand's eyes. Perfect, that's how, she thought. The place was the epitome of contemporary luxury, clean but not fussed over (even though she had fussed over every little thing for days), tasteful but not decorated (even though she had planned it obsessively).

In the taxi ride from midtown, Olivia had gone over and over the scenario in her mind until she was nearly giddy with anticipation. In less than an hour, Rand would come through the door and step into this ideal setting. He probably wouldn't go down on one knee; that wasn't his style. Instead, he'd wear that raffish, have-I-got-a-deal-for-you grin as he reached into his jacket for the gleaming black box with the emerald-shaped logo of Harry Winston. Rand was a Whitney, after all. There were perks.

Forcing herself to move with attractive dignity, she paused at the sideboard and checked the angle of the champagne bottle in the ice bucket. The label didn't need to be turned all the way out. Any practiced eye could pick out the mark of Dom Perignon, just from the silhouette.

She spared only a glance—half a glance—into the mirror above the sideboard, which was actually a tansu chest she'd rented from a furniture warehouse. Mirrors were important in her line of work, not for studying one's reflection, but for creating light and dimension and ambience in a room, and for checking—oh so briefly—one's teeth for lipstick. Anything more than that was a waste of time.

Then she saw it—a flicker of movement in the reflection. Even as a scream erupted from her, she grabbed the Dom Perignon by the neck of the bottle and swung around, ready to do battle.

'I always did want to split a bottle of bubbly with you, darling,' said Freddy Delgado, 'but maybe you should let me do the honors.'

Her best friend, incongruously good-looking even in a borrowed apron and holding a feather duster, strode across the room and took the bottle from her.

She snatched it back and shoved it into the ice bucket. 'What are you doing here?'

'Just finishing up. I got a key from your office and came right over.'

Her 'office' was a corner of the sitting room in her apartment, which was even farther downtown. Freddy had his own keys to her place, but this was the first time he'd abused the privilege. He removed the apron. Underneath, he was wearing cargo pants, Wolverine workboots and a tight *Spamalot* T-shirt. His stylishly cut hair was tipped with white-blond highlights. Freddy was a theater-set designer and aspiring actor. He was also single, well-spoken, and he dressed with exquisite taste. All reasons to suppose he was gay. But he wasn't. Just lonely.

48

'I get it. You've lost your job again.' She grabbed a cloth from his back pocket and dried the water spots from the spilled ice.

'How did you guess?'

'You're working for me. You only work for me when there's no better gig around.' Scanning the apartment, she couldn't help but notice he'd done a stellar job putting the finishing details on her design work. He always did. She wondered if their friendship would change after she got married. Rand had never liked Freddy, and the feeling was mutual. She hated it that loyalty to one felt like betrayal to the other.

'The funding fell through for the show I was working on. I hate when that happens.' Although he was a talented set designer, Freddy tended to get hired by shows with thin-to-nonexistent financing, and he often found himself abruptly out of a job. Fortunately for Olivia, he was a world-class builder, painter and all-around creative talent. 'By the way,' he said, charming her with a smile. 'You really outdid yourself with this place. It looks like a million bucks.'

'One point two million, to be exact.'

He gave a low whistle. 'Ambitious. Oops, cobweb.' He went to the built-in media shelves and fluffed at a high corner with his feather duster. 'And oops again,' he added. 'I almost missed this.'

'Missed what?'

'The DVD collection.'

The slender cases and boxed sets were lined up neatly on the shelf. 'What about it?' she asked.

'You've got to be kidding. You'll never sell this place with *Moulin Rouge* in full view.'

'Hey, I liked that movie. Lots of people liked that movie.'

Freddy was a movie buff. A major, annoying-to-the-point-of-snobbery movie-trivia champ. If it had been put on celluloid, Freddy had seen it and probably memorized it, too. He made short work of the DVD shelf, tucking *Moulin Rouge* into a drawer, along with *Phantom of the Opera* and *Ready To Wear.* 'They're turnoffs,' he said. 'Nobody wants to make a deal with a guy who watches dreck like that.' He squatted down and peered into a cupboard where the rest of the movies were stored. 'Aha. This is much better,' he said.

'*Night Nurses From Vegas?*' Olivia asked. '*Flight of the Penis?* No way. You're not putting porn out where people can see it.'

'Spine out,' Freddy insisted. 'It's subtle, but it says the seller is just a regular guy who doesn't put on airs. What are you doing dating a guy who watches porn, anyway?'

The discs had been party favors from a bachelor party, but she didn't feel like explaining that to Freddy. She smiled mysteriously and said, 'Who says Rand is the one watching porn?'

'Give me a break.'

'I am,' she said, 'whether I like it or not. Next time you decide to get back on the payroll, clear it with me.'

'You would have said yes.' He jammed the handle of the feather duster into his back pocket. 'You always say yes. That's another reason I'm here.'

'I don't get it.'

His customary sunny smile disappeared. He fixed his sincere, brown-eyed gaze on Olivia and sank to one knee before her. Reaching into his apron pocket, he drew out a small black box. 'Olivia. I have something to ask you.'

'Oh, please. Is this a joke?' She laughed, but there was an intensity in his gaze that unsettled her.

'I'm deadly serious.'

'Then get up. I can't take you seriously at all when you're on the floor like that.'

'Fine. Whatever you like.' With a long-suffering sigh, he stood up and opened the jewel box. Inside lay a pair of silver earrings. From one dangled the letter N and from the other, O. 'A friendly reminder to just say no.'

'Come on, Freddy.' She gave him a playful shove. 'You've had a problem with Rand from day one. I wish you'd get over that.'

'I'm begging you, Livvy. Don't marry him.' He swept her dramatically into his arms. 'Come away with me instead.'

51

'You're unemployed.' She pushed away from him.

'Not so. I have the best employer in the city—you. And he's late, isn't he? The scoundrel. What sort of man shows up late to pop the question?'

'A man who's stuck in rush-hour traffic from the airport.' Olivia went to the window and looked down—way down—at the avenue, so crammed with taxis that it resembled a river of yellow sludge. 'And nobody says scoundrel anymore. Don't write him off just yet, Freddy.'

'Sorry, you're right. Bad, Freddy. Bad.' He made a self-flagellating motion. 'It's just that I don't want you getting hurt.'

Again. He didn't say so aloud, but the word hovered in the brief silence between them.

'I'm fine,' Olivia said. 'Rand is nothing like—' She struggled to quell the emotional flurry in her gut. 'No. I won't say it. I won't mention them in the same breath.'

She physically shook herself. Don't go there. The trouble was, there was here. She couldn't escape her own life. The fact that she had been engaged and dumped twice before was as much a part of her as her gray eyes, her size-seven feet. In her circle of friends, her ill luck with men was something people joked about, like in the old days, when they used to joke about Olivia's weight. And just like in the

52

old days, she laughed right along with them, bleeding inside.

'Smart girl,' Freddy said. 'Rand Whitney is his own brand of disaster, unlike any other.'

'Oh, now you're being melodramatic.'

'He's all wrong for you, sweetheart.'

'You know what?' she said. 'I don't need this. You're fired.'

'You can't fire me. You didn't hire me in the first place.'

She tapped her foot. 'In case you haven't noticed, I'm trying to get you to leave.'

'In case you haven't noticed, I'm trying to get you to dump Rand.'

They glared at each other, and the strain on their friendship thrummed between them. They'd met as seniors at Columbia, and had been best friends ever since. They'd even gotten matching tattoos one night before graduation, sipping liquid courage from a bottle of Southern Comfort while Jorge, the tattoo artist, created a butterfly in the small of each of their backs, a blue one for Freddy and a pink one for Olivia. Freddy had never known the old, fat, miserable Olivia. He believed she had always been fabulous. It was one of her favorite things about him.

Muttering warnings and dire predictions under his breath, he handed over his apron and duster and left. Olivia stowed the cleaning supplies, took out her cell phone and checked her messages. The least Rand could do was let her know if he was going to be late. Of course, if he was on a plane, he couldn't very well do that, could he?

She could always call the airline, check his flight status, but she didn't know his airline or flight number. What kind of girlfriend doesn't know her boyfriend's flight number? A busy one, she thought. One who's used to having a boyfriend who travels half the time. He'd be here any minute, she told herself. She slipped a hand into her pocket and fingered the silly earrings Freddy had given her. What did Freddy know? This was right. She was ready to settle down with Rand, to make a life, have babies. The urge was so palpable that her stomach clenched.

Turning in a slow circle to survey the apartment, she felt a surge of pride and satisfaction. It was remarkable, she mused, the way minor details could matter so much, the way a shade of color or angle of light could set a mood. These things had a huge impact on buyers. A property that had been skillfully staged nearly always fetched a higher price.

Many people scratched their heads, claiming they didn't know why there should be a pair of flip-flops haphazardly parked by the shower, or why a well-thumbed paperback copy of *A Man In Full* should be open and placed facedown on a nightstand. Olivia did, though. It had nothing to do with aesthetics and everything to do with human nature.

54

People liked to think of themselves as living a certain way, being surrounded by certain things. Creature comforts, signs of sophistication, evidence of success and, probably most important and least tangible, that sense of home, of safety and belonging. And even though what she did was all smoke and mirrors, the feelings her best work produced were real.

In her business, the key question was, When I walk into this place, do I feel like taking off my shoes, pouring a glass of sherry at the sideboard, then settling into a cushy chair with a good book and sighing, 'I'm home'?

Forty-five minutes later, she was trying out the cushy chair and struggling to stave off a yawn. She tried Rand's cell phone and his voice mail picked up on the first ring, indicating that his was still turned off. He was probably still in the air.

She waited another thirty-one minutes before heading into the kitchen. This was also beautifully arranged, right down to the retro apple design on the tea towels from a vintage-linens shop she frequented. One of the keys to staging was to find authentic things that had lost that artificial sheen of newness. The tea towels, faded but not shabby, perfectly fit the bill.

Olivia headed for the pantry, stocked with imported pasta from Dean & DeLuca, cold-pressed olive oil, pomegranate juice and dolphin-safe tuna. The stuff Rand usually ate, like Lucky Charms and canned ravioli, now lay hidden in covered wicker baskets that looked as though they wanted to go on a picnic.

She pulled out a basket and grabbed a bag of Cheetos. One of the many nutritionists she'd been sent to as a chubby teenager had counseled her about mood eating.

Screw that, she thought, ripping into the bag of Cheetos, which opened with a cheese-flavored sigh. Screw everything.

For good measure, she grabbed an Alsatian beer—another contrivance; he usually drank Bud—from the stainless-steel Sub-Zero fridge. She took a long, defiant swig and belched aloud.

She was about ten minutes into the Cheetos-and-beer-fest when she heard the front door open and close.

'Hey?' called a voice from the entryway.

Uh-oh. She looked at the orange dust clinging to her fingertips. It was probably crusted around her mouth, too.

'I'm back,' Rand called unnecessarily. Then: 'Wow. Hey, this place looks awesome.'

Olivia threw the Cheetos bag and the beer bottle in the trash and rushed to the sink to wash her hands. 'In the kitchen,' she answered, her voice a tad shrill. 'I'll be right out.'

She was bent over the sink, her hair falling

56

to one side as she rinsed her mouth, when he walked in.

'Olivia, you're a freaking genius,' he said, opening his arms.

She hastily wiped her mouth with a tea towel. 'I am, aren't I,' she said and walked into his arms.

He held her for a moment, then kissed her forehead. 'You need to bill my real-estate agent for everything you've done here.'

Olivia froze. Her heart knew, even before her mind caught on. The awareness prickled up her spine and over her scalp. There was something in the way a man held a woman when he was about to let her go. The knowledge was in his frame and in his muscles—a tangible stiff reluctance. The air of discomfiture hovering around him was unmistakable.

She stepped back, stared up at his handsome face. 'Oh, my God,' she said. 'You're breaking up with me.'

'What?' Her blunt observation clearly took him by surprise. 'Hey, listen, babe. I have no idea what you're talking about.'

The protest only underscored her conviction. She was right, and they both knew it. Many women with more powerful denial mechanisms than Olivia were able to shut out the warning sign. Not Olivia, not with her sensitive radar, not after two previous failures had left her bleeding. She was like one of

57

those dogs trained to an electric fence. She only had to be popped twice, and then she got it.

The Cheetos and beer formed a cold, unpleasant knot in her stomach. *It isn't going to happen again,* she thought. *Not even if I have to do it first.* 'I completely misread you,' she said. 'God, what an idiot.' She took another step away from him.

'Slow down,' he said, and the hand he laid on her arm was gentle and made her want to cry.

'Do it fast,' she snapped at him. 'Like ripping off a Band-Aid. Get it over with quick.'

'You're jumping to the wrong conclusion.'

'Am I?' She folded her arms across her middle. Don't cry, she told herself, blinking away the tears that boiled behind her contact lenses. Save the crying for later. 'All right. How about telling me exactly what you intend to do after selling this apartment?'

His gaze flirted ever so briefly with the light fixture on the ceiling, the one she'd replaced at two o'clock this afternoon. That was another symptom of man-on-the-run. He didn't want to meet her eyes. 'Something came up while I was in L.A.,' he told her, and despite his obvious discomfort with her, his face lit with enthusiasm. 'They want me there, Liv.'

She held her breath. He was supposed to

say, I told them I couldn't make a decision until I talked to you. She already knew, though. With a dry laugh of disbelief, she said, 'You told them yes, didn't you?'

He didn't deny it. 'The firm's going to create a new position for me.'

'What, asshole-in-residence?'

'Olivia, I know we talked about a future together. I'm not ruling that out. You could come with me.'

'And do what?'

'It's L.A., Liv. You can do anything you want.'

Marry you? Have your babies? She knew that wasn't what he meant.

'My whole life, my family, my home, my business, everything is here in New York. I put the last five years of myself into Transformations,' she said. 'I built it. I'm not going to just walk away.'

'L.A. needs a company that does what you do,' he claimed. 'The market's just as hot there as it is here. Hotter.'

She thought about starting over from scratch, all over again. Networking, cultivating contacts, doing public relations, getting out the word of mouth. The idea exhausted her. She had finally whittled her work hours down to a manageable number, but it had taken years to get there. Starting over in L.A. would be even harder. There, her name and connections wouldn't open any doors for her

59

as they had in Manhattan. This can't be happening, she thought. Not again.

'Say you love me,' she challenged him. 'Say you can't live without me. And mean it.'

'When did you turn into such a drama queen?'

'You know what?' she said, shaking back her hair and squaring her shoulders, 'if I loved you enough, I would do it. I wouldn't care. I'd be packing my things right now, and gladly.'

'What do you mean, love me enough?' he demanded.

'To follow you anywhere. But I don't. And that's a very liberating notion, Rand.'

'I don't get you.' He ran a hand through his hair. 'It's a simple situation. You can move to L.A. with me or not. Your choice.'

My choice, thought Olivia. Surprisingly enough, she realized she did have a choice. 'All right, then,' she said, somehow getting the words past a sudden, breath-stealing agony. 'Not.'

And with that, she headed for the door. She'd done well this time—this third time. But if she lingered any longer, her control might waver. She passed through the foyer, noting the artful placement of the red plum blossom plant, which added an auspicious *je ne sais quoi* to the entryway. It was hard to miss the irony of this beautifully composed, staged setting. She considered kicking the damn thing over, but that would be so...so un-

60

Bellamy-like.

She took the stairs to avoid waiting for the elevator. She had tried that the first time, with Pierce. She still remembered standing in the lobby, willing him to come bursting out the door, shouting, 'Wait! I was wrong! What was I thinking?'

It never worked that way except for people like Kate Hudson or Reese Witherspoon. People like Olivia Bellamy took the stairs.

She didn't even remember the taxi ride home. She blindly overpaid the cabby and, shell-shocked, climbed the stairs to her brownstone.

'Oh, this is not good,' her neighbor, Earl, said, not bothering with hello as he stepped out into the foyer between their first-floor apartments. 'You're home way too soon.'

A silver-haired older man who had come up through school with Olivia's father, Anthony George Earl the Third owned the brownstone. Since his second wife had left him, he claimed Olivia was the only woman he wanted in his life. In a flurry of midlife ambition, he was taking cooking lessons. At the moment, the rich scent of coq au vin wafted from his kitchen, but it only made Olivia feel queasy. She wished she hadn't told him she thought Rand was going to pop the question today.

Although Earl was divorced and lived alone, he turned and called to someone in his

61

apartment. 'Our girl's back. And it's not good.'

Our girl. He only referred to her like that to one person—his best friend. She scowled at Earl. 'You told him?' Without waiting for a reply, she pushed past Earl and stepped into his apartment. 'Daddy?'

Philip Bellamy rose from a wing chair and opened his arms to Olivia. 'The rat bastard.' He pulled her into a hug. Her father was her rock, and probably the sole reason she had survived her turbulent adolescence. She leaned against his chest, breathing in the comforting scent of his aftershave. But only for a moment. If she leaned on him too hard, she'd lose the ability to stand on her own.

'Ah, Lolly,' he said, using the old nickname. 'I'm sorry.'

There was something phony in her father's tone; didn't he know she could hear it? Pulling back, she studied his face. He looked like Cary Grant, everyone had always said so because of the cleft in his chin and those killer eyes. He was—had always been—a tall, elegant man, the sort you saw at museum fund-raisers and at weekend house parties in the Hamptons.

'What's going on?' she asked him.

'Does something need to be going on in order for me to visit my only child and my best friend?'

'You never come downtown unannounced.' Olivia glared at Earl again. 'I can't believe you

62

told him.' She also couldn't believe both Earl and her father knew it would go badly, that she would come home upset and in need of comforting. She supposed that, this being the third time, they had learned to expect false alarms from her. 'I need to check on Barkis,' she said, fumbling for her keys and stepping out into the hallway.

She let herself in, and despite the blow she'd taken, Barkis was Barkis. He came bursting through his little dog door and sailed into her arms. Olivia's parents thought the dog door was a security breach, but she deemed it necessary, given her crazy work schedule. She didn't worry about break-ins anyway. Earl was a playwright who worked at home and had the watchdog instincts Barkis seemed to lack.

What the little dog had in abundance was exuberance. Just the sight of her caused him to do a dance of joy. Olivia often wished she was as fabulous as her dog thought she was. She set him down to pet him, which sent him into paroxysms of ecstasy.

Just being home lifted her spirits a little. Her apartment wasn't all that special, but at least it was hers, filled with a profusion of color and light and texture, created in layers over the three years she'd lived here. This was as un–New York as an apartment could get, according to her mother, and that was not a compliment. It was far too warm, even

63

dangerously cozy, painted in deep glowing autumn colors and filled with overstuffed furniture that owed more to comfort than to fashion.

'You're such a fine designer,' her mother often said. 'What happened here?'

Plants in colorful pots bloomed on every windowsill—not the spare, sleek-tongued tropicals that indicated taste and sophistication, but Boston ferns and African violets, primroses and geraniums. The back garden surrounding the tiny flagstone-paved patio was no different, its candy-colored blooms brightening the brick privacy wall on all three sides. Sometimes she sat out here and pretended the rush of traffic was the sound of a river, that she lived in a place with room for her piano and all her favorite things, in a setting of green trees and open space. As her relationship with Rand progressed, children entered the picture, tumbling into her fantasy in laughing profusion. Three or four of them, at least. So much for that, she thought. Right dream, wrong guy.

Her father and Earl barged in and went to the not-very-well-stocked liquor cabinet. 'What'll it be?' asked Earl.

'Campari and soda,' her father said. 'Rocks.'

'I was talking to Olivia.'

'She'll have the same.' Her father lifted one eyebrow, looking young and mischievous, and Olivia was grateful for once that he was not a sentimental man. If he offered sympathy right now, she might just melt. She nodded, forcing a wan smile, then looked around the apartment. If things had gone the way she'd anticipated today, this would be a much different moment. She'd be looking at her place through new eyes and feeling bittersweet, because she would soon be moving on with her life, planning a future with Rand Whitney. Instead, she saw the place where she would probably live forever, turning into an odd spinster.

Olivia and her father sat down at the bistro table by the window overlooking the garden and sipped their aperitifs. Earl managed to rustle up a tray of pita triangles and hummus.

Olivia had no appetite. She felt like a survivor of some disaster, shocky and tender, assessing her injuries. 'I'm an idiot,' she said, the ice clinking in her glass as she set it on the wrought-iron table.

'You're a sweetheart. What's-his-name is a world-class heel,' her father said.

She shut her eyes. 'God, why do I do this to myself?'

'Because you're a...' Always careful with words, her father paused to find the right ones.

'Three-time loser,' Olivia suggested.

'I was going to say hopeless romantic.' He

smiled at her fondly.

She knocked back the rest of her drink. 'I guess you're half-right. I'm hopeless.'

'Oh, now it starts,' Earl said. 'Let me take out my violin.'

'Come on. Don't I get to wallow for at least one night?'

'Not over him,' her father said.

'He's not worth it,' said Earl. 'No more than Pierce or Richard was worth it.' He spoke the names of her previous two failures with exaggerated disdain.

'Here's the thing about broken hearts,' Philip said. 'You can always survive them. Always. No matter how deep the hurt, the capacity to heal and move on is even stronger.'

She wondered if he was talking about his divorce from her mother, all those years ago. 'Thanks, guys,' she said. 'The whole you're-too-good-for-him-anyway routine worked once. Maybe twice. This is the third time, and I have to consider that the fault might be with me. I mean, what are the odds of meeting three rat bastards in a row?'

'Honey, this is Manhattan,' her father said. 'The place is crawling with them.'

'Quit blaming yourself,' Earl advised. 'You'll give yourself a complex.'

She reached down and scratched Barkis behind the ears, one of his favorite spots. 'I think I already have a complex.'

'No,' said Earl, 'you have issues. There's a

difference.'

'And one of those issues is that you mistake your need for love for actually being in love,' her father observed. He watched a lot of *Dr. Phil.*

'Oh, good one,' Earl said, and they high-fived one another across the table.

'Hello? Breaking heart here,' Olivia reminded them. 'You're supposed to be helping me, not practicing armchair psychology.'

Both her father and Earl grew serious. 'You want to go first, or me?' Earl asked.

Her father fed another tidbit to the dog. Olivia noticed he wasn't eating or drinking, and felt guilty for upsetting him. 'Take it away, maestro,' he said to Earl.

'There's really not that much to say,' Earl told her, 'except that you didn't love Rand. Or the others. You only think Rand was special because he seemed so perfect for you.'

'He's moving to L.A.,' she confessed. 'He never even checked to see if that would be all right with me. He just expected me to go along.' She felt her chest expand, and knew she was inches from tears—because it was true that she didn't love Rand enough... but she had loved him a little.

'You're...what, twenty-seven years old?' Earl continued. 'You're a baby. An emotional newborn. You haven't even scratched the surface of what love is.'

67

Her father nodded. 'You never got past the early-crush phase. You were strolling in Central Park and fixing candlelit meals for each other, and he was parading you in front of his friends. That's not love, not the kind you deserve. That's like…a warm-up exercise.'

'How do you know that, Dad?' she demanded, crushed that he had managed to sum up her entire relationship with Rand so handily. Then she caught the look on her father's face, and backed off. Even though her love life was always under the microscope, her parents' marriage and divorce were protected by a conspiracy of silence.

'There's a kind of love that has the power to save you, to get you through life,' her father said. 'It's like breathing. You have to do it or you'll die. And when it's over, your soul starts to bleed, Livvy. There's no pain in the world like it, I swear. If you were feeling that now, you wouldn't be able to sit up straight or have a coherent conversation.'

She met her father's gaze. He so rarely spoke to Olivia about matters of the heart, so she was inclined to listen. His words grabbed at something deep inside her. To love like that…it was impossible. It was frightening. 'Why would anyone want that?'

'It's what living is about. It's the reason you go through life. Not because you're compatible or you look good together or your mothers attended Marymount at the same time.'

Clearly, these two had studied and discussed Rand Whitney's résumé.

'I still feel like crap,' she said, knowing somehow that they were right.

'Of course you do,' her father said. 'And you're entitled to feel that way for a day or two. But don't mistake that feeling for grief over lost love. You can't lose what you never had in the first place.' He swirled his glass, the ice clinking against the crystal.

Olivia rested her chin in her hand. 'Thanks for being so great, Dad.'

'He's the mother you never had.' Earl made no secret of his dislike for Pamela Lightsey Bellamy, who still used her married name, years after the divorce.

'Hey,' Philip warned.

'Well, it's true,' Earl said.

Olivia drank the rest of her Campari and gave the ice to a thirsty-looking African violet. 'So now what?'

'Now we have coq au vin for dinner, and you'll probably have more *vin* than *coq,* but that's okay,' Earl said.

'Mom is going to hate this,' she said. 'She had high hopes for Rand. I can just hear her now— 'What did you do to run him off?''

'Pamela has always been such a lovely woman,' said Earl. 'Are you sure you're an only child? Maybe she ate the others when they were young.'

69

Olivia grinned over the rim of the highball glass. 'She would never do that. Mom has too much fun messing with people's heads. I bet she'd like to have ten of me if she could.'

It had taken Olivia's entire adolescence to finally lose the weight that had made her such a target for bullies, and gain the approval of her mother. Ironically but not surprisingly, all it had taken was the loss of forty or sixty pounds, depending on how much she was lying to herself. Once the slender, chic Olivia emerged from her cocoon of obesity, Pamela had a whole new set of ambitions for her only daughter. It never occurred to Pamela to wonder why Olivia had only found success in losing weight when she left home for college.

'I wish there were ten of you,' Earl said loyally, clinking his glass to hers. 'You're adorable, and it never would have worked out with Rand Whitney anyway.'

'Still, it would have been fun if she was married to a Whitney,' her father mused.

'Bullshit. She'd be so busy with charity fund-raisers and gallery openings, we'd never see her. Plus, she'd be an alcoholic in a few years, and where's the fun in that?'

'I don't believe you guys,' said Olivia. 'If you were so convinced I'd be miserable with Rand, why didn't you tell me months ago?'

'Would you have listened?' Her father cocked an eyebrow.

'Are you kidding? He's Rand Whitney. He

looks like Brad Pitt.'

'Which should have been your first warning sign,' Earl pointed out. 'Never trust a man who gets collagen injections.'

'He doesn't—' Olivia cut herself off. 'It was just the one time, for that *Vanity Fair* feature.' The magazine had made her even more crazy about him, emphasizing his blond good looks, his effortless charm, his insistence that being a Whitney didn't define him, his assurance that he worked for a living just like everyone else. Well, like everyone else, except for that handy trust fund.

In the article, Olivia had been reduced to a single line: 'Rand Whitney is protective of his privacy. When asked about romance, he says only, "I've met someone special. She's wonderful, and that's all I can tell you." '

There was only one problem. A dozen other women also thought the statement was about them. When the article came out, Olivia and Rand had laughed about it, and she had been touched by the pride that lit his face. He had his insecurities like everyone else.

And now he had his freedom.

She resigned herself to spending the evening with her father and Earl. It was one of the first warm spring nights of the season, so Earl insisted on bringing over the coq au vin to the patio for dining alfresco. She, her dad and Earl even played the toasting game. They went around the table, taking turns finding

71

one thing to drink to, the goal being to prove to themselves that no matter what else happened in the world, they had something to be grateful for.

'Voice dictation software,' Earl said, raising a glass. 'I despise typing.'

'I'm toasting guys who can cook,' Philip said. 'Thanks for dinner.' He turned to Olivia. 'Your turn.'

'Once-a-month heartworm pills,' she said with a fond glance at Barkis.

Her father regarded her with kindly eyes. 'Too bad they don't make them for humans.'

He and Earl had seen her through this two times before. They knew the drill. And the depressing thing about that was, so did she. She felt...stuck. There was a point in her past that still held her captive. She knew what that moment was. She'd been seventeen, spending her last summer before college at camp, working as a counselor. That had been the only time she'd truly given her heart—fully, fearlessly, without reservation. It had ended badly and she didn't know it at the time, but she had gotten stuck there, mired in emotional quicksand. She still hadn't figured out how to move on.

Maybe her grandmother was offering her an opportunity to do that. 'You know what?' she said, jumping up from the table. 'I don't have time to sit around and wallow.'

'So we're practicing speed breakups now?'

72

'Sorry, but you guys will have to excuse me. I need to pack my bags,' she said, taking Nana's photo album out of her briefcase. 'I'm starting a new project first thing in the morning.' She took a deep breath, surprised to feel a beat of hopeful excitement. 'I'm going away for the summer.'

Three

'This is a bad idea,' said Pamela Bellamy as she opened the door to let Olivia in. The opulent apartment on Fifth Avenue had a museum-like quality, with its polished parquet floors and beautifully displayed art. To Olivia, however, it was simply the place she had grown up. To her, the Renoir in the foyer was no more remarkable than the Tupperware in the kitchen.

Yet even as a child, she'd felt like a visiting alien, out of place amid the Gilded Age elegance of her own home. She preferred cozy things—African violets and overstuffed chairs, Fiestaware and afghans. There was a long history of disconnect between mother and daughter. Olivia had been a lonely child, her parents' one and only and as such, she'd always felt a certain pressure to be all things to them. She'd applied herself diligently to her studies and her music, hoping that a perfect report card or a music prize would warm the chill that seemed to surround her family for as long as she could remember.

'Hello to you, too, Mom.' Olivia set her bag on the hall table and gave her a hug. Her mother smelled of Chanel No. 5 and of the cigarette she sneaked on the east balcony after breakfast each morning.

'Why on earth would you take on such a project?' her mother demanded.

So far, all Pamela knew was what Olivia had told her on the phone the previous night—that it was over between her and Rand, and that she was going to spend the summer renovating Camp Kioga. 'Because Nana asked me to,' she said softly. It was the simplest explanation she could come up with.

'It's absurd,' Pamela said, straightening the shawl collar of Olivia's sweater. 'You'll wind up spending the entire summer in the wilderness.'

'You say that like it's a bad thing.'

'It *is* a bad thing.'

'I tried to tell you and Dad that every summer when I was growing up, but you never listened.'

'I thought you liked going to summer camp.' Her mother held out her hands, palms up, in a helpless gesture.

Olivia had no reply. The misconception summed up her entire childhood.

'I assume you've already discussed this

74

with your father,' Pamela said, her voice iced with indifference.

'Yes. Nana and Granddad are his parents, after all.' Olivia felt weary already. Her mother had a way of wearing her down with a steady rain of words. Yet Olivia was determined not to be talked out of this. At least her father hadn't tried to stand in her way. Last night, when she'd explained her sudden decision to take on the Camp Kioga project, he'd been supportive and encouraging. By noon today, arrangements were already under way. She had leased a huge SUV for the summer, organized her office for her absence and arranged for another real-estate enhancement firm to take referrals and maintain her current properties.

'You're running away,' her mother said. 'Again.'

'I guess I am.' Olivia took out her day runner and flipped it open to a lengthy list she'd made in the taxi ride over here.

'Darling, I'm so sorry.' Her mother looked genuinely crestfallen.

'Yes, well. It happens.' Just once, Olivia wished she could snuggle up to her mother and cry on her shoulder. It didn't work like that, though. Not between her and Pamela. 'I'm sorry too, Mom,' she said. 'I know you had your hopes up this time.'

'Oh, for heaven's sake, never mind me.' Her mother made a clucking sound. 'I simply want you to be happy, that's all. That's my main concern.'

'I'll be all right,' Olivia assured her. To her amazement, a telltale gleam of tears flashed in her mother's eyes. She realized Pamela was taking this harder than she was. 'It's not the end of the world, right?' Olivia said. 'There are worse things in life than being dumped by your boyfriend. And now that I think about it, I wasn't even dumped.'

'You weren't?' she patted her forehead and cheeks with a tissue.

'Rand asked me to move to L.A. with him.'

'I didn't know that. Dear, perhaps you ought to consider—'

'Don't even go there.'

'But once you take that step, once you're sharing a life, you'll both realize you're happy together.'

'I think I've realized we're happy apart.'

'Nonsense. Rand Whitney is perfect for you. I don't know why you're giving up without a fight.'

Olivia's heart sank. This was what made Pamela Lightsey Bellamy tick—the quest to look happy and successful at all costs, even if it meant a fight. Even if it meant hiding the fact that you still hadn't gotten over a divorce, seventeen years earlier.

Once, long ago, Olivia had asked her mother if she was happy. The question had excited a short laugh of disbelief. 'Don't be

76

silly,' Pamela had said. 'I am supremely happy and it would seem ungracious to appear any other way.'

Which wasn't even close to providing the answer Olivia sought, but she had dropped the subject.

'I'm done with Rand Whitney,' she concluded, 'and you're sweet to worry about me. But my mind is made up. I'm going to do this for Nana. I wanted to grab a few things while I'm here.'

'This is insane,' her mother said. 'I don't know what Jane was thinking, asking you to do such a thing.'

'Maybe she was thinking that I'm good enough at my job to make a success of this.'

Pamela stiffened her spine. 'Of course she was. And she is a very lucky woman, because that place is going to look amazing once you finish with it.'

'Thank you, Mom. You're absolutely right.' The distress on her mother's face wasn't all about Rand. Olivia knew that the upcoming anniversary put her mother in an awkward spot. Pamela's father, Samuel Lightsey, was best friends with Charles Bellamy. This was probably another reason her mother had finalized the divorce on paper but never in her heart. Her family's close ties with the Bellamys created a bond she couldn't escape.

'Mom, do you think you'll go?'

'It would be petty to do otherwise.'

'Good for you,' Olivia said. 'It'll be fine. Listen, I have to dig out some things from the basement.' She studied her mother's lovely, composed face. 'My duffel bag and sports equipment. And I need Dad's old footlocker,' she added. Then her heart sank. 'Tell me you didn't throw it out.'

'I never throw anything away. Ever,' her mother said.

Which explained much about Pamela. Fresh as yesterday, Olivia could remember the day her father had moved out. She could still picture the way he looked through a blur of tears, as if he was on the other side of a rain-smudged window. He'd sat down so he could look her in the eye. 'I have to go, honey,' he'd told her.

'No, you don't. But you're going to, anyway.'

He'd refused to be dissuaded. The unspoken tension that had always existed between Olivia's parents had finally reached the breaking point. It should have been a relief, but Olivia could never recall feeling relieved.

'I'm leaving some boxes of my stuff in the basement,' her father had told her, 'including all my sports equipment and camp gear. It's all yours now.'

Every once in a while, she'd take out his old Kioga sweatshirt and put it on, or wrap

78

herself in the Hudson's Bay blanket, which smelled of mothballs.

She took the service elevator, descending alone into the bowels of the old building, and let herself into the storage unit. She found her duffel right away. The stiff canvas was covered with a patchwork of badges from Kioga, marking every summer from 1987 to 1994. Most campers avidly collected the coveted patches, each of which represented a magical summer at sleepaway camp. Not Olivia. Though she had dutifully sewn on her patches in order to keep from offending her grandparents, the colorful badges held no sentimental value for her. Nana and Granddad were convinced that the camp was Shangri-la and it would hurt their feelings to say otherwise.

Olivia set aside the duffel bag and looked around the crowded but well-organized basement room, dank with disuse and old memories. There were framed photographs of Olivia and her father and leather-bound albums labeled Bellamy. Pulling out the large, heavy footlocker her father had left behind for Olivia all those years ago, she opened the lid and was hit with a musty smell she could immediately put a name to: camp. It was an unforgettable combination of mildew, wood smoke and outdoors, an essence that resisted laundering and airing out.

Rifling through the locker, she helped

herself to a lantern and a book on wilderness survival, and grabbed a vintage Kioga hooded sweatshirt with the words Camp Counselor stenciled on the back. In the Bellamy family, it wasn't enough to be a camper. As each individual came of age, working as a counselor was a rite of passage. Olivia's father, all her aunts and uncles had spent college summers there, leading camp activities by day and partying at night with the rest of the staff. Olivia and the next generation of cousins had done the same, right up until the camp had closed nine years ago. It was a summer that had begun with great promise but ended in disaster. She was surprised by how vividly she recalled the sounds and smells, the quality of the light and the stillness of the lake, the dizzying joy and nauseating disappointment she'd experienced that summer. I'm crazy for going back there, she thought.

She stuffed a few key items of memorabilia into the duffel bags—the striped Hudson's Bay blanket, the sweatshirt, an old tennis racquet that needed to be restrung. There were wooden pins with campers' names burnt in, canoe paddles that had been painted with surprising skill, the shafts autographed by other campers. Songbooks, friendship bracelets, dipped candles and birch-bark craft projects—it was a treasure trove.

The key to staging a property was in the details—the more authentic, the better.

Things like this would bring the camp back to life, and she was counting on her aunts and uncles to contribute to the collection. In the bottom of the footlocker, she found a tennis cup, tarnished and battered. It had a pedestal, a domed lid and double handles. The piece would look handsome in the glass trophy case in the dining hall of the camp, assuming the display case was still there.

When she picked up the tennis cup, something rolled around inside it. She pried off the lid, and an object fell out. A button? A cuff link. It, too, was wrought of tarnished silver, with a fish design—maybe a zodiac sign? She looked around for its mate, but there was only the one. She put the cuff link in her pocket and rubbed the trophy, trying to make out the engraving: Counselors Classic. First Place. Philip Bellamy. 1977. Apparently her father had won the cup at the annual staff games while working as a counselor at Camp Kioga that year. He would have been twenty-one, getting ready to go off for his senior year at college.

She found an old photograph stuck down inside the cup. The edges of the picture were curled, the colors fading, but the image made her catch her breath. She saw her father as she had never seen him before, holding the sparkling new trophy aloft. He appeared to be laughing with joy, his head thrown back and his arm around a girl. No, a young woman.

Olivia wiped the dusty photograph on her sleeve and angled it toward the light. On the back, the photo bore the date—August 1977—and nothing else. She studied the woman more closely. Long dark hair, cut in feathery layers, spilled loosely over the shoulders of her camp shirt. The abundant waves of hair framed an attractive face and a smile that might be tinged with a hint of mystery. With her full lips, high cheekbones and dark, almond-shaped eyes, the stranger was an exotic beauty whose looks contrasted with the ordinary shorts and shirt she wore.

There was something in the way the man and woman in the photograph seemed bonded together that sent a chill of curiosity through Olivia. A certain familiarity—no, intimacy—was evident in their posture. Or maybe she was reading too much into it.

Olivia knew she could ask her father who the stranger was. She was quite sure he'd remember a woman who could make him laugh the way he was laughing in the photograph. But she didn't want to upset him, asking about an old girlfriend. There was probably a very good reason she was a stranger.

Something about the old photograph bothered Olivia. She studied it a moment longer. Looked at the date again. August 1977. That was it. By August 1977, her father was engaged to her mother, and they married later that year, at Christmastime.

So what was he doing with the woman in the photograph?

CAMP KIOGA CODE OF CONDUCT

Display of overly affectionate attention between males and females is discouraged. This applies to campers, counselors and staff members alike.

Four

August 1977

'Philip, what are you doing?' asked Mariska Majesky, stepping into the bungalow.

He stopped pacing and turned, his heart lifting at the sight of her in a beautiful chiffon cocktail dress and platform shoes, her dark, wavy hair swept up off suntanned shoulders.

'Rehearsing,' he confessed, his chest filled with joy and dread, the intense emotions waging an undeclared war.

She tilted her head to one side in that adorable way she had of conveying curiosity. 'Rehearsing what?'

'I'm practicing what I'm going to say to Pamela when she gets back from Europe,' he explained. 'Trying to figure out how to end our engagement.' Since his fiancée had gone overseas, there had been only a few brief, unsatisfactory phone conversations, a hasty flurry of postcards and aerograms. The Italian telephone system was famously unreliable, and destroying her dreams over a crackling transatlantic wire or in a letter didn't cut it.

Next week, she would return and then he'd tell her in person. It was going to turn him into the heel of the century.

The only thing worse was spending the rest

84

of his life with someone who didn't own his heart the way Mariska did.

Now Mariska grew serious, her full mouth forming a sad smile. Philip hugged her. She smelled fantastic, a heady mixture of flowers and fruit, and she fit just right in his arms, as though heaven itself had made her for him, exactly like the song said. Her nearness made him forget his worries about Pamela.

'I picked these up at the one-hour-photo place today.' Mariska took an envelope out of her purse. 'There's a shot of us. I ordered double prints, so you can keep a copy.' Flipping through the snapshots of the day's sporting events at the camp, she pulled out one of her and Philip, laughing in triumph as he held a bright silver trophy cup aloft.

His heart constricted. He looked so damn happy. In that moment, he had been happy. Taking the tennis trophy down from the luggage rack, he put the snapshot inside it and replaced the lid. 'Thank you,' he said.

She crossed the room and kissed him. 'We should go. It's the last dance of the summer, and you know how I love dancing.'

Each summer, the season ended with a series of rituals. Yesterday, the campers had all gone home. Today was the staff's farewell, a dinner dance that would end at midnight. By this time tomorrow, nearly everyone else would be gone, the college-age counselors all heading back to school.

'Let's go,' she urged him, pulling back and taking his hand. 'I don't want to muss my hair.' She eyed him with a mischievous gleam in her eye. 'Not yet, anyway.'

Even that oblique promise was enough to send him into overdrive. As they left the bungalow, he buttoned his sports coat and hoped his physical reaction to her nearness wasn't too obvious. As he had since the beginning of summer, he cast a furtive glance around the area to make sure they hadn't been spotted. Kioga had strict rules about fraternizing among counselors and other workers, and just because his parents owned the place didn't mean he was exempt.

Mariska wasn't a counselor, but she was supposed to be off-limits, too. She and her mother, Helen, supplied the baked goods to the camp. From the age of fourteen, Mariska had driven the white panel van up the mountain every morning at dawn, bringing bread, pastries, muffins and cookies to the dining hall. The local police looked the other way when the delivery truck lumbered past. Mariska's mother, a Polish immigrant, had never learned to drive. Her father was on swing shift at the glassworks down in Kingston. They were a working-class family and the authorities were sympathetic to their plight. They weren't about to ticket an underage girl for helping out with the family business.

As Philip and Mariska strolled through the forest at twilight, he couldn't resist slipping his arm around her. She tucked herself against his shoulder. 'Careful,' she said softly, 'someone might see.'

'I hate all this sneaking around.' A sick guilt flurried in his gut. It was definitely not cool, falling in love with another girl while your fiancée was overseas. He couldn't help himself, though. He had been helpless to resist Mariska, even though he wasn't free to be with her. She was so understanding, complicit in the secrecy, but he suspected she was as eager as he was to stop hiding it. The moment Pamela returned, he'd end it with her and then he could finally show the world what was in his heart.

'You're looking at me funny,' Mariska said. 'What's that look?'

'I'm trying to figure out the exact moment I fell in love with you.'

'That's easy. It was that night back in June after Founders' Day.'

He couldn't help smiling at the memory, even though she was wrong. 'That was the first time we had sex. I fell in love with you way before that.'

They reached the end of the gravel path and, out of habit, separated, keeping their distance. In the pavilion across the field, the farewell dance was already in full swing. A disco ball spun slowly from the center, its facets creating a strobelike effect on the crowded dance floor. People seemed more frenetic than usual, at least they did to Philip. But perhaps that was his imagination.

Outside the pavilion, he stopped walking.

'What's the matter?' she asked.

'Dance with me. Right here, right now.'

'These shoes aren't doing so well in the grass,' she protested.

'Then take them off. I want to dance with you in private where no one can see, so I can hold you exactly the way I want.' Once they made an appearance at the pavilion, they would have to go their separate ways, pretending they were just friends. For now, he wanted to dance with her like a lover.

With a silky laugh, she kicked off her shoes and slipped into his arms. The house band was playing a passable rendition of 'Stairway to Heaven,' and they danced in the dark, where no one could see them. She felt wonderful in his arms, and his heart soared at the thought that, very soon, the whole world would know she was his.

Pulling her close and swaying to the music, he bent and whispered in her ear, 'It didn't happen all at once. Me, falling in love with you. I think it started four years ago, when you first started delivering stuff to the dining hall.' He could still picture her, sun browned and serious, a hardworking girl who couldn't quite hide her envy of the privileged city kids whose parents could afford to send them to summer camp. She had moved him then, a beautiful girl wanting something she couldn't have. And she moved him now, a beautiful woman whose dreams were finally within reach.

'Each summer when I came here,' he said, 'I was more and more into you.'

'You never did anything about it until this summer,' she pointed out, a note of gentle chiding in her voice.

'I didn't think you wanted me to.'

'Oh, I did. I wanted you to sweep me off my feet.'

He laughed and did exactly that, scooping her up with one arm under her knees, the other behind her shoulders. 'Like this?'

She made a sound of surprise and clung to his neck. 'Exactly.'

He kissed her then, slowly and hungrily, and wished he had acted on his feelings long before this summer. What an idiot he'd been, thinking those feelings weren't real, expecting each summer that the attraction would be gone. Maybe he'd spent a little too much time with his father's parents, the redoubtable Grandmother and Grandfather Bellamy, who claimed it was impossible to love someone from a different class. They were fond of reminding Philip that he was a young man of sophistication, with a first-class education and the brightest of prospects for his future. A girl like Mariska, who attended a small-town high school, who worked at her family's bakery and part-time at the local jewelry store, would be considered an unfortunate mismatch for him.

Pamela Lightsey, on the other hand, seemed to have been created just for him. She had everything a man in his position wanted in a wife—brains, beauty, heart, social status. Her parents were best friends with his own. The Lightsey fortune came from a jewelry empire, and they had given their daughter all the same advantages Philip enjoyed—private school, personal coaches, foreign travel, Ivy League college. She was blond and beautiful and accomplished, having mastered two languages and piano. This summer she was in Positano, perfecting her Italian.

Yet Philip had discovered one missing ingredient. When he looked into Pamela's eyes, he didn't get dizzy with love. That only happened with Mariska.

He forced himself to stop kissing her and set her down. 'We should get a move on,' he said. 'People will start to wonder where we are.'

By people, he meant his fellow counselors and staff. Most were guys like him who had spent their childhood summers at Kioga, guys who were jealous of Philip because he was going to marry Pamela Lightsey. Or so they thought. It was comforting—just a little—to know so many of them would be willing to catch her on the rebound.

His stomach churned every time he thought of breaking their engagement. He didn't have a choice, though. It wouldn't be fair to anyone—not to Pamela, nor to Mariska—to pretend nothing had changed over the summer. It wouldn't be fair to the children he and Pamela had talked about having one day; kids deserved to grow up in a house full of love.

He should never have proposed to her last spring, on her birthday. But she had wanted him to, so much. One of the designers who worked for Lightsey Gold & Gem had created a one-of-a-kind ring, a 1.3 carat marquise-cut solitaire in a free-form setting of gold. He had knelt down before her in the middle of New Haven Green on campus—and in that starry-eyed moment, he could have sworn he loved her.

He was a fool. It had taken Mariska Majesky to finally show him what love was.

Outside the pavilion, he paused and squeezed her hand, then leaned down to say, 'I love you.'

She rewarded him with a smile, then freed her hand. They walked into the dance side by side, like a couple of old friends.

The party was in full swing. His parents were circulating among the guests, always the perfect hosts. Even more perfect, he observed, trying not to cringe—the Lightseys were here. Pamela's parents and his own were lifelong friends, another factor that complicated Philip's plans. They went way, way back. Mr. Lightsey had been the best man at the Bellamys' wedding, and the couples had been close ever since. It was almost as if a match between Philip and Pamela had been preordained. Each year, Pamela's family came up at season's end to help close up the camp and steal a few final days of summer before heading back to the city.

With the Lightseys around, he had to be extra careful. He had to be the one to tell Pamela, face-to-face. If she heard the news from her parents... He didn't even want to think about that. And just to complicate matters, Mariska's mother stood behind the buffet table, keeping the dessert trays filled. Helen Majesky's berry pies and kolaches were legendary, and they didn't last long.

Spying Mariska, Helen waved, though her smile appeared forced. Philip was pretty sure Helen suspected something was going on between him and Mariska, and disapproved. Of course she did. She knew he was engaged to Pamela and undoubtedly feared he'd break her daughter's heart.

He wanted to reassure Helen, let her know he meant to spend the rest of his life making Mariska happy. Soon, he thought. I'll straighten everything out soon.

Under the pavilion, he and Mariska went their separate ways, though he had a hard time keeping his eyes off her. A glow seemed to surround her, and even though he knew it came from the fairy lights strung along the railing, he thought it made her look magical, like someone from another world.

'Yo, Phil.' Earl, his best friend and college roommate, clapped him on the back. 'You just missed the staff meeting at the boathouse.' That was code for getting high. Anthony George Earl the Third was extremely fond of weed, and indulged in it nightly. Sucking a bong almost seemed like another camp ritual.

'I'll live. Let's get something to eat.'

'Good plan. I'm starved.' His eyes were puffy and bright, evidence that he'd made the most of the staff meeting.

They moved along the buffet table, raising their voices to be heard over the music. 'I'm going back on the morning train,' Earl said, munching on a mouthful of Bugles. 'Man, I hate to leave this place.'

'I hear you.' Philip sneaked a glance at Mariska. She was dancing with Terry Davis, a local kid who did maintenance work around the camp. As usual, Davis was toasted. Built like a linebacker, he was known to drink a six-pack of beer in only minutes.

'She's something, huh?' Earl commented, adding an extra scoop of potato salad to his plate.

'What? Who?' Philip played dumb. He'd been doing it all summer long.

'Sweet Mariska. Damn. Look at her.'

It took all of Philip's self-control to keep from smacking the leer off Earl's face. That, too, had been going on all summer long. Every guy in camp had the hots for Mariska.

'Man,' Earl continued, 'I'd kill to have a piece of her.'

'Yeah, I'm sure,' Philip said, hanging on to his patience by a thread.

Unperturbed, Earl shrugged. He balanced his plate on one hand, grabbed a box of Screaming Yellow Zonkers with the other and found a seat at one of the tables placed along the periphery of the dance floor. 'Well,' he said, 'I would.'

'You are so full of shit,' Philip said, joining him.

'Nope, just horny. I think it's affecting my mental health. I don't know how you stayed so calm all summer long without getting laid.' Earl shoveled in several bites of potato salad. Like Philip, he was engaged, and his fiancée was overseas. Lydia had gone to Biafra to work as a Red Cross volunteer. Unlike Philip, Earl had stayed faithful, though he complained loudly about his noble sacrifice.

'So when does Lydia get back?' Philip asked.

'Two more weeks. Damn, I can't wait. What about Miss America?' Earl called Pamela Miss America because she embodied the qualities of a beauty queen. She bore herself with a regal self-assurance, as though walking down a pageant runway. And there was always an invisible but impenetrable distance between her and the rest of the world.

'Next week,' Philip said.

'The waiting is hard, eh?'

'More than you know,' Philip admitted.

Earl dug into the barbecued ribs. 'I don't get it,' he said. 'How do you know you've found the right girl? I mean, sometimes I know Lydia's perfect for me. But other times, I see something like that—' he gestured at Mariska, who was now fast-dancing with a group of her local girlfriends "—and I can't imagine sticking with one girl for the rest of my life.'

I can, thought Philip. But it's not Pamela.

'Your parents make it look easy,' Earl said, giving them a wave.

Philip watched his mom and dad as they stepped onto the dance floor together. Despite the fact that they claimed to know nothing about rock and roll, they were lost in each other's arms while Eric Clapton's voice rasped from the speakers.

'See what I mean?' Earl commented. 'I wonder how they knew.'

'Nobody knows for sure,' Philip said. 'That's why so many people make mistakes. Not because they're stupid, but because they can only hope they've made the right choice.'

Although his parents did indeed have a happy marriage, Philip knew for a fact that they'd gotten off to a rough start. The Bellamys had been completely opposed to the marriage. Philip's dad, Charles, had defied his family to be with Jane Gordon, whose family had founded Camp Kioga. Charles had dropped out of Yale in order to marry her and take over the running of the camp.

Eventually, there was a reconciliation between Charles and his parents. Maybe it was the four kids Jane had in quick succession, or maybe it was that the Bellamys finally understood that Charles and Jane's love would not be denied.

That was how it would work for him and Mariska. He was sure of it. They would encounter doubts and resistance at first. Then the world would come to realize what he had discovered for himself this summer. He and Mariska belonged together forever.

'Dance with us,' ordered the Nielsen girls, striding over to the table as the music changed. 'No way can you guys sit through "Bohemian Rhapsody."'

'Okay, you twisted my arm.' Earl got up, wiped his mouth with a napkin.

Sally and Kirsten Nielsen were fraternal twins. Guys at Kioga nicknamed them the Valkyries because of their size and handsome Nordic features, and their fearless tendency to grab guys they liked and carry them off. Philip was glad enough for an excuse to get out on the dance floor where Mariska was.

He noticed his parents and the Lightseys watching him, and felt a crushing weight of responsibility. There was so much he was expected to do once he finished college— Marry Pamela. Go to business school or law school. Have a family.

Mariska was dancing with Matthew Alger now. Philip felt a surge of possessiveness when he saw them together. Although he was heavyset, with straight blond hair, Alger tried to emulate his idol, John Travolta, right down to the blow-dried hair and polyester shirt open to display his chest. What a loser. Yet girls seemed to like him, for no reason Philip could figure.

The music glided into a slow song and Philip caught Mariska's wrist, slipping between them. 'My turn.'

'Back off,' said Alger, always spoiling for a fight. 'You're not wanted here.'

'That's up to the lady.'

'You two.' Mariska laughed, then turned to Alger. 'I haven't danced with Philip yet, and you're all leaving tomorrow.'

'Not me,' Alger informed her, squaring his shoulders with self-importance. 'I'm going to be living in Avalon. Doing my senior thesis on city administration, and Avalon is the subject.'

Alger didn't come from money but apparently had his share of brains. Suddenly

Philip was on fire with envy. Alger got to stay in Avalon while Philip would be exiled to campus for another year.

With phony expansiveness, Alger backed off. 'I guess I'll see you around anyway, Mariska.'

Alger was sharp, an ambitious guy, Philip supposed, though a little off. Despite working as a bookkeeper and counselor for the camp all summer, he never quite fit in. 'He's a weirdo,' Philip said. 'You should stay away from him.'

'I have to live in this town,' Mariska reminded him. 'I can't afford to make enemies.'

'Don't be silly. After I finish school, we'll live anywhere you want—New York, Chicago, San Francisco.'

'I'll hold you to that,' she said, excitement sparkling in her eyes. Then her gaze darted to the sidelines. 'So those are Pamela's parents. They're scary.'

Philip frowned. 'Not really. They're just—'

'Just like your family,' she said. 'They're made of money.'

'They're people, same as anyone.'

'Sure. Anyone with Gold & Gem after their name.'

He didn't like it when she talked like that, as though coming from a working-class background set her apart from him. 'Forget it,' he said. 'You worry too much.'

The deejay announced that everyone should head down to the lakeshore for the final bonfire of the year, and everyone surged out of the pavilion en masse. The fire had a practical function as well as a traditional one. It was a way to get rid of the wooden delivery pallets and scrap lumber that had accumulated over the summer.

As people moved toward the pyramid of fire, Philip pressed his hand to the small of Mariska's back and veered off the path.

'What are you doing?' she whispered.

'As if you didn't know.'

'Someone will see.' All summer long, she'd been as concerned about discovery as he was, determined not to earn a reputation for stealing other girls' fiancés.

He took her hand and steered her toward the row of bunkhouses. 'No, they won't.'

Someone did see, though. As they headed away from the lake, a match flared, illuminating the contemplative, inebriated face of Terry Davis. He held the match at arm's length so that its weak light winked over Philip and Mariska.

' 'Night, kids,' he said, an ironic smile on his face.

'Shit,' Philip said under his breath. 'She's not feeling well,' he explained to Davis. 'I'm walking her...to her car.'

Davis's gaze flickered. 'Uh-huh.' He brought the match to the tip of his cigarette.

Philip and Mariska kept walking. 'Never mind him,' Philip said. 'He probably won't remember anything tomorrow, anyway.' Despite the conviction in his words, he felt a thrum of apprehension in his chest. Over the summer, he and Mariska had grown increasingly inventive when it came to finding places to make love. They'd done it not just in the boathouse, but in some of the boats. In the panel van Mariska drove on her bread deliveries. On the bridge over Meerskill Falls.

Tonight, they decided to risk sneaking into the bungalow. As a senior counselor, he had private quarters, and there, illuminated only by a single night-light, he took her in his arms, leaning down to bury his face in her fragrant hair. 'I can't wait to be with you forever.'

'You're going to have to. I better not stay out too late tonight. I've got a doctor's appointment first thing in the morning.'

He pulled back, studied her face. 'Are you okay?'

'Just a checkup,' she said.

A sigh gusted from him. 'Whew. I'm going to miss you so much.'

With delicate fingers, she unbuttoned the front of his shirt. 'How much?'

'More than you know.' He caught his breath as she parted his shirt and pressed her lips to his throat.

'You'll probably forget all about me once you're back at college with your rich fiancée and high society friends.'

'Don't talk like that. You know it's not true.'

'All I have is your word for it.' Despite the accusation, a teasing note lightened her voice. 'The rich boy's word. What do rich girls do all the time, anyway?'

'They let rich boys make love to them,' he said, unzipping her dress in a smooth, practiced motion. He was excited now, but forced himself to slow down. He undid one cuff link and slipped it in his pocket.

'Those are pretty,' she said, admiring the glint of silver.

'They were my grandfather's.' He removed the second one and placed it in her hand. 'Tell you what. You keep one, I'll keep the other. After I...when I come back for you, I'll wear them again at our wedding.'

'Philip.'

'I mean it. I want to marry you. I'm giving you this little hunk of silver now. After this is all straightened out, it'll be a diamond ring.'

Her eyes sparkled up at him as she dropped the cuff link into her handbag. 'I'll hold you to that, too. In fact, I've got my dream ring all picked out.'

'At Palmquist's, where you work?'

'Very funny. At Tiffany's.'

'Ha. I can't afford Tiffany's.'

'Sure you can. Your parents are loaded.'

'But I'm not. In this family, we make our

own way in the world.'

'You're kidding, right?'

He laughed and skimmed her dress down over her shoulders, watching it pool on the floor. Then he reached around and unfastened her bra. 'You're going to be the bride of a poor but noble public defender.'

'Okay, now you're scaring me.'

He caught his breath as the bra came away; then he found his voice again. 'The only thing that scares me is leaving you tomorrow.'

CAMP KIOGA SONGBOOK

The bear went over the mountain,
The bear went over the mountain,
The bear went over the mountain,
And what do you think he saw?

Five

'Why do I keep flashing on scenes from *The Shining?*' asked Freddy Delgado. He hummed an ominous sound track as Olivia drove their leased SUV up the narrow, patchwork-paved country road toward the town of Avalon.

'Believe me,' she said, 'that's not as horrific as the flashbacks I'm having. I spent a lot of excruciating summers here.' She still couldn't quite believe she was doing this. The simple act of driving felt foreign to her, since she never drove in the city. Right up to the last minute, her mother had tried to talk her out of the renovation project, but Olivia was determined. Her father had been more supportive. When she'd told him goodbye the previous night, he'd held her close and wished her luck.

'Why excruciating?' asked Freddy. 'It looks like the perfect place for summer.'

She eased up on the accelerator as a chipmunk darted across the road. There were things she'd never told Freddy—or anyone—about her life. 'I was sort of a misfit.'

'You?' He snorted with a disbelief that made her feel flattered. 'What is this, a camp for freaks and geeks?'

She gestured at the photo album, which lay on the seat between them. The thought of him getting a glimpse of her past was discomfiting, but she had to trust him. Who besides Freddy would drop everything and agree to spend the summer at a remote Catskills camp, trying to bring back the charm of a bygone time? Of course, being jobless and homeless was a clear incentive, but now it was too late. He was already flipping through the old photos.

'Find the group shot from 1993. Saratoga Cabin, Eagle Lodge,' she instructed him.

He flipped it open and scanned the collection of photos. 'Looks like a breeding program for the Aryan nation. Geez, did everybody have to be tall, blond and hot to go to camp here?'

'Look closer. Back row, on the end,' she said.

'Oh.' The tone of Freddy's voice indicated that he had spotted her. 'Went through an awkward phase, did you?'

'I wouldn't call it a phase, I'd call it my entire adolescence. And I wasn't awkward. I was fat. The Coke-bottle glasses and braces were just kind of a bonus.'

Freddy let out a low whistle. 'And look at you now. The ugly duckling became a swan.'

'The ugly duckling got contacts, went blond and did year-round intramural swimming in college. The ugly duckling worked for two years to get to her ideal weight. And you don't have to be polite. I was horrible. I was an unhappy kid and I took it out on myself. Once I figured out how to be happy, everything got better.'

'Kids aren't supposed to have to figure out how to be happy. They just are.'

'Some families are different,' she told him. 'And that's all I'm going to say about the Bellamys, so don't bother to pry.'

'Ha. I've got you to myself the entire summer. I'll learn all your secrets.'

'I have no secrets.'

'Bullshit. I think you're keeping secrets even from yourself.'

'It's going to be a real picnic, spending the summer with Dr. Freud.'

'Well, I'm glad we're doing this project. And I'm glad Rand Whitney is history now.'

'Thanks,' she said, her voice sharp with sarcasm. 'That means a lot, coming from you, Freddy. You wanted me to fail.'

'Olivia. You set yourself up for failure every time. Ever wonder why that is?'

Ouch.

'You have a habit of picking the wrong guy,' he went on. 'I think it's because you wouldn't know what to do if you actually found the right guy. You say you figured out how to be happy. Why don't I believe that?'

She didn't want to discuss this. 'I think Barkis needs a bathroom break.'

'No, he doesn't. He just peed in Kingston. According to the map, we're almost there. I'll

105

shut up, I promise.' True to his word, Freddy fell silent and went back to studying the photos. Olivia had already done so, poring over the old Kodachromes and black-and-white photographs in order to remind herself what the place used to look like. Fortunately, her grandmother kept a concise history of the camp, from its humble beginnings in the 1930s to its heyday in the late 1950s, which was the time period she wanted to replicate in honor of the golden anniversary. She hoped to evoke the simple pleasures of summers past, to make Camp Kioga look like the sort of place people used to go—or wish they had.

Freddy flipped the book shut. 'Seeing you as a kid explains a little more about you.'

'What do you mean?'

'You're a master of the art of transforming things. No wonder you're so good at what you do.'

She'd certainly had plenty of practice. As a child, she had been obsessed with changing things—her room in her mother's Fifth Avenue apartment, her locker at the Dalton School, even her cabin at Camp Kioga each summer. At camp, it was the one thing she was good at. One year, she'd raided a storeroom above the dining hall and found a stash of old linens. Her cabinmates had returned from a hike to find the bunks covered in handmade quilts, soft and faded with age. The windows were draped with calico curtains, the sills decked with freshly picked wildflowers in jelly jars.

'We'll see how good,' she cautioned Freddy. 'I've never staged an entire wilderness camp before.'

'Your grandmother gave you a big fat budget and the whole summer to get the job done. It'll be an adventure in itself.'

'I hope you're right. And thanks for agreeing to do this with me. You're a godsend, Freddy.'

'Trust me, honey, I needed this gig,' he said with self-deprecating candor. 'You're going to need more than me on this renovation, though. Who are you going to use for labor?'

'My grandparents budgeted for a general contractor. We need to find someone as soon as possible. You're going to meet a few more Bellamys, too. My closest cousin, Dare, is coming. So are my uncle Greg and my cousins Daisy and Max. Greg is a landscape architect, and he'll be in charge of the grounds. He's going through a rough spot in his marriage, so spending the summer up here might be good for him and his kids.'

'See, marriage is a bad idea,' Freddy said.

'So I shouldn't even bother, is that what you're saying?'

He ignored the question and went back to the photo collection. 'What a place. The older pictures look more like a family reunion than

107

summer camp.'

'Way, way back, before our time, the camp was for families,' she said. 'Sometimes, it was the only time of year that relatives got together. The moms and kids would stay the entire time, and the dads would come up on the train every Friday. Weird, huh?'

'Maybe. I hear family retreats are coming back in vogue, though. You know, the overscheduled family in search of downtime together, yada yada yada.'

She glanced over at him. 'You sound really taken with the idea.'

'Babe, I retreat *from* my family, not with them.'

'Whoa, where did that come from?' she said. 'I didn't realize you had issues with your family.'

'I have no issues. I have no family.'

She gritted her teeth. Though they'd been friends for years, he'd never told her about his family, except that they lived in Queens and hadn't been in touch since he left home. 'You've been poking and prodding at me for the past ninety miles, so now I get a turn.'

'Believe me, it's not that interesting, unless you're a huge Eugene O'Neill fan. Now, shut up. I need to navigate.'

Just before they reached the village of Avalon, the railroad-crossing barriers descended, and she put the car in Park as the local train took its time passing by.

'I used to take that train from the city to Avalon.' Olivia could still remember the noise and the excitement streaming through the passenger cars. Some of the more experienced campers would sing traditional songs or boast about past victories at archery or swimming or footraces. There would be nervous speculation about who would wind up in which cabin, because everyone knew that bunkmates could make or break the entire summer. When she was in the eight-to-elevens, she had looked forward to camp. She had three girl cousins in her age group, and the train ride and then van up the mountain was a magical journey into an enchanted world.

Everything changed the year her parents split up. She emerged awkwardly from the cocoon of childhood, no lithe butterfly, but a sullen, overweight preteen who distrusted the world.

The train passed by, the last car disappearing, and the curtain opened on the perfect mountain town of Avalon.

'Cute,' Freddy observed. 'Is this place for real?'

Avalon was a classic Catskills village. It looked exactly the way tourists yearned for it to look—a world apart, separated from time itself by the railroad tracks on one side and a covered bridge on the other, with brick streets lined with shade trees, a town square with a courthouse in the middle and at least three church spires. It changed very little from year to year. She remembered Clark's Variety Store and the Agway Feed & Hardware, Palmquist Jewelry and the Sky River Bakery, still owned by the Majesky family, according to the painted display window. There were gift shops with handmade crafts, and upscale boutiques. Restaurants and cafés with striped awnings and colorful window boxes lined the square. Antiques shops displayed spinning wheels and vintage quilts, and almost every establishment featured homemade maple syrup and apple cider for the tourists who came in the fall for the autumn colors.

In the backseat, Barkis woke up from a nap and stuck his nose out the window as they passed the picnic grounds by the Schuyler River. The most beautiful street in town was Maple Street, which boasted a collection of Carpenter Gothic homes from the Edwardian era, some displaying plaques from the National Historic Register.

'Very *Age of Innocence*,' Freddy declared. The pastel-painted houses had been converted to bed-and-breakfast inns, law offices, art galleries, a day spa. The last one on the street had a hand-painted sign: Davis Contracting and Construction.

'Olivia, watch out!' Freddy yelled.

She slammed on the brakes. In the backseat, Barkis scrambled to stay upright.

'It's a four-way stop,' Freddy said. 'Take it easy.'

'Sorry. I missed the sign.' Just the sight of the name Davis left her shaken.

Get a grip, she told herself. There are a zillion Davises in the world. Surely the construction firm wasn't... No way, she thought. That would just be too crazy.

'I'm taking down the number of that construction firm,' Freddy said, oblivious.

'Why would you do that?'

'It's probably the only one in town, and we're going to need their help.'

'We'll find another.'

He twisted around in his seat as they passed. 'The sign says they're bonded and insured, and they give free estimates and references.'

'And you believe that?'

'You don't?' He clucked his tongue. 'A cynic, at such a tender age.' He scribbled down the number.

It was highly unlikely that Davis Construction had anything to do with Connor Davis, Olivia told herself. Even if it did, so what? He probably didn't even remember her. Which was a strangely depressing relief, considering what a fool she'd made of herself over him.

'Okay, tell me that's not a covered bridge,' Freddy said, grabbing for his camera.

'It is a covered bridge.'

'I can't believe it,' he said. 'This is better than *Bridges of Madison County.*'

'A lobotomy is better than *Bridges of Madison County.*'

He snapped away, marveling over the sign that dated the original structure to 1891. It even had a name—Sky River Bridge. Spanning the shallow rapids of the Schuyler River, it had a postcard-pretty quality. Olivia recalled that the camp van from the train depot to Camp Kioga always honked its horn when they entered the shadowy tunnel, creaky and festooned with swallows' nests. It was the last man-made landmark before the camp itself.

Beyond the bridge, the road meandered along the river, past a chain of mountains with names and elevations posted. Freddy, a city boy through and through, was beside himself. 'This is incredible,' he said. 'I can't believe you have a place like this in your family, and you never told me about it.'

'It's been closed as a camp for the past eight—no, nine—years. A property management company looks after the place. Some of the family come for vacations and get-togethers every once in a while.' Olivia had been invited to the occasional family gathering, but she never went. The place held too many bad associations for her. 'In the winter,' she added, 'my uncle Clyde brings his family up for cross-country skiing and snowshoe hiking.'

'Crazy,' Freddy murmured. 'Almost makes me want a normal family.'

She glanced over at him. 'Well, if what you see today doesn't send you screaming back to New York City, you'll have a tribe of Bellamys all summer long.'

'Works for me. And, ah, did I mention the situation with my apartment?'

'Oh, Freddy.'

'You got it. Jobless *and* homeless. I'm a real prize.'

'You're working with me this summer, and you're living at Camp Kioga.' He was her best friend. What else could she say?

She slowed down as she saw the white flicker of a deer's tail from the corner of her eye. A moment later, a doe and a fawn appeared, and Freddy was so excited, he nearly dropped his camera.

In the shuttle van years ago, camp regulars used to call out landmarks along the way, each sighting greeted with mounting excitement as they drew closer and closer to their destination.

'There's Lookout Rock,' someone would announce, pointing and bouncing up and down in the seat. 'I saw it first.'

Others would be named in quick succession—Moss Creek, Watch Hill, Sentry Rock, Saddle Mountain, Sunrise Mountain and, finally, Treaty Oak, a tree so old that it

113

was said Chief Jesse Lyon himself had planted it to commemorate the treaty he signed with Peter Stuyvesant, the colonial governor.

Her twelfth summer, Olivia had ridden in silence. With each passing landmark, her stomach sank a little lower and dread became a physical sensation of cold, dead weight inside. And outside, she reflected. The weight she gained represented the stress of her quietly warring parents, the demands of school, her own unexpressed fears.

They passed a glass art studio with a whimsical sign by the road and then a stretch of riverside land, where the meadows were almost preternaturally green and the forest deep and mysterious. High in a sunny glade sat, of all things, a small Airstream travel trailer with a black-and-chrome Harley parked outside.

'Interesting place,' Freddy commented.

'There are still a lot of counterculture types around here,' Olivia said. 'Woodstock's not that far away.'

Passing Windy Ridge Farm, with yet another whimsical sign, they came around the last curve in the road, turned onto a gravel drive marked Private Property—No Trespassing, which wound through woods that grew thicker with every mile. Finally, there it was, a hand-built timber arch looming over the road—the entrance sign to the property. Built on massive tree trunks, it was the signature trademark of the camp. A sketch of the rustic archway bordered the stationery kids used for their weekly letters home. Across the arch itself was Camp Kioga. Est'd 1932 in Adirondack-style twig lettering.

On the bus, kids would hold their breath, refusing to take another until they passed beneath the arch. Once they were inside the boundaries of the camp, there was a loud, collective exhalation, followed by war whoops of excitement. *We're here.*

'You all right?' Freddy asked.

'Fine,' Olivia said tightly. She slowed down as the dry, sharp gravel crackled under the tires. As they drove along the ancient road, shadowed by arching maple and oak, she had the strangest sensation of stepping back through time, to a place that was not safe for her.

The pitted drive was overgrown, branches swiping at the lumbering SUV. She parked in front of the main hall and let Barkis out. The dog skittered around in an ecstasy of discovery, determined to sniff every blade of grass.

The hundred-acre property was mostly wilderness, with Willow Lake as the centerpiece. There were rustic buildings, meadows and sports courts, cabins and bungalows lining the placid, pristine lake. Olivia pointed out the archery range, the tennis and pickle-ball courts, the amphitheater and hiking trails that were now completely overgrown. Already, she was making mental notes, assessing what it would take to restore the camp.

The main pavilion housed the dining hall. Its deck projected out over the lakeside, where dancing and nightly entertainment used to take place. The lower part of the building housed the kitchen, rec room and camp offices. Now everything had a neglected air, from the weed-infested drive to a patch of rosebushes around the three bare flagpoles. Astonishingly, the roses had survived, growing in riotous profusion on leggy, thorny branches.

As he surveyed the main pavilion and some of the cabins, Freddy said, 'I had no idea a place like this still existed. It's so *Dirty Dancing*.'

'It's a ghost town now,' she said, though her imagination populated it with kids in regulation athletic gray T-shirts with the Kioga logo. 'Up until the early 1960s, there was dancing every night. There was even live music.'

'Right here in the middle of nowhere?'

'My grandparents claimed the players weren't half-bad. You could always find talent because of the New York musicians and actors looking to do summer stock. After the camp converted to kids only, there were sing-alongs and dancing lessons here.' She shuddered at the memory. She was always picked last and usually ended up with another girl, a cousin or a boy who mugged for his friends, his face expressing disgust at finding himself with Lolly, 'the tub of lard,' as she was known back in those days.

'Let's open up the main pavilion, and I'll show you the dining hall,' she said.

Using the key her grandmother had given her, she unlocked the place, and they opened the heavy double doors. In the foyer, glass display cases were draped in dustcovers, and the walls were hung with glass-eyed trophy heads——moose, bear, deer, cougar.

'That's disturbing,' Freddy said.

Barkis appeared to agree. He stayed close, casting suspicious glances at the animals' staring eyes and artificially bared teeth.

'We used to give them names,' Olivia said, 'and steal each other's underwear and hang it from the antlers.'

'That's even more disturbing.'

She led the way into the dining hall. Timbered cathedral ceilings soared overhead. There were enormous river-rock fireplaces at either end, long wooden tables and benches, tall glass doors leading out to the deck and another railed gallery around a loft. A faint odor of burnt wood still lingered in the air.

'It's a wreck,' she said.

Freddy appeared to be struck silent by the magnitude of the project. His eyes were wide as he turned in a slow circle, taking it all in.

'Listen,' she said, 'if you don't think we should take this on, you need to tell me now. We could probably subcontract it out—'

'Get out of town,' he said, walking toward the long wall of French doors facing the lake. 'I am never leaving here.'

Olivia couldn't help smiling at his enchantment. It took some of the sting out of her own memories.

As if in a trance, he went to the glass doors that faced the lake, cranked the lock and stepped outside onto the vast deck. 'My God,' he said, his voice soft with wonder. 'My God, Livvy.'

Together, they stood for a long time, gazing at the lake. Edged by gracefully arching willows, it resembled a golden mirror, reflecting a ring of forested mountains. It really was beautiful. Magical, even. She didn't remember that about this place. No surprise there. When your life was completely unraveling, you tended not to notice the charm of your surroundings.

'There, in the middle,' she said, pointing. 'It's called Spruce Island.' It was large enough to house a gazebo, a dock and picnic area yet small enough to still seem like something conjured, a gleaming emerald in the middle of a sea of gold. 'My grandparents were married there, fifty years ago. That's where they're going to renew their vows in August, provided we get things whipped into shape.'

'What, there's a question in your mind?'

'Hey, I like your attitude, but we need to face facts. This is not a two-thousand-square-foot prewar needing some paint and ambient lighting. It's a hundred acres of wilderness with a bunch of old structures, some of them dating back to the 1930s.'

'I don't care. We can do this. We have to.'

She gave him a hug. 'And here I thought I'd have to twist your arm.'

He held her just a bit longer and a little tighter than necessary. She was the first to pull back, and she smiled up at him, pretending to see only friendship in his eyes. For the first time, she started to understand what it felt like to be Rand Whitney, looking into her worshipful eyes and unable to return the feeling.

'Thanks for coming, partner,' she said, walking to the deck rail and feeling the cool ripple of a breeze off the water. The blue-green scent of the lake and the woods brought back a swell of memories, and surprisingly, not all of them were bad.

'I don't think I've ever been to such an isolated spot,' Freddy said. 'It's like we're the only people on earth. The first man and first woman, Adam and Eve.'

'Just so you don't turn weird on me,' she said.

'What, no "Here's Johnny" routine with

119

the ax?' He gave her a wild-eyed look.

'I think I can do without that, thanks.'

'Fine. But if I had a book in me, this would be the perfect place to write it.'

She headed back inside. 'Let's go figure out where we're going to sleep tonight.'

*   *   *

Olivia and Freddy ended up sharing a cabin that first night. Neither of them relished the idea of lying in a cavernous bunkhouse, alone in the wilderness, wondering about every secret rustle and snuffle they heard from the impenetrable darkness that closed over the place after twilight. When the others arrived, they'd move to the private cottages, but for the time being, neither wanted to be alone.

The bunkhouses were all named for historic forts and battle sites—Ticonderoga, Saratoga, Stanwix, Niagara—and Olivia picked Ticonderoga for its proximity to the dining hall and to the big, communal bathroom.

After unloading their supplies and luggage, and fixing a meal of canned soup and crackers in the cobwebby but still functional kitchen, they used an air compressor from the utility shed to fill their mattresses. The camp had switched to flocked air mattresses years ago to avoid the problem of being chewed by mice. Then Olivia and Freddy made up their bunks at opposite ends of Ticonderoga cabin and embarked on a thorough decobwebbing and general cleaning.

Evening crept over the forest slowly, the sky turning from iridescent sunset pink to layers of deepest violets and then finally, a darkness so complete that it was like being in a cave. Once night fell, Barkis was completely intimidated. He feinted from every mysterious rustle of leaves or lonely birdcall.

After a harrowing battle with two spiders in the large, institutional bathroom located outside the bunkhouse, Olivia got ready for bed, returning to the cabin in lilac pajama crop pants and a matching tank top. The night breeze through the window swept over her.

Freddy stared at her boobs. 'I do love Mother Nature,' he said.

She dived for a sweater and wrapped it around her.

'Okay, now I'm bored,' he complained. 'This is usually my night to watch *Dog the Bounty Hunter.*'

'I told you there was no TV. No phone, no Internet, no cell phone signal.'

'What the hell are we going to do?' Freddy asked in despair.

'Talk. Play board games. Read books. Sleep.'

'Kill me now.'

They sat on their respective bunks and stared at each other. Then she reached up and turned off the overhead light. 'It's strange, not hearing the city,' she commented, snuggling under crisp sheets and a thick woolen blanket. 'I'm so used to horns and sirens.'

Barkis seemed to miss the sounds of the city as well. He was completely cowed by the beating of wings and the hoot of owls. He tucked himself under Olivia's bunk and curled into a tight ball.

She stared into blackness and willed herself to sleep. Instead, she felt restless and uneasy. The minutes seemed to crawl by, and instead of getting sleepier, she felt more alert than ever, her mind racing with plans for the project. 'Freddy,' she whispered.

No answer.

'Freddy. Are you awake?'

'I am now,' said a disembodied voice. 'Where the hell are you? It's too dark to see.'

'We're getting more flashlights,' Olivia said.

'Tomorrow,' he agreed.

Barkis whined, and she recognized the note of urgency in his voice.

'He needs to go out one more time.' Olivia found her flip-flops and a flashlight. 'Come with me.'

'I was just getting warm.'

'Chicken.'

He heaved a long-suffering sigh, and she shone the beam of light toward him. He looked unexpectedly cute in boxers and a

122

white T-shirt, his hair rumpled. He pulled on a pair of sweats, grumbling the whole time.

In the vast wilderness, drowning in darkness, Barkis stayed within range of the light beam as he skirted the overgrown field surrounding the bungalow area.

'You're different here,' Freddy remarked. 'You're more at home here than in the city.'

'Oh, right,' she said.

'You are. Mark my words.' He grabbed her hand with sudden urgency. 'Turn the light off for a second,' he said.

'What?'

'Humor me, just turn it off.'

She shrugged and clicked it off. 'What the—'

'Shh. Look up at the sky, Livvy.'

As she tilted back her head, a blanket of stars seem to rush over them, the Milky Way bright and thick yet filled with mystery. Next to her, she could hear Freddy breathing; it was that quiet.

'Like it?' she asked.

'I've never seen the sky like this before. Where the hell did all these stars come from?'

'They've always been there. You just have to find a place dark enough to see them.'

'I guess we found it.' He squeezed her hand.

'My grandfather had a telescope,' she said. 'It's probably around somewhere. We could see if it still works, have a closer look.'

'I feel close enough to touch them already.' Without warning, he slipped his arms around her and pulled her close.

Olivia was so surprised that she giggled. 'Freddy—'

'Shh.' He kissed her, very carefully and gently, his lips finding hers through the darkness.

The kiss was so unexpected that she struggled a little, pushing her hands against his chest. 'Whoa,' she said. 'What's this about?'

'Now that you've finally gotten rid of what's-his-name, it's about time we did something about us.'

She pushed back farther, surprise giving way to mild panic. 'Freddy, you are the best friend I've got. Don't spoil it by trying to turn it into some kind of romance.'

'Why not?'

'I suck at romance. I have a terrible track record. You said so yourself. I set myself up for failure.'

'You'd be great at it if you'd just pick the right guy.' He kissed her again. His mouth was warm and sweet, and the kindness of the gesture made her feel like weeping.

'Oh, Christ,' he said, pulling back. 'Now you're crying.'

'Sorry,' she said. 'I didn't mean... God, Freddy, I'm such a mess.' She hadn't cried over Rand Whitney, yet here she was, the tears boiling from her eyes simply because Freddy had kissed her.

'I know you are. So am I. Maybe it's something else we'll work on this summer besides renovating the camp.' And with that, he released her.

She felt both bereft and relieved. Freddy was wonderful, she adored him, but a romance? She pressed her sleeves to her eyes. Impossible.

Edging away from him, she studied the reflection of the stars on the lake. 'Is it going to be all awkward between us now because we tried kissing and it didn't work out?'

'Who says it didn't work out?'

Oh, God. 'Freddy, I—'

'Shut up, Livvy.' He patted her gently on the back. 'I'm pulling your leg. I wasn't feeling it from you.' He cleared his throat. 'But you understand, I had to try.'

She wondered, if she shone the flashlight on him, what she would see in his face. But she wasn't sure she wanted to know, so she kept the beam turned off.

*   *   *

When the sun rose, neither Olivia nor Freddy mentioned the previous night. Fortunately, they found plenty to keep them busy. She pulled on sloppy denim cutoffs and a sweatshirt over a tank top, and looped her hair into a messy ponytail. This was going to be a workday.

Over mugs of coffee, they held a typical consultation, just as they might in the city when they were starting a project, with Olivia making lists and Freddy creating sketches on big sheets of butcher paper. They worked at a long table of scrubbed pine in the dining hall, with a view of the lake as their backdrop.

'It's going to be incredible,' she said, standing back and admiring their shared vision. 'All we need now is the right contractor to get the job done.'

Freddy tore a slip of paper out of his notepad. 'Here's the number I took down when we passed through town yesterday. Davis Construction.'

'I'll ask around for others.' Catching his expression, she said, 'You know, to get some competitive bids.'

'Don't be surprised if this is the only game in town. And with the budget your grandmother gave us, we don't exactly need to pinch pennies.'

'I'll ask around,' Olivia said stubbornly. 'Wish me luck.'

*　　　*　　　*

She had no luck. Cell phone service was nonexistent and the camp-office phone had been disconnected years ago. To make a call, she had to hike out to the main entrance and use the antiquated pay phone at the gatehouse. Until she set up the old business office in the main building, it would be the camp's only phone service. According to the directory assistance operator, there was only one general contractor in Avalon, just as Freddy had predicted.

Gritting her teeth, she dialed the number. Like most small-time contractors, Davis Construction's answering service consisted of a male voice saying, 'Leave your number and I'll get back to you.' The first time she heard the message, she hung up without saying anything.

Come on, Olivia, she pep talked herself. It didn't really sound like him. It couldn't be him. What would he be doing with a construction business in Avalon, New York? And even if it was him, so what? She was a professional. She dealt with contractors all the time.

None of them, however, had ever made her hyperventilate when she dialed his number. That was new.

Grim with determination, she plugged another quarter into the pay phone and dialed the number again. And once again, she got the voice mail. This time, she left a clear, distinct message: 'My name is Olivia Bellamy, and I'm calling from Camp Kioga. I'd like to discuss a...sizable restoration project, if you're interested...'

*　　*　　*

'Any luck?' called Freddy.

'No. I left a voice mail.' It took her a moment to find him, following the sound of his voice. He was in the storage loft above the dining hall. The high gallery featured an impressive peeled-log railing that was badly in need of dusting.

'But no one can call you back.'

'I left directions and said to just show up if he's interested in the job. If no one shows by tomorrow morning, we'll work on finding someone else.' She said this with a small measure of relief. 'What are you doing?'

'Getting started,' he said. 'I'm digging up all kinds of treasures here.'

'Like what?'

'Like the telescope you told me about.' It was his only reference to last night, and Olivia pretended not to hear. She suddenly became fascinated by a collection of painted paddles that used to be displayed in the foyer.

'Check these out.' Freddy dropped something unwieldy over the railing. A large bundle fell in a heap on the floor, throwing up a storm of dust.

'The flags,' said Olivia, gagging on the dust. She bent down and unwrapped the old,

128

brittle fabric, jumping back as a spider scuttled out. 'I don't think you're supposed to let them touch the ground.'

'There's a five-second rule,' he said.

'Right.' She gingerly picked up the bundle and laid it on an empty table. There were three of them—the flags of the state of New York and of the U.S., and Camp Kioga's signature banner. The faded fabric was covered in cobwebs and creepy-looking spider-egg cases. She rolled the flags up and brought them outside to the commercial Dumpster that had been delivered first thing in the morning.

You weren't supposed to put the flag in a Dumpster, though. She remembered that from civics class. You were supposed to burn it to show reverence, though she had no idea why that showed more reverence than putting it in a Dumpster.

Then she had another thought. In front of the main pavilion at the entrance circle, the three flagpoles stood, stark and denuded as trees in winter. The sight of the three flags flying would certainly be an improvement.

Decisively, she shook out each flag with a snap. The cables on the flagpole seemed to be in working order. Within minutes, she had raised the Camp Kioga flag, which depicted a kitschy tepee by a lake. Then came the state flag, with its two goddesses holding a shield. Finally, on the center and tallest pole, she raised the U.S. flag. She felt oddly virtuous and patriotic, tugging at the cable and humming the national anthem under her breath. This flag was a true antique, because it had forty-eight stars. Like her grandparents, it had seen a half-century of history—wars and the birth of rock and roll, disaster and abundance, social movements and national crises.

This flag...was upside down.

In her patriotic fervor, Olivia had raised it the wrong way. An upside-down flag was a sign of distress. She didn't want to give that impression, surely.

She reversed the direction of the cable, but the pulley seemed to be snagged. She tugged a few times and swore at the thing, but it did no good.

'A ladder,' she muttered, heading for a storage shed. She found one, brushed away the cobwebs and marched back to the flagpole area. By now, the sun had burned away the cool of the morning, and she peeled the sweatshirt down to her tank top. It took some maneuvering to lean the ladder against the slender pole, but she found that by keeping herself centered, it didn't wobble too much.

Halfway up, she heard the wind in the trees and paused to survey the area from her high vantage point. She could see the layout of the camp from here, the quaint wooden structures in the distance, the lake shimmering

130

in the sun and the wind. From here, the view was majestic and intimidating. It struck her then that this job was bigger than she'd ever imagined. It would be a miracle if she could pull it off.

I can do this, she thought, moving up each rung with determination. Nana liked to say that everything happened for a reason, and you don't always get to know what that reason might be.

Olivia climbed as high as she dared, and then reached, stretching to her limit. As she extended her arm upward to tug at the snag, she felt the ladder shift.

No, she thought. No. But before she could even open her mouth to yell for help, the ladder canted sideways. She hugged the pole, cringing as she heard the ladder hit the ground with a crash.

Six

Connor Davis couldn't remember ever meeting an Olivia Bellamy. There were a bunch of Bellamys and in the past, he'd encountered his share, but not lately. Thank God. High-strung and overbred, the Bellamy women he'd known were the French poodles of the fairer sex. Most of them, anyway.

Still, her message had intrigued him. The

131

promise of a project intrigued his bottom line. So far, it had been a lean spring season on the heels of a brutal winter. The weather that had turned the landscape into a regular Currier and Ives postcard had also put the big freeze on most building projects. He was ready for the dry spell to end. There were a dozen guys on the payroll and he wasn't keeping them busy enough.

Because the work truck was in use by one of his crews, he rode up to Camp Kioga by the only other means he had, his Harley. To someone who didn't know his situation, the bike looked like a huge extravagance. In reality, a cash-poor client had given it to him a few years back as payment for a project.

Connor was happy enough to ride today. It was the kind of late-spring day that promised that winter was finally over. The sky was a deep blue bowl and sunlight sliced down through the tree branches, dappling the road with coins of gold. Chilly, though. He was glad he had taken the time to put on all his gear—jacket, gloves, boots, chaps. And hell. Might as well admit it. People like the Bellamys tended to pay closer attention when he dressed head to toe in scuffed black leather.

He didn't get up this way very often, not anymore. No one but the most dedicated autumn leaf-lookers did. But as a kid, the road to Camp Kioga represented an emotional roller-coaster ride. Each summer he'd come here, it was the same. He made the journey with a heart full of hope and possibility. This year, it would be different. This year, his father wouldn't let him down. This year, his father would keep his promise to stay sober. This year, his father wouldn't humiliate him and make him wish he could disappear. This year, he could just be a kid, instead of taking care of the man who was supposed to take care of *him*.

That was a long time ago, though. Now the camp was closed and its boundaries posted Private Property—No Trespassing.

The sign arching over the main entrance looked the same. A little more rusty, maybe a tad crooked. But it had been built to last, and seemed to be as much a part of the landscape as the rocks and trees.

Time fell away as he rolled under the arch. He was a kid again, clutching his duffel bag and making a run for it, hoping he got a good cabin this year.

The three flags that flew in front of the main hall looked…Connor touched his sunglasses. Something was wrong. On the tallest flagpole, the U.S. flag hung crookedly by one corner. And someone—a very blond someone in extremely short shorts—clung to the pole as though hanging on for dear life.

Connor accelerated, the Harley blasting an announcement of his arrival. This should be interesting.

CAMP KIOGA CODE OF CONDUCT

The use of alcohol, tobacco and drugs is strictly prohibited.

In matters of dress, *modesty* must prevail. Halter tops, short shorts, etc., will not be allowed. Wear shoes at all times. See the Official Camp Dress Code.

Radios, tape players, magazines, comic books, etc., are a distraction to camp. The dean has the privilege of confiscating such items.

No camper is to be out of his or her cabin after lights-out.

Food is not allowed in the cabin at any time; it attracts bugs and animals.

The camp kitchen is off-limits except at mealtimes.

Do not push the beds together; it's a state law.

Seven

His first summer at Camp Kioga, in the middle of water-safety practice, Connor Davis discovered firsthand what a woody was. Sure, guys talked about it all the time, and a morning woody was nothing new, but the actual wide-awake experience was... startling. All it had taken was one look at Gina Palumbo in her red swimsuit, and his elastic warrior instantly got a mind of its own. His regulation dark blue swim trunks were suddenly way too tight. Tent pole time.

Schwing. And worse, Connor couldn't make it go away.

He and a group of kids had been sent up to the top of the lookout tower, a platform thirty feet above the swim and dive area. They were supposed to be watching the swimmers as part of their safety-certification training. Instead, he found himself staring at Gina Palumbo, whose boobs belonged in the hall of fame.

Some of the guys in the cabin told dirty stories about her. Connor doubted if any of them were true, the stuff they said she did behind the boathouse or on the floating dock at night. Sometimes there was even an extra

135

girl in the story, or a German shepherd, which was plain gross. Anyway, he wasn't even thinking about the late-night, whispered stories when he saw Gina and two of her friends strolling down the beach. It was the furthest thing from his mind. But once he spotted her and her friends, he couldn't think of anything except those stories.

Why was it that hot girls always went around in packs of three? he wondered, biting his lip to keep in a groan. It made it three times harder not to stare. *Down, Simba.*

But Connor couldn't help himself. Even though there was a rule—universally hated by the girls—that they had to wear one-piece regulation camp suits, Gina still looked like a Madonna CD cover. The stretchy fabric showed off those huge melons and pulled tautly over the curves of her rear end.

It was said that guys weren't even supposed to look at Gina. Her father was this mafioso gazillionaire whose goons would break your kneecaps if they caught you having impure thoughts about his daughter. Impure didn't even begin to describe what Connor was thinking. If there was a mafia goon around, Connor Davis would be toast.

Fordham, the swim and dive safety instructor, was droning on and on about how to methodically scan the area in an invisible grid pattern so you didn't miss anything. A good lifeguard could quickly spot trouble, distinguishing between normal horsing around and genuine distress.

'So where's the trouble?' Fordham asked the group, gesturing at the busy swimming area.

In my damn pants, that's where, Connor thought, hanging back and praying no one would notice. Once you were busted, the guys gave you no peace. Earlier in the week, J. J. Danforth had popped a woody in the shower, and ever since, the guys called him flagpole and saluted when he went past.

Go away, Connor thought, feeling the sweat break out on his forehead and in his armpits. That was another weird change in his body lately—sweating armpits. Sweating, hairy armpits.

He wasn't even looking at Gina now, but the damage was done. He tried diverting himself, thinking about stuff that didn't excite him.

Like his mother getting married to her boss at the club in Buffalo. Or that his new stepfather, Mel, wanted Connor gone for the summer. Or the fact that Connor had a baby brother in New Orleans he never got to see, and a completely pathetic father, who could build practically anything with his hands, when they weren't shaking from needing a drink.

Even thinking about his screwed up family didn't help. Nothing would help. Connor was dizzy now, so filled with an urge he'd never felt before that he almost couldn't breathe. And—shit—Fordham was going down the line, quizzing everybody about the safety features of the tower. And suddenly, it was all about sex. The round holes of the life rings. Mouth-to-mouth artificial respiration. Pumping a victim's chest. Geez, everything was pure sex. In a second, it would be Connor's turn to be questioned, and then they'd notice him and he would be totally busted.

He couldn't let that happen. Glancing around like a trapped animal, he tried to concentrate on the view of the lake and the camp, the bunkhouses connected by a network of paths, the main hall, where a white panel truck from Sky River Bakery was making its daily delivery. A little farther out was a cluster of cottages and bungalows in the trees, where the counselors and workers lived, including his loser father, who told Connor to pretend they weren't related if he knew what was good for him.

And Connor hadn't told. So far, only that stupid Lolly Bellamy knew, and she wasn't talking. Maybe she wasn't so stupid after all. Maybe he was the stupid one, with his stupid shorts sticking out a mile. He needed to escape, and fast.

His gaze fixed on the dive platform. They had been told repeatedly that the platform was never, ever to be used except under supervision or in cases of extreme emergency. Like when someone was in distress.

Well, hell. If this wasn't an emergency, Connor didn't know what was. He sure as hell was in distress.

Except...the platform was ten meters above the diving area. That was like skyscraper height. Okay, maybe it wasn't exactly the Empire State Building, but when you were looking down at the surface of the lake, it looked like forever.

Dang it. His turn was coming up and the situation in his pants was not improving. In fact, it was getting worse. He had seconds to make up his mind. Take action now, or spend the rest of the summer as the joke of Ticonderoga Cabin.

That did it. Without another thought, he broke for the diving platform. The breeze whipped over him as he sped past the others. He ran to the end of the platform with shouts and warning whistles ringing in his ears, but he ignored them and kept running, even when there was nothing but thin air beneath his paddling feet.

He didn't dive, of course. Who the hell would dare to do this headfirst?

He forgot to be scared but remembered to tuck one leg up in a jackknife—a position he'd been told would protect the family jewels. Although at the moment, they didn't feel that fragile.

The fall took forever. He was a skydiver without a chute, plummeting toward the earth. He hit the water so hard it slammed up his nose and snapped his neck back. It felt as if his head was about to explode. He kept going down, down, down, deeper than he thought the lake could ever be, so deep he didn't think he'd ever reach the surface alive.

Then he felt the soft sand and algae of the bottom beneath his feet, and pushed off with all his might. He could see the murky darkness of the depths growing lighter and lighter, and he followed the glow of the sunlight upward. It seemed to take forever, but at last he broke the surface, instantly gulping in a giant breath of air with a loud and desperate gasp.

With that breath of air, his brain kicked in. He was in deep shit now. He had just majorly violated a camp safety rule. They would put him in solitary for hours. Or worse, they'd kick him out. It wasn't like he was a paying customer, anyway. They'd send him to stay at his dad's pathetic caretaker's cottage, and the rest of the summer nights would be filled with the queasy crack and hiss of a beer can opening, his dad sliding nightly into drunkenness and talking, endlessly talking about nothing, nothing at all.

Connor swam as if there was a giant alligator after him, and grabbed the first swimmer he could find, winding his arm around the designated victim in the rescue hold they'd been taught.

'Just relax,' he shouted. 'I've got you. I'll take you to shore.'

The surprised swimmer fought like a mad cat, writhing and scratching. Crap, thought Connor. Of all the kids in the lake today, he had managed to grab loudmouthed Lolly Bellamy.

'Let go of me, you freak. Who do you think you are?'

'I'm your new best friend,' he told her, mimicking something she'd once said to him.

'Let me go,' she spluttered, blowing droplets of water from the braces on her teeth. 'What do you think you're doing?'

'Rescuing you.' He was struggling toward shore, awkwardly dragging his victim along. Her rubber swim cap and goggles made her look like a Teletubbie.

'I don't need rescuing.' She fought with a sturdy determination and a strength that took him by surprise.

'Too bad,' he said, trying to subdue her. 'I'm doing it anyway.'

'You're crazy. Let go of me, you stupid freak.'

'When we get to shore.'

She was pretty much the most annoying girl at camp. The most annoying girl he had ever met. She was a complete know-it-all and a diehard when it came to stuff she was good at, like Scrabble and cribbage and playing

141

piano and reciting every rule of the flag. When she couldn't do something, she pretended it was beneath her.

Except swimming. He saw her practicing every day, doing laps from the shore to the floating dock, back and forth, back and forth. Clearly, the practice had made her stronger. She fought him all the way to shore, spluttering and telling him he was crazy, a freak and an idiot.

She did do him one favor, though. By the time he slogged ashore to make his excuses for going off the platform—*I really thought she was drowning, honest*—Lolly Bellamy had proven she was good for one other thing. His woody was completely gone.

CAMP KIOGA CHRONICLES, 1941

Camp Kioga was founded on the principles of good sportsmanship, equality, the value of hard work and the importance of character.

Eight

'Holy shit.' Connor Davis's voice was incredulous, echoing across the flagpole yard. *'Lolly?'*

All right, thought Olivia as she dusted off her hands after her climb down the ladder, so maybe it was a little bit fun, watching the expression on his face, a mildly amusing look of wonder and confusion.

The flags, now properly hung, snapped in the brisk morning breeze, and somewhere hidden in the woods, a bobwhite called. Time felt frozen, suspended somewhere between the past nine years. What a temptation it was to summarily dismiss him, announcing that she would be giving the project to his competitor. But she hadn't located a competitor, and she wasn't likely to find one.

Besides, Olivia had to be honest with herself. This was Connor Davis. Why would any normal, red-blooded American girl want to work with anyone *but* him?

So here he was, in the flesh. In old black leather and faded denim, to be more accurate. He was still freakishly good-looking, not in the polished, privileged way of, say, a Rand Whitney. There was nothing pretty about Connor Davis. His features were too rough-hewn, his black hair was a little too long, his piercing blue eyes too intense. He had always been the bad boy from the wrong side of the tracks and he'd always looked the part. She found the sight of him disconcerting and, appallingly, she felt a warm little thrum of physical awareness. She didn't want to be attracted to him. He was a member of the same club as Rand Whitney, Richard and Pierce, she reminded herself. The four of them belonged to a fraternity whose membership was expanding. Men who had dumped her. Connor was simply the first—and admittedly, the most inventive.

'Can you give me a hand with this ladder?' In truth, she didn't need help, but she was desperate to find some kind of equilibrium. Seeing him again was like having a flashback to a nightmare. When she looked at him, she still felt that same crazy crush of attraction, the feeling that had driven her to make a complete and total fool of herself, once upon a summer.

He didn't give her a hand. He simply grabbed the ladder and carried it to the main utility shed. Olivia had to hurry to match his long strides.

'You can lean the ladder against the building,' she told him. 'It's all got to be cleaned out, anyway.'

Connor nodded. 'I need to peel off some of this stuff,' he said, unzipping his jacket as he strode back to the Harley, the chains on his boots ringing with every step. 'It's hot.'

She stood and watched as he unbuckled and unzipped the military-style jacket and chaps, draping them over the handlebars of his bike. Underneath, the white T-shirt molded to his body, outlining the cut of his pecs. His arms, thick with muscles, already looked tan from working outside, even though summer had barely begun. She glanced away, determined not to appear too interested.

She felt perversely satisfied that he had not recognized her. On the one hand, it was nice to know she had transformed herself from the gawky, overweight girl she had once been.

On the other hand, it was infuriating to see how intrigued he was by her new look. Because no matter what she looked like on the outside these days, that incredibly insecure girl was not so very far away. She was a part of Olivia, living just beneath the surface of polish and confidence.

Only she was older now, and she didn't let her feelings show. She sidestepped to put some more distance between them. 'You know, no one's called me Lolly in years,' she said, her voice sounding lightly amused. Casual, as though he was an old acquaintance rather than the person who had ripped out her heart and left it bleeding on the floor. 'When I went away to college, I switched exclusively to my given name.'

'I never knew your name was Olivia.'

There's a lot you never bothered to learn about me, she thought. 'It's the name I was born with. Olivia Jane Bellamy. Sophisticated, huh? Not really a kid name. One of my cousins christened me Lolly. She was just learning to talk and couldn't say Olivia, so Lolly's the name that stuck.'

'You never told me that story. When I was young, I thought all rich kids had names like Binky and Buffy and Lolly, and asking why made me look ignorant, so I never asked.'

'How did you wind up in Avalon?' she asked him.

'A guy's got to live somewhere.'

'That's not what I'm asking.'

'I know. After that summer—'

She knew which summer he meant, but she didn't make him say it—*The summer I destroyed you.*

'After that last summer, my dad got pretty...sick. It...just made sense to stick around.'

'I'm sorry about what you had to deal with,' she told him. It must be horrible to lose a parent, she thought. Maybe she should tell him so, but the words stuck in her throat.

'We all deal with things.'

'All righty, then,' she said with forced brightness. 'How about we take a look around and I'll tell you about my project.' She was aware that he probably knew Camp Kioga as

146

well as she did. 'When was the last time you came up here?'

'I never come here. Why would I?'

She figured it was a rhetorical question that didn't need an answer. Hurrying, she led the way to the deck of the dining hall, which projected out over the lake. The weathered wooden stairs creaked, and the railing felt as wobbly as a loose tooth. Connor took a small notebook from his back pocket and scribbled something. When they reached the deck, she shaded her eyes, looking for Freddy and Barkis, but saw no sign of them. When she turned to Connor, she was startled by the slightly insolent way he was studying her.

'You're staring,' she said, feeling his eyes trace her body and trying to deny the sensation.

'Yeah,' he said, resting his hip against the deck railing. 'I am.'

At least he was willing to admit it. 'Don't,' she said.

'Why not?'

She folded her arms. 'It makes me uncomfortable.'

'If being stared at by a guy makes you uncomfortable, you must spend a lot of time squirming.'

This, she supposed, should be taken as a compliment, yet she didn't feel flattered in the least. She knew he was wondering how the fat chick nobody liked had turned out to be her.

'What's going on?' he asked.

'I came to fix up the place. My grandparents want to celebrate their fiftieth anniversary here.' She pointed at the lake. 'They were married on the island, under a gazebo that isn't there anymore. I have until August to get this place ready for a hundred guests.'

'I don't blame them for wanting to celebrate. I don't know anyone who's been married that long.'

His statement made Olivia feel wistful. It was a rare thing, to love someone that long. It warranted a celebration. From where she was in her life right now, a fifty-year marriage seemed impossible. How did it happen that two people fell in love and stayed that way, growing old together, not just keeping their bond intact, but strengthening and deepening it through all the trials and triumphs life had to offer? She found herself wondering if she would ever celebrate such a milestone, if she'd ever meet a man she wanted to grow old with.

Given her track record, the likelihood was as distant as the moon. She glanced at Connor, who appeared to be checking for wood rot. She thought she saw—yes, she wasn't imagining it—a telltale gleam through his dark, glossy waves of hair. In one ear, he wore a very small silver loop. My Lord, she thought. He'd kept the earring. She wondered what it meant. Was it because he liked having an earring, or because she had—

'I don't see anything to worry about here,' he said.

'Let's go down by the lake and take a look around,' she said, telling herself to quit thinking about the earring, and things that had happened years ago, things that didn't matter now. She led the way along footpaths that were overgrown with sticker bushes that scratched at her bare legs.

'Let me,' Connor said, eyeing her legs. He pushed ahead so he could hold the long, thorny fronds out of the way to let her pass.

Memories of summers past waited around every turn—midnight pranks, the dazzle of nature in full bloom, the sights and sounds of campers singing and talking around a crackling fire. She studied Connor, his big, broad form cutting a swath through the wilderness. She wondered what sort of memories this place evoked in him. Was he reliving past glories or remembering the darker, more difficult times?

She pointed out the sagging boathouse and dock, and a timbered, Adirondack-style cabin, set off by itself beside the lake. It was the camp's most comfortable cabin, originally built to house the camp's owner. It had running water and utilities year-round, a river-rock fireplace and wood-burning stove. In the winter, even when the rest of the camp was closed, it was accessible by snowmobile, and sometimes by road if the snows weren't too bad. 'This is the cabin I want to redo especially for my grandparents when they come in August for their anniversary,' she told Connor.

'All right.'

'My uncle Greg spent Christmas here one year, when his wife threw him out.' She flushed, wishing she hadn't blurted that out. 'Sorry,' she said. 'Too much information.'

'So how is it you're in charge of the whole renovation?' he asked, diplomatically changing the subject.

'And here you thought I was destined to spend my life lying around eating bonbons and reading *Town & Country.*'

'I never said that.'

'I bet you thought it.' She was used to people having low expectations of her.

'Nope,' he said simply. 'I figured you'd be married by now, driving the kids to preschool in Darien.'

It wasn't for lack of trying, but she knew she wouldn't tell him that. 'I'm not married,' she admitted. 'No kids, no house in the suburbs.' Although she was quite sure she knew the answer, she asked, 'You?'

'Never married.' His gaze touched her in a strangely intimate way, considering he was simply walking beside her. 'Not seeing anyone, either.'

Which, of course, was her invitation to

offer him the same information. She didn't, though.

'And didn't you want to be a teacher?' he asked.

Startled, she almost tripped over a tree root. She couldn't believe he remembered that old dream. She barely remembered it herself. As she reinvented herself and rebuilt her life around the new Olivia Bellamy, the idea of teaching school had gotten lost in the shuffle. 'I started a business in Manhattan. I'm a real-estate stager.'

He looked blank.

'When a property's up for sale, it's my job to make it look as appealing as possible. Usually, it's a process of decluttering, picking fresh paint colors, rearranging furniture or bringing in new pieces.'

'And people pay for this service?'

'You'd be surprised. I'll show you what I mean.' She led the way back to the dining hall, knowing the best way to get rid of his skepticism was to show him. Walking over to a corner table by the window, she said, 'Help me move this. We want to set it at an angle so it catches the morning light.' She shook out a vintage oilcloth she'd found in a cupboard. 'I try to use things that belong to the owner because that gives the space an air of authenticity. Sometimes I rent furniture and accessories. This summer, I'll keep my eyes peeled for bent willow and Adirondack

151

furniture. I go to a lot of estate sales, too.' She cringed inwardly when she thought of the vintage tansu chest she'd rented for Rand's place. It had looked so perfect as a sideboard.

She finished spreading out the tablecloth and added a few other simple touches—the jar of wildflowers she'd picked while taking Barkis for his walk at sunrise. A pair of thick china coffee mugs and a checkered napkin.

'It's mostly smoke and mirrors,' she told Connor. 'For each property, I try to picture who the ideal owner will be, and then I create his or her fantasy.' She folded yesterday's newspaper and laid it on the table. 'I worked on a listing in Greenburgh not long ago, and I had this vision that it would sell to one of the Nicks. It had ten-foot ceilings and everything was larger than life. So I staged the whole place to appeal to a star athlete.'

'And?'

'Kwami Gilmer bought it the same week the listing went on the market.' She climbed up on a chair to let down the drapes. The fabric was dry and brittle with age and disuse, and when she pulled the cord, a cloud of dust went up, causing Olivia to sneeze.

'Careful there,' he said. 'This chair is rickety.' He hovered nearby as though ready to catch her if she fell.

She cleared her throat, intensely aware of the cutoffs and tank top she was wearing. 'I'm fine. And thank you. I don't usually require rescuing more than once a day.' Very carefully, she stepped down, ignoring his chivalrously proffered hand. Then she straightened the chair, fluffed out the drapes and waited for the dust to settle. The tableau now resembled a café table with a view of the lake. Vintage posters, she thought. Vintage Catskills posters from the Borscht Belt days would awaken that ache for the sweetness of summers past. 'All right,' she said, 'you get the idea.'

'You're into creating other people's fantasies.'

'I suppose you could put it that way.'

'What about your own?'

'My fantasies?' She tried not to choke on the dust. 'Never gave it much thought.'

And boy, are you ever a liar. In her mind, there was a fantasy as vivid as the sky over the mountains. And it wasn't the trust-fund-baby, celebutante lifestyle some of her friends and cousins favored. Instead, Olivia fantasized about a big, rambling house with a wraparound porch and sturdy old rosebushes, a sunroom and music conservatory, cookies baking in the vintage oven, kids laughing and playing in the backyard. And of course, the husband. A big, laughing man who would swing her around and nuzzle her neck when he got home from work. It was funny. In the fantasy, he wasn't anyone in particular.

He was just someone who loved her.

Someone who would hold her at night, who would make her laugh and keep her safe, witness the passage of years by her side, grow old with her.

'So what do you want?' Connor asked, breaking into her thoughts.

She felt her cheeks flush, and wondered if the yearning she felt was written on her face. Then she realized what he was asking.

'Let's go over the plans. This place is going to require a lot more than decluttering and flying the old flags, and we've only got one summer.'

The notes and sketches she and Freddy had made were spread on a long table and pinned to a wall. 'I have more family members coming up to help,' she said. 'My cousin Dare is a professional event planner, so she'll be in charge of the celebration itself. My uncle Greg's a landscape architect, so he'll be working on the grounds. His daughter, Daisy, just finished her junior year in high school, and she and her brother, Max, can do...whatever needs doing. Detail work. The goal is to make this place look like the camp in everyone's mind,' she said. 'The kind of place people dream about—'

'As opposed to the camp as it really is.'

'Such a cynic,' she said. 'I thought you liked camp.'

'I did like camp. For the most part.' A small, delicate muscle twitched in his jaw.

Olivia tried to read his expression, but she simply didn't know him anymore. 'Should I be looking for another contractor?'

'You'd be crazy to look for another contractor.'

She pretended to be unimpressed by his self-confidence. 'And why is that?'

He leaned back, crossing his ankles, hands behind his head. 'Because in the first place, you won't find anybody in a fifty-mile radius. And in the second,' he said, 'you need me. Not somebody else.'

'I need you. And how do you know that?'

'Because I remember you, Lolly. It's all coming back to me now and I know exactly what you want.'

Nine

'I have to hand it to you,' said Olivia's cousin Dare. 'I didn't think you could pull this off, but you're actually doing it.'

The camp's extreme makeover was well under way. Just as he'd said, Connor Davis *did* know what Olivia wanted. He'd brought in heavy equipment and an experienced crew, and had already made visible progress. He also knew every subcontractor in the county— plumbers, electricians, painters, roofers.

Dare stepped out of the rental van and

surveyed the main part of the camp compound, her eyes bright with appreciation. Olivia had always regarded her cousin as a slightly older, slightly better-adjusted Bellamy than Olivia had ever been. The daughter of Aunt Peg and Uncle Clyde, Dare was one of those people who made life look fun and easy. She'd sailed through college, dated effortlessly and had launched a successful career as an event planner. She looked like Barbie's shorter, more likable sister and dressed with a breezy sense of style. So many reasons to envy her, and yet Olivia adored Dare.

'Come on, you guys. Check it out.' Dare slid open the panel of the van, and Uncle Greg got out of the driver's side. Greg had two kids of his own—ten-year-old Max, and Daisy, who was seventeen. They were Olivia's youngest cousins, and the fact that their parents were on the verge of divorce resonated painfully with Olivia.

'My Lord,' she said, beaming at Max. 'Look how tall you are. I guess I won't be winning any more games of one-on-one against you. Where's your sister?'

Daisy emerged through the rear door of the van. As sunny and cheerful as her namesake, she beamed at Olivia. At seventeen, she was heartbreakingly adorable, with silky blond hair and cornflower-blue eyes. It was hard for Olivia to see the troubled girl Greg had described on the phone when she had called to ask for his help with the project. The Daisy he'd described was struggling in school, sneaking out at night and sneaking back in, reeking of cigarettes and booze. The Daisy he'd described was having just as hard a time with her parents' breakup as Olivia had with hers.

'Hello, you,' Olivia said, hugging her. She didn't smell of anything but youth and trendy body splash. 'I'm so glad you decided to come.' Barkis came to greet everyone, squirming with delight as Max hunkered down on the ground to play with him.

'What a cute dog!' Daisy exclaimed.

'Thanks. I adopted him from a shelter.'

Daisy looked around at the camp, and suddenly seemed overwhelmed. 'So this is it.'

'Yep. You never got to come here when it was up and running.'

'What are we going to do all summer? I mean, like, besides fixing the place up?'

'There's a piano in the dining hall,' Olivia said. 'A library and rec room. All the board games you'd ever want.'

She watched her cousins' expressions turn dubious. 'Did you explain to them that they'll be spending the summer unplugged?' Olivia gave her uncle a nudge.

'Yeah, but I don't think they believed me.'

'Unplugged means no TV, no Internet, no cell phone service. We won't even have regular phone service for another week or

157

two. They keep putting me off. There's one radio station that comes in when the wind is calm.'

The kids' eyes widened. 'Welcome to the gulag,' said Dare.

* * *

Max and Daisy headed off to explore the bunkhouses. Olivia and Dare lingered with their uncle, organizing the luggage and supplies. There was one working electric cart, which they would use to deliver the bags. Greg was her father's youngest brother, the baby of the family. He had been the fun-loving uncle, the prankster, the one who never took anything seriously. Now that he was an adult and the father of two, Olivia suspected that wasn't working so well for him. 'How long do you think they'll last?'

'I have a feeling they'll surprise us,' he said. 'They'll be okay.'

She and Dare exchanged a glance. 'How about you, Uncle Greg?' Dare asked. 'Are you okay with this, too?'

'I need this time with my kids,' he said, flexing and unflexing his hands. He was dressed like a teenager himself, in board shorts and a Flay-Vah T-shirt, a baseball cap turned backward on his head. 'Your aunt Sophie... She, uh, her plans for the summer are still up in the air. The kids have been so jerked around by this. I'm hoping that being here will, I don't know, help them feel less fragmented.'

Olivia was struck by the pain that shook in his voice. 'Uncle Greg, I'm so sorry.'

'What happened?' asked Dare.

'It's hard to describe. Things just...unraveled, and the whole family was too busy to notice until it was too late. Between Sophie's work and mine, and all the kids' activities, we...lost touch with each other. When Sophie's firm offered her a huge case in Seattle, she took it, even though it could last six months, maybe a year. She didn't leave just for work, though, and we all know it.'

'Are you splitting up for good?' Dare asked.

'We haven't said so officially. Feels that way, though.' He stuffed his hands in his pockets.

'How are Max and Daisy coping?' Olivia asked.

'Hard to say. They're not talking.'

'You'll have plenty of time for talking this summer,' Olivia assured him. There was a special kind of pain that happened to a fragmented family. She knew this. She knew the way it lodged under the heart, casting even moments of hope and happiness into shadow. 'What can we do?'

'Just being here will help. God. I hope.' Some of the bleakness lifted from his face.

159

'We need this time. Max should learn to paddle a canoe. He still hasn't caught his first fish.'

'You came to the right place, then,' Dare said.

'How did I luck into two nieces like you?'

'You said it. Luck.'

He loaded up everyone's luggage and got into the cart. For a moment, he looked as lost and bereft as an abandoned puppy. Then the sound of the kids' voices—laughter and chatter—drifted across the lake, and he straightened up, squared his shoulders, gave them a thumbs-up sign and took off.

Olivia and Dare busied themselves in the kitchen. In addition to planning the anniversary celebration, Dare had assumed the duties of provisioning the camp kitchen for all the people who would be spending the summer. 'No more Spaghettios out of the can,' she said, briskly reorganizing the industrial-size pantry. 'No more mandarin oranges in heavy syrup and please, no more ramen noodles.'

'There go my three major food groups,' Olivia said.

Dare explored the huge camp kitchen with its walk-in fridge, commercial grills and stainless steel countertops and appliances. Although out of date, everything worked. The stainless-steel fixtures and surfaces gleamed. This had been the first cleanup job after the bathrooms. Olivia and Freddy had made it a priority. In order for the rest of the summer to run smoothly, they needed a functional kitchen. A few basic repairs and upgrades done by Connor's workmen had transformed the kitchen into an updated, efficient-looking work space.

'Nana is going to love this,' Dare said. 'Your contractor must be a god.'

'No,' Olivia said quickly. 'He just looks like one.'

Dare fixed her with a speculative stare. 'Oh, really? Someone I should meet?'

Olivia didn't allow herself to look away. 'You've already met him, a long time ago. Connor Davis.'

Dare's jaw dropped. As Olivia's closest cousin, she was well aware of the heartbreak Olivia had suffered as an unhappy young girl, thanks to Connor Davis. 'He's here? In Avalon?'

'Yes.' Beyond inquiring about his father, Olivia hadn't asked him why he'd stayed. She hadn't asked him much at all because she didn't want to seem as if she cared.

'I can't believe you're working with him.'

'It's fine,' Olivia assured her. 'This is working out just fine.' She told herself so every day, and on the surface, it was. She showed Dare the progress she'd made so far. She had removed the dust coverings from the display cases and heavy lounge furniture in

161

the foyer of the main pavilion, setting out camp gear and memorabilia, turning the space into a reflection of the bygone days she knew her grandparents remembered so well.

'So is it weird, seeing him again after all these years?' Dare asked, refusing to drop the subject.

'What do you think?'

Dare laughed. 'All right. Dumb question. But... oh, my.' Her voice trailed off as she looked out the window.

Olivia followed her gaze to see what she was oh-mying about. It was Freddy, pulling a hand truck laden with lumber. The city boy had taken to camp life with surprising aplomb, and looked completely at home in the landscape. The afternoon sun highlighted the blond tips of his hair. He wore a muscle shirt and painters' pants, the waistband dragged low by the weight of his fully loaded tool belt.

Dare moistened her lips. 'That can't be Connor Davis.'

'No, that's Freddy. I've told you about him.'

'That's *the* Freddy? The theater geek?'

'He still calls himself that, sometimes. He's a set designer these days. His latest production closed down, so he's working with me this summer.'

'Oh, my,' Dare said again. Then she seemed to catch herself. 'I mean, he's very cute, but is he... gay?'

162

'Everybody asks that. *No.*'

'Then, are the two of you…?'

'Definitely not,' Olivia assured her. She thought about their first night here. They'd moved into separate cottages soon after, and now that night was a distant memory. 'As far as I know, Freddy is unattached. Come on outside and meet him.'

She made the introductions and watched her cousin and Freddy fall instantly into a highly charged mutual attraction. And why not? They were both adorable, he with his trendy metrosexual look and she with her trademark bubbly charm. They were even the right height for each other, both on the short side. Dare and Freddy made things like attraction, dating, maybe even falling in love, seem simple and natural rather than fraught with peril. Olivia envied them their instant ease with one another.

She gave them a bit of time to chat; then she checked her watch. 'Sorry to interrupt, but I need to pick some things up from the building supply in town. And don't you have a meeting with the caterer?'

'You bet,' said Dare. 'I believe in hitting the ground running.' She regarded Freddy with a tragic expression. 'Sorry. We've got to go. Can we bring you anything from town? I'm stopping at the caterer, and then the Sky River Bakery.'

'How about a cannoli?'

'A what?'

'You know, one of those long tubular pastries filled with white cream. If you haven't tried one, you don't know what you're missing.' He winked at her.

'Let's go,' Olivia said, linking arms with her cousin and heading for the parking lot. 'God, I don't believe him.'

'What?' Dare asked.

'He's totally hitting on you.'

'You think?'

'A long tubular pastry filled with white cream? Come on.'

'Good. I was hoping he'd hit on me.'

So was Olivia. Dare and Freddy were two of her favorite people in the world, and it made her happy to see that spark of attraction between them. As they drove down the mountain to the town of Avalon, she and her cousin chattered away about everything. It was always like this with Dare. No matter how much time had passed, they talked as though they saw one another every day. By the time they reached the Avalon city limits, they had worked through Rand Whitney's feet of clay and Dare's pregnancy scare, which turned out to be quite a scare.

'One thing I know for sure now,' she said. 'I am *so* not ready to have kids.'

Olivia smiled, brushed by wistful longing. 'Funny. I'm so *ready* for kids. Definitely more than one.'

'Come on.'

'I mean it. It's totally bizarre. Out of the blue, I get hit with these...urges.'

Dare shrugged. 'I get urges to consume Richart chocolates by the kilo, but that doesn't mean I should.'

Olivia sent her a wry smile. 'I'd better work on getting a date first.'

'With Connor Davis,' Dare readily agreed.

'Not in this life,' said Olivia. 'Probably not in the next. I can't believe you'd even suggest it.'

'You're different people now. Maybe—'

'And then again, maybe not,' Olivia said. Then why, she wondered, did she feel such a painful tug of yearning whenever she imagined the two of them together?

Dare had a gift for knowing when to leave a topic alone. She rode in silence for a while, watching the scenery swish past the windows. Summer unfurled in the mountains with lazy extravagance, the forest floor carpeted by shade-loving ferns, the trees reaching for sunlight above the gently rounded hills. 'Has this place changed at all?' she asked when the speed limit decreased at the edge of town.

'Not so you'd notice,' Olivia said. They passed a real-estate office. The marquee identified it as Alger Estate Properties and advertised something called Brookwood Acres, homes from $450,000. 'Property values are up.'

'So do you think Nana and Grandpa will sell the property after this summer?' Dare asked.

'I can't imagine them doing that. I know they'd love to keep it in the family if they can. Maybe Uncle Greg will take it over. He seems to be at loose ends.'

'I think he's probably got enough on his plate without taking on a white elephant.'

'I don't know. I've had plenty of time to take a long hard look at things. It's completely idyllic, the sort of place you just don't find anymore. Maybe its days as a summer camp are over, but...' She waved her hand, laughing at herself. 'Listen to me. I'm all about 'repurposing' these days.'

'So what would be the new purpose? A conference center? Executive retreat? Those are in vogue right now.'

'Maybe something more like a place for families. You know, to unplug, get to know one another again.'

Dare smiled. 'You're still the idealist, kiddo.'

'Right. That's me.'

As they pulled into a parking slot in front of Camelot Catering, Dare pulled out a folder. 'Do me a favor. Drop this off at Sky River Bakery. The woman there is doing the cake for the anniversary and I promised to bring her pictures of the original.'

'No problem. I'll meet you back here in a

few.' Olivia grabbed the folder and crossed the street. The Sky River Bakery was a thriving business that had been around for decades, having been started by immigrants after World War II. Under its hand-lettered sign, it said, Leo & Helen Majesky, prop. since 1952. The white step van with its picture of the river painted on the side used to make a daily delivery to Camp Kioga, Olivia recalled. She had a vague memory of a dark-haired girl in a white jumpsuit and white baseball cap, wheeling bread racks into the camp kitchen.

Even though local rumor had it that this was the best place in town for coffee and pie, she'd been avoiding it. She had to steer clear of pie or wear the evidence on her hips.

A bell jangled as she pushed the door open. She nearly stumbled over the raised threshold as she stepped inside, and held on to the door handle to steady herself. A hand-lettered sign on the door warned, Watch Your Step.

Olivia felt a little sheepish but quickly recovered. A moment later, she nearly fainted from the fragrance. The bakery smelled of all that was sinfully delicious in the world—fresh bread and cinnamon rolls, homemade pies and delicate kolaches, savory rolls and the dizzying rich smell of doughnuts. She inhaled, breathing the heady scent of paradise. This is where I'm coming when I die, she thought.

It was an old-fashioned family bakery with

167

glass display cases and a big brass cash register. On the wall behind the counter was a display of framed photographs and memorabilia—a dollar bill, a business license, newspaper clippings, an array of what appeared to be family photos. A sleepy-looking, heavy-set teenager looked up from reading the sports pages at the counter. He had straight blond hair, a sullen expression and a name badge that identified him as Zach Alger.

'Can I help you?' he asked.

'I have something to drop off. It's about a special order.'

'Just a sec.' He pushed through a door to the back.

A few minutes later, a young woman of about thirty came through the door. She was quietly attractive, with dark hair and brown eyes, full lips and a ready smile. She definitely had an air of being in charge. 'Hi,' she said. 'Can I help you?'

Olivia felt an odd little twinge of awareness. She studied the pretty face—creamy skin, vivid, beautiful features—and tried to place her. Back in the days of the camp, perhaps they had crossed paths.

The dark-haired woman offered a polite smile. She wore a lot of jewelry, Olivia noticed, indicating she probably wasn't involved in production at the bakery. Graceful gold hoops dangled in her ears, and she wore a silver necklace from which a pendant dangled. No wedding band. 'I'm Jenny Majesky.'

'I'm Olivia Bellamy,' she said. 'I'm dropping something off—a picture of a wedding cake.'

Jenny brightened. 'The special order. I spoke to someone on the phone about it.'

'My cousin Dare, the event planner. We're hoping you'll be able to do the cake for our grandparents' fiftieth anniversary celebration.' Olivia opened the folder to reveal a black-and-white photo of her grandparents on their wedding day, about to cut the cake, a towering confection covered in sugar flowers and doves. 'This is a shot of my grandparents back in 1956,' Olivia explained. 'They were married up at Camp Kioga. Maybe you know them— Jane and Charles Bellamy.'

Jenny Majesky's mouth softened into a bemused smile. 'I remember them well. How are they?'

'They're doing great. Looking forward to a big party up at the camp at the end of August.'

Jenny held the photograph by the edges. 'They look wonderful, like movie stars. And so young and happy. I love wedding pictures.'

'You have a lot of pictures of your own.' Olivia indicated the display on the wall.

'Uh-huh. My own grandparents started this place back in the early fifties.'

Olivia scanned the pictures—a grinning

woman with a thick braid arranged in a coronet around her head, a man in coveralls, a young slender girl and... Olivia did a double take. One of the shots looked eerily familiar. It showed a laughing girl in a camp shirt and shorts, her head thrown back, her feathered hair shining. Then she realized where she'd seen that picture before. It was the same shot Olivia had found among her father's things, the picture from 1977. Only the photo on the wall had been cropped, showing the woman only. She glanced from the picture to Jenny Majesky, seeing a strong resemblance there, except she had a small, rather attractive dimple in her chin.

Olivia felt strangely detached from reality. This woman. Jenny Majesky. She... *Get a grip, Olivia,* she coached herself.

'Miss Bellamy?' Jenny prompted, and Olivia realized she'd let a long silence stretch out.

'Please, call me Olivia.' She regained her composure, although she knew her face was flushed a bright, probably unattractive red. 'Anyway, the whole idea behind the anniversary celebration is to re-create the camp as it was fifty years ago. Dare and I thought we'd have you create a replica of this cake.' She flipped the picture over. Someone had written 'cake by Mrs. Majesky.'

'That would be my grandmother, Helen Majesky.'

'Of course. I see. So is she…is your grandmother retired now?' She didn't want to ask the obvious.

Jenny rescued her from saying it, though sadness haunted her deep brown eyes as she spoke. 'My grandfather passed away several years ago, and Gram had a stroke.'

'I'm sorry.'

'She's disabled, but I bet she'd coach me and the master baker through making this cake.' Jenny smiled, and again Olivia was struck by a sense of familiarity, maybe déjà vu. Or something else. She found herself staring at the pendant dangling from Jenny's necklace. It looked just like the odd cuff link she had found among her father's things, at the same time she found the photograph. A small, stylized fish.

'That would be wonderful,' Olivia said, flustered now. 'Dare will be thrilled to hear you think it can be done. And keep the photograph for reference. It's a copy.'

'I'll show it to my grandmother.' Jenny beamed and closed the file. 'You know, Zach's dad, Matthew Alger, might be a good resource for details about the camp. He went to Kioga as a kid, and then he worked there. He's lived in Avalon for decades.'

'I'll look into that.'

'Thanks for stopping in.'

Olivia left feeling a little unsettled by the encounter. She didn't mention it to Dare, and was quiet as they drove back to the camp. When they arrived, Uncle Greg and the kids were busy exploring, with Barkis trotting at their heels. Greg was like the Pied Piper, leading them around the lake to the boathouse and dock. Max sent up whoops of glee, clearly thrilled with everything. Even Daisy looked eager as she skipped stones across the water.

'So far so good,' Dare said.

'Yes, but they've only been away from their TV, cell phones and Internet for half a day.'

'I never missed TV when I was a camper here,' Dare mused. 'I think kids are kids. Put them around a campfire and start telling scary stories, and they'll have a ball. If you don't hand them their fun on a platter, they figure it out for themselves.'

Laden with parcels, they went into the main pavilion. 'Looks like trouble,' Dare murmured as they entered the dining room. Freddy's design plans were laid out on tables and tacked to a wall. In front of a big drawing of an elevation, Freddy and Connor Davis were locked in a stare-down.

Dare lowered her voice even more. 'My Lord,' she said, sizing up Connor, from his shoulder-length black hair to his battered work boots. 'He's Conan the Barbarian.'

'Hey, guys,' Olivia said cheerily, ignoring the fury on their faces. 'What's up?'

'I quit, that's what,' Freddy snapped, still

172

glowering at Connor.

They hadn't liked each other from the start, and Olivia suspected she knew why. They were like two aggressive dogs, marking their territory.

'You can't quit,' she said simply. 'You need this job, and I need you.'

'Tell that to him,' Freddy said, jerking his head in Connor's direction.

In a calm voice, she said, 'I need him, too.'

Equally calm, Connor said, 'It appears we're mutually exclusive.'

'Come on,' she said. 'You're both here for different reasons. I need you both. What's going on?'

'I already told you, I'm quitting. He's already ruined my vision for the gazebo.' Freddy made an inarticulate gesture at his marked up plans. Then he brushed past her and strode out of the hall.

'I'll go,' Dare said, patting Olivia's arm.

Ten

Connor was just as glad to be rid of the annoying little shit for a while. Freddy, with his city-boy hair and two-hundred-dollar jeans.

Olivia appeared to be unaware of the fact that he had just been inches from rearranging Freddy's pretty face. She was probably used to working with girlie-men who had hissy fits when somebody messed with their 'vision.' Studying the elevation of the gazebo, which now bore Connor's modifications in permanent marker, she said, 'I take it you didn't like Freddy's design.'

'It's structurally unsound. The first big wind would sweep the thing away. He makes stage sets, for chrissake. I build things to last awhile.'

She thought for a moment, pushing a finger against her full lower lip in a gesture Connor found unsettling. 'We'll go with your design because we don't want it getting blown away. But do me a favor. Try to get along with Freddy. He's important to me.'

How important? Connor pressed his mouth shut to keep from asking, and offered only a noncommittal grunt. It didn't matter. It shouldn't matter.

They headed out together to inspect the

staff cottages at the far edge of the property. No work had been done here yet. This was where the help had lived when the camp was in operation. It was a row of plain cottages that had housed the dishwashers and groundskeepers, the security guards and laborers. And, of course, the maintenance man and caretaker, Terry Davis, who lived at the camp year-round.

The sight of the bungalow on the end had a curious effect on Connor. He slowed his steps, balking. He didn't want to be here. There were too many memories of darkness, of humiliation and despair.

Olivia clearly had no inkling of his thoughts as she wrote a list on a clipboard. Then she headed to the cottage on the end, up the three steps to the door. 'We should check out these buildings,' she said. 'See what needs to be done.'

He stayed where he was. *No.*

The screen door screamed on its hinges as she opened it and then used the master key to unlock the main place. 'Stuffy in here,' she said, turning back to him. 'Are you coming?'

My God. Didn't she remember that this was where his father had lived?

Apparently not. Connor forced himself to move, climbing the stairs, crossing the porch, brushing past her to step into the musty bungalow. Immediately, memories flashed in nightmare images through his head. There

175

was the fridge, which never held much more than a pack of baloney and several cases of beer. The broken-down sofa was gone but there was a pale rectangle on the linoleum where it had been, and against his will, he could see his father passed out on the gray cushions, a dozen or so beer cans lined up on the floor.

'Something the matter?' she asked with phony innocence. 'You're cranky today.'

'What the hell did you think I'd feel like?'

She took a step back, flinching a little at his tone. 'Let's see,' she said. 'A building contractor, maybe?'

Her very confusion put Connor in his place. To imagine even for a moment that she would remember who had occupied this particular bungalow, and to suppose she was sensitive to the effect it would have on him was definitely a stretch. Yet somehow, he had imagined that he'd been important enough to her to rate this consideration.

Maybe, on the other hand, maybe she knew exactly what she was doing. Maybe this little guided tour was supposed to serve as a reminder to him: This is who you are. This is why I walked away from you and never looked back.

'Right,' he said. 'That's me. The building contractor.'

Her frown deepened. 'Look, if you want me to talk to Freddy, I will, but—'

He laughed bitterly, splayed a hand through his hair. 'You do that, Olivia. You talk to Freddy.'

She backed away, seeming more mystified than ever, and went through a doorway to the kitchen area, which was barren except for an ancient calendar pegged to the wall, its picture faded beyond recognition. Even from the doorway, Connor recognized his father's shaky handwriting in some of the squares. Up to his final days as a drunk, Terry Davis had struggled to function normally. He wasn't a bad guy or even a bad drunk. He'd never raised either a hand or his voice to Connor. In a way, it would have been easier for Connor if his dad had been abusive. At least then Connor could have hated him, stopped wishing he'd get sober. Maybe Connor could have walked away that night nine years ago, instead of sacrificing himself to protect his father.

Olivia surveyed the room, opening a cabinet here and there. Finally, she figured out where she was. Connor could tell the moment she put two and two together. Something written on the faded, yellowed calendar clued her in. She turned to him, set her clipboard on the counter. 'Oh, God. Connor, I didn't realize... Why didn't you say something?'

'Say what?' he asked evenly. That this was where he'd spent some of the worst, most painful hours of his youth? That his helpless, broken father still haunted the place like a ghost?

'I am so, so sorry.' She crossed the room and took one of his hands between hers. 'I truly had no idea this was your father's place, I swear it.' Her touch was tender, oddly expressive.

He hadn't been expecting this. Compassion and even understanding. She couldn't have known, he realized. As a youth, he'd taken great pains to distance himself from his father, to keep the family secret, as all good sons of alcoholics were wont to do.

He looked down at their joined hands, hers dainty and his rough, and then he looked at her face. Since he'd last seen her, she had effectively banished the funny, smart, awkward Lolly he used to know, the one he'd fallen in love with. In her place was a cool-eyed, beautiful stranger, poised and successful, and yet the moment she'd understood what was going on with him, the compassion came back.

'Please forgive me, Connor,' she whispered. 'Please.'

Very carefully, without letting his gaze waver, he disengaged his hand from hers. At the same time, his anger drained away. Simply looking into her eyes made his heart lighter. She was the only person who had ever affected him this way. 'There's nothing to forgive, Lolly.'

She let out a sigh. 'Really? You're not going to quit on me?'

'Nope. That seems to be your buddy Freddy's specialty.'

'It's just that he's really passionate about his designs. I, um, I need him, Connor. He came here with me after something...after I went through a really rough time, and...I need him,' she repeated.

He had no idea what to make of that. A rough time? He waited but she didn't explain herself. 'We'll get everything done,' he assured her. 'And I'll try to be nice to your boy.'

'Freddy is not my boy.'

'He's a she?'

She laughed and shook her head. 'You haven't changed much,' she said.

'You have.'

'Not really.' Again, she didn't elaborate, but turned away, picked up her clipboard and left.

As he watched her lock the bungalow, Connor had a funny feeling he'd said the wrong thing. All right, he thought. Clearly this arrangement would work better if they kept it on an impersonal level.

*　　*　　*

Not possible, he quickly discovered. Each day, their work brought them together, and it was

179

clear that keeping things impersonal was simply not going to work for them. There was no way to deny what they'd once been to one another, or to ignore a shared past.

Between the two of them, they had been assigning tasks like a pair of battle commanders. Everyone had a job, even Max. He and his sister were in charge of getting the big pontoon deck boat shipshape, so it could be used to ferry guests back and forth to and from the lake island.

Connor listened and made notes, but he was often distracted by Olivia, this self-possessed blond bombshell who was both a stranger and hauntingly familiar. She smelled like fresh flowers, and he wanted to bury his face in her shiny hair. *Down, Simba.* He reminded himself to concentrate on their discussions of the gazebo, the main pavilion, the outbuildings and physical plant. Most of the time, he found it pleasant—in an unsettling way—to work with her side by side. Sometimes he noticed her looking at him with quiet absorption. Like now. She seemed to have lost her train of thought as she rested her arms on the worktable and studied him.

'What?' he asked.

'I forgot what we were talking about.'

He loved it when she said things like that. It reminded him of the old Lolly, who was blunt and awkward. 'Then let's talk about something else,' he suggested.

She paused, looked at him a bit longer. Briefly, she pressed her teeth into her lower lip, then looked away. 'Do you know Jenny Majesky, from the bakery?'

'I know who she is. Why?' He tried to read Olivia's expression but couldn't. Not anymore.

'I met her the other day. She... So you don't know anything about her or her family?'

'Her grandparents have had the bakery in town forever. A few years ago, there was a big expansion to a commercial facility over in Kingston. I think Jenny was in charge of that, which I'm sure she'd tell you herself if you asked.'

She got up and poured herself another glass of tea. 'Sorry. I must sound horribly nosy.'

'Just nosy,' he said, and grinned.

'I'm surprised you don't know her better.'

'Why surprised?'

Her cheeks flushed, and for a second she looked like she was a kid again. 'It's a small town. I thought maybe you'd dated her.'

'Nope.' He wasn't about to tell her more.

'You were the one who was going to see the world, never spend more than one night in the same place. What happened to those plans?'

'I did that,' he said. 'For a while.'

She sat back down across from him. 'Really? Where did you go?'

He paused, looked at her. Hell, it wasn't a

secret. But he didn't feel like answering more questions.

She figured out that he wasn't going to tell her more, so she said, 'You kept your ear pierced.'

He touched the little silver loop. 'Uh-huh.' Christ, she had to know why. Didn't she? He made an observation of his own: 'You named your dog Barkis.'

She folded her arms, probably in a protective gesture. Yet instead of shielding her, the stance only accentuated her incredible female curves. 'It's a perfectly good name for a dog.'

'Yeah. Sure.' He grinned because he suspected she had used the name for the same damn reason he'd kept the earring. It was a part of their history—together. For the time being, he dropped the subject. He crossed to the dais where the musicians had played, back in the days of live music. A baby grand piano still occupied the space, draped with a thick padded vinyl cover that zipped up the sides.

He unzipped the piano cover and pulled it off the old baby grand. 'What are the chances that this still works?'

'I'll get the tuner up here ASAP. We'll definitely need a working piano, the sooner, the better.'

She flipped up the keyboard cover and a mouse ran out. At least he assumed it was a mouse. The thing moved so fast he could barely tell. He expected Olivia to do what most women did, to scream as though the mouse were an armed assassin. Instead, she simply went over to one of the French doors and propped it open, and the panicked mouse skittered out.

Then she turned back to him. 'God. Am I crazy, thinking we can pull this off by the end of the summer?'

'We'll get it done.'

She stepped up to the dais ahead of him, giving him an excellent view of her ass. Was that sway in her hips natural or did she exaggerate it for his benefit? He couldn't tell, but regardless, it was working. There was something about the way the afternoon light through the windows struck her, adding a soft, golden glow. She was wearing jeans rolled up to midcalf, and a sleeveless pink blouse and little white sneakers. He was abruptly overwhelmed by the need to touch her. Really touch her, not just graze her accidentally, or brush past her like some loser in an Edith Wharton novel.

'...used to be the last one picked,' she was saying, and he realized he'd barely heard a single word she had said.

He had to pretend great interest in a scrolled wooden music stand. 'Sorry, what's that?'

'Never mind. Just going over the defining moment of my youth, no big deal.' She laughed at his expression. 'Kidding. I was talking about all my fond memories of dance lessons at camp.'

'I liked the dance lessons.'

She sniffed. 'You would.'

'I found them weirdly entertaining.'

'I'm not surprised. You always won the talent contests, too, you big show-off.'

'Why enter if you don't intend to win?'

She studied him for a moment, her gaze misty with memories. 'Do you still sing?'

'All the time.'

'Maybe you can sing at the anniversary celebration,' she said, brightening.

Which was his cue to point out to her that he wasn't invited, nor did he want to be. 'Do you still play piano?' he asked her.

'Almost never.'

Well, now, that was odd. Or maybe not. The fact was, he needed music in his life—he needed to sing—the way some people needed air. It was vital for survival.

Obviously, Miss Olivia Bellamy had found enough fulfillment in her life so far and didn't have to fill the empty places inside her with noise and light.

'I'm surprised,' he said. 'You used to be pretty passionate about your piano playing.'

'It was one of the few things I could do better than the other kids.' She propped open the lid of the piano, coughed a little at the dust. 'I don't need to keep proving myself

184

constantly anymore.'

'Maybe you never did,' he pointed out.

'Easy for you to say, winning all the firsts like you did. You always won the quadrathalon prize and the talent show. You were such an overachiever.'

'Competitive,' he corrected her. 'And I don't remember that.'

'What, winning all the time?' She grinned and shook her head. 'Didn't it get boring after a while?'

'Yeah, sure.'

'The girls in my bunkhouse used to stay up half the night, trying to figure out how to be your partner for the dance competitions.'

That made him laugh. 'No way.'

'Huh. Remember Gina Palumbo?'

'Nope.' Actually, he'd lost his virginity to her, his third and final year as a camper, the summer after eighth grade. She'd been sexy and scary and wildly exciting.

'Gina told everyone in the bunkhouse that you'd promised every dance of the summer to her.'

He probably had. 'Is that so?'

Olivia nodded. 'I always wound up dancing with another girl or one of the counselors who felt sorry for me.'

He looked at her now, in the spill of afternoon light, her hair soft and her smile a little shy. Then he found the remote to the iPod dock, scrolling until he found 'Lying

185

Awake,' an old sixties tune sung with irresistible smoothness by Nina Simone. 'Okay, I feel sorry for you,' he said. 'Dance with me.'

'I didn't say that to get you to—'

'Doesn't matter,' he said, and caught her in his arms. It had been a while, but he had an instinctive memory of the dance frame. She was a perfect fit, though he could feel her pulling back, resisting him.

'Hey,' she said.

'What's the matter?'

'I used to despise ballroom dancing so much. Every year, I begged my grandparents to take it off the schedule.'

'It wasn't so bad,' he said.

'Maybe for you it wasn't. For me, it was excruciating. I still cringe just thinking about it. The choosing of a partner was always torture for me, pure torture.'

'You know, for being such a miserable kid, you managed to turn into a normal, well-adjusted grown-up.'

'Thank you.'

'Not to mention an incredibly hot babe.'

'Fine. Don't mention it. But honestly, we've got a lot of work to do here, so maybe we shouldn't be—'

'Shut up and dance, Lolly, and I'll show you why I always won,' he said. In addition to the classic hold, he had a couple of other tricks up his sleeve. The eye contact, the look

186

that said, *I wish we were naked.* So much of dancing had to do with being a good faker. Except at the moment, he didn't have to fake anything. He loved looking into Olivia's eyes. He *did* wish they were naked.

She clung to his neck, trembling, which was actually a good thing, because that way, she might not notice that Connor was trembling, too. He felt her soft, warm body against his, inhaled the scent of her skin and felt a jolt of attraction. Even though the dance was a slow one, she was breathing fast, pulling in panicky gasps of air through her teeth. Her mouth was maybe four inches from his, and half-open.

Connor wanted to kiss her so bad it hurt, and even before their lips met, she had a look on her face as if he was already kissing her— eyes shut, lips parted, inches from his...oh, God... 'Lolly—'

A door slammed and Freddy strode into the room. 'Working hard, kids?'

They broke apart, and he could see the color pouring into Olivia's cheeks. Connor grinned at Freddy. 'That wasn't hard at all. But I need to get going.' He strode out to the yard, where his Harley was parked, and was surprised when Olivia followed him. He strapped on his gear, piece by piece, but kept his eyes on her.

'What?' she asked.

'I didn't say anything.'

187

'You were staring.'

'I still am.' He let a slow smile unfurl.

'I'd prefer you didn't.'

He looked at her a moment longer. When she blushed, she looked younger, more vulnerable, more like a girl he once knew. 'Do you ever think about us, Lolly?' he asked. 'About the way we used to be?'

The blush turned an even deeper shade of red. 'No,' she said emphatically. 'Not any more than I think about anything else from nine years ago.'

Of course. It was a reminder that they didn't know each other at all anymore. With unhurried movements, he zipped his leather jacket. 'I'd better go get ready for my unexpected company.'

'I never would have picked you out as the biker type,' she said.

'Sure you would have,' he said, and let the motor drown out her reply.

CAMP KIOGA SUMMER EVENING SAIL

One of the most beloved traditions at Camp Kioga is the weekly summer evening sail on Willow Lake. There is no better way to enjoy a peaceful Catskills sunset. Campers are instructed to gather on the dock promptly at 7:30 p.m.

Eleven

It was Connor Davis's third year at camp, and he knew it would be his last. For one thing, he was going into eighth grade next year and after that was high school, and his mom and Mel always said guys in high school got jobs, period. For another thing, he didn't know what in holy hell to do about his dad, and coming here each summer, watching Terry Davis stagger and stumble through his days, the laughingstock of the camp, made Connor feel pissed off at the world.

Living with Mel and his mom pissed him off, too, but it was different with his dad. Because here was the saddest, sickest thing of all. Connor loved his dad. Terry Davis was a good man with a bad problem, and Connor just didn't know how the hell to fix things for him.

What the fuck, he thought. It's my last summer at Camp Kioga. I'm going to make the most of it. He made a mental list of things he wanted to do. Win the quadrathalon. Go rock climbing at the Shawangunks. Do the wilderness-survival trek, where you had to spend two days on your own with nothing but a compass. Maybe take on Tarik in a chess

189

tournament. Get his ear pierced, just to tick off his stepdad. Kiss a girl and feel her up. Maybe even get to third base or score a home run.

Yeah, he wanted to do all that and more. When school started in the fall and he had to write the requisite 'How I Spent My Summer Vacation,' he wanted it to sound so cool, his teacher would think he was making it up.

On the way to the dining hall, he saw Mr. Bellamy, the camp dean and owner, an older guy with a craggy face and a voice like Lawrence Olivier in those old black-and-white movies.

'Hello, sir,' he said, squaring his shoulders and holding out his hand. 'Connor Davis.'

'Of course, Davis. I remember you well. How are you, son?'

'Excellent, sir.' What the hell else would he say? That his life was shit, that he still missed his baby brother every day, that he hated his stepfather, hated living in a trailer park in frigging Buffalo? His mother, who had spent his entire childhood dreaming of a career onstage, had taught him to be a good faker, so he pasted on a grin. 'It's good to be back, Mr. Bellamy. I really want to thank you and Mrs. Bellamy for letting me come.'

'Nonsense, son, Jane and I consider it a privilege to have you here.'

Yeah, right. Whatever.

'Well, anyway. I'm real grateful.' He
190

wished there was some way to show the Bellamys his appreciation. He couldn't think of a thing, though. These people had everything. There was all that Bellamy-family money. And they had the camp, this amazing place in the wilderness where you could stand on a mountaintop and touch the stars. And they had each other, and a bunch of grandchildren who were nuts about them, and they had a perfect, sweet life. There wasn't a thing Connor Davis could offer them.

The first night's supper was always a feast, and this year was no exception. Connor sat at a long table with his cabinmates, a loud gang of guys in all shapes and sizes. They consumed huge amounts of something called beef Wellington, guzzled big pitchers of milk. Even kids who didn't normally like vegetables went for the steamed broccoli and tossed salad at camp. For dessert, they had the renowned berry pies from the Sky River Bakery.

'Didja see the hottie who drives the bread truck?' asked Alex Dunbar, who occupied the bunk under Connor.

Connor shook his head. From his perspective, pretty much everyone with an X chromosome was a hottie. Lately, he had this almost feverish sex drive, one that made him feel like a maniac inside.

'She's this high-school girl, looks just like Wynona Ryder.' Dunbar reached for the big bowl of buttered potatoes. 'Her name's Jenny

Majesky, I found out that much. Now all I have to do is find out how to get her to—'

'Hey, Dunbar.' Their counselor, Rourke McKnight, propped his foot on the bench between Dunbar and Connor. 'Word to the wise.'

'Yeah? What's that?' Dunbar tried to act cool, but Connor knew he was intimidated by McKnight. Everyone in Fort Niagara Cabin was. Though just out of high school, McKnight had this hard edge, a scary side that might or might not be a put-on. None of the guys in Niagara wanted to get on his bad side.

'Don't finish that thought,' McKnight said. 'Not about Miss Majesky or anyone else of the female persuasion. Got it?'

'Sure,' Dunbar said, glowering. 'Got it.'

'Good.'

When McKnight was gone, Dunbar snickered. 'He's probably doing her himself.'

'He hears you talking like that,' said Cramer, who sat across the table, 'he'll do you, and it won't be pretty.'

The stupid joshing and joking started up again, but Connor wasn't listening. When it came to his dad, he had this weird sixth sense. He felt his scalp prickle, felt something like a cool shadow sweep over him. Then he heard it. The crash of breaking glass.

Without asking to be excused, he flung his napkin on the table and bolted for the door. Sure enough, there was his father in the foyer, standing there looking totally bewildered at a glass ceiling fixture, which now lay shattered at the base of a stepladder.

'Dad, you all right?' Connor murmured, grabbing the sleeve of his shirt.

'Justa little blood,' Terry Davis said, swaying ever so slightly on his feet as he studied the back of his hand. 'All I was doing was changing the dadgum lightbulb.'

Connor's heart sank. He was such an idiot. Every year he hoped this wouldn't happen, but every year it did. His father smelled like a malt-liquor brewery, and the worst part of it was, he tried to pretend everything was fine.

Inevitably, the crash had brought curious onlookers. Most of them didn't know Connor and Terry Davis were related. Terry always told Connor not to advertise that fact, but it made Connor feel totally weird to pretend.

'Hey, how many drunks does it take to change a lightbulb?' some kid asked. 'One to pour the martinis, and another to read him the directions in twelve steps.'

Connor cringed inwardly, but didn't let it show as he leveled a deadly glare at the kid. He knew it was deadly because he'd spent all his middle-school years perfecting it. Often it was his only defense. 'Back off,' he said.

'What's it to you?' the kid challenged.

'Yeah,' another kid said, 'what's your problem?'

'Go sit down.' The order came from

Rourke McKnight, who appeared in the doorway, drawing himself up to his full height, well over six feet. His appearance caused the kids to scatter. 'I'll clean this up.'

'No, wait,' Terry Davis protested, 'I gotta change that lightbulb. I gotta—'

'Hey, Mr. Davis, that's a pretty bad cut. Let me go with you to the infirmary and we'll clean it up.' Out of nowhere, Lolly Bellamy showed up. Earlier in the day, Connor had barely had time to say hi to her, but he'd nodded at her from across the room. She was the last person in the world he pictured himself being friends with, but he was glad to see her. Over the past couple of summers, they'd become friends, sort of. He liked her because she was funny and smart and genuine. And because she was the kind of person to take his dad by the arm and lead him out the door and to the infirmary, talking the whole time, calmly averting disaster.

Humbled by her simple act of kindness, and too grateful for words, he followed them into the pristine office, which had a well-stocked medical cabinet and four cots, made up with crisp white sheets. Lolly's manner was brisk as she turned on the tap. 'Just hold your hand under that, Mr. Davis. We need to make sure there's no glass in the cut.'

'Yeah,' said Connor's dad. 'You bet.'

Connor knew she was all but bathed in the brewery smell, but she didn't flinch as she cleaned the wound, sprayed antiseptic on it and applied a neat bandage.

'I surely thank you,' Terry said. 'You're a reg'lar Florence Nightingale.'

Lolly beamed at him. 'Yep, that's me.'

While she put away the supplies, Connor said, 'Listen, Dad, why don't you go on home. You want me to help you?'

'Hell, no.' Terry looked glum. 'I think I know my way home after all this time.'

'Home' for Terry Davis was the year-round caretaker's cottage at the edge of the camp. It had the advantage of being on the premises, so he didn't have to drive to it. That was one worry Connor wouldn't have tonight. His dad already had a DUI, and another one would land him in jail.

'You want me to come with you?' Connor offered.

'Hell, no,' his dad said again. He seemed ticked off now, and stomped out of the infirmary without another word, slamming the door behind him.

Connor didn't move. Neither did Lolly. He didn't look at her, but felt her nearby, waiting. Breathing softly. And all of a sudden, it was too much—her kindness, her complete acceptance of the situation, her refusal to make a big deal of something so huge that it was ruling his life. Connor felt the humiliating burn of tears in his throat and eyes, and knew he was about to lose it. 'I need to go,' he

195

mumbled, groping for the door handle.

'Okay' was all she said.

There was a world of meaning in her 'okay.' Connor was pretty sure she knew he realized that. She was Lolly, after all. Even though they were only summer friends, she understood him better than anyone else in his life, maybe even himself. The notion made him drop his hand. He'd conquered his emotions. Four years of living with Mel had taught him to do that. Never show emotion, because some asshole is bound to make you regret it.

I hate this, he thought. I hate it when my dad drinks.

'Know what I feel like doing?' he asked Lolly all of a sudden.

'Putting your fist through a wall?' she suggested.

He couldn't help flashing a rueful grin. God, she *did* know him. Then the grin faded and words he'd never dare utter to another soul came out before he could even stop them. 'I wish the bastard would stop,' he said. 'I wish he'd just get sober and be himself. If he did that, I wouldn't care what else he did with his life. He can play cribbage and build birdhouses all day, for all I care, just so long as he quits drinking.'

'Maybe he will one day,' she said, not at all perturbed by what he'd said. 'My grandmother Lightsey—that's my mom's mom—is an

196

alcoholic, but she doesn't drink now and she goes to these special meetings at her church. My mom acts like it's this big family secret, but I don't know why that is. I'm proud of my grandmother for getting better.'

He couldn't decide whether or not he was glad she'd told him that. On the one hand, it gave him hope that maybe his dad would change. On the other hand, it seemed so unlikely that his father would simply make up his mind to quit drinking and go to meetings that Connor felt like a fool, wishing it could happen.

'I don't know why your grandparents keep him on,' Connor muttered. 'It's not like he's this totally reliable worker.'

She frowned behind her glasses. 'He never told you?'

'Told me what?'

'God, Connor, you should let him tell it. Or my granddad. Your grandfather and mine were in the Korean War together. Your grandfather saved my grandfather's life.'

Connor had never known his grandfather, whose name had been Edward Davis. 'I knew he'd been killed in Korea when my dad was a baby, but that's all my dad ever said.'

'You ought to ask my granddad. There's this whole big story about how they were fighting in something called the Walled City, and your grandfather saved a whole platoon, my granddad included. So when my granddad got back from the war, he made a promise that he'd always look after your grandfather's family, no matter what.'

Even if Edward Davis's son grew up to be a drunk, Connor thought. Yet somehow, Lolly's story made him feel marginally better.

'So anyway,' she said, in her semi-annoying, bossy way, 'you should ask my granddad to tell you the story.'

'I might,' he said.

They were quiet for a long time after that. Then he crossed to the supply cabinet and slid open a white enamel drawer. 'I was thinking of piercing my ear.'

'I beg your pardon?'

Now he let out an actual laugh. She was so funny when she got all formal like that. 'I was just thinking I'm going to pierce my ear.'

'You're completely insane.'

'You don't think I'd dare?' In the drawer, he found a lancet in a sterile packet. 'This ought to work.' He started to rip the packet open with his teeth.

'Wait.' She looked wild-eyed with fright now, her glasses comically askew on her face. 'Don't be stupid, Connor. You don't need any more holes in your head than you already have.'

'If that's the case, then one more won't matter.' He paused, digging in his pocket for the small silver hoop earring he'd been carrying around for weeks, trying to get up the nerve to go for it. Mary Lou Carruthers, who'd had a crush on him since second grade, had given it to him last year. The hoop was attached to a black plastic card. He pried it off and set it on the counter.

'You can't be serious,' Lolly said. Her cheeks were bright red.

'Serious as a heart attack,' he said.

'You'll get an infection. Your ear will fall off.'

'Bullshit. People pierce their ears all the time.'

'At the doctor's, or they get it done by a professional.'

'Or they get some smart-alecky girl to do it.'

'No way,' she said, taking a step back and shaking her head. She no longer wore her hair in brown pigtails, but had it in some kind of knot held with a cloth-covered elastic. Stray locks sprang free, curling around her face.

'Fine. I'll do it myself.'

'We could both get expelled.'

'Only if we get caught. We're not going to get caught, Lolly.' He opened the lancet and leaned toward the mirror. Shit. This wasn't as simple as he'd thought. If he poked the lancet through his ear, what would stop it from poking a hole in his skull? And once it was through, was there going to be blood? And how the heck did you get the earring in?

In the mirror, he saw Lolly watching him.

199

All right, no backing down. He'd give it a swift poke and hope for the best. He took a breath and held it. Caught himself squeezing his eyes shut. No, that wouldn't do. He had to see what he was doing.

Behind him, he heard a snapping sound and almost dropped the lancet. It was Lolly, putting on a pair of rubber surgical gloves. 'All right, Boy Wonder,' she said. 'Don't blame me if your ear turns black and falls off.'

FISHING ON WILLOW LAKE

Willow Lake is an abundant source of delicious trout. The limit is three trout per licensed sportsman. Over and above that, catch and release is required.

Twelve

'Come on, lazy Daisy! Rise and shine.'

When Daisy heard that phony, cheerful note in her dad's voice, she knew it couldn't mean anything good. He was outside the bunkhouse she shared with him and Max, and it was still dark. She heard his footstep on the porch, heard the door creak open. 'Daze?' he cajoled. 'Come on, kiddo. It's time.'

'No,' she moaned very softly, burying her head under the pillow. Couldn't he see that it was not even the crack of dawn? Not even the *pre*crack. What in the world made people so eager to wake up early? Maybe if she didn't respond, he would give up and go away.

No such luck. The tapping became more insistent and the screen door creaked on its hinges as he opened it. Oh, crap, thought Daisy. He's coming in. He's not giving up on me.

'Crap,' she muttered aloud, the lovely numbness of sleep now driven completely out of her. Forcing herself awake, she crept out of bed and picked a path around piles of clothes strewn about, books and decks of cards, soda cans and food wrappers.

'Daisy?' he said again, a hulking silhouette in the doorway.

'I'm up, Dad. Geez. Don't make so much

noise.'

'Okay,' he said. 'I'll wait right outside.'

'Great.'

'Don't be long.'

'Wouldn't dream of it.'

The last thing she wanted to do was to go on some sort of predawn outing with her dad. Fishing, ugh. He'd been after her ever since they got here to do all this stupid family-bonding stuff, and very quickly, she had run out of ways to avoid him. There were few places to hide at Camp Kioga without getting lost in the forest or attacked by mosquitoes.

She and her cousins, Olivia and Dare, had stayed up late last night playing whist with Freddy. Whist was a card game that was dangerously close to bridge. If she ever learned bridge, Daisy would know she had officially turned into the dork of the century. Whist. If her dad had told her what actually awaited her here at Camp Kioga, she would have asked somebody to shoot her, which was preferable to the slow, lingering death-by-boredom that the summer was in danger of becoming.

She had believed the stories Dad and her grandparents told about Camp Kioga, where the fun never stopped. Cluelessly, she had not questioned the picture they drew of an idyllic private retreat by a pristine lake. It hadn't occurred to her that once she got here, she would need to find something—besides work—to actually *do* at the idyllic private retreat.

Except the funny thing was, she wasn't that bored. Thank God her older cousins had a sense of humor. Olivia in particular seemed sensitive to the fact that Daisy's family situation currently sucked in the extreme. It was slightly encouraging that Olivia had survived her own parents' divorce and seemed to be okay with it. And when Daisy's boredom and frustration started to seem unbearable, she had a few tricks up her sleeve, those tricks consisting of a carton of cigarettes stashed under her bed, a bag of weed and even a small, red-gold chunk of hashish from Lebanon. One of the benefits of going to a high school with an international student body was that many of her friends had diplomatic immunity, and they took advantage of it.

Thinking of her friends back in the city, she gave a restless sigh. She missed hanging out with kids her age. Yet at the same time, now that senior year was coming up, she noticed a slight bit of relief. Her friends were all so focused and driven. A number of them had known exactly what they wanted to do with themselves since kindergarten. They'd all set their sights on an Ivy League college or the Julliard School, or some incredible place overseas like the Sorbonne. In the face of her friends' talent and ambition, Daisy felt like a complete phony. Sure, her grades were all right, she went to one of the best high schools in the country, she played piano and guitar and lacrosse. But even with all that, she was drifting. She didn't know where she wanted her life to go. She'd overheard her mom—a high-powered, type A international lawyer—tell her grandmother that Daisy was like her father. This was not a compliment. Although her father was really talented at being a landscape architect, the family's affluence sure as heck didn't come from that. It was family money and her mother's giant salary that financed the Upper East Side co-op and the private schools. Yet for all that, her parents still couldn't manage to stay happy with each other.

Maybe if I was more focused, they would stay together, she thought. *Maybe if I got some horrible disease, they wouldn't split this family apart.* The ideas swirled through her head like so much useless dust. Deep down, she knew there was no point in trying to force them together. She'd just go on doing her thing. She had a stack of college catalogs and brochures. This summer, she was supposed to figure out where she was going to apply to college.

Daisy bent forward at the waist to tug a brush through her hair. She used a cloth-covered band to make a ponytail and finished dressing in a pair of jersey shorts with Pink written across the butt, a tank top and a hooded school lacrosse-team sweatshirt.

Shoving her feet into flip-flops, she stood and automatically grabbed for her iPod. Then, regretfully, she set it down. Although her dad claimed he knew what he was doing, a little warning voice in her head advised her to leave the thing at home. If she drowned it, her music source for the summer would be gone, completely, and then she really would have to shoot herself.

As she washed her face and brushed her teeth, she felt grateful that there was no mirror over the sink, no mirror anywhere. The sight of herself was bound to be depressing. Casting a last envious look at her cozy bunk, she stepped outside into the quiet darkness and stood on the stoop. An oppressive fog shrouded the camp.

A cigarette pack lay under the stoop next to the old Mason jar she used as an ashtray. Although anybody with half a brain knew how stupid it was to smoke, Daisy did it anyway. Smoking was so forbidden, so incredibly, shockingly *bad* that of course she had to do it. Smoking was considered worse than sex or recreational drugs. Therefore, it was the perfect thing to do in order to drive her parents crazy.

And of course, that was Daisy's mission— to drive them crazy. Because God knew, they had been doing it to her for years.

Yet her dad never told her to quit. Didn't he understand that she wanted him to *order* her to quit, so she could fight with him and tell him no and rail at him that it was her life, and her lungs, and her health, and she could do what she wanted with them, and then he would point out that she was still his daughter, and her health was very much his concern, and if she didn't quit, he was going to make her. That was all he had to do. She would fight with him, and then she would quit.

'"Good morning, Merry Sunshine," her dad sang, dredging up the song from her childhood, "'and how are you today?"'

'I'll give you a hundred bucks to stop singing,' she grumbled.

'You don't have a hundred bucks.'

'Shows how much you know. Nana told Olivia to pay me in cash, every Friday. I've made almost six hundred bucks so far.'

Her dad gave a low whistle. 'You got it, then. I won't sing a note. Not even to say good-morning to my best girl.'

She knew he wouldn't make her pay up. He never made her do anything. 'Besides,' she pointed out, 'in case you haven't noticed, the sun is not even up yet, so technically, it's not morning.'

'I know.' He made a great show of taking a bracing gulp of morning air. 'It's great, huh? My favorite time of day.'

She shivered in the clammy chill. 'I can't believe we're doing this.'

'I had no choice. Neither of my children

has ever caught a fish. This is a sacred quest.'

'I don't get it,' she said. 'How can it matter what time of day we do this great deed of catching a fish? Don't tell me fish can tell time—'

'It's got to do with the light and water temperature. The trout feed when the bugs are out, dawn and twilight.'

'Yeah, that's my favorite time of day, too. When the bugs are out.'

There was an eerie quality to the quiet that settled over the compound. The shroud of fog insulated the sound of their voices and the slap of her flip-flops against the soles of her feet. The camp looked like the setting of a creepy horror movie where an ax murderer lurked in the deep woods.

'How did you sleep last night?' her dad asked.

'It's still last night. I was sleeping fine. It's not like there's anything else to do around here.'

'Oh, I think you've definitely done a good job amusing yourself.' He gestured down at the lake-shore, where the blackened remains of last night's fire were barely visible. 'We used to do that, too, when we came to camp. We'd build a big fire down on the beach and get high.'

'I don't—' Daisy glared at him and stiffened her spine in defiance. Why deny it? He obviously knew, and he obviously didn't give a shit, so why should she? A part of her wished he would put his foot down, order her to stop, but he never did. Instead, he took the fun out of getting high by acting like it was no big deal, because it was something he himself had already done. Yelling at her to behave herself was her mom's job, and her mom was out of the picture now. Just for the summer, Mom said, a trial separation, but deep in her gut, Daisy already knew.

'Whatever,' she muttered, pushing into the kitchen ahead of him. 'What's for breakfast?'

Max was already there, entranced by something on the back of a box of cereal as he mechanically shoveled each bite into his mouth.

'Hey,' Daisy said. 'Where'd you get the Cap'n Crunch?'

He didn't look up. 'Dad and I went to town for supplies last night. Dare has this place stocked up with too much healthy stuff. Want some?'

'No, thanks. That much sugar is addictive, in case you haven't noticed. It's pretty much the worst thing you can put into your body.'

' 'Cept cigarette smoke,' Max said. 'So don't go criticizing me.'

'Shut up,' she said, and took a carton of low-fat Greek yogurt from the industrial-size fridge. She topped it with a scoop of Dare's muesli.

'Dad, you should make her stop smoking,'

Max said.

Their father found a big bowl and filled it with Cap'n Crunch. 'She should stop on her own,' he said.

'She should be in bed, sound asleep, instead of being up at this hour with a couple of morons,' Daisy said.

'Morons,' Max repeated, and high-fived their dad across the table.

Daisy cut a peach into chunks and added it to the yogurt and muesli. That was the kind of morning it was going to be—just peachy.

They finished breakfast and piled their dishes in the sink. Her dad and Max headed for the boathouse. Daisy took a minute to wash the dishes. The huge stainless-steel sink was equipped with a showerlike commercial dishwashing apparatus, and she had everything clean in about half a minute. She put away the cereal and milk—did they think it would put itself away?—and then went outside to find the guys and nag them about cleaning up after themselves. They weren't being rude. They just didn't think. And that habit was harder to break than rudeness.

She stepped outside and headed along the path to the boathouse and dock. All right, she thought, now fully awake, she had to admit, there was something about this place at this hour of the morning. A special hush hung in the air and there was a mystical quality to the lake at sunrise. The mist moved as if it had a life of its own, sneaking across the perfectly still water. With the light from the rising sun shining through, everything took on a soft, magical glow. Everything smelled so fresh, of clean water, wildflowers and dewy grass, and the birdsong was somehow muted by the air around them. If the Lady of the Lake herself rose up, holding Caliburn aloft, Daisy wouldn't be surprised.

Every so often, a trout rose to grab a bug, its movement forming gentle concentric rings that gradually subsided. Poor, unsuspecting trout, Daisy thought. Why would anyone want to rip the poor thing from the peaceful lake, gut it and fry it up in a pan?

Because she and her brother had never caught a fricking fish, and their goofball dad thought it was important.

'Daisy, look!' Max said, running toward her. 'Look what Dad and I got last night!' He held out a large coffee can for her inspection. She saw a mound of dark, moist dirt, braided through with flesh-colored earthworms, gleaming and undulating with mindless creepiness.

'Golly, that's great, Max,' she said with false brightness. 'Now, if you'll excuse me, I need to go yark in the bushes.'

'What a baby,' he mumbled. 'They're just night- crawlers.'

She swallowed and took a couple of gulps of air, and if she didn't look at the can, the queasiness subsided. *Nightcrawlers.*

The thing her dad refused to see about this whole family bonding, let's-go-fishing expedition was that it was all such BS. On the surface, he might look like Father of the Year taking the kids fishing, but there was still a can of worms to deal with. There was always a can of worms.

Next to the boathouse was a big storage barn filled with sports equipment. 'Whoa,' said Max, his eyes wide. 'Look at all this stuff. They got everything here.'

'That they do, buddy.' Dad lifted a dusty canvas shroud to reveal a row of parked bicycles.

'Bikes!' Daisy exclaimed. She loved riding bikes.

'There are even a few tandems,' Dad said. 'We'll have to pump up the tires later.'

There was a ton of other stuff, including nets and raquets and balls, floating goals for water polo, bows and arrows and targets, croquet sets, you name it. Daisy made a mental note to check it out later. With none of the usual entertainment available, she and Max were learning to be creative when it came to amusing themselves. She never thought she'd get excited about a game of badminton, but the prospect took on a new appeal.

One whole section of the barn was devoted to fishing gear, with poles and reels of every size, boxes of hooks and lures, waders and vests with every pocket imaginable. There was a big tackle box filled with equipment and an even bigger box marked Majesky.

'What's this stuff?' Max asked.

'Ice-fishing gear,' Dad explained. 'Old Mr. Majesky from town used to come up here during the off-season to fish. He and Granddad were fishing buddies a long time ago, so I guess that's why his stuff has been left up here.'

'What's that sign say, Dad?' Max pointed.

'It says—'

Daisy hushed her father. With Max, they were supposed to seize on teachable moments whenever possible, in order to help him with his reading. Since he'd been in first grade, he had struggled with reading. A bunch of testing and daily tutors had ensued, but her brother's reading didn't improve.

'What's the matter?' her dad asked, frowning.

Did he really not know? 'You read the sign, Max,' she said. 'You tell us what it says.'

'Never mind,' he grumbled, his temper foul now. 'Sheesh, you're as bossy as Mom.'

'No, I'm not. For Mom, you'd try to read it.'

Max stormed out, muttering something about checking the can of worms.

Their father looked completely astonished. 'Wait a minute. The sign says Fishing Regulations for Local Residents. Are

212

you saying Max can't read it?'

Daisy folded her arms and thrust up her chin. 'Hello? This is news to you?'

'I knew he was having a little trouble in school, but I thought his tutor was taking care of that.'

Typical, she thought. Her dad always figured the solution to every problem was to hire someone to solve it. You'd think by now he would realize that the strategy didn't always work. Her mother wasn't much better. Her solution was to hire someone and then run away, clear to Seattle. Sometimes Daisy felt like the only member of this family who realized something needed fixing, and not by the hired help. Oh, they did all that bullshit family counseling, but it never worked. Dr. Granville was all, 'How did that make you feel?' He had a knack for making people break down and cry, but so what? Oprah had that same talent, but it never seemed to help the situation, so big deal.

'Did you even read his IEP?' She could tell from her dad's expression that he needed remedial help, too. 'Individualized educational plan,' she said, exaggerating each word. 'The main component of the plan for summer is that you read with him every day for at least an hour. I can't believe Mom didn't tell you.'

'You're kidding,' Dad said.

'Right,' she agreed. 'Kidding. I thought it

213

would be hilarious to tell you Max can't read and then lie to you about how to deal with it.'

Her dad either didn't pick up on the sarcasm, or he was ignoring it. 'So I'm supposed to read to him? That's great,' he said, and he grinned. He actually grinned from ear to ear.

Daisy wasn't sure she had heard correctly. 'Excuse me? Great?'

His face lit up with boyish enthusiasm. 'There are all kinds of books I've always wanted to read to Max. To both of you.'

Then why didn't you? she wanted to ask.

'I mean, I know you can read just fine, right?' Dad said.

'You're asking me?' She grabbed three canoe paddles from the pegs on the wall. 'Do you really not know?' He looked so crestfallen that she relented. 'No worries, Dad. I can read just fine.' He acted like he was the world's coolest father just because he didn't freak even though he knew she smoked cigarettes and pot. But really, he didn't realize how much he didn't know about her—that she'd won the Dickinson prize for poetry this year and had earned a key in the National Honor Society. That she had scored a record number of goals in lacrosse last season. That her favorite jazz pianist was Keith Jarrett and that she'd tried cocaine at a party.

'There's a ton of stuff we could read,' Dad said. '*The Once and Future King* and *Treasure*

214

Island. There used to be a camp library in the main pavilion by the rec room. We'll go check it out tonight.'

One thing about Dad, he never lacked for enthusiasm.

They picked out rods and reels, lead sinkers and red-and-white bobbers, and headed out to the dock. Dad had launched a big canoe, one that had six bench seats going across. He had brought along a cooler of drinks, sandwiches and snacks, enough for an army. She pictured him up before first light, putting all this together for them, and her heart lurched. He was trying. He really was.

She noticed a bundle of towels and a tube of sunscreen. Sunscreen? Did he think they were going to be out on the water long enough to need sunscreen?

'You said you wanted us to plant flowers all along the front drive and around the main pavilion,' she reminded her dad.

'That's right,' he said, tossing her a life jacket. 'Flowers will really dress the place up. In the garden plan, I went with traditional red and white geraniums.'

'So I shouldn't stay out too long,' she added.

'Don't worry about that. The flowers won't care what day you put them in the ground. What good is summer camp if you can't play a little hooky once in a while?' He grinned. 'Looks like you're trapped with Max and me.'

215

'Super.'

The canoe was more wobbly than it looked, floating placidly alongside the dock. When they got on board, the hull lurched ominously from side to side, which Max thought was hilarious.

'Sit still,' Daisy said as she picked up a paddle. 'If you make me fall in, I'll make you sorry.'

'It's only water.'

'Yeah, but have you felt it?'

Max trailed his hand in the water. 'Feels great to me.'

'Just paddle, numb nuts.'

'My nuts are not numb,' he said.

'Come on, Max. Grab a paddle and start paddling,' she said. 'Or don't you know how?'

' 'Course I know how.' Belligerently, he picked up a paddle as their dad pushed off from the dock.

Daisy dug in, setting the pace from her spot in the front of the canoe. She didn't really know what she was doing, but she had done some paddling in PE at school, so that helped a little. It really wasn't hard, although she and her dad and Max were hopelessly out of sync. Their paddles clacked together in midair, splashing sun-sparkled droplets in the water. Daisy imagined herself telling Dr. Granville about the outing. He would point out that the lack of coordination was a metaphor of the family's issues. He was into all this metaphor crap. He'd explain how Dad's immaturity and detachment, Daisy's looking for boundaries and Max's need for reassurance were coming out in the way they paddled the canoe.

'When I was a kid here,' Dad said, 'we used to have a team quadrathalon. A race with four parts. First we had to paddle—once around the island and then back. Then we'd have to swim from the starting blocks to the buoys and back. Then there was a leg of the race on bikes for about three miles, and finally, a cross-country footrace for a mile to the finish line. First to finish won the prize.'

'What was the prize?' asked Max.

'I don't even remember. Probably something like extra s'mores.'

'That's a lot of work for s'mores.'

'Son, we didn't do it for the s'mores.'

'Then why did you?'

'To win. To own bragging rights as the fastest team.'

'Geez, I don't get it.'

'Come on, Max. Where's your competitive spirit?'

'I guess I forgot to pack it.'

'When are we going to start fishing?' Daisy figured the sooner they got started, the quicker they'd be done.

'We need to get to the perfect spot,' Dad said. 'It's a place called Blue Hole.'

It took forever to get there because it was clear on the far side of the lake, and they were

217

so lame at paddling. All their splashing and noise probably scared every single fish in the water into hiding, anyway.

Finally, just before blisters started to form on Daisy's hand, Dad declared that they had arrived. She had to allow that it was beautiful here. The deep fishing hole was bound by a sheer wall of rock plunging into the water. Here, the lake was as still as a sheet of glass.

'Now what?' asked Max.

'Now we bait our hooks and hope for the best. Grab that can of worms, will you, Daisy?'

'I wouldn't touch that can of worms with a barge pole,' she said.

'Chicken.' Max clambered toward her, jostling the canoe.

'Careful, numb nuts,' she said, bracing her hands on the sides.

To her surprise, Max showed a bit of grace as he grabbed the can and passed it to their dad. In just a few minutes, their hooks were baited—by Dad, who somehow appeared to know what he was doing—and their lines were cast.

And then...nothing. The three of them sat like dunces, staring at their bobbers, watching for a bite. Every once in a while, Dad would reel in a line and put a fresh worm on the hook, as if the trout would turn up their noses at a dead, bloated worm. Once in a while, a bobber would stir, dipping a little. When that happened, one of them would reel it in with wild excitement, only to discover that the bait had been stolen from the hook.

'Clever little devils,' Dad said.

'What, the trout?' asked Daisy. 'Since when is a trout clever?'

'Since it can steal a worm without swallowing the hook,' Max explained reasonably. 'I'd call that clever. Wouldn't you?'

'Yeah, real clever.'

By the end of the first hour, boredom gave way to silliness. The three of them played verbal games, dumb stuff she remembered from when she was really little, like 'I Spy' and 'Who Am I?' The sound of Max's giggles trilled like birdsong across the water, and Daisy felt something strange and unexpected come over her. A sense of relaxation, of...peace.

A bit later, Dad started to tell stories. He talked about the old days when he was a boy, and what it had been like spending every single summer of his childhood here. 'It was the only life I knew,' he said, 'and I didn't realize how great it was. Kids never do.'

Yeah, but they notice if their life is in the toilet, she thought.

Max got hungry and unwrapped a sandwich. 'My favorite.'

'You didn't,' Daisy said.

Dad shrugged. 'It's his favorite.'

A blissful look came over Max's face as he

ate the disgusting baloney-and-peanut-butter sandwich. 'Tell us about the time Uncle Philip put catfish bait in the girls' bunkhouse,' he said, although he knew the story by heart.

The minutes slipped by as they listened to their dad tell stories. Max idly picked off the crust and dropped the pieces over the side. Daisy watched as a fat trout swam up and sucked the peanut-buttered bread crust from the surface. She watched like an idiot as another fish came, and then another....

'Hand me the net,' she said in an urgent whisper.

'Do you have a bite?' Max asked.

'No, you do. Look in the water. They're coming for your sandwich.'

His eyes grew comically wide. 'Dad, look.'

Daisy grabbed the net. She held it above the two fish feeding on the discarded, soggy bits of sandwich. All she had to do was reach down and scoop them into the net.

'Go for it, Daisy,' Max whispered. 'Come on, you can do it.'

As quickly as she could, she dipped the net beneath the surface. The fish darted away.

'Dang it,' she said, plopping down heavily in the canoe. 'That's the closest I've had to any action at all.'

'Look,' Max said, tossing in another bit of his sandwich. 'They're back. Three of them now.'

Daisy didn't hesitate. She scooped again

with the net. 'I got one! Daddy, look! I caught a fish,' she said. Its silvery body writhed and flopped inside the net.

'Fantastic, Daisy,' he said. 'Good for you. Now, let's get it in the creel here....'

'A trout! Daisy caught a trout!' Max bobbed up and down with excitement.

'Take it easy, buddy,' their dad cautioned him. 'You don't want to capsize the—'

'Dad!' Daisy's trout somehow managed to flip itself out of the net. She lunged to recapture it.

Which was, of course, her fatal error. She felt the canoe lurch to one side, and was powerless to stop its momentum. She went in headfirst, arms pinwheeling. The shock of the cold water, and the buoyant life vest, propelled her instantly to the surface, a scream of outrage on her lips.

But she didn't scream. She surfaced in time to see Max flailing, and their dad reaching for him in midair. They both went in, sending up a fountain of lake water, creating a temporary rainbow as the sunlight shot through it.

'Holy shit,' Dad said. 'Holy shit, this water's cold.'

'You said shit,' Max pointed out, his lips already blue.

'Twice,' Dad reminded him. 'I said *holy* shit.' He swam over to the canoe and rescued the net, the bundle of soggy towels and two of

221

the paddles that were floating in the lake. There was water in the bottom of the boat, but it was in no danger of sinking.

Max leaned his head back against the collar of his life vest and looked up at the sky. 'It's f-f-freezing!' he said, laughing and spinning in a circle. 'Freezing! *Now* my nuts are numb.'

Daisy was shivering, but as she swam off in pursuit of her stray flip-flops, she found herself enjoying the weightless sensation of floating. If she kept moving, the water didn't feel so cold. She played a game of water tag with her dad and brother, and they ducked each other under, yelling and laughing and no doubt scaring away every last fish in the lake for good. After a while, Max's teeth started chattering so much he couldn't talk, so they decided to head back.

Easier said than done, that was for sure. They couldn't get in the boat. She and her dad managed to hoist Max up and over the side, but then they couldn't get in without tipping it over again. It was crazy, and pretty soon they were laughing so hard that her arms felt like jelly, completely useless. They gave up and swam the boat to the nearest shore, a thick wilderness of birch trees and tall grass. By then, all three of them were shivering.

'I'll make a fire,' Dad said. 'We can warm up a little, then paddle back.'

'Right, a fire,' Daisy said. 'With what?'

222

Their dad surprised them. Amazed them, actually. Who knew he was able to make a fire starter with a shoelace, two short branches and some dry grass? Somehow, he rigged the apparatus so that a quick tug on the string would drill in the point of the branch fast enough to create sparks. After a bunch of tries, the dry grass caught and they gently blew on the little nest of fire to coax a real flame from it. Finally, with careful tending, they had a perfect little campfire right there at the lakeshore. The heat felt delicious, and they managed to salvage a bag of Fritos and some grapes from the picnic, and they had a small feast. Eventually, they warmed up and dried out sufficiently to paddle back to camp.

By the time they arrived, all three of them drunk from exhaustion and from singing endless, made-up verses of 'The Bear Went Over the Mountain,' Daisy felt cleansed by the lake water, her skin tingling with a slight sunburn.

After they tied up the canoe and brought in all their soggy gear, Olivia came to greet them. 'Any luck?' she asked.

Daisy, Max and Dad looked at each other, and then burst out laughing.

*   *   *

That night, Max practically fell asleep in his macaroni and cheese, and Dad carried him off to bed. Daisy ducked into the library of the main building, a cozy room with built-in benches and reading nooks and rustic twig furniture. The shelves were crammed with every sort of book—novels with funny names like *The Egg and I,* and nature guides and what appeared to be every Dr. Seuss book ever written. She grabbed a book and went after her dad and brother.

The cabin was messy, and they were already in bed, crammed into a bunk together. She got in next to Max and handed their dad a book. 'We should start with something short,' she said.

Dad clicked on the lamp and opened *Horton Hatches the Egg,* reading with such hilarious drama that Daisy hung around to hear him. ' "I meant what I said and I said what I meant," ' Dad read in a voice of ponderous gravity, ' "an elephant's faithful one hundred percent." '

Thirteen

'So what's up with you and Olivia?' Connor asked Freddy Delgado. He figured he needed to ask, and now was probably a good time. They were rebuilding the gazebo and so far had managed to work together without killing each other.

There was something between Freddy and Olivia, but Connor couldn't put his finger on what. Ever since he'd pulled her into his arms and nearly kissed her, nothing further had happened. Did he want something to happen? Well, besides the obvious. He didn't know, he honestly didn't. He sure as hell wanted to kiss her, that was for sure.

As for Olivia, she was either avoiding him, or was genuinely too busy.

Freddy measured a four-by-four and marked it off with a flat carpenter's pencil. 'What's *up* with us?'

'That's what I asked.' Connor spoke around a mouthful of nails.

'Why do you want to know?' His face was pinched with suspicion as he set down his pencil. He went over to the big red-and-white cooler and pulled out two bottles.

'Wondering if the two of you are involved, because if you are, I respect that.'

'And if we're not?' Freddy asked, handing him a bottle.

'Then that opens up my options.' It was city-boy water in a cobalt blue teardrop-shaped bottle. He took a big gulp, then grimaced, not expecting the sharp carbonation. 'What is this piss?'

'Tynant, from a spring in Wales,' Freddy said, as if any fool should know. 'Look, all you need to know about Olivia and me is that she's the best friend I've ever had. She's taken some hard knocks, which makes me feel like shit, because I should be able to protect her from that.'

'What kind of hard knocks?' Connor asked.

Freddy glowered a warning. 'The kind I can't protect her from.'

*   *   *

Olivia stood on the deck of the main lodge, staring out at the lake island and watching Connor Davis work on the gazebo. She had a dozen things to do this afternoon, but she couldn't stop thinking about that kiss. The kiss that wasn't. The almost-kiss that Freddy had interrupted and that Connor had not bothered to reprise, even though she'd given him plenty of opportunities. Clearly he regretted making that move. She didn't blame him. When she'd dragged him to the place where his father had lived, he probably thought she'd done it to torture him. Even so, she could still hear the question he'd asked her. *Do you ever think about us, Lolly?*

'*Not any more than I think about anything else from nine years ago,*' she'd replied. It was such a huge lie, the words had probably stained her teeth.

'What do you suppose they're talking about?' Dare asked, joining Olivia. 'They actually seem to be having a conversation for a change rather than arguing.'

'Who knows? At least Nana's gazebo is going up,' Olivia said.

They decided to paddle out to the island with lunch in a cooler. Dare made the most incredible picnic lunches. Sandwiches, white grapes, mocha brownies, lemonade. She did everything with a peculiar elegance, a trait she seemed to have been born with. The camp kitchen had an abundance of picnic baskets, and she used a classic wicker one with a liner of checkered cloth. They arrived at the work site just in time to see Freddy peel off his shirt. Dare emitted a little whimper of yearning.

'He probably saw us coming and did that on purpose,' Olivia said, well acquainted with Freddy's vanity. What he lacked in height, he made up for in physical fitness, his arms and abs carefully sculpted by a daily routine involving an obscene number of push-ups.

As they glided closer, Freddy wiped his chest and underarms with the shirt.

'Well, maybe not,' Olivia amended, watching in disgust.

He shook out the shirt and then hung it from the branch of a tree.

'Definitely not,' said Dare.

Olivia regarded her cousin thoughtfully. Dare seemed quite taken with Freddy. She was about to mention it when Connor came into view, a stack of boards balanced on his shoulder.

Her own whimper of yearning was not so little.

Dare tossed a line around a cleat on the dock. 'So you're still into him after all these years? After what he did to you?' she asked.

'I'm a different person now. I always wish I'd handled things differently that summer,' she said.

'Well, here's your chance for a do-over. Not many people get that.'

Freddy spotted them coming along the dock. When he saw Dare's picnic basket, he clutched his heart and said, 'I think I'm in love.'

'A man of simple needs, then,' she observed.

'Simple and few. A hearty meal and a willing woman. That's pretty much it.'

'Then today is your lucky day. Go wash your hands and put your shirt back on.'

Olivia felt Connor's eyes on her as she watched her cousin flirting with Freddy. She took two cold bottles of lemonade from the cooler and handed him one.

'You've gotten a lot done,'she said.

'I'll show you around. Watch your step.' He held out his hand, palm up, and she flashed on an image of the way he had looked years ago, on the last night she'd seen him, dressed up and asking her to dance. She blinked, and the image went away, and she

228

was whisked back to the present. He was Connor Davis of the here and now, in Levi's and a T-shirt, a bandanna trailing from his back pocket.

She stared briefly at his hand, wondering if just touching him would cause her to melt. Probably, she thought. She was halfway there already.

She put her hand in his, and it happened exactly the way it had when he'd pulled her into his arms the other day. A peculiar, irresistible warmth flooded through her. It wasn't something she trusted or particularly wanted, nor was it something she could deny.

He drew her up to the octagonal platform he and Freddy had built, and she tipped back her head, gazing up at the open rafters. 'I feel like Cinderella at the ball.'

'Right. And I'm Prince Charming.'

'A girl can pretend.'

He let go of her hand. 'She sure as hell can.'

She leaned against the railing of the gazebo and inhaled the aroma of cut lumber. Shading her eyes, she said, 'They were probably married on a day like today. My grandmother said it was a perfect summer day.'

An old black-and-white photograph had been tacked to a post. It was a shot of her grandparents, young and dazzlingly in love, with their wedding party, under the original gazebo. The new structure appeared to be a close replica.

Connor mistook her expression. 'Don't worry. It's a copy.'

'You put the photograph here?'

'That surprises you?'

'It's just…yes.'

'Well, I did it. What's that look?'

'Nothing. You turned out to be a cool guy, Connor. That surprises me, too.'

'And you turned out…sexy,' he countered, 'which doesn't surprise me at all.'

She sniffed. 'You didn't even recognize me when you first saw me.'

'You were hanging from a flagpole. I wouldn't recognize my own mother under those circumstances.'

She felt herself opening up to him. Trusting him. And wasn't that a curious development? For some crazy reason, she harbored a palpable trust for Connor Davis.

She studied the photograph. It showed a moment of such joy, naked on their faces, bright in their eyes. Her grandfather looked so proud and handsome in his tuxedo, her grandmother utterly blissful. Their friends, gathered around, wore clothes so crisply tailored and pressed that they had the flat, cartoonish look of drawings. Both her grandparents were younger than Olivia herself was now. Even though the shot was clearly staged, there was an innocence and purity in

230

their faces that touched the heart. It must be magical, she thought, to share a moment of such simple happiness and hope, to know you had found the person with whom you wanted to spend the rest of your life.

They were young and totally in love. There was no hint of the struggles they had endured with Granddad's family, who had bitterly opposed the marriage. There was no foreshadowing of the life that awaited these two, the good times and bad. Vietnam and the oil crisis, unimaginable prosperity and unbearable tragedy. The moment the photograph was taken, there was only the innocent, soaring joy of embarking on a lifelong adventure together.

She recognized her other grandparents in the photograph, too. Samuel Lightsey was the best man in the wedding. A few years after the photograph was taken, he had married his date, her maternal grandmother, Gwen.

With a wistful smile, she said, 'I want the day of their anniversary to be as perfect as their wedding day.'

'I have a feeling you and Dare are going to make sure of it.'

She sank deeper under his spell, trusting him more with every word he spoke. All right, she thought. Deep breath. 'I was engaged,' she said softly, watching his face. 'In case you were wondering.'

His expression didn't change. 'I take it

231

things didn't work out.'

'That's right.'

'Freddy told me you'd been hurt, but that's all he would say.'

She shuffled her feet, cleared her throat. Why not? He'd probably hear the story anyway, eventually. 'Three times,' she added.

'I don't get it.'

'Three times. That's how many times I was engaged. To three different guys. Well, the third one wasn't technically an engagement. I sort of…headed that one off.' And Freddy was right. She *had* been hurt, and with each successive failure, she became more and more convinced that the trouble was with her. She seemed to have a knack for picking the wrong guy. She made herself hold Connor's gaze. She searched his face for some kind of reaction but saw nothing. 'Well?'

'Well, what?'

'Aren't you going to say anything?'

'What do you want me to say?'

'I don't know. How about, 'Sorry to hear that'?'

'I'm not sorry to hear it.'

'What?'

'If any of those engagements had worked out, you'd be married now, and that would mean I'm standing here lusting after a married woman.'

His bluntness took her breath away. 'You're lusting after me?'

232

He laughed. 'Isn't it obvious?'

'Who says *lusting* anymore?'

'Pretty much any guy who's being honest.'

'Lusting,' she repeated, feeling her skin heat with embarrassment. 'You should quit right now.'

'Yeah,' he said, 'I'll get right on that.' He laughed at her. Laughed. 'Not going to happen, no way.'

'You're never going to get any satisfaction,' she said.

'Damn, Lolly, you're so quick to take offense. I'm not trying to get engaged to you. I just thought you might want to be my girlfriend for the summer.'

An unbidden spasm of response reverberated through her but she quelled it. 'What a treat.'

'I take it that's a no.'

'With a capital *N*. God, Connor. Why would I want to be your girlfriend?'

'So we can hang out, have some laughs, make love in every conceivable way and then some.'

She nearly choked on her lemonade.

'You all right?' He patted her on the back, and she nodded but couldn't speak. He asked, 'Was it something I said?'

Another nod. 'Guys don't talk to me like that.'

'I guess that's the problem. No wonder you dumped the last three.'

'It's kind of you to assume I dumped them.'

'Doesn't matter. The good news is, they're gone.'

She reluctantly had to agree. As perfect as Rand had seemed for her, she didn't actually miss him. She kept bracing herself for moments of weakness, when she thought about calling his voice mail just to hear his voice, but those moments never came. She didn't lie around with a hole in her heart, missing him, wishing they could still be friends, aching to feel his arms around her. This was not good news to Olivia. It meant she didn't know her own heart. The only man she had ever yearned for that deeply was—

Connor handed her a bandanna. 'It's clean,' he said. 'Wipe your face.'

Fourteen

Olivia's most unsettling memories tended to hit in the darkest hours of the soft summer nights. Most days, everyone worked themselves into exhaustion and turned in early—with the exception of Olivia. Ordinarily, she had no trouble sleeping, but here at Camp Kioga, she often found herself wide awake. Her mind was on fire. Not just with unanswered questions about Jenny

Majesky or with enthusiasm for a challenging job, but with memories. She walked outside with them. They flickered in the stars, which were so plentiful they seemed to spray the night sky with glitter. Through the mist, the white sliver of the moon cut an arc upon the black table of the lake.

A breeze rippled the water and she shivered, drawing her denim jacket more securely around herself. Living in the city, she forgot that there were places like this, places where she could be completely alone while her thoughts swirled through her head like a scream. It felt strange to hear only the singing of frogs and the rustle of wind through the trees. Strange, and maybe a little ominous.

She ought to head for bed. Tomorrow was going to be a busy day. Connor Davis was coming first thing in the morning with contracts from the plumbing and electrical subcontractors. A business meeting, she told herself. It was just a business meeting. Yet in her mind, she was already picking out her outfit. How pathetic was that?

Connor Davis. Why did she remember every touch, every kiss they had shared, years ago? Why could she still feel the exact imprint of his lips on hers, the precise taste of him, the rhythm of his heart as they embraced? It was crazy. Life had given her so much since she had come of age here at Camp Kioga, and then walked away. Why did she still feel trapped in that moment with him?

Because, when he'd taken her into his arms that day on the dance floor, all those feelings had come rushing back at her.

She sighed and turned to go into the dining hall, now the command center for the project. Might as well get some work done, since sleep was impossible. She turned on a light and perused the sketches and plans laid out on the tables and tacked to the wall. Maybe she would fix a pot of tea and mull things over.

She was going over her uncle's plan for the gardens when a loud noise nudged her from her reverie. It took less than a second to identify it as a motorcycle engine. Oh, boy, she thought, unable to quell a thrill of nerves as she went to the front of the building to wait for him. She checked her watch—10:30 p.m. What was going on?

He drove up to the main entrance, killed the engine and light, and pulled the bike up on its kickstand. 'Hope I didn't wake you,' he said, taking off his helmet.

'I was up.' Mystified, she followed him inside. He smelled of old leather and wind, and his boots thudded on the planks of the floor as he crossed to the dining hall. He peeled off his gloves and flexed his fingers. 'Colder than I thought tonight,' he said. 'Froze my nuts off driving up here.'

'Sorry to hear it,' she said, feeling

awkward.

'You planning on putting in phone service anytime soon?'

'It's scheduled for next week.'

'Good. I don't like driving ten miles up the mountain every time I need to talk to you.'

'So you need to talk to me.' She sat down on a bench. 'What's up?'

'I've got unexpected company coming for the summer. Just found out about it.' He sat down beside her, steepled the tips of his fingers together. 'My brother, Julian.'

'You're kidding. I remember Julian.' Did she ever. He was Connor's half brother, and they'd grown up separately, Connor with their mother in Buffalo, and Julian...Gastineaux— she still remembered that name—with his dad in New Orleans. 'That's great,' she said. 'Isn't it?'

'Who knows? It's Julian, after all.'

He was a good ten years younger than Connor, she recalled, and had been a camper at Kioga back in 1997, the summer she and Connor had been counselors. 'He was a handful when he was little,' she said.

'He's seventeen now, just finished his junior year in high school. He and our mom live in California now, since she divorced Mel. Julian's father died a few years back, so he's with Mom now.'

To Olivia, the idea of losing her father seemed like something she would not survive.

237

'How is he doing?'

'He took it hard, and yeah, he's still a handful.'

'So he's coming to visit you.'

'All summer long. He's going to be working for me.'

'Well, that's good. I'm sure we can keep him busy on this project.'

'It's court ordered,' Connor said.

'Excuse me?'

'Julian tends to get in trouble. A lot. After his latest stunt, the juvenile-court judge gave him a choice—time in juvey, or he could remove himself to a different environment for the summer. This is a hell of a lot different from Chino, California.'

She couldn't imagine taking in a teenager in trouble, even if he was a brother he barely knew. The responsibility must feel crushing. 'That's...very nice of you.'

'Yeah, well. I'm a very nice guy.'

'You always were.' She almost added, *Up until you humiliated me and walked away,* but refrained.

'He's flying into LaGuardia on a red-eye and will take the early train up from the city, and I have to meet him.'

'Of course,' she said.

'I didn't see this coming.' He blew out a weary-sounding breath.

'You couldn't have. So, um, what sort of trouble is he in? If you don't mind my asking.'

238

He flashed a grin. 'How long have you got?'

'All night. Remember, no TV at Camp Kioga.' She shivered, hugged herself against the chill night air.

'I'll make a fire.'

Now she was totally intrigued. And for the first time in her life, she was thrilled to be without phone service. If he had been able to call her, he wouldn't be here now, lighting a cozy fire and pulling two armchairs close to the hearth. There was something elemental and, all right, fundamentally sexy, about a guy building a fire for a woman. Maybe it went back to caveman times. She felt a natural attraction to a man with the instinct to make a fire for her.

The dry logs caught quickly, and flames and sparks danced up the chimney. She watched the play of light on Connor's broad shoulders. The flames danced over him, and her gaze was drawn inexorably to the shadows the firelight carved in his face.

All right, she thought. The first step was admitting it. She had a thing for Connor Davis. Again. Still. And this would not do at all. She was supposed to hold herself aloof, showing him what he'd missed out on when he'd blown his chance with her all those years ago.

'You all right?' He was looking at her strangely.

239

She realized she had been caught staring. 'So you were going to tell me about your brother.'

'Right.' He lifted one hip and took out a wallet that had shaped itself to his body, a detail Olivia tried not to notice but couldn't help herself. Connor handed her a photograph. 'His school picture from last year.'

Julian Gastineaux had turned into one of the most singularly attractive boys she had ever seen. He had a perfect symmetry of bone structure and his smile was a sweet Cupid's bow. He was biracial, with creamy skin the color of café au lait, dark eyes fringed by long thick lashes and an abundance of dreadlocks.

'He's gorgeous,' she said. 'Looks like an angel.'

Connor pulled a folded sheet of paper out of his jacket pocket and spread it on his knee. 'He was cited for skateboarding down a spiral parking lot ramp, which actually sounds kind of fun to me, except he hit an oncoming car and went flying over the hood and roof.'

'Was he hurt?'

'No, but he damaged a late-model Lexus and scared the crap out of the driver. He was ordered to pay for repairs to the car, so he got a job as a lifeguard.'

'Makes perfect sense.'

'He was fired from that when they caught him doing gainers off the ten-meter diving platform.'

'I thought that was what a diving platform was for.'

'After hours, in the dark.'

'All right, maybe not that. So what else?'

He ran down a list of hair-raising adventures, each more dangerous than the last. Julian had 'borrowed' a hang glider and went soaring off the Sansovino cliffs, dislocating his hip on landing. He had gone surfing in twenty-foot waves, bungee jumping off a bridge, spray painted his initials on a water tower and, on a dare, had ridden a stolen bike into the La Brea Tar Pits.

'And those are just the things we know about,' Connor finished. 'When he turns eighteen, the record will go away, but only if he keeps his nose clean this summer. That's where I come in.'

'The judge feels he'll stay out of trouble if he spends the summer with you.' It sounded logical enough to Olivia.

'Honestly, I think the judge is trying to keep my mother from throwing him out.' He wadded up the printout and tossed it in the fire. 'Anyway. Looks like I have a new project for the summer. And you've got a decision to make.'

'About…'

'Working with me.'

'You don't think you can juggle Julian and this project?'

'I'm going to have to.'

'Then there's nothing to decide. He'll probably love it here.'

'Maybe you'd better think about it. The kid's a maniac for risk taking.'

'This will work. And if his thrill seeking gets him in trouble, well, we have liability insurance.'

Connor looked startled, as if he hadn't expected her to be so cooperative. 'Thanks for understanding. I'll be back tomorrow after I pick Julian up from the station.' Then he frowned.

'What is it?'

'Trying to figure out where to put him.'

'He won't be staying with you?'

'I'll have to find a rental for us in town, because I don't have room. My place is a bit on the small side.'

'Your place.'

'It's on the river road, between the glass art studio and Windy Ridge Farm.'

She now knew exactly where he lived. It was riverside land, a high meadow and sunny glade surrounded by maple and birch trees. The tiny Airstream trailer in the woods. 'That's your place?'

'Uh-huh.'

She tried not to appear startled, but failed.

He noticed her expression, and offered a grin that disappeared too quickly. 'Home sweet home.'

242

'I didn't mean—'

'I know.'

She felt badly, though, and blurted out, 'Your brother can stay here. We've got nothing but room. Bunkhouses, staff cabins and that whole row of bungalows—'

'Thanks, but he's going to need close supervision.'

'You could stay with him.' She tried to act as though this was all about being accommodating. In reality, it was all about getting Connor Davis to spend the summer at Camp Kioga instead of driving down the mountain every day at sunset. 'It makes perfect sense,' she said. 'You're working here every day, anyway, and this will save you the commute.' *Oh, smooth, Olivia. Very smooth.*

'This is your family's place,' he said. 'You don't need to provide housing for the help.'

She recognized the look on his face. It was the same look he'd worn when he was a kid, and people talked about his father. Terry Davis used to be the 'help.' 'Listen to you,' she said lightly. 'Are you really that uncomfortable with this arrangement?'

He sat back in his chair, stretched his booted feet toward the fire and crossed them at the ankles. A silence stretched out to the point of discomfort. Each crackle of the fire sounded like a gunshot.

'I guess I'm not, Lolly,' Connor said finally, amusement evident in his voice. 'And

243

what's that look?'

'I wasn't giving you a look.'

'Sure you were.'

She was, and he'd caught her. 'You could have told your mother no,' she said. 'You don't have to take care of your brother for the summer. You know what I think? I think you act like a tough guy but it's just a cover.'

He scowled. 'A cover for what?'

'Your sweet, creamy center.'

'Oh, yeah. That's me. Sweet.'

He was, she thought, even though he'd die before admitting it. Ever since she'd known him, he was keenly aware when someone was hurting. 'Julian is the same age as Daisy,' she said, intending to seal the deal before he changed his mind. 'They can keep each other from getting bored. It'll be the bungalow colony all over again. Just like when we were their age.'

'That's what I'm afraid of.'

'Hey, we survived, and kids these days seem a lot more sophisticated than I was. If you share a cottage with Julian, you can keep tabs on him. Assuming,' she quickly added, 'we have a deal.'

He stared at her for a long moment. His gaze seemed to be lingering on her mouth, and then her eyes. She had nearly forgotten his silences, forgotten that way he had of studying her as if he actually cared about was going on in her head. She felt her neck and

244

cheeks growing warm.

'I guess we do, Lolly,' he said. 'I guess we have a deal.'

Oh, God, she thought. What have I done?

'Now you're staring,' he pointed out.

'Oh.' She blinked. 'Sorry.'

He turned to walk out the door.

'Connor?'

He turned back.

'Do you—' She swallowed, cleared her throat. 'I have the same question you asked me the other day. Do you, um, ever think about...us?'

'Nope,' he said, shrugging his shoulders. 'Things happen. Life gets busy. I haven't thought about us in a long time.'

All right. She'd asked for that. She shuffled her feet, stared at the floor, the door, her gaze seeking neutral territory.

He grinned easily, touched her shoulder. 'But I am now.'

Fifteen

Connor hadn't told Olivia half of it. From the moment he had first spotted her, stranded atop a flagpole, he'd been intrigued. As time went on, he became consumed by memories of the past, good and bad, of the time he'd spent with her.

He wasn't sure why he was being so guarded around this woman. He could have explained the Airstream and the Harley to her easily enough. Maybe he even could have explained why he'd hurt her all those years ago. He hadn't, though. For some reason, he felt he was better off letting her think he was a born son of a bitch, a biker who lived in a trailer. Maybe so she wouldn't fall for him. Because even though he found himself wanting to go to every forbidden, sensual place with her, he knew they didn't stand any better chance together now than they had when they were kids.

Last night, he had wanted to explain everything to her, but it sounded too intense. Obsessive, maybe.

There was really no point in wondering why they had parted ways, all those years ago. They were just seventeen and eighteen, fresh out of high school. She was desperately unhappy and he was scared to death, saddled with way too much responsibility. Not exactly a firm foundation for a relationship. Still, that wasn't the reason the relationship had failed.

Over the past nine years, she had changed everything about herself. Her looks, her hair, her attitude, even her name. She simply wasn't Lolly anymore. Lolly might as well be a figment of his imagination—shy, self-conscious, a dreamer who once wanted to be a teacher. A girl with a kind heart, a girl who

246

turned out to be the only person in the world who loved him.

For the tenth time, Connor checked his cell phone: 11:15 a.m. No new messages. That was good news, he told himself, slipping the phone into his shirt pocket. Julian was supposed to arrive on the eleven-thirty train.

Connor wondered what Julian would think of Avalon. The place could be a stand-in for Mayberry, populated with folksy types and ex–flower children, earnest ecoactivists, artists and poets. Connor had never imagined himself settling down here, making a life for himself in a town where people didn't bother locking their doors at night. Yet when life had taken him to the brink of disaster, it had been his connection to Avalon—and to the Bellamy family in particular—that had saved him.

Rourke McKnight, chief of police of Avalon, showed up at the train station. Connor knew he was off duty because he had his two favorite off-duty accessories with him—a woman who was built like a lingerie model, and a pair of dark aviator glasses to hide the evidence of last night's party. Spotting Connor, he offered a brief wave, and Connor nodded to acknowledge it.

The lingerie model said something to Rourke and headed for the restrooms in the lobby. Connor decided to use the opportunity to offer a heads-up on Julian. 'Hey, Rourke,' he said.

'Connor.' They shook hands.

'Got a minute?' Connor asked.

Rourke glanced toward the lobby. 'Sure. You know women and their primping.'

Not really, but Connor nodded. Rourke was notorious for his romantic revolving-door policy with women. They were always gorgeous, and they always went back to the city after a brief time—usually a weekend— never to return. Some of the town busybodies thought it outrageous behavior for the chief of police, but most people figured what he did in his own time, so long as it was legal, was none of their business.

'I wanted to let you know that my younger brother's coming to spend the summer with me,' Connor explained. 'Complicated family situation. The two of us will be staying up at Camp Kioga, at the work site.'

'Okay.'

'He's coming here at the order of a judge,' Connor added. 'He's seventeen and has a few incidents of delinquency in California.'

'What, did you lose a bet?' Rourke flashed a brief grin.

'Something like that. Anyway, his name's Julian Gastineaux, and he should be in on the next train.'

'I'll keep it in mind.' With that, McKnight removed the dark glasses and held Connor's gaze. 'You let me know if there's anything I can do to help.'

'Thanks.' They shook hands again, and a tacit understanding passed between them. Most people in town—including Rourke McKnight—knew Connor Davis had done time. But no one knew what that time had done to Connor Davis.

Since his mother had put him in the position of taking Julian for the summer, Connor was fiercely determined to make sure his brother never faced that.

When Julian had first gone to live with her, Connor had hoped the kid would do better than Connor had in the Mom department. Judging by the current situation, that was unlikely. Connor would make it a point to tell the kid the problem was not with him. That it wasn't his job to get his mother to love him. This was something Connor himself had spent considerable sums of his own time and heart on, only to discover for himself that it couldn't be done.

Rourke's date returned and he put the sunglasses back on. 'See you around, Connor.'

'You bet.' He nodded politely to the woman and moved away on the platform.

The southbound train arrived, and the lingerie model gave Rourke a lingering kiss, then boarded. A moment later Connor's phone rang. He checked the number on the incoming call and flipped open his phone. 'Ma. I was just thinking about you.'

'Is he there yet?'

'His train gets in any minute.' Connor watched the southbound disappear through a cleft in the mountains rising against the sky. He tried to picture her view in Chino, California, where she'd moved after Mel had left her. Freeways, stockyards and strip malls.

'Are you sure he's on it?'

'You mean you're not?' Connor frowned. Was she suddenly having an attack of maternal concern? 'What's going on?'

There was a pause. 'Sometimes he runs away,' she said quietly.

'Great. Thanks for telling me.' Connor's jaw tensed. She'd probably have to pay a hefty fine if the kid went AWOL. He wasn't sure what bothered him more—the fact that his mother had manipulated him into taking Julian for the summer, or the fact that he had let her. 'What else you hiding, Ma?' he asked.

'God, Connor. I'm not hiding a damn thing from you. Just checking on your brother.'

'Right.'

'Look, if you're going to be so pissed off about this, you should have told me. I nearly went broke getting him a ticket at the last minute.'

'How is it that you're broke, buying a plane ticket?' He wondered if she'd given the kid enough for train fare as well.

'I had to pay full fare.'

His mother was fifty-five years old. She

ought to have enough for a plane ticket from L.A. to New York without going broke. Yet she simply could not hold on to her money. She was as addicted to spending it as his father had been to alcohol.

'Tell you what,' he said. 'I'll have him give you a call when he gets here. And if he doesn't get here, I'll call you myself.'

A long pause. Through the silence, he sensed an unspoken warning. 'What else are you keeping from me, Ma?'

He heard her gather in a long breath. 'I, er, didn't exactly explain to your brother how long he'd be staying out there.'

'How long does he think he's staying?' Connor didn't need to ask. Not really. He already knew his mother had lied to get her way. It was what she did.

He only half listened to her lengthy, self-justifying explanation. She'd told Julian it was only for a week or two, and that if he didn't cooperate, she'd be fined into bankruptcy and he'd wind up in detention.

Connor had heard it all before, or some version of it. He tuned his mother out and focused on the arriving train. A handful of passengers disembarked—a nun with her overnight bag, a teacher he recognized from the local high school, a businessman, a family of tourists who headed for the rental-car counter.

And that was it. No one else disembarked.

Connor paced up and down the platform. A conductor stood at the door, looking up and down the tracks and platform. He put a whistle to his mouth, about to give the all-clear signal.

Still no sign of Julian. Connor cursed under his breath, waving at the conductor to wait.

At the same time, a tall, slender teenager with dreadlocks got off the train. *Julian.*

He didn't use the normal exit but emerged between cars, heaving an overstuffed duffel and backpack onto the platform and then jumping down after it.

His gaze riveted on the impossibly tall kid, Connor lifted the phone to his mouth. 'Ma, he's here. We'll call you later.'

He ended the call and pocketed the phone. 'Yo,' he yelled to his brother. 'Over here.'

Julian stiffened, assuming a defensive posture as though he feared a physical assault. It was the posture of someone who was used to getting hurt. Someone who had spent the night in jail, maybe.

The last time they'd seen each other, Julian had been about fourteen, still on the child's side of puberty. Connor had gone out to California because his mother, in despair after the collapse of her marriage, had begged him to come.

The Julian he'd seen that year had a

broken arm, a crooked grin and a heart full of grief, having just lost his father.

Three years later, Connor found himself looking at an extremely tall stranger with a sullen, hostile expression. 'Hey,' he said, stopping a few feet from Julian.

His brother jerked his head to clear his overly long locks from his eyes. 'Hey.' He had a man's voice now, a man's anger burning in his eyes. And more tattoos and body piercings than a sailor in the merchant marine.

'I just got off the phone with Ma,' Connor said. 'She was worried that you might not show.'

Julian shrugged into his army-surplus backpack. 'I showed. Lucky you.'

They didn't shake hands. They sure as hell didn't embrace like brothers who hadn't seen each other in three years.

'The truck is over here.' Connor indicated the Dodge Power Wagon, circa 1974. 'Throw your stuff in the back and get in.'

'Nice wheels.'

'Shut up.'

The duffel bag made a clanking sound when it landed. Connor wondered how the kid had ever made it through airport security. Julian kept the backpack with him, his gangly limbs sprawling over the sides of the bench seat and the pack between his knees. He unzipped the top, took out a Power Bar and stuffed it into his mouth in two bites. Connor glanced at the contents of the backpack—clothes and a surprising number of books. The thing probably weighed a ton, but Julian carried it as if it were nothing. Good. He was going to need his strength this summer.

'So I've got good news and bad news,' Connor said. 'The good news is, you don't have to spend a summer in juvenile hall.'

'And the bad?'

Connor threw the truck in gear and left the train station behind. 'The bad news is, you're spending the summer with me.'

Sixteen

For Julian Gastineaux, life reached a new level of suckitude when he passed through the gates of Camp Kioga. Camp-freaking-Kioga, where summers go to die, he thought, looking around with contempt. It resembled the set of a Disney movie, the kind of place that made white folk burst into song.

He had been here only one time before, the summer he was eight years old. Except back then he'd actually regarded camp as an exciting adventure. Then, like now, he'd been sent away because his mother had better things to do than take care of him, and his father... He thought for a minute. That year, his father had gone on sabbatical. To Italy, as

Julian recalled.

His father's people, as they were referred to, lived in a forgotten town of shanties and lottery-ticket stands in southern Louisiana. They were always happy to look after Julian, but both he and his father were misfits there. A Tulane professor and his son found little in common with the rest of the Gastineaux family, so when Julian's father went away that one summer, he was supposed to go live with his mother. But back then, she hadn't wanted him around any more than she did now, so Camp Kioga became his temporary home. History repeating itself, he thought, only this time he was a hell of a lot more pissed off about it.

As a little kid, he had been totally blown away by summer camp. Raised in an ancient, musty-smelling house in New Orleans, Julian recalled a childhood was filled with yellowing books stacked high on every available surface. All the desks and tables were riddled with papers, notes, journals and every possible gizmo known to man. This was the trailing edge of a district that was just barely genteel, separated only by a couple of mews from an area where smart women didn't walk alone after dark, where his father forbade him to go, on those occasions when Louis Gastineaux remembered Julian was around.

Louis often forgot, because he was an eccentric genius. He was a bona fide, pocket-protector-wearing, bad-haircut, Coke-bottle-glasses geek. He had the brilliant mind and dorky personality to back it up. The only thing that was not uncool about Julian's father was that he was black, and built like a linebacker.

Julian used to try everything to get his father's attention, but nothing ever worked. Not making straight A's in school, or flunking every class. If he tried to fake illness or injury, he got bored with bedrest before his father even noticed.

'I'll be with you in a moment,' Louis Gastineaux used to say, his face bathed in the misty glow of a computer monitor. Although his scientific calculations were precise to the eleventh decimal place, the guy had no clue how long a 'moment' was supposed to be. Professor Gastineaux inhabited the universe inside the computer much more comfortably than he fit into the everyday world of school lunches and PTA meetings, remembering birthdays and shopping for groceries. Sometimes he seemed to forget he had a son at all.

Julian entertained himself by seeking out physical thrills. He climbed to high places—treetops and fire escapes, tall bridges and rope swings. He learned to love the sensation of danger screaming through his blood, and to crave the weightless thrill of flying, whether by taking a jump on his skateboard, or para-surfing in the hot wind over the Gulf of

Mexico.

There was no possible way Julian could imagine his parents in the same room, much less the same bed. His mother, the blond bombshell, and his father, the nutty professor. About that fateful meeting, his father had little to say. 'It was at a jet propulsion conference in Niagara Falls,' he said. 'She was performing at a club, and I'd presented a paper on a breakthrough my research team had achieved in solar and laser sail technology. We had plenty to celebrate.'

When Julian was little, he'd been unfamiliar with the term 'one-night stand' and his father failed to enlighten him. Julian's dad had been an embarrassing fifteen years younger than his mom. It skeezed Julian out just thinking about it.

Later, Julian's mother filled in a few more blanks in the story. 'After you were born, I realized I couldn't support another kid, so I gave Louis full custody.' Julian suspected there was a good deal more to the situation than that. Ultimately, he drew the conclusion that he had been an accident, an unwanted child who fell into the hands of the parent who had drawn the short straw.

Years ago, his father did remember to explain the perils of unprotected sex. He had done so in his trademark detailed fashion, as though he was delivering a lecture on propulsion mission concepts. Then he'd handed Julian a box of condoms.

The life of a college professor was not supposed to be hazardous, but an eccentric genius driving a rusted-out Duster in rush hour traffic was an accident waiting to happen.

The day Julian's life had changed had been completely ordinary. The last thing Louis had said to him that morning was nothing profound or prescient. He'd simply told Julian he wouldn't be home for dinner.

It was the next morning by the time someone remembered to call him. Louis Gastineaux barely escaped the wreck with his life, and when he awoke from a coma induced by a swelling of the brain, he was a quadriplegic, his body no more than a life-support system for his brilliant mind. He was eerily comfortable with this turn of events, for with some training on a modified system, he could still operate a computer, could still think like a genius. And one of the first things he thought was that he couldn't look after a fourteen-year-old son. Julian would have to go to live with his mother.

She agreed, and once again he suspected there was a lot more to the story. He was pretty sure there had been a generous financial incentive, and Julian was sent to Chino, California, a charmless freeway town where his mother lived and worked as a cocktail waitress at a dinner theater, never quite giving up her hope of a stage career. There, he joined a crowd of skaters and baby outlaws, and spent most of his time seeking thrills and evading capture. When the call came, a few months later, that his father had passed away due to complications from his condition, Julian's fate was sealed. He was stuck.

Now, resentment boiled in every cell of his body as he crossed the main compound of Camp Kioga with his brother. Connor-fricking-Davis. Other than being the same height—six-foot-two—the two of them looked as though they were from different planets instead of the same mother. Connor had that long-haired-biker-meets-Paul-Bunyon thing going on, while Julian cultivated the hip-hop dreadlock look. It helped him blend in at school, while setting him apart from his Nordic queen of a mother.

He couldn't believe she had tricked him into coming here. Just a week, she'd wheedled. Just so the judge thinks we're taking his advice. He should have known better.

A blue lake in the middle of the woods might be some people's version of paradise, but not Julian's. Not even close. A concrete skateboard park would be good. Back home, he had his best times flying his board over a freeway divider or surfing at Huntington Beach during a storm. Here, he had no clue what to do with himself. With his luck, his brother would have him digging latrines or something. Because that was another thing about Connor. Although Julian barely knew him, he understood somehow that his older brother had that thing known as the 'work ethic.' As in, the harder you work, the more ethical it makes you. The logic simply didn't follow. Julian could even prove it using a deductive model, but every time he used his brain for something like that, it seemed to get him deeper in trouble.

They passed by Meerskill Falls and the bridge arching above the gorge. Oh, man, did he remember that bridge. At the age of eight, he'd made his first bungee jump from it. There had been hell to pay after, but the ride had been worth it. The stunt had even earned him a nickname from the other kids—the Birdman of Meerskill Falls. He'd earned a different name from his brother—shit-for-brains dumb ass. Connor had always worried about Julian in a way Julian's parents never had.

'We're bunking here,' Connor said, indicating a row of cabins tucked against the brow of the hill and surrounded by miles of forest. The cabins were identical, made of weathered wood, each with windows facing the lake and a rock-clad chimney, steps leading up to a front-porch area. 'The whole camp's been shut down for years,' Connor explained, unlocking the cabin on the far end. 'We've got some cleaning up to do.'

Julian set down his backpack and duffel with a sigh. Clouds of dust rose from every surface. 'Dude,' he said in his best surfer imitation, 'this is awesome.'

'Uh-huh.' Connor headed for the larger of the two bedrooms. 'I'm taking this one,' he said. 'You get the other.'

'I can't believe you're making me stay here.'

'Hey, considering the alternative, you're in fine shape.' Connor didn't take the bait, didn't lash back. 'You can take the whole day off. Make your bed, get going on the cleaning. Rest up after your trip, check out the camp, grab something to eat.'

If that was his idea of a day off, Julian thought, then work was going to be a bitch.

'Ma e-mailed me a list of recommendations from family court,' Connor continued. He took some folded pages out of his back pocket. 'There's, like, forty-seven rules and guidelines.' He tossed them on the shelf in Julian's room. 'As far as I'm concerned, you only have to remember one rule while you're with me.'

Julian narrowed his eyes, thrust up his chin. 'Yeah? What's that?'

Connor stuck the wad of keys deep in his pocket. 'Don't fuck up,' he said.

It was close to sunset when Julian's hunger overtook his pride. Sadly, it didn't take much. He ate all the time, his appetite like some insatiable monster with a ravenous need for sustenance. Initially, Julian had planned to keep to himself the entire time and go to bed hungry, just to show Connor what he thought of this suck-ass summer.

Connor probably thought it made him seem cool to reduce all the house rules to a single one—*don't fuck up.* What Connor didn't know was that he was taking away the only thing Julian was good at.

Now, with hunger gnawing at his belly, he made his way to the dining hall, which was in the main pavilion. It didn't seem as big and palatial as it had when he was little, entering the place with the other Fledgling boys.

A bell rang to signal mealtime, just like it used to when the camp was operational. Connor said that if Julian missed out, he was on his own. Julian had every intention of skipping this pukefest of a meal, but as usual, his stomach betrayed him. He was hungry enough to start gnawing on his own leg. When the dinner bell sounded, he made a beeline for the dining hall, salivating like Pavlov's dumbest dog.

Connor introduced him to everyone— Olivia Bellamy, who had hired Connor's firm to renovate the camp, was a complete blond hottie. She said she remembered him from years ago, but he didn't recall her. In his mind, all the counselors were a blur of bland, smiling white folks who listened to bad music and sang lame campfire songs. There was some guy named Freddy, and some combo of relatives—Cousin Dare, the event planner, who also prepared the meals, a guy named Greg and his annoying-looking kid, Max. The apple-cheeked boy, who was about ten, resembled one of the von Trapp children in the most horrifying film on record—*The Sound of Music.*

'Daisy should be here any minute,' Olivia said. 'Go ahead and get something to eat.'

Daisy? *Daisy?*

Trying to quell his curiosity, Julian sauntered over to the buffet table. All right, he had to admit, Cousin Dare was a phenomenal cook. He shamelessly loaded his plate with chicken potpie, mashed potatoes, salad and rolls. Beside him, Max watched with an open mouth.

'You going to eat all that?' the kid asked.

'For my first course,' Julian said. 'For my second course, I eat little boys.'

It didn't work on Max. Instead of scurrying away to the protection of his father, the kid snickered. 'Oh, I'm shaking.'

Ah, well. The fun in scaring a little kid was limited, anyway. Julian set down his tray at a table just as Daisy—apparently the missing cousin—arrived. Maybe it was a trick of the light, and maybe Julian was hearing things, but the moment she appeared in the arched doorway of the dining hall, everything changed. There was a hush, like an indrawn breath of anticipation.

As she stood there, her feminine silhouette backlit by the setting sun, he was sure he heard a chorus of heavenly voices blaring in perfect harmony. *Hallelujah.*

Usually, he had to shut his eyes in order to conjure up a fantasy this good. But now here it was, in three-dimensional living color, walking straight toward him. The chorus in his head switched to 'Pretty Woman' as she approached with a runway-model rhythm, as if she heard the music, too.

Some latent lesson in manners kicked in, and Julian rose to his feet as the introductions were made. Daisy was from New York and like Julian, she had just finished her junior year in high school. She offered him a smile that lit up the world, her amazing blue eyes sparkling. 'Mind if I share your table?' Though it was a question, she didn't wait for an answer but sat beside him as though bestowing a royal favor.

He wasn't about to argue.

Daisy's family resemblance to her father and brother, Max, was unmistakable. She, too, was a von Trapp—blond and Germanic, with features so appealing they should probably model a Barbie doll after her. However, Julian observed, the girl-next-door cuteness masked something else, something he couldn't quite identify, like the shadow of a troubled spirit.

During dinner, he learned that she went to some snooty-sounding New York prep school, one she insisted everybody should have heard of. Her mother was a lawyer who practiced international law, and her father was a landscape architect who had taken the summer off to renovate Camp Kioga.

All right, *that* was annoying, thought Julian. Bragging on your parents. Who did that? Not him, that was for damn sure, and the nosy blonde had better not ask him about his family.

Fortunately, she dropped the subject when Dare brought out dessert—thick slices of peach pie with vanilla ice cream. The pie was so good, Julian almost wept. He looked around the table and everyone else clearly felt the same way. They had the closed eyes and ecstatic expressions of people in the throes of a religious experience.

'The pie's from Sky River Bakery,' Dare said.

'No, it's from heaven,' Greg amended.

The only flaw in the perfect dinner was that Julian and Daisy had to do the dishes. Even that wasn't so bad. The big, industrial kitchen had walk-in coolers, tall steel racks and a commercial dishwashing system. They made short work of everything, laughing and teasing as they scraped, soaped, rinsed and dried everything. By the time they finished, it was dark outside. Freddy took Max and the little mutt called Barkis to the rec hall for a game of Ping-Pong. Connor and the others sat around drinking coffee and looking over plans and schedules. It was all so frigging wholesome, Julian wanted to puke.

'Can we go make a fire on the beach?' Daisy asked.

'You and Julian?' her father asked.

'Duh. Yeah, Dad. Me and Julian.'

So here was something interesting, Julian observed. Some sort of power struggle between Daisy and Greg Bellamy. Julian decided to speak up. 'I promise I'll be on my best behavior. Sir.'

Girls' dads were suckers for 'sir.' One little syllable, and they acted like their daughter was dating Dudley Do-Right.

'He will,' Connor said. No further words passed between them, but Julian caught a repeat of the warning: *Don't fuck up.*

'I guess it's all right,' Greg said. 'I might come out to check on you later.'

'Sure, Dad,' Daisy said with forced brightness. 'That'd be great.'

Olivia handed her a box of kitchen matches. 'Just keep it in the fire pit, okay?'

Making a fire was actually harder than it

looked on *Survivor.* They used up the whole box of matches before their pile of twigs finally caught, creating more smoke than fire. Trying to avoid the thick billows of smoke, Julian found himself wedged comfortably next to Daisy. *Score.*

'So what's your story?' she asked.

Julian thought about inventing some high-class-sounding boarding school just to impress her. He was too damn tired to make up a story and stick to it, though.

'My mother's an out-of-work performer—sings, dances, acts,' he said, and decided not to explain about his father. When people heard what happened, they got all sympathetic and mushy, which Julian hated.

'I got in trouble with the law in May,' he confessed.

The truth worked like an aphrodisiac. He thought he could maybe even feel Daisy's boob pressing on his arm as she leaned toward him and whispered, 'So what was the incident? Did you steal a car? Deal drugs?'

Of course. That was what people thought when they looked at Julian Gastineaux. A big black kid with dreadlocks and an attitude. What else could he be but a small-time criminal?

'I raped a girl,' he said. 'Maybe I raped three.'

Daisy tried not to be obvious about scooting away from him, but he noticed when

267

the warm tension between them slackened.

'You're lying.' She looped her arms around her drawn-up knees.

Damn, but she was an annoying girl. She not only knew he was lying; she knew he was already regretting characterizing himself as a rapist. It had been a stupid thing to say. 'I got caught bungee jumping off a highway bridge,' he admitted.

'Whoa. Why would you go bungee jumping off a bridge?' she asked in horror.

'Why wouldn't you?' asked Julian.

'Oh, let me see. You could break every bone in your body. Wind up paralyzed. Brain dead. Or just plain dead.'

'People wind up dead every day.'

'Yeah, but jumping off bridges tends to hasten the process.' Daisy shuddered.

'It was awesome.' His gaze tracked a spark to the sky. 'I'd do it again in a heartbeat. I've always liked flying.' Anything that even remotely resembled flying was his dream, and always had been.

'Then you'll like this.' Daisy reached into her pocket and took out an eyeglasses case. She opened it up to reveal a fat, misshapen joint.

Holding the glowing end of a twig to it, she lit up and inhaled. 'This is my kind of flying.' She took a second expert hit and held it out to Julian.

'I'll pass,' he said. 'I need to watch myself.

See, the judge in California gave my mother a choice—I had to leave town for the summer or do time in juvenile detention. By coming here, I get the incident wiped off my record.'

'Fair enough. You won't get caught.' She offered the joint again.

So now he had to admit the truth again. Even though it made him seem like a Boy Scout. 'I don't partake.'

'Come on. It's really good weed,' Daisy said. 'No way we'll get caught. We're out in the middle of nowhere.'

'I'm not worried about that,' he said. 'Just don't like getting high.'

'Whatever.' Daisy added a twig to the fire, watched it burn. 'A girl's got to find her fun where she can.'

'So are you having fun?' he asked.

She squinted at him through the smoke. 'So far, this whole summer has just been...weird. It's supposed to be a lot more fun. I mean, think about it. It's our last summer as regular kids. Next year, we'll graduate and have to spend our time working and getting ready for college.'

'College. That's a good one.'

'You're not planning to go to college?'

At first he was so stunned by her question that he just laughed.

'What?' she asked, seeming to forget the smoldering joint.

'No one's ever asked me that before,'

269

Julian admitted.

'You're going to be a senior, aren't you?' she pointed out.

'That's right,' he said.

'And your teachers and advisers haven't been hounding you since ninth grade?'

He laughed again. 'That doesn't happen at my school. People don't go to college. At my school, they figure they're doing a good job if a kid makes it through without dropping out, having a baby or being sent up.'

'Up where?'

'It's just an expression. Sent up means doing time at juvenile hall.'

'What a nightmare,' Daisy said. 'You should change schools.'

Julian was amazed. This girl did not live in the real world. She just didn't get it. 'Where I'm from, you go to the public school that's close to you. And after that, you get some crappy job at a car wash and play the lottery and hope for the best.'

Daisy got the giggles then. 'I do admire a boy with ambition.'

'Just being realistic.'

'I'm not saying that college is, like, some nirvana or something, but it sure as hell beats working at a car wash.'

'College costs money. Even if you get financial aid—which I'd never qualify for because of my mom's sucky financial records—you still have to come up with all kinds of dough I don't have.'

She shrugged. 'Then get into the ROTC. God, even I know that.'

ROTC. He'd heard of it, vaguely. Some recruiter had come to his school to talk about it, but Julian had taken the opportunity to skip class and head for the dirt bike track. Reserve Officer Training...something.

'The military picks up all the cost of your schooling,' Daisy continued. 'You could also apply for an appointment to a service academy, but that's, like, really hard. You have to have, like, a fifteen-hundred-plus on your SAT.'

Despite the fact that he'd already taken the SAT, and had earned a score that had school officials convinced he'd cheated, Julian felt totally ignorant. Appointment? Service academy?

'Those schools are free,' she continued. 'Actually, they even pay you to go there.'

'No way.'

'Way.'

'Name one.'

'West Point. Ha, I'm right. You could go to West Point.'

'About as easily as I could go to the moon.' He'd seen the place in a movie one time. West Point. Guys marching around like toy soldiers, screaming into one another's faces. And it was a college? 'So you're saying they give you a four-year college degree for free?'

'You actually collect a paycheck while you're there. This kid from my school, his dad's, like, a colonel in the air force or something. He's trying for an appointment to the Air Force Academy.'

Air force, thought Julian. *Flying.* The idea grabbed hold of him, vivid as a daydream.

'It sounds really extreme.' Daisy evidently tired of trying to get high. She put the cold joint in a Ziploc bag. 'I think in addition to all the military stuff, you have to study to be an engineer or a scientist or something. Who wants to do that?'

Julian thought about his father, missing him with a pang as sudden and sharp as a stab wound. Science had consumed Louis Gastineaux. It was his passion. Julian understood it because he felt passion, too. Not for science but for flight and danger and speed. 'So what's the catch?' he asked.

'You don't pay tuition, but you definitely owe them something. You give them, like, five years of your life, minimum.' She studied Julian with knowing, sympathetic eyes. 'It must be weird to go to a high school where no one helps you get into college,' she said.

'I never really thought about it.' Julian didn't know which was worse—that no one cared, or that the possibility of college was so remote that he hadn't even considered it himself.

'Well, just because no one's helping you

doesn't mean you can't help yourself.'

'Sure,' he said, and tossed another dry branch on the fire. 'Thanks for the public-service announcement.'

'You've got a chip on your shoulder,' she said.

'And you've got your head in the clouds.'

Daisy laughed aloud, and her voice was as light as the sparks and smoke from the fire. He sat still, watching appreciatively.

All right, he thought, maybe this summer wasn't going to suck so bad after all.

Seventeen

For Olivia, each morning began with a magical hour. The birds sang the forest to life and the sun touched the world with gold. A mist gathered on the lake, the layered swath steered by the gentle morning breeze and slowly burned off by the rising sun. She went jogging every day, just as she did back in the city. Only back home, she did so on a treadmill. At Kioga, she ran an uninterrupted five-mile course through the woods, along a trail that had been newly bush-hogged by her uncle's landscaping crew.

To keep from getting bored on the treadmill, she used to tuck an iPod into the inner pocket of her shorts. Out here, she didn't need Radiohead or Cake in her ears during the morning jog. The trill of awakening birds, the occasional bugle of an elk and the rustle of the morning breeze were entertaining enough.

As she emerged from the woods to the dining hall, she spotted Connor Davis pulling his truck around to a storage shed, and nearly tripped over her own feet.

'You're up early,' she remarked, trying not to pant too hard. She smiled pleasantly, but inwardly she was cringing. He had a habit of catching her at her worst—up a flagpole, clad in painter's coveralls and now in her jogging bra, no shirt, neon-orange shorts. To complete the look, she was drenched in sweat, out of breath, her hair caught carelessly in a ponytail. Just once, she'd love for him to see her looking smart, in her favorite Marc Jacobs sheath and new Manolo flats.

He didn't seem to be focusing on the sweat and unwashed hair, though. He was checking out her legs and her boobs and bare midriff. And yes, she saw the moment he noticed it— her pierced belly button. 'So this is what I've been missing every morning?' he asked.

'Pretty much.'

'I ought to start setting my alarm earlier.'

She wasn't sure if he was pulling her leg or flirting with her. Regardless, she wished it wasn't so stupidly entertaining. Trying to seem nonchalant, she opened her water bottle, took a swig, then dabbed her mouth with the back of her hand. 'How's your brother doing?'

'He's all right.'

Guyspeak drove Olivia nuts, and Connor was one of the worst offenders. 'All right' could mean anything from 'He still has a pulse' to 'He just won the lottery.'

Maybe Connor's very guyness was the reason she found him both infuriating and sexy. His truck was a perfect example. She suspected that the papers and invoices littering the cab were the closest thing he had to a filing system, yet his collection of CDs was perfectly organized so that he could access his favorite Rush album without even taking his eyes off the road.

When she looked into the bed of the truck, she was startled to see not the expected tools and equipment, but a load of birdhouses in every conceivable size and shape. Each one looked unique and handcrafted, with far more detail than the average bird needed. One had a little waterwheel on the side, another had a striped awning. A few had Victorian-style scrollwork, and several were perfect twig-and-timber replicas of Adirondack lodges.

'Did you make these?' she asked Connor.

'Right,' he said. 'In all my spare time.' He shook his head. 'They came from the hardware store in town.' He picked up four at a time and carried them into the shed.

'Can I ask what you're doing with all these

birdhouses?' She grabbed a couple and followed him.

'You can ask. If they're in the way here—'

'Of course not. I just wondered if you had something in mind.'

'Nope.' He continued placing the birdhouses in neat rows inside the shed. 'Maybe Dare can use them to decorate something.'

'You must really like birds.' Mystified, Olivia helped out, though she didn't question him again. He appeared to be ignoring her. As she cooled down from her run, she felt the chill of the morning air. Immediately, Connor took off his jacket and held it out to her. Okay, so he wasn't ignoring her.

'No way,' she protested. 'I'm covered in sweat.'

'Like that's going to bother me,' he said. 'Hands in the sleeves.'

Olivia pulled the jacket around her like an embrace. It shouldn't feel this good, she thought, inhaling as she sensed his body heat lingering in the fabric. He shouldn't smell this good.

'So what's it like,' she asked, trying to fill an awkward silence, 'being back at Camp Kioga?'

'It's not all that different from my Airstream.'

'How long have you lived there? Did you spend the winter there?' She immediately regretted asking. It sounded judgmental, somehow. 'Sorry,' she said. 'I never got over my nosiness.'

'I've had worse winters,' he said, and didn't elaborate.

Shoot. She'd offended him or ticked him off. One of these days, she ought to figure out that sometimes it was best to keep her questions to herself. Accordingly, she took care not to bring up the topic of his father. Or was it weird that she didn't ask about him? She didn't know. Terry Davis had been a big factor in Connor's life—a defining factor. And the shameful truth was, Olivia was a coward. She was afraid to hear his sad story—that his father had passed away. She didn't want to hear that he'd finally drunk himself to death. She was afraid of Connor's sadness because she knew she'd be helpless to comfort him.

'Well,' she said briskly. 'I hope you and Julian had a good night.'

He shut the door to the shed. 'I just hope I can keep him out of trouble this summer.'

'You did it before,' she reminded him. 'That last summer we…' Poor choice of words. 'He gave you a run for your money when he was a little kid, but you managed to stay ahead of him.'

'He can probably outrun me now, but I'll give it my best shot.'

Connor was a caretaker. She knew that

277

about him. Growing up the way he had, his character had been forged in the crucible of his father's drinking and his mother's neglect. Sometimes Olivia wondered what sort of person he might have become if his parents had nurtured him instead of leaving him to raise himself. Then she thought of other people she knew, people who had been nurtured and given every advantage. Many of them blew the opportunities they had been granted and became the kind of trust-fund babies who were fodder for the tabloid press.

'How is it between you and Julian?' she asked.

'We hardly know each other. He's not too keen on taking orders from me.'

'And how do you feel about him?'

'He doesn't want to be here, and he's acting like a little shit.'

She ducked her head, hiding a smile.

'What?' he asked, noticing her amusement.

'It's good that you're being honest. I was a little worried that you're too saintly.'

'I've never had that problem. Julian is family, though. I was eleven years old when he was born, and he was the best thing that ever happened to me. For six months, I got to be a brother. Then he went to live with his dad, and it was all over, just like that. Nobody warned me, God knows nobody consulted me. I just came home from school one day, and he

278

was gone. I didn't speak to my mother for days afterward, maybe weeks.' He looked down at his hands, callused and nicked with hard work, and flexed his fingers. 'I've never told anybody that.'

It was then that Olivia recognized the hurt he was masking. 'Maybe I could talk to Julian. I mean, if you don't mind—'

He shook his head. 'Why would I mind?'

'I like talking to him.' She had stayed up late last night, and when Julian and Daisy came in, she'd had a long talk with him. 'Did you know he took the SAT last spring and scored a fifteen hundred fifty? Eight hundred in math, seven-fifty verbal.' She watched surprise trace across Connor's face.

'A sixteen hundred is a perfect score, right?' he said.

'Yep.'

'He failed half his classes,' Connor pointed out.

'Sounds to me like the school's failing him.' It felt curiously adult, discussing his teenage brother. This was new—relating to Connor Davis as an adult, with some experience under her belt. Suddenly their relationship felt much more complicated. When she'd first encountered him, she'd been interested only in flaunting her new self in front of him, making him regret letting her out of his life all those years ago. Now that attitude seemed childish and superficial—and

279

blessedly simple. It hadn't lasted, of course. Her heart had no defenses when it came to Connor Davis. Almost against her will, their relationship was changing and deepening every time she was with him.

They went into the kitchen together. As she measured coffee into the basket of the coffeemaker, she felt his eyes on her but pretended not to notice. 'Remember the year we did a midnight raid and found those institutional-size buckets of peanut butter?' she asked.

'Falk St. John is probably still trying to get the stuff out of his hair.' He picked up the tarnished tennis cup she'd brought from her father's old footlocker. 'What's this?'

Olivia bit her lip. She'd left the thing out in plain sight, and every day, she half hoped someone would ask her about it. Correction. Every day, she hoped *Connor* would ask her about it. Unanswered questions were burning a hole in her. 'An old trophy of my dad's. I keep meaning to get some silver polish for it.'

He found the photograph and cuff link that had been stuck inside. He put the cuff link away but studied the snapshot with a bemused expression on his face.

'That picture,' she said, trying to sound casual, 'that's the reason I asked you about Jenny Majesky that day.'

'Looks like her. A younger version of her,' he agreed. 'It's probably her mother.'

'It is. The same picture is on display at the bakery, only the guy in the shot has been cropped out. Recognize him?' she asked. Without waiting for a reply, she said, 'It's my father. Back in 1977. I'm dying to know the story behind it.'

'So ask him about this woman,' Connor suggested reasonably.

'I don't think so.'

'Why not? You're close to your dad. He probably wouldn't mind.'

Connor was right, but still, Olivia just couldn't. A parent's personal life was a tricky thing. Sometimes she asked her dad if he was seeing anyone, if he thought he might remarry one day. He always looked at her with a sad-sweet smile and shook his head, declaring that he'd never had much luck in the romance department. Olivia was starting to think the trait ran in the family.

'I'd feel awkward doing that,' she told Connor. 'And don't tell me to show it to Jenny. I'd feel awkward doing that, too.'

'I know someone we can ask.'

Eighteen

Connor hoped he was doing the right thing, helping Olivia pry into old business. It was too late to back down, though. A few days later, they drove down to Avalon together, with Julian in the backseat. He wanted to be dropped off at the library, though he offered no explanation as he shrugged his arm through the strap of his backpack and got out at the curb.

'I'll be back to pick you up in an hour,' Connor said, then turned to Olivia, who sat in nervous silence in the passenger seat beside him. 'I guess he can't get into too much trouble there.'

'The library doesn't seem too hazardous. He's probably desperate for an Internet connection,' she said. 'Has he told you much about the friends he left back home?'

'Not really. You think I should be asking him?'

'No,' she said quickly. 'If you start to pry, he'll clam right up.'

He studied her for a moment. She'd taken an interest in Julian, and he wasn't sure why. It felt surreal, sitting with her beside him again. Since she'd been back, he'd thought a lot about the past, about how close they'd been, how much they'd shared. And how

282

much they had hurt each other.

Now they had to face different questions, such as whether or not to get involved in each other's lives again.

Don't, he cautioned himself, trying not to remember the way she used to feel in his arms, her cheek pressed against his chest as she listened to the beating of his heart. He thought he barely remembered her, but with every moment he spent with her, more memories came back, and now all he had to do was close his eyes and drift a little and he was back there, in the days of Camp Kioga, when life seemed so simple and anything seemed possible.

'Does he play a sport in school?' Olivia asked.

'He's on the dive team, I think.'

'That makes sense, since he loves heights so much. He's an interesting kid. I'm glad he's here for the summer.' She smiled, still looking a little nervous.

'You're glad?'

'Sure. I like kids. I especially like teenagers, even their angst and traumas.' She sighed and looked out the window. 'Maybe it's because I remember it so well, how raw every emotion feels, how big and crucial things seem at every crossroads. And how nobody in the world understands you.'

'And yet, here you are.'

'Here I am.'

'Whatever happened to you wanting to be a high-school teacher?' he asked.

Olivia shrugged. 'I changed a lot, those four years of college. At first, I really did want to teach high school. I wanted to come back and do it right. It was my chance to turn high school into a happy experience, to be popular.' She smiled softly. 'Then during college, I stopped needing that. I stopped needing the do-over.'

As she spoke, he watched her lips. When her mouth formed the words *do-over*, it was like she was getting ready to kiss him.

Wishful thinking, he thought. She'd said it herself. She didn't need a do-over.

'And you wanted to be a coach,' she reminded him.

'You have a good memory.' His rationale differed wildly from Lolly's, though. School— and sports teams in particular—had been the one place where he felt successful, accepted and safe. Being a coach would make him part of that world forever. He knew why he had abandoned his dream, but he wasn't ready to explain it to Olivia.

He pulled away from the curb and headed toward Indian Wells, a few miles north of town, where his father lived in the seniors community. Terry Davis wasn't sick, and he wasn't even that old, but he seemed to enjoy life there, liked the meddlesome women who dominated the place, and, as a recovering alcoholic, he liked the 12-step meetings that took place on the premises daily.

Olivia had lapsed into silence again. 'You all right with going to visit my dad?' Connor asked.

'Sure. Of course. When you first told me he was still…around, I was startled. You never mentioned him.'

'You never asked about him.'

'I know. I'm sorry, I mean, I'm glad…' She was flustered. 'I didn't ask about your father because I was afraid something bad had happened to him, and I didn't want to make you sad by asking.' She paused. 'I'm such a chicken. I've never done well with other people's sadness.'

Maybe, Connor thought, that factored into her three broken engagements. He didn't want all the gory details, but he figured if you couldn't handle someone else's troubles, you weren't going to get too far in a relationship. He turned into the parking lot. 'FYI, he's doing fine,' Connor added, feeling more than a touch of pride and relief. Connor wished his dad's recovery hadn't been so long in coming, but there was no point driving himself crazy over it. The fact was, his parents' problems had virtually stolen his childhood from him, but brooding over that was pointless. His father was in recovery. His mother was in denial. Things could be worse.

'He's really good these days,' Connor said.

'He stays busy and goes to meetings and wishes he had grandkids, but I guess I've disappointed him in that department so far.'

Oops, thought Connor. Too much information.

Olivia got out of the car. 'Let me guess,' she said, scanning the row of town-house units, each with a small patio. 'Your father's place is the one with all the birdhouses. You sneaky thing. He builds them for the hardware store, and you buy them.'

Busted, thought Connor. 'Do me a favor and don't let on,' he said.

'Of course not.' Her gaze softened, and his heart sped up. She used to look at him like that, long ago. And that look had meant the world to him.

His father greeted them at the door. 'Hey, son. Good to see you.' He held out a hand to Olivia. 'Terry Davis, ma'am.'

'Olivia Bellamy.'

'Miss Bellamy. How are you, ma'am?' It always made Connor uncomfortable, the way his father tended to bow and scrape. When Connor pointed it out, his father always offered the same explanation. 'It's the way I was raised,' he said. 'You have to be polite to your betters.'

'How the hell do you know they're better than you?' Connor used to ask.

'It's just an expression. When somebody comes from money, when they're maybe in a position to offer you something, they're your betters.'

'That's nuts, Dad.'

'It's the way the world works, son.'

And now when Terry Davis greeted Olivia, he automatically put her in the group of 'betters.' She did have that polished, neat-as-a-pin look. It was there in the details—the small gold earrings, the sleek hair, the crisp white shirt with the collar turned up just so, the khaki shorts.

Connor expected her to feel ill at ease, here in the small, spare apartment. Yet when she greeted his father, there was nothing but warmth in her smile. 'I hope we're not interrupting anything.'

'Not at all.' He led the way to the kitchen and hastened to turn off the radio. 'Glad for the company.' He bustled around, clearing piles of mail and clipped coupons off the table.

As she watched him, her expression turned thoughtful and, Connor suspected, relieved. He didn't blame her. The Terry Davis of the past had been, in the eyes of the world, a hopeless drunk. Except to Connor. Even as a kid, Connor had refused to give up hope. He had gotten his heart broken countless times because of it, but he was his father's only kin. Out of foolish loyalty or desperation or maybe unwavering filial love, he persisted in believing his father could recover. He had believed it so fiercely that when it came to making a choice between his father and Lolly, he had chosen his dad without hesitation, on a summer night nine years ago, a night that was burned forever into Connor's memory.

'I'm happy to see you again,' Olivia said politely. 'You probably don't remember me. Everyone used to call me Lolly.'

'Now, there's a name I remember,' Terry assured her. 'You were that cute, chubby one Connor used to run around with.'

Connor stifled a groan. Drunk or sober, his father had never balked at saying exactly what was on his mind. 'Dad—'

Olivia's smile didn't falter. 'I don't know about cute, but I was definitely the chubby one.'

'Lost your baby fat, I see.'

'Dad.'

'How about a soda?' Terry asked her.

'I'd love one. Thanks.' She didn't seem the least insulted by his candor as she graciously accepted a blue bottle of Saratoga Springs water and had a seat at the round table.

'So here you are, all grown-up,' Terry said. 'Been what, ten years?'

'Nine.'

'Man. Connor sure was crazy about you. Still single?'

'Dad, for chrissake—'

Terry waved him silent. 'All right, all right, I'm sure you didn't come here to get teased about your old girlfriend.'

'It's fine,' Olivia assured him. 'Really. I don't mind hearing that Connor was crazy about me, although that's not quite the way I remember it.'

Bringing her here was a bad idea, Connor thought. Why the hell had he brought her here?

Terry chuckled. 'He's had other girlfriends since you, but none of them lasted.'

'Neither did I,' she reminded him.

'Yeah, but that was because—'

'Hey, Dad.' Ready to change the subject, Connor said, 'Olivia found this old photograph. We were wondering if you could tell us anything about it.'

Olivia handed over the yellowed snapshot. 'It was developed in August 1977. The guy in the picture is my father.'

When Connor's father saw the photograph, his face changed. He went from mild and congenial to tense and agitated. He quickly handed the print back to Olivia. 'That's a picture of Mariska Majesky,' he said. 'She's Helen and Leo's daughter. She's been gone twenty years, maybe thirty.'

'You mean she passed away?'

'I mean she's gone. Took off one day and no one ever saw her again. She was always the restless type,' he added. 'Had a habit of taking off for a while, but she always came back to see her kid. Up until that last time, I guess.

Mariska up and left, and no one ever saw her again.'

'She had a kid.' Connor looked at Olivia and they both had the same thought. *Jenny.*

'Was she married?' Olivia asked, her voice unsteady. 'Or…involved?'

'I reckon you should talk to your father, ma'am,' Terry said.

*　　　*　　　*

As she left the small, cluttered apartment, Olivia felt as though something had been sucked out of her. She must've looked that way, too, because Connor put one hand at the small of her back to steady her. She wasn't sure how he had come by this latent sense of chivalry, but he was careful with her in a way no other man had ever been.

'I keep thinking there must be a zillion explanations,' she said to him, 'but they're all just excuses.'

'We could still be drawing the wrong conclusion,' Connor cautioned. 'Maybe there's no mystery at all about who Jenny's father is.'

'Your dad knows,' Olivia insisted. 'You saw his face. He just didn't want to say.' She'd hoped it was some local guy—anyone but Philip Bellamy—but based on Terry Davis's discomfiture and his insistence that she talk to her father, her certainty was hardening fast.

290

She stopped walking and held the photograph in front of Connor. 'Take a good look. See my dad's chin?' She pointed out the Cary Grant–style dimple. 'Jenny has that, but her mother doesn't.'

He smiled. 'It's not exactly unique.'

'It's a recessive trait, like blue eyes. According to the laws of genetics, a person with a cleft chin always has at least one parent with one.'

'You won't know anything for sure until you ask your father about her,' Connor said, digging his keys out of his pocket.

Olivia couldn't forget the way Terry Davis had avoided her eyes. She looked around the parking lot, at the world that hadn't changed one iota in the past few minutes. It was an illusion, though. A fundamental shift had occurred. The earth had slipped its bonds and was slowly spinning off course. 'I don't really need to ask. I know. The laws of genetics aside, you can see by the way he looks in this picture that he was with this...Mariska when he was engaged to my mother. God, maybe even after he married my mother. And Jenny Majesky is...'

She wobbled a bit, and Connor helped her into the truck. She felt like the victim of a violent accident as she spoke her next thought aloud. 'I have a sister.' A sister. A sister. The word reverberated through her on a wave of disbelief.

'This is all speculation.'

'We both know it'll be confirmed.'

'And what if it is? Would that be such a bad thing, having a half sister?'

'God, no. The bad part is that we grew up not knowing each other.' *I have a sister.* She wondered what her life would have been like, had she known Jenny through the years. Someone to share secrets and jokes, to give her advice or quarrel with her. Maybe Olivia's childhood wouldn't have been so lonely. Maybe she would have had more self-confidence.

'What do I do now?' she wondered aloud. 'Is it possible Jenny doesn't know who her father is? I can't just walk up to her and ask.'

'Call your father,' Connor suggested. 'Ask him yourself.'

'I can't do it by phone. I need to talk to him in person. I need to see his face.'

Connor nodded. 'You're right.' He turned on his signal and headed up the river road. 'What time do you want to leave?'

'I beg your pardon?'

'Tomorrow,' he said. 'For the city. I think we should leave by seven in the morning. Can you be ready that early?'

'What are you talking about?' she asked.

'Taking you to see your father.'

Olivia was incredulous. 'Why would you do that?'

'Because I'm a good guy. Always have

292

been, which is something we haven't really talked about yet.'

'Wait a minute. You're taking me to the city?'

'First thing in the morning. This secret's been kept for a long time. It can keep one more night.'

'Just like that? We're going to drop everything and go to the city?'

He balanced his wrists casually atop the steering wheel. 'That's the beauty of being self-employed. We get to drop everything if we want to.'

'But you don't have to drive me. I could always take the train.'

'Not this time.'

Her heart lifted. She didn't know why he was offering this kindness. She was almost afraid to trust it. 'It's a three-hour drive.'

'You don't think we can find something to talk about for three hours?' Though he kept his eyes on the road straight ahead, he grinned. 'I think we've got plenty to talk about, Lolly.'

CAMP KIOGA TRADITIONS

Camp Kioga serves young people, ages eight to sixteen. One of the most important Kioga traditions is continuity. Campers of good character are invited to serve as counselors as soon as they earn their high-school diploma and are certified in lifesaving and water-safety techniques.

Nineteen

Summer 1997

Following high school graduation, Lolly had mixed feelings about returning to Camp Kioga to be a counselor, but as a Bellamy, she didn't have much choice. It was a family tradition that all Bellamys served as camp counselors, and Lolly was no exception.

And maybe it wouldn't be so bad. After the summer she was twelve, she had learned to hate camp just a little less. The reason for this could be summed up in two words: Connor Davis. What took root and grew that first summer was an unexpected friendship, and for the next two summers, the friendship flourished. Even though she thought he was rude and he said she was a prissy know-it-all, somehow they just clicked.

When she was with him, hiking or kayaking or serving on breakfast duty or facing off over a rainy-day game of Scrabble, she was content in the moment. With Connor, she didn't have to be a certain way. He didn't expect her to have good grades or important friends or prizes for piano and art. He didn't expect her to act like the class clown. She just acted like herself. Just Lolly.

Subsequent summers—following seventh

and then eighth grades—were no exception. Even though she and Connor might circle each other warily and trade insults back and forth, their taunting was built on a bedrock foundation of something mutual and unexpected—respect and friendship.

There was no obvious reason that they should be friends. He was this giant boy, an athlete, with a difficult mother and stepfather in a working-class life in Buffalo, and a father who kept breaking his heart, year in and year out. She was an unhappy girl with too much riding on her shoulders. In other words, a total mismatch. Except they clicked. From the first day they'd met at the age of twelve, and learned too much about each other, they had shared a quirky friendship.

Each summer, they would meet again and pick up where they had left off, as though they had never been apart. Then it would be a long season of kitchen raids at midnight, dumb but hilarious pranks played on counselors or other campers. They would team up for anything requiring skill and brains because he always had the skill and she had the brains.

Eventually, they told each other even more secrets. Connor confessed his shame over his father's drinking and his unrequited crush on Evelyn Waller. Lolly admitted her favorite subject in school was fiber arts and that she was obsessed with her idol, Martha Stewart. He challenged her to be better, braver and more confident than she was, and he supported her when she was down. He treated her like an equal. Like one of the guys. She liked that because it was a way to get close to him without the awkward boy-girl tension.

Each Labor Day, Connor returned to Buffalo and she to New York, and they didn't speak or see each other between summers. Sometimes she would think about writing him a letter but she never had anything to say: *Dear Connor. My life sucks.* Who wanted to read that?

She supposed she could make stuff up. Some of the girls she knew at school did that. But she couldn't imagine how making up stories about her fabulous life would make it suck less.

Then, without warning or explanation, the friendship ended. The summer following ninth grade, Lolly arrived at camp expecting to meet Connor again, but he never showed up. When she screwed up enough courage to ask his father about him, Mr. Davis would say only, 'My boy's got a job in Buffalo this summer. He won't be coming.'

When Lolly finished tenth grade, her mother thought it was time for her to see the world, and took her to visit the capitals of Europe. Not to be outdone, her father claimed the entire summer after eleventh grade, whisking her off on a Mediterranean cruise.

It all sounded fantastic. It should have been fantastic. Yet the pressure robbed something from the experience. Her parents expected everything of her— perfect grades, perfect test scores, prizes at music competitions and science fairs. 'I just want you to get into a good college,' her mother maintained, though she never explained why. As far as Lolly could tell, going to Yale and marrying a Yale man had brought Pamela Lightsey no joy, just a lot of money and a divorce. It made Lolly wonder why her mother insisted getting into the perfect college was the key to some magical kingdom.

Now she was done with high school and had been accepted to Columbia, which she hoped would fulfill her obligation to be her parents' trophy daughter. This was to be the last summer of her childhood, and she had come back to Camp Kioga.

She considered staying away, knowing her grandparents would understand. Then a phone call from Nana made up Lolly's mind for her. 'Connor Davis will be working at Camp Kioga this summer,' Nana had said. 'I thought you'd like to know.'

*   *   *

'This year, things are going to be totally different,' declared Dare Yates, Lolly's closest cousin.

'No shit, Sherlock,' said Frankie, who was Dare's sister, older by a year. 'We get to be in charge.'

'I just hope being a counselor is as good as it looked when we were kids,' Lolly said, walking out on the porch of their bungalow to shake the mud from her hiking boots.

Frankie looked around the cottage the three of them would be sharing for the summer. 'This is nice,' she said. 'Why is it so nice in here?'

'You can thank Lolly for that,' Dare said. 'She got here a day early and fixed up our cabin.'

Lolly was pleased that her cousins had noticed. It had taken so little to make their army-barracks-plain cabin more pleasant. She'd raided the camp's storage sheds and trunks, reclaiming treasures from summers past. She'd covered the bunks with colorful tartan blankets, added a braided rug, some old Adirondack twig chairs and a rustic table. Nana had encouraged her to help herself to left-behind crafts projects—a birch-bark sign with Kioga spelled out in twigs, some lanterns with parchment panes, even a handwoven doormat. Jars of wildflowers brightened the windowsills.

'It's great, Lolly,' Frankie called through the screen door. 'I think you have a flair for this.'

299

'That's me,' Lolly said. 'The girl with the flair.'

She and her cousins were in charge of the youngest group of campers—the Fledglings. The little girls had arrived the day before, and had survived the first night with just a few tears and no hysteria. Lolly loved the way the girls giggled and shrieked when they were having fun. She even liked bandaging their hurts and comforting them when they were afraid—and for some of these kids, she suspected, that was going to be every night. She thought particularly of little Ramona Fisher, who had cowered in her bunk last night like a bivouacked soldier under fire.

Dare joined Lolly on the porch and lifted a pair of field glasses to her eyes, aiming toward the lake. 'God, I love this view.' She wasn't talking about the lake, though. Lolly knew that. The lenses were trained inexorably on the swimming area. The male counselors and Fledgling boys were already there, doing routine swim tests in order to form skill-level groups.

The three cousins lined up at the porch railing, passing the binoculars between them. The counselors wore shorts, muscle shirts and whistles around their necks. They joked around with the kids, trying to put them at ease.

Even from a distance, and without the binoculars, Lolly felt a thrill of recognition.

The tall, dark-haired boy was Connor Davis.

She hadn't seen him up close yet. The arrival of the campers had been too chaotic, taking up all their time and attention. And when it was her turn with the field glasses, she had to pretend she was giving all the guys equal scrutiny. She wasn't, of course.

Connor Davis had grown taller than ever, and although he was still skinny, his shoulders were broader. He was tanned already, maybe from working outdoors with his father, and he looked completely at ease with the kids, as though he was born to do this.

Lolly suppressed a sigh, wondering what had changed between them, and what would stay the same, if there was any remnant of their friendship left or if they'd be strangers now. She knew she'd changed in some obvious ways. She was nearly eighteen now, and she'd seen a good bit of the world. She spoke French and had passed five Advanced Placement exams.

The fundamental Lolly hadn't changed, though. She was still the overweight sidekick to prettier, more popular girls. Instead of going to school dances with boys, she always served on the decoration committee and was almost embarrassingly good at it. During her high-school years, she had magically transformed the gym into a Wild West wonderland, an undersea fantasy, even a scene from the hit movie *Men In Black*. She

301

had grown adept at hiding the fact that she was lonely and unhappy. Her good humor and can-do attitude were a careful facade. People thought she was perfectly content being the gym decorator, the best friend, the brainy but unattractive honor student. Lolly tried to accept herself as such. She tried to be happy—or at least content. Sometimes it even worked and she forgot herself for a while, but then something would happen to remind her.

Like today. She had to put on a swimsuit, possibly the least-flattering garment ever invented. The entire morning was going to be devoted to water-safety skills, a key component of the Kioga experience. It had always been a point of pride with Lolly's grandparents that every single camper learned water safety, even if it meant the fat ones had to stuff themselves like sausages into skins of spandex.

Frankie propped her elbows on the railing to steady the field glasses. 'Is it totally strange to like a guy's legs?' she asked in a dreamy voice.

'Probably,' Dare replied, equally dreamy. 'Hand me the binoculars and I'll let you know.'

Lolly picked up her clipboard and looked over the day's schedule, pretending not to listen. Sometimes it was amusing to hear her cousins mooning over various guys. Most of the time it was just tedious. She didn't understand how they—how every girl their age—could be so totally obsessed with the way people looked. Then, sneaking a glance at the tall, dark-haired boy at the lakeshore, she felt a deep inner tug, and realized maybe she understood, just a little.

'We'd better get going,' Dare said, grabbing her makeup bag. 'We've got to get the girls in their swim groups, and after morning snack, I want to start on the choral reading for Friday night. I thought maybe a Little Mermaid theme would be fun.' Dare loved making a production of things. She was good at it, the way Lolly was good at transformation and illusion. Together, they'd make a good team this summer.

Frankie put away the field glasses, and they went into the cabin, pulling her T-shirt off over her head as she crossed the room. Lolly felt a familiar twinge of envy. It must be nice, she thought, to be so unselfconscious about your body. Frankie and Dare deserved to be. They were both slender, and Frankie had secretly had her belly button pierced.

Lolly could hear her cousins horsing around in the adjacent room as they got ready. She envied them being sisters, too. Even though the two of them fought, they were loyal about the things that mattered, and shared a bond that would endure all their lives.

Lolly changed in the bathroom. She didn't bother pretending she wasn't modest. It was silly, these were her cousins, but all the same, being fat turned her into a very private person. As quickly as possible, she slipped on her camp swimsuit.

Connor. I'm going to see Connor Davis again. She tried to quell a thrill of anticipation but couldn't quite manage. She told herself to take it easy. Maybe he wasn't as cute as she remembered. Maybe he was all bulging from steroids or had a face full of zits, or maybe he'd turned into a skank or an obnoxious jock. Pulling on a heather-gray T-shirt over her swimsuit, Lolly conceded that there was really only one flaw in the otherwise perfect friendship they used to share every summer. And that flaw was such a deeply buried secret that sometimes she even forgot she was keeping it. But something always happened to bring the truth back home to her.

And the awful, piercing, deeply concealed truth was that she was hopelessly in love with Connor Davis.

Of course she was. How could she not be? He was strong and fast and kind, and you always knew where you stood with him because he didn't play games and he didn't lie. He was the perfect friend and theirs was the perfect summer friendship—except for that one little problem she had with being completely over-the-top gaga about him.

It didn't matter that she hadn't seen him the past three summers. If anything, that made him even more perfect in her mind. Sometimes she tried to figure out the precise moment it had happened. Had there been a tipping point, when she'd shifted from simply liking him to swooning over him as Prince Charming?

If she had to pick a moment, an instant when she knew beyond a doubt that her heart was lost, it would have to be the night of the ear piercing. She hadn't known it at the time, but it was their last summer together, so perhaps there was something symbolic in the act of marking him permanently. He'd wanted his ear pierced for reasons she suspected had to do with rebelling against a hated stepdad. Connor would have done the piercing himself, except that she knew he'd make a mess of it, maybe even damage himself. She'd stepped in, pretending to be stoic when she wanted to faint the whole time. In the camp infirmary, using a sterile lancet and a rubber reflex mallet, she'd pierced his ear, weeping openly as tears of pain squeezed reluctantly from his clamped-shut eyes.

He'd worn the silver hoop earring all summer, and every time she looked at it, she felt a secret flash of pleasure. She didn't doubt for a minute that some other girl would be his first love, but in a weird way, Lolly felt as if she'd staked some sort of claim on him.

She liked him so much that when she wrote about him in her diary, her hand shook, and the passage of time since she'd last seen him didn't diminish her feelings. She was shaking now, getting ready to go down to the swimming dock.

As she headed out the door, she grabbed her windbreaker and tied it by the sleeves around her waist so that it covered her butt. She was fooling no one, of course. Least of all herself.

*   *   *

They hiked down to Saratoga Cabin and rounded up the Fledgling girls.

'Aren't we supposed to march in a line?' asked one of the campers, a little girl named Flossie.

'Probably.' Dare ruffled the girl's blond hair. 'Think we'll get in trouble if we don't?'

Lolly scanned the girls, an excited, giggling mass of all shapes and sizes. 'They should definitely walk in a line, at least until I do a head count.'

Despite some grumbling, they lined up two by two and sure enough, someone was missing.

'I'll go,' Lolly said, heading into the cabin. Its familiar smell enveloped her—shampoo, bubble gum, and the faint but ever-present whiff of mildew. She was always on the lookout for misfits, and she knew right where to look, because she knew all the hiding

306

places. She found the stray camper curled up on a lower bunk, facing a wall from which hung a calendar. The first day of camp had been x-ed out, but the rest of the boxes stretched out in a long, seemingly endless string.

'Ramona?' Lolly asked. 'We're going to the lake now.'

Ramona gave a tragic sniffle. 'I have a stomachache.'

'I'm sorry to hear that. Did you know that in the counselor's manual, it says that a stomachache is the most common ailment of all campers?'

'It's the most common ailment of *me*,' she said miserably.

'When I feel scared, that's usually when my stomach starts to hurt,' Lolly confessed. 'The good news is, the bellyache goes away when you quit being scared.'

'That's not such good news,' Ramona said. 'I'm scared of camp and I'm stuck here for the whole summer, so it's not going away.'

'Oh, yes it is,' Lolly assured her, gently prying the girl's white-knuckled grip from the edge of the bunk. 'There are hundreds of ways to get over being scared. Believe me, I know them all because I'm an expert at being scared of things.'

Ramona looked dubious. 'I'm scared to swim.'

'So am I,' Lolly said, 'and I do it anyway.

And the more I swim the less scared I am. I've already decided that when I go away to college in the fall, I'm going to join the intramural swim team.'

'No way.'

'Way.'

'Why would you want to be on swim team?'

'Because it's hard. And scary.'

'Then why do it?'

'Good question. I've heard you should face your fears. It makes you grow as a person. For me, that would be making swim team.' She offered Ramona a conspiratorial smile. 'You're the first person I've told.'

'I don't see what's good about doing something hard.'

Lolly held out her hand. 'Let's get your swimsuit on and go down to the lake and see if we can figure that out.'

The little girl whimpered, and then surrendered, tucking her hand into Lolly's.

'Will you go in the water with me?' Ramona asked.

'Of course, if you need me.'

'Oh, I know I will.'

Great, thought Lolly. While all the other counselors were high and dry, standing on the dock and flirting with one another, she'd be in the drink with this kid.

She and Ramona were the last to join the swarm of campers, counselors and lifeguards.

The long dock was equipped with starting blocks, and the swim course was marked with buoys every twenty-five meters. In the distance was the diving tower, its tallest platform ten meters high. Keeping hold of Ramona's hand, Lolly scanned the crowd. Counselors were blowing whistles, yelling at the kids to form lines at the starting blocks. And there, supervising a squirming tangle of restless boys, was Connor Davis, looking like something out of a dream.

At first, it was too chaotic to do anything but wave at one another over a sea of little kids. Even so, Lolly felt her bones melt when he looked at her. It was a wonder she was still standing upright. He was far and away the best-looking guy she had ever seen.

The thing about Connor Davis was, he seemed to have no clue that his looks were anything special. Maybe that natural humility was a function of growing up hard and having a father like Terry Davis. Maybe things like that kept him from focusing on appearances.

Girls focused on his looks all the time, Lolly knew. She could see it happening right now. The female counselors were already circling like lipsticked buzzards, checking out his shoulder-length glossy black hair, his sapphire-blue eyes, his big shoulders and easy, attractive grin. Some of them were undoubtedly already plotting ways to seduce him.

By the time he jostled his way through the milling kids and moved close enough to greet Lolly on the dock, it was too late. Girls were nudging one another, pointing, staking their claim. Connor stayed focused on Lolly, though.

'Hey,' he said. His voice was much deeper than she remembered, but still melodic. She wondered if he was still a good singer.

'Hey, yourself.' Lolly knew every bit of delight she was feeling shone on her face, and she didn't even care.

'I was hoping you'd be here this summer,' he said with his customary blunt honesty.

'Too bad I didn't have your e-mail address. I would have sent you a note, asking you.'

'I don't have an e-mail address. I hear you can use the library for that, but I don't get there too often.'

Lolly was mentally kicking herself. She always did this. Always took it for granted that the whole world had stuff like computers and mobile phones and such at their fingertips.

'E-mail isn't that reliable, anyway,' she conceded, and much as she hated to admit it, she liked it as a method of communication. E-mail seemed like a hybrid between a paper letter, which was a deliberate act, and a phone call, which presumed a level of intimacy between parties. To Lolly, e-mail would have been the ideal way to contact him. Except he never would have received her note.

A whistle sounded, and the water-safety captain yelled at everyone to form lines along the swimming dock. Ramona Fisher grabbed Lolly's hand and clung desperately.

Connor flashed another grin. He still didn't seem to notice that every female counselor in sight was fixated on him. Could he possibly be that clueless, or did he really not know?

'So we'll catch up later,' he said to Lolly.

'Yeah. Later.' She saw that he still had his pierced ear. Oh, God. He'd kept it. That had to mean something, didn't it?

'Yo, help me out here,' someone bellowed.

'Julian,' Connor said under his breath, and then he shouted the name as he ran. The small boy named Julian had climbed a tree beside the lake, and he was crawling along a limb that hung out over the water. He was a remarkable-looking boy, wiry and quick and clearly filled with mischief. Balancing on the end of the limb, he thumped his chest, Tarzan style, and let out a bloodcurdling yell before leaping like a frog into the water.

Lolly got busy as well, helping to sort the girls into their skill groups. Ramona stood shivering on the dock, regarding the beautiful, clear water with misery and terror.

'I can't,' she whispered.

'You're going to amaze yourself with what you can do,' Lolly said.

'I'm not going in.'

311

'If you put it off today, it'll only be harder tomorrow.'

'I'll take my chances,' Ramona said.

'Tell you what, how about if I get in the water first, and you can jump in and swim to me. Think you could do that?'

Ramona shrugged. At least it wasn't a flat-out refusal.

Wonderful, thought Lolly, dropping her windbreaker, then peeling off her T-shirt. I get to be the first counselor in the water. Ramona looked so grateful that Lolly forgot to be self-conscious, though. She showed her how easy it was to jump in, just a short drop.

'Right here to me,' she urged. 'Come on, Ramona. Think how proud of yourself you'll be.'

'You promise you'll catch me?'

'Promise.'

Ramona shut her eyes tightly, screwed up her face and hurled herself off the dock. For such a tiny, birdlike girl, she made a huge splash, drenching Lolly. But she succeeded. She went all the way in over her head and came up dog-paddling, bursting with wonder and pride. 'I did it! Lolly! I did it!'

And so did I, Lolly thought, seeing Connor on the dock again. He was being checked out and fawned over once again, and appeared to be completely ignoring Lolly. Fine, she thought. She didn't need or want his attention.

'Let's swim over to that ladder,' she

312

instructed Ramona, heading for the swim ladder at the end of the dock.

'It's too far. I'll drown.'

'I'll be right by your side the whole time,' Lolly promised.

The wooden ladder attached to the dock had seen better days, and its rungs were slimy and waterlogged. Ramona scrambled out of the lake and did a little jig of triumph. Behind her, Lolly slipped and nearly fell on her face, coming down heavily on the dock.

'Graceful,' someone said, and snickered. Lolly recognized the voice of Jazzy Simmons, one of the other counselors. 'Have a nice trip, Lolly?'

Her face burning with humiliation, Lolly ignored her and started to climb to her feet. A large hand took hold of hers and helped her up, and her face burned even hotter when she found herself gaping up at Connor Davis.

'You okay?' he asked.

'Fine.' She couldn't bear to look at him. After he walked away, she looked down at Ramona, now shivering inside a towel. 'See? It's not the end of the world.'

Twenty

Unofficially, the staff common room at Camp Kioga was known as the party shack. This was a large, all-purpose room where counselors and workers came after work to hang out and play music. As Connor approached the shack, he felt a base beat rattling the walls and rafters, and knew the party was already in full swing.

He stepped inside, letting his eyes adjust to the darkness, which was illuminated by the glow of the stereo equipment and a couple of candles on a table with some bags of chips and bowls of salsa. Undulating bodies clustered in the middle of the room, creating an impromptu mosh pit. Others stood around the periphery of the building, drinking contraband beer and trying to hold conversations despite the volume of the music. Connor scanned the place for Lolly, but he couldn't find her.

Maybe she was…mad at him? He couldn't quite figure out why, but when he'd helped her up off the dock today, she'd seemed pissed off, dismissing him with a curt, 'Fine.' Girls, he thought. Who the hell could figure them out?

A leggy blonde in a windbreaker that was unzipped to her belly button sidled up to him, holding a longneck bottle of beer. The music subsided as the CD changed. 'Here's to getting through another day with the ankle biters,' she said in a low, sultry voice. Her tongue slipped out to moisten her lips. 'I had no idea little kids were so much work.' She lifted the longneck to her mouth and took a swig, then drew the bottle away with a kissing sound and offered it to him.

The music started up again, 'Do It With A Stranger,' the metal beat banging hard against the walls of the place.

'Want some?' she asked, leaning up to shout into his ear over the loud music.

'No, thanks.'

'People call me Jazzy, by the way,' she said with a smile.

Maybe you should tell them to stop, he thought. 'I'm Connor.'

'I know.' She winked. 'I asked. You got a girlfriend, Connor?'

He saw Lolly come in with her two cousins, and the three of them started waving and greeting people. 'Nope,' he said.

'Excellent. It's going to be a great summer. I'm from L.A.'

'Buffalo,' he said. Big deal.

She laughed as if he'd said something funny, then did that dumb-girl thing where she pretended to be tipsy, and staggered into him. She smelled of beer and fruity shampoo. Her boobs felt unnaturally firm—which he'd heard was a telltale sign of a boob job. He slipped

315

one arm around her and helped her to a bench. She apparently assumed he wanted to make out with her, and wound her arms around his neck.

'I'm going to grab something to drink,' he yelled in her ear. 'Nice to meet you, Jazzy.'

He looked around, part of him wanting to escape, the other part wanting to stay and party, and of course, yet another part wanting to jump her bones. But no. Not with Jazzy from L.A. Or with the other girl—Mandy or Mindy—who hit on him as he wended his way to the refreshments table, laden with soft drinks and chips.

It wasn't that he had anything against hooking up. Far from it. He practically had a hard-on right now, just from the thought of Jazzy leaning against him. But he didn't want to start the summer hooking up with some random girl, that was for sure. He needed to scope out the territory first.

And now two more girls were bearing down on him. The one with the big tits and the Mount Holyoke tank top, and her giggling friend, whose father manufactured a line of overpriced clothing.

He spotted a lifeline in the form of Lolly Bellamy. She stood at the fringes of the crowd, watching with a bored expression on her face. Connor crossed the room to her, cutting a path through the crowd, which was now freak dancing to Metalopolis.

'Hey,' he said, acting casual.

'Hey.' Her smile was brief, and he wondered if she was still mad about something.

'So we said we'd catch up,' he reminded her.

'What's that?' She cupped a hand around her ear.

'Catch up,' he repeated, and gestured for her to follow him to a far corner of the room, out of the blare of the stereo speakers. She smiled up at him with a look that was soft and genuine. He'd always liked her face. She had nice skin and pretty eyes behind the glasses.

'I was surprised when I learned you'd be here this summer,' she said.

'I hadn't planned to come back,' Connor explained. He was a man now, as Mel was fond of reminding him. Old enough to leave home, to get out of his stepfather's life. And of course, he couldn't escape fast enough. It wasn't as if he liked living at his mother's. It was simply the best option he had in order to save every possible penny for college. Because it was a given that he'd get no help from his mother and Mel, or from his father, in that department.

Which was fine with Connor. He didn't mind paying his own way. He would have been long gone the minute he tossed his graduation mortarboard in the air, except that his mother had other plans for him.

'What made you decide to come back?' Lolly asked.

He hesitated, wondering how much to tell her. 'I figured after graduation, I'd get a job and a place of my own. I figured I'd get a life.'

'And here you are.'

'Just couldn't stay away.' There was plenty more he could have said to her, and probably would, except it was almost impossible to have a decent conversation amid all this noise. Maybe that was for the better. Maybe there was no need for Lolly to hear the real reason he was back here once again. His mother's other son, eight-year-old Julian, had come up from Louisiana for the summer. Their mother needed Connor to look after him.

That was code for keeping the kid out of her hair, and out of the way of Mel's fists.

Connor had only ever known his brother as a baby, and then their mom had given Julian away like an unwanted puppy. It had taken Connor years to get over that, and maybe it made Julian a little odd, too. At eight years of age, he was a bundle of energy, simmering with seldom-denied impulses. According to his school records, private diagnostic testing would be required to determine Julian's specific needs, but that had never been done. His level of intelligence had never been measured; it was that far off the charts.

The other thing that came through on

school records was a multipage litany of conduct infractions. These were not your garden-variety episodes of schoolyard horseplay or sassing the teachers. They were, for the most part, bizarre and dangerous acts that affected only one person—Julian himself.

Connor's mother claimed the boy would turn her into a nervous wreck. The solution had come from an unlikely source—his father, who still worked at Camp Kioga. The Bellamys offered Connor a job for the summer, and invited Julian to camp. He wondered if they'd told Lolly that there was yet another scholarship camper, courtesy of Terry Davis. He suspected they hadn't. Charles and Jane Bellamy were discreet when it came to such matters.

'So what've you been up to?' Lolly asked. 'Why didn't you come back until now?'

'My stepfather told me I was old enough to bring in some money.' Connor did his working-class Mel imitation. ' "You get a job, son. I don't want to see you sitting around all day, eating us out of house and home." '

So many levels of irony to choose from. In the first place, he was not Mel's son. Like it or not, Connor had a father. 'And the thing about house and home?' he snorted. 'It assumes we have them—a house and a home. The truth is, we live in a trailer park and it's nobody's home. Just a place to stay for a while.'

He tried to figure out the expression on

319

her face. Was it disgust? Superiority? What did someone like her think when she heard how someone like him lived?

'It sounds kind of amazing,' she concluded.

'It does?'

'Well, heck. Think about it. You can walk away anytime you want. Just…walk away. Believe me, if my parents had been able to do that when they split up, their divorce would not have turned so ugly and painful.'

'It was ugly and painful?'

'Ha. They wrote the book on ugly and painful. And the thing was, all their fights— the Cold War Years, I call it—were about things. Stuff. Like a painting or a lamp or an antique. You know?'

'They didn't fight over custody of you?'

'As if. There was no way my mother would have considered giving me up. I was the one thing they didn't fight over. It was just a given that my mother would keep me, same as she would keep her ovaries.'

More irony, he thought. Lolly couldn't escape her parents' expectations. He couldn't imagine parents who expected anything of him.

'So what about you?' he asked her. 'What've you been up to?'

'The last two summers, I did some traveling.'

'Where to?'

'Overseas.'

'You could be more specific. I think I remember some of my geography.'

She offered a joyless smile. 'Let's see. Summer after sophomore year, I spent with my mother and her mother—my grandmother Gwen—in London, Paris and Prague. In the summer after my junior year, not to be outdone, my father took me to Alexandria, then Athens and Istanbul.'

'Sounds awesome,' he said. 'Man— Istanbul. And Egypt. Did you see the pyramids?'

'I did. And it was just like I imagined. No, better. Those summers, the places I went, the things I saw, were…like a dream.'

'You're lucky, Lolly. Lucky Lolly. Sounds like the name of a racehorse up at Saratoga.'

'Yeah, that's me. Lucky.'

'You mean you had a bad time?'

'No. Trust me, you can't go to Paris and have a bad time. But…it was just lonely and strained. I felt the way I've felt ever since the divorce, as if I'm supposed to be or act a certain way. God, I sound like a baby, whining about this stuff.'

'Don't worry,' he said. 'I don't feel too sorry for you.'

'Good, because I don't feel sorry for you, either.'

'I know. You never have.' Another thing he liked about her.

'What are your plans?' Lolly asked.

321

'I wish I had a nickel for every time someone's asked me that.' What he really wished was that he had an answer he actually liked, travel or college or a kick-ass job he couldn't wait to go to every day. Reality was much less appealing. He was going to have to get a job, live on the cheap and go to community college part-time. 'I haven't made up my mind yet. What about you? I bet you've had a plan since you were in grade school.'

'Why do you say that?'

'You're a planner. That's how it always seemed to me.'

'Well, now that I've survived high school, I'm going to shock the world with a bold move,' she said with exaggerated drama.

'How's that?'

'Wait for it. College.'

'You're right. I'm shocked.' College was, of course, the next logical step for people like the Bellamys, and most of the people at this camp. Rich kids learning how to be rich grown-ups, so they could perpetuate the species.

'I think I'd like to be a high-school teacher,' she said. 'An art teacher.' In the shadows, he could see her smile turn kind of shy, flickering at him through the darkness. 'You're the first person I've told that.'

'Is it some big secret?'

'Not really, but it's not the kind of thing that would thrill my mother. She'd rather see me in the foreign service, something exciting like that.'

'It's your life. Your decision.'

'Kind of. I hate disappointing my mother. I haven't even told my therapist.'

He chuckled. 'You still have a therapist.'

'Always. And as you can probably tell, I like talking. Dr. Schneider's like a friend who charges by the hour.'

'I'd be your friend for free,' he told her.

That smile again. It flashed at him through the shadows, kind of shy, kind of pretty. 'Thanks,' she said. 'That, um, it means a lot to me, Connor. I've never had a lot of friends.'

Even though a few years had passed, Connor still felt as if he could talk to her. When they were younger, he found her bossy and annoying, but he quickly learned that her bossiness was a front. Underneath, she had a good heart and a great sense of humor, and he knew for a fact that you couldn't have too much of that.

He liked their silences, too. He never felt as if he had to fill the lulls in their conversations with small talk. With Lolly, he could be quiet, and she didn't make him feel as if he should be kissing her or trying to get into her pants. Not that he had anything against kissing and getting laid, hell no. He had plenty of luck in that department. For whatever reason, scoring with girls had never been a challenge.

323

Having it mean something. That was the challenge.

Or maybe it wasn't supposed to mean anything. Maybe that was all bullshit for books and movies.

He liked the fact that Lolly was honest with him, and the fact that he could be just as honest with her. There weren't many people in his life he could tell things to, but she was one of them. 'I've got another reason to be back this summer,' he said.

'What's that?'

'My little brother.'

He heard her gasp in the darkness. 'I never knew you had a brother.'

'Julian is eight. He's in the Fledglings. Julian Gastineaux.'

The expression on her face was comical. 'I did see that kid today—jumped out of a tree into the lake.'

'That's the one.' Connor nodded. Julian was always climbing to high places where he didn't belong. No wonder he drove their mom nuts. Connor supposed the tactic made just about as much sense as Connor's method of trying to be a good son, keep his nose clean, get good grades. Neither approach was going to win her love. He'd come to terms with that quite a while ago, but he still remembered how much it had hurt, back when he'd believed it was possible to get her to love him. Julian was probably still at that stage, and clearly it was making him squirrelly.

'I never would have taken the two of you for brothers,' Lolly said.

He grinned. 'We get that a lot.'

'You don't look much alike,' Lolly said, clearly trying to be diplomatic. 'You must be…half brothers?'

'That's right. His dad's African-American. Mine is…' *A drunk.* 'Mine isn't.'

She gave him a light slug in the arm. 'I can't believe you never said anything.'

'I was eleven years old when Julian was born,' he told her. 'To me, there was nothing unusual about him. He was just a baby, you know? Then Julian's biological father showed up and I was, like, damn. The kid's half African-American.'

'What happened?' Lolly asked. 'Why didn't your mom raise you together?'

'Nobody explained it to me at the time. When Julian was about six months old, my mother started dating Mel. He convinced her that she couldn't afford a baby, and that Julian would be better off being raised by his father.'

Connor discovered that the memory still had the power to hurt. By the time Gastineaux came for Julian, the baby was old enough to squirm and coo and laugh at Connor, who had loved him with a fierce, intense joy. When Julian was taken away, Connor had felt his heart being ripped out. He'd raged at his mother for weeks afterward. 'How could you?'

he asked her over and over again. 'He's my brother. How could you?'

'It doesn't do to get attached,' his mother had told him, her eyes red rimmed with tears. 'Julian is better off with Louis, anyway.'

She might have been right about that. Gastineaux was not a man of great means, but he had a town house and a serious job, which was more than most kids' fathers had.

'So now Julian lives in New Orleans with his father,' Connor told Lolly. 'He's some kind of college professor, a rocket scientist, and this summer he's on sabbatical overseas, so Julian came to stay with my mom and me. She was going to let him sit around all summer and watch TV, probably get into trouble. So she called my dad and told him we were both coming. I can only imagine what my old man thought of that—having his grown kid and his ex's other kid coming up for the summer.' Connor's relationship with his dad was complicated by the fact that Terry Davis was a man completely without judgment or pretense, and he'd do anything to have Connor with him. When Connor's dad was sober, he was the best guy on earth. Things would be simpler, Connor thought, if his dad was an asshole. That way, drunk or sober, Connor could simply hate him.

'So your dad's okay about…?' Lolly's voice trailed off, as if she sensed herself heading into unknown territory.

'He and my mother never talk anymore, but he'd never make Julian feel weird about being here.'

'He must be a tolerant guy,' she said.

Very diplomatic, thought Connor. In fact, Connor's dad and Julian had hit it off. Connor figured that, although completely unrelated by blood, Terry Davis and Julian Gastineaux had something elemental in common. They were both destroying themselves, Terry with his drinking and Julian by jumping from high places.

'I have your grandparents to thank for this summer. They gave me a job and invited Julian to camp. That's cool of them.' He wondered if Julian would appreciate the chance he'd been given. He wondered if spending the summer at Willow Lake would change Julian's perspective on life the way it had Connor's.

Back when Connor had been a camper here, enjoying a camper's rights and privileges, he knew he'd been given a rare opportunity. The Bellamys had no idea what those summers had meant to him. Living with a dozen other guys in a bunkhouse that smelled like a hamster cage by the end of week one didn't sound like much. But to Connor, it was huge. It was a chance to live a different life, even if it was only for the summer. For ten whole weeks, he got to experience the kind of summer a kid was supposed to have: a string of sunny days filled with fun and laughter, practical jokes, sports that stretched strength and endurance to the limit, incredible meals every day, goofy talent shows, ghost stories whispered in the dark, singing around a bonfire. They were the kind of summers a kid had in his mind somewhere, whether or not they were real. And for those three years, Connor's summers had been like a dream.

It was too idyllic to last. Summer pleasures were fleeting, and so was childhood.

Calvin, the head counselor, came over to their table. 'I need a volunteer for lights-out duty.' He held out a police-style nightstick. 'Lolly, I volunteer you.'

'Ha-ha,' she said, though she took the Maglite and headed for the door willingly enough.

Connor watched her for a few seconds. Then he spotted Jazzy, with the big lips and the boob job, coming toward him again.

'I'll go, too,' he said, ducking out just in time to evade Jazzy as she moved in for the kill.

Despite the loud music blaring from the stereo, he could hear someone say, 'No accounting for taste.'

Idiots, he thought. When he reached Lolly, he was a little out of breath.' Hey, wait up.'

She looked surprised, her eyes illuminated by the faint starlight. 'You didn't have to leave the party early on my account.'

'There'll be plenty more this summer. In fact, if you'd rather hang out at the party,' he said, 'I can do the rounds myself.'

'No, I'm good. It was too loud in there, anyway. Too hot.'

'My thoughts exactly.' They walked along a path, picking their way through shadows. The Milky Way arched in a swath across the night sky and they stopped just to look up at it in wonder. That was when Connor started— finally—to feel the old connection with Lolly, the friendship that used to mean so much to him.

'Really?' she said. 'You weren't having any fun, getting hit on by a different girl every five minutes?'

'I wasn't—'

She chuckled. 'It was hard to miss.'

He was glad for the darkness to hide his red face. 'Lots of people were hitting on each other.'

'Not me.'

'Yeah, well, you're smart,' he said. 'I don't know why everybody rushes into things.'

'Because they don't want all the hotties to get away,' she said. 'Ever think of that?'

'No,' he said.

'I know of at least three girls who called dibs on you. Nobody wants to get stuck with a loser.'

'Are you saying you're a loser?'

'Did you see anyone trying to hook up with me?'

No, he thought, I would have run them off.

'It sucks,' she said, 'the way everything's based on looks. Don't you think?'

'People say my mom looks like Sharon Stone, and it's never brought her anything but assholes who treat her like shit.'

'Jeez, Connor,' Lolly said.

She made him smile in spite of himself, simple as that. He liked being with her, and if the other counselors had to wonder why, it was because they were idiots. He felt perfectly content, walking with her along gravel paths that had been there for generations of campers. It was an hour past lights-out, and through the screen windows of the bunkhouses, they could hear the expectant whispers from the Fledgling group. Lolly lingered under the window of Saratoga Cabin, and Connor went to check on the boys, in Ticonderoga. They didn't go in because that got the kids all excited. They were only supposed to go in if something seemed wrong. When he came back for her, she held a finger to her lips.

The sound that reached them was the titter and hiss of little girls who thought they were getting away with something. Which, of course, they weren't. Lolly hesitated for a few more moments. Then she motioned for Connor to move on.

'There's a little one named Ramona I'm keeping an eye on,' she said. 'Homesick.'

It was a concept with which Connor was totally unfamiliar. He had no idea what it would be like to have the kind of home you actually missed when you were away. He wondered if Julian was missing his dad and New Orleans. From what little he knew of the kid's life, it wasn't so bad. Louis Gastineaux had never been married, and according to Julian, didn't go out on dates. As far as Connor could tell, they lived like a couple of bachelors.

Lolly didn't seem to be in a hurry to get back to the party, and Connor didn't blame her. He liked it out here, where it was dark enough to make out stars you couldn't see from the city, and quiet enough to hear the whir of an owl's wings and the water lapping at the dock pilings and canoe hulls. From a distance, the sounds of the party were muted and pleasant, carrying across the lake.

The moon had risen and now washed the compound in an eerie pale light. The distant roar of the falls sounded like a cheering crowd at a football stadium. Through the trees, the lights of the staff cabins glimmered, and Connor thought about his father, spending another night drinking beer and listening to old songs on the radio. As he had for the past two decades, Terry Davis lived alone in one of the all-season cabins at the fringes of the

331

camp, losing pieces of himself while life passed him by.

Pushing aside the depressing thought, Connor tracked the flight of an owl, and then something else caught his eye. A flicker of light, maybe a flashlight. He grabbed Lolly's arm. 'Look up on the footbridge over Meerskill Falls,' he said. 'Do you see anything?'

'No, just shadows, but—yikes, I think you're right. Someone's up there.' She switched on the nightstick and headed up the trail, as fearless and focused as a cop on patrol. 'Let's go check it out.'

The trail rose steeply alongside the rocky gorge. The falls crashed down over the boulders, throwing up a needle-fine mist that cultivated a lush fringe of moss everywhere it touched.

As they climbed, passing switchbacks and rocky outcroppings, nocturnal animals scuttled in the underbrush. He heard Lolly stumble. 'You okay?' he asked.

'Yes. I'm wearing flip-flops. I didn't think I'd be taking a hike tonight.'

'You don't have to come.'

'You think I'd miss this?' She gave a familiar, snorting laugh.

He knew she'd say that. Lolly Bellamy knew how to be annoying, but she wasn't a quitter, no matter what she said. 'Grab on to me if you feel like you're going to fall.'

'Huh,' she said. 'You just want someone to grab your ass.'

'Yeah, that's the plan.' They fell easily into their old pattern of bickering, a pattern that had been set years before when they were twelve years old. It felt familiar. Comfortable, like an old shirt.

Connor could make out two shadowy silhouettes on the bridge now. One of them seemed to be on the outside of the safety fence. A very bad feeling clutched at his gut. 'You stupid little shit,' he muttered under his breath.

'What?' Lolly asked.

'Julian!' Connor burst into a run.

At the same time, an exuberant yell split the night: 'Gee-ronimo!'

Lolly shone the light on the bridge and they watched in horror as a small figure detached itself from the concrete railing and hurtled through the darkness. Lolly made a terrible sound, something between a gasp and a scream.

The long beam of the Maglite illuminated a small, fleeing figure on the bridge—not Julian but another boy Connor didn't recognize. Then the beam started to tremble as Lolly aimed it at the area under the bridge.

'Julian,' he said, pulling in stinging gasps of air.

The light wobbled through the forest as Lolly searched. Panic hammered so wildly in

Connor's ears that he couldn't hear anything. Then he realized that she was talking, grabbing his arm to steady him, and finally, he made out what she was trying to say.

'Okay,' she gasped. 'I think he's okay.'

Shrieks of boyish glee drifted through the night forest. Lolly took Connor's hand and guided the flashlight beam to a long rope attached to the bridge.

His heart rate slowed, though his blood felt as if it were about to boil up through his head. 'The little son of a bitch,' he said, striding up the last part of the trail. 'The stupid little son of a bitch.'

A moment later he reached the bridge deck and collared the accomplice, a kid named George from Texas who babbled like a coward that he had nothing to do with this, that Julian had forced him to come along.

'Shut up,' Connor barked, and young George subsided. Lolly shone the light on a spot where the safety fence had been clipped. She slipped the beam downward to the small, swaying figure at the end of what appeared to be a bungee cord.

'You are so busted,' he said to his dangling brother.

'Shee-it,' Julian replied.

*   *   *

It was a half hour later by the time they had

reeled Julian in, marched him and his accomplice down the mountain. 'You crazy-ass little fucker,' Connor said, unfastening the elaborate system of harness and carabiners with which Julian had secured himself to the bungee cord.

'I don't think you're supposed to call me that,' Julian said. 'Kioga Rule 11. "Under no circumstance will foul or vulgar language be tolerated from either campers or staff." '

'Yeah? So what rule prohibits dumb asses from jumping off bridges?' Connor demanded.

'What on earth were you thinking?' Lolly asked.

Julian gazed up at her, and in the moonlight, the kid looked as guileless and angelic as a choirboy. He gave her a sweet, vulnerable little smile and Connor imagined Lolly's heart melting into a puddle on the ground.

'Ma'am,' said Julian, his voice quivering with sincerity, 'I wanted to know what it feels like to fly.'

Connor expected Lolly to be taken in by his little brother's infectious charm. Instead, she said, 'Ha. That wasn't flying. That was a free fall.'

*   *   *

Another half hour had passed by the time they

put the boys to bed, warning them that they both faced disciplinary action, maybe even expulsion. Great, thought Connor, knowing that if his brother left, Connor was a goner, too. Summer would be over before it had a chance to begin. As he and Lolly left the bunkhouse, he said, 'Sorry about that. You probably should have stayed at the party.'

'Are you kidding? It's not every night I get to see somebody jump off Meerskill Bridge. I wouldn't have missed it for the world.'

'What the hell am I going to do?'

'Talk to him about a career as a stuntman?'

Counselors were supposed to report infractions to the dean. Connor tried to see Lolly's face, but it was too dark to tell what she was thinking.

'I didn't see a thing,' she said. 'You have to admit, he was pretty creative and resourceful.'

True enough. Julian and George had helped themselves to the camp's rock-climbing harnesses, ropes, slings, bungee cords and hardware. Working from a diagram they'd found in a book, they'd constructed a workable apparatus. Connor's kid brother was an awkward combination of child prodigy, stuntman and idiot. 'According to his dad, he started jumping off things as a toddler,' he told Lolly. 'He's always been obsessed by heights.'

'Let's put him in high-dive lessons

tomorrow. If he's going to be jumping off things, he might as well be safe about it. There's also zip-lining and rock climbing.'

Sweet relief unfurled inside him. Connor was tempted to kiss her at that moment. The last thing in the world that he wanted was to lose his brother again. 'That would be completely...terrific,' he said.

She shrugged. 'No big deal. I believe in following your impulses even if it takes you to a weird place.'

'I'll make sure he doesn't screw up again.'

'All right.'

He indicated the dining hall. 'Hey. You up for a kitchen raid?'

'Always.'

The kitchen was locked every night, mainly to guard against raccoons and bears, but there was a key kept above the lintel, and they were inside in seconds. The camp kitchen, with its fragrance of spices, yeasty fresh bread, the stacks of institutional-size cans, the packed walk-in fridge, seemed like a place of endless abundance.

Connor grabbed a loaf of bread, cracked wheat from Sky River Bakery, the same kind they'd served when he was a camper here. That was one of the things he'd grown to like about Camp Kioga. Nothing ever changed, year in and year out. You could always count on bread from the local bakery, milk delivered in reusable glass bottles and fresh produce

337

from the farms of Ulster County.

Lolly opened an institutional-size jar of peanut butter and pushed it down the counter to him. He slathered peanut butter on thick slices of bread, added honey from a squeeze bottle and pushed a sandwich across the counter to her. He poured himself a glass of milk, then offered the jug to Lolly. She shook her head.

'You have an interesting family, Connor,' she said. 'I think it's great that you're spending the summer with Julian now.' She licked a drop of honey from the corner of her sandwich.

Hearing her say so made Connor feel better about Julian. He was a crazy little kid, but Connor was glad, too. They finished their snack and cleaned up the evidence.

'It's late,' Connor said. He held out a hand to help her up from the table. She didn't really need help getting up. It just seemed like the polite thing to do. After turning out the lights, he closed and latched the kitchen door and they stepped out into the cricket-filled night.

'I'll walk you back to your cabin.'

'I know the way back,' Lolly said.

'You should know that's just code,' he said, taking her hand again.

'Code for what?' she asked.

'When a guy tells a girl he'll walk her home, that means he wants to kiss her good-night.'

'Very funny.' She gave her trademark snorting laugh, the one that used to annoy him when they were younger. 'You don't want to kiss me good-night, Connor,' she said.

'You're right,' he agreed, stopping in the path and slipping his arms around her. 'I want to kiss you now.'

SCOUT VESPERS (TRADITIONAL)

Softly falls the light of day
As our campfire fades away.
Silently each Scout should ask,
Have I done my daily task?
Have I kept my honor bright?
Can I guiltless sleep the night?
Have I done and have I dared,
Everything to be prepared?

Twenty-One

'What do you wear when you go to confront your father about his secret love child?' Olivia asked Barkis. The little dog had skittered into her room as she was drying her toenails, freshly painted a luscious candy pink.

'Lilly Pulitzer,' she concluded, reaching into the closet. It was a crisp summer dress in a cool aqua-and-lime print, one that would be comfortable during the long drive but that would also look smart in the city. As she stepped into wedge sandals, grabbed a Longchamps bag and put on earrings, she realized that it felt absurdly good to dress up, even at six-thirty in the morning. The weeks of grubby renovation work had turned her into a frump. Now, with her hair and nails done and makeup on, she felt like a new person.

The last thing she expected, however, was for Connor Davis to dress for the city, too. When he came to pick her up, she scarcely recognized him. He was wearing slacks that looked as though they had been specially tailored for his narrow hips and waist. He had on a good white shirt with the sleeves rolled back, and a jacket and tie hung on a hook in the backseat of the car. He'd left his customary Agway Feed cap at home and had done something to his hair, something involving gel and finger combing, she suspected. In his clean-shaven, suntanned face, his eyes looked bluer than the lake under a clear sky.

'Wow,' she said, startled to feel a warm pulse of attraction, 'Look at you. You clean up real well.'

'Wow, yourself,' he said. 'You look like an episode of *Sex and the City.*'

Compliments from men always made Olivia suspicious. Do guys watch that show? she wondered. Then she thought of Freddy. Yes, they did.

Julian showed up from the direction of the cabin he shared with Connor. In loose sweats and no shirt, he had the softly blurred look of someone whose older brother had just nudged him from a sound sleep. 'Morning,' he said to Olivia.

'You're up early,' she said, smiling at him.

'Not by choice.'

'I wanted to make sure you were up by the time my dad gets here.' He turned to Olivia. 'He's coming up to do some maintenance work.'

'Huh,' said Julian. 'He's going to be supervising me.'

'No offense, but the way you've been acting, you need supervision.'

'That's such bullshit. When we first got here, you said my only rule was not to fuck up. Have I?' He glared at Connor, then Olivia.

341

'Have I fucked up?'

'Watch your damn mouth,' Connor warned him.

'You've been enormously helpful,' Olivia said, 'and I'm grateful for that.'

'We'll be back around dark,' Connor said. 'Maybe later.'

'I'll try not to miss you too much.'

'I'm just saying—'

'I know.' Julian waved a hand, offered a brief smile.

Olivia clipped a leash on Barkis. 'Can you take him? He gets a scoop of food at lunchtime and another at dinner.'

'No problem.' Julian took the leash. 'Um, does that fax machine in the office work?'

'I think so, now that we have phone service. Do you need to fax something?'

'Some paperwork.' He avoided Connor's eye. Olivia hid a smile. She had been talking to Julian about some options for his future, and the boy was surprisingly open to suggestion. He himself had brought up the idea of the ROTC and the Air Force Academy, and Olivia had urged him to explore further, to learn what was involved. Once he'd discovered that he might have a chance to fly high-tech fighter jets, he was sold on the idea.

'You can fax anything you want.' She ducked into the passenger side of the car, slinging her sweater over the headrest and

342

putting on her sunglasses. 'Ready,' she said to Connor.

'Look,' he said, 'I'm glad you hit it off with Julian, but he's my responsibility. There's no need for you to try to...rehabilitate him, or whatever it is you're doing.'

'Meddling,' she said simply. 'I'd call it meddling. I've been telling him that going to college is not so impossible.' Olivia saw, too late, the effect her words had on Connor. She knew he had once dreamed of going to college, too. But that hadn't happened, and she couldn't find a way to ask him why.

'He doesn't have the money or the grades,' Connor said flatly.

'Wasn't there a settlement from his father's accident? Social security? A pension from Tulane?'

'I'm not privy to all the details, but I understand there was no negligence in the accident. Julian's portion of the settlement was gone by the time the lawyers, the relatives and our mother took their cut. Even if he had the money, I don't think college is an option. Because mainly, he doesn't have the attitude.'

'Don't give up on him up,' she said. 'He's only seventeen.' She liked Julian, with his face like an angel and the brains of a Nobel Prize winner, his obsession with heights and danger. 'And don't rule out an ROTC scholarship. He could actually do something with all that energy.'

Connor's expression turned skeptical. 'That takes a lot of motivation.'

'Maybe he has a lot of motivation.' She studied Connor. Lord, but he was good-looking, his profile clean and masculine, his piercing eyes watching the road. 'You don't think he should go into the military, is that it?'

'I don't think he understands the risks.'

'How would being in the military be riskier than what he's doing now?' she asked.

He frowned. 'Good point.'

'Are you upset that I've been talking to him about these options?'

'Hell, no. It just seems like a long shot.'

Of course it would to someone who had grown up the way Connor had. In his world, just having a decent place to live had probably seemed like a long shot. But there was something else, she thought. 'You're worried about him, aren't you?' she said. 'About your brother.'

'Sometimes I think I'm the only one.'

'He's lucky to have you,' she said, recognizing the pain in his voice. 'Do you think he's going to be all right?'

'That depends on whether or not he can keep his record clean and figure out something to do with his life.'

Which was exactly what Olivia was trying to help the boy do. It appeared her efforts were not wholly welcome. She was a born meddler, and she was headed to the city in order to meddle some more. Surreal as it seemed, she was going to ask her father if he'd had a baby out of wedlock when he was in college. The thought caused her stomach to cramp, and she tried to concentrate on the scenery out the window, a rapidly changing slide show of bucolic villages, farms nestled in the rolling hills, gas stations and strip malls.

'You're too quiet now,' he said. 'You've barely said a word in forty miles. Don't be so tense.'

'I can be tense if I want,' she said. 'You think it's going to be easy, asking my dad if he has a daughter he never told me about?'

'Maybe he doesn't know about Jenny Majesky.'

Olivia wanted to throw up. It was bizarre, imagining this whole alternate life for the father she thought she knew. Once she put together the pieces of the puzzle—the photograph, the silver pendant, the information from Terry Davis—everything she'd once believed to be true flew out the window.

'I'm completely freaked out about this,' she confessed. 'If I'm right, and Jenny's my sister, then she's been missing from my life when she could have been a part of it.'

'It's better you never knew,' he told her in a low voice. 'For me, growing up and knowing I had a little brother, well, it just…hurt.'

Oh, God. She tried to picture him as a

little boy, with a baby brother one minute, and an only child the next. Maybe he was right. Maybe it hurt too much to know.

He drove with surprising ease into the city, navigating the flow of traffic with patience and skill. Under different circumstances, she might have given him a quick tour of her father's neighborhood—the deli and newsstand, the gardens and quirky neighbors. Her stomach was in knots, though, and her throat ached. As he pulled up to the curb in front of the extended awning of her father's building, she said, 'I have a huge favor to ask.'

He grinned and shook his head. 'Uh-uh.'

'Please…'

'You don't want me there, Lolly. I promise you don't.'

He was right, of course. No way could she ask him to come inside with her. It was already too awkward, the questions she had, the answers she was afraid to hear. 'You're stronger than you think,' Connor said.

Olivia couldn't believe how good it felt to have someone believe that about her, not with high expectations but with a sturdy certainty in her innate abilities. A wave of tenderness eased through her, dissipating the tension a little. This was new—being with a man who made her feel both relaxed and capable.

'Call me when you're finished here,' he said. 'I'm heading downtown.'

'Downtown?' She tried to picture him

sightseeing in the Village, perhaps, or at Chelsea Piers. 'Do you have a particular destination in mind? Or are you open to suggestions?'

'I'm not playing tourist,' he said. 'I've got an appointment downtown, at Greenwich and Rector.'

'Oh. Is it anything…God, listen to me. I'm horrible. Totally nosy.'

'With my broker,' he said.

She must have betrayed a look of amazement, because he chuckled. 'Even backwoods contractors sometimes have equity funds.'

'I wasn't—'

'Sure you were. It's all right. Go, Olivia. Have a nice visit with your father.'

'Thanks.' She picked up her purse and shoulder bag.

He turned to look at her, and once again, she was bowled over by his lake-blue eyes, dark hair, shirt open at the throat. She could have sworn he wanted to kiss her. There was a moment of tension, and plenty more to be said, but not now. She unclipped her seat belt. Then, on impulse, she leaned over and kissed his cheek. Well, shoot, she thought. She wanted a kiss. The moment she felt his warm cheek with her lips and inhaled the scent of his shaving cream, she wanted more than that.

'For luck,' she said hastily, then got out of the car. If he said anything, she didn't hear it.

Though aware of the doorman's eyes on her, she stood on the sidewalk and watched Connor go. Downtown. To meet with his broker. It shouldn't surprise her that he had a portfolio at such a young age. For someone growing up with no security or control at all, keeping control of finances was probably second nature. Seeing him each day at the camp, she often forgot he had a whole separate life she knew nothing about, other clients with other projects. He might even have a girlfriend, for all she knew, though a part of her would be devastated if he did.

Who was she kidding? *All* of her would be devastated if he did. He couldn't, she told herself. No way could he look at her the way he just had if he had a girlfriend. The heat in his gaze alone would have constituted a betrayal.

Adjusting her shoulder bag, she turned and went into the building. 'Miss Bellamy.' The doorman bobbed his head.

Her father had moved here after the divorce. As a child, Olivia spent the night only occasionally, perhaps after attending a Yankees game with him, a night at the opera or on the eve of the trip together. For the most part, it was understood by all of them that her place was at her mother's, amid the muted luxury of the Fifth Avenue flat. That was where she had kept all her things, including her piano, her beloved books, her adored cat named Degas. Still, her father tried hard to make room for her in his life. His sleek, midcentury modern condo had a small bedroom just for her, with a built-in desk, bunk beds and a white shag rug.

Bypassing the elevator, she took the stairs. Her father, having been called by the doorman, stood waiting with the door held wide open. Although the day was warm enough for open windows, he wore a light cardigan. It was funny, she'd never seen him in a cardigan sweater before. It made him seem older. She didn't like to think of her father as an old man. Until very recently, she'd simply thought of him as 'Dad.' Now she had to wonder about him as a person, someone with urges and passions and motivations she'd never considered. What made him tick? He was a successful lawyer, a dutiful son, a devoted father, but what else? He'd always wanted to write. She knew that, but they'd never talked about it, and now she wished they had. She wished they'd talked about so much more.

'Hey, Dad,' she said, lifting up on tiptoe to kiss his cheek.

'How's my happy camper?' he asked.

'Amazingly happy,' she said, 'considering it's Camp Kioga. Giving the place an extreme make-over is a lot more fun than camping.'

'What can I get you?' he said. 'Lemonade? Seltzer?'

'I need to freshen up, and then I'll help myself to something.' She visited the powder room, then afterward stopped in the kitchen, studying the selection in the fridge, helping herself to a bottle of plain seltzer. Then she joined him in the living room.

Her father sat back in his favorite wing chair. 'So spill. Something about Camp Kioga must agree with you. You're glowing.'

Three hours in a car with Connor Davis will do that to a girl, she thought.

She took a sip of seltzer and brought him up to date on the past several weeks. 'It's amazing, Dad,' she said, 'how the place unlocks so many memories. For all of us. Maybe it's the lack of technology. We have to entertain ourselves the old-fashioned way.'

'How's Greg doing?'

'At first, not so hot.' She watched her father's brow pinch together with disappointment. Though Greg was a decade younger than Philip, the brothers were close. She hastily added, 'He's doing better every day. All three of them are. I think a big part of Uncle Greg's trouble was that he lost touch with his kids. When they first got to the camp, he and Daisy barely spoke, and he and Max were like two strangers. Now they're paddling around in canoes, going fishing, playing games, reading books together. They're going to be all right, Dad.'

'And you?' he asked. 'How are you doing?'

She set down her drink. 'You know, it's a funny thing. I was over Rand quickly. Too quickly. It was like getting a really bad hangnail. At first it hurts so much, you can't think about anything else. But if you put the right kind of salve on it, the pain goes away so fast, you forget you were ever hurting in the first place.'

'Renovating the camp is the right kind of salve, then. Either that, or he wasn't right for you in the first place.'

'Then why did I think he was?'

'Wishful thinking is a powerful force.'

Olivia had to wonder if it was just her pride that was hurt. That worried her, that she could be so superficial. She'd envisioned a life for herself and made choices that fed into that vision—the home, the husband, the family. But was it all, as her father suggested, wishful thinking?

'Have you been to see your grandparents?' her father asked her.

'I'm not sure I'll have time today. I thought I'd call them. And Mother, too,' she added cautiously. It had crossed her mind to stop in and check on her apartment, but there was no need. Earl was keeping the place in order, watering the plants and looking after things there. And, all right, she was also unsure about taking Connor Davis there, giving him a glimpse of the way she lived.

She felt herself circling around the real

351

reason she'd come here. Just say it, she coached herself. She took a deep breath…and chickened out. 'I don't know if I told you this or not. The contractor doing all the work is Connor Davis.'

Her father frowned, rubbed his chin. 'Connor… that would be Terry Davis's boy, then.'

'He's not a boy anymore.'

'You think I don't remember,' Philip said.

'Do you?' She was amazed.

'What kind of father would I be if I didn't remember my only child's first broken heart? I wanted to kill the little son of a bitch.'

'Dad. I never knew.' The phrase *only child* swirled in her head. 'Well, I got over that one, just like I did the others,' she said. Liar. She was not over Connor Davis. Pieces of herself—important pieces—had been left behind, and she was only now coming to realize that. Excellent time to change the subject. 'About the only-child bit. I need to ask you something. It's kind of personal.'

'Anything. My life is an open book.'

He really seemed to mean it. She'd never regarded her father as a deceptive person. Yet secrets swirled around him, secrets and lies. All right, she pep-talked herself. Just come right out and say it. 'I was wondering, Dad. About your days at camp.'

He grinned. 'You'll have to be more specific. I spent a hell of a lot of days there.'

She took a deep breath. The pause felt big and heavy, and it was. 'Tell me about the summer of 1977.'

His expression softened to thoughtfulness. 'Let's see. I would have been a counselor that year. Why do you ask?'

'I found an old snapshot of you, dated August 1977, and I was curious.' She took a manila folder out of her bag and passed it to him.

His hand was unsteady as he put on his reading glasses and took the faded photo from her. 'Well, I'll be. I'd nearly forgotten…'

Something—maybe the softness of his voice or the mistiness in his eyes—told Olivia that he was lying.

'Forgotten what?' she prompted.

'Winning that trophy. I still like tennis. I need to get back on my game.'

'There's a copy of this picture in the Sky River Bakery. But you've been cropped out of it.'

'I…didn't know that.'

'How close were you and Mariska Majesky?' Olivia asked, watching his face.

He turned the snapshot over. She knew it was blank except for the date.

'Terry Davis told me you two were an item,' Olivia explained.

'You showed this picture to Terry Davis?'

'That's right. He lives in Indian Wells these days.' Olivia didn't want to get sidetracked from Mariska. 'She was very beautiful,' Olivia ventured. 'Were you...a couple?'

He sighed and leaned back in his chair. 'I guess you could say we were.'

'You were with her the summer of 1977,' she reiterated. 'And later that year, you married my mother.'

He turned pale, his gaze avoiding hers.

'Oh, God. *Daddy.*' She'd wanted him to deny it. To defend himself.

'Olivia, this is ancient history. It all happened before you were born. I don't see how it can possibly matter now.'

She took out another picture, this one printed off at the Avalon Public Library. She had found it by searching the archives of the *Avalon Troubadour.* The caption read Sky River Bakery Celebrates 50th Jubilee. Pictured are owners Mrs. Helen Majesky and her granddaughter, Jennifer Majesky.

It was an excellent likeness of Jenny, showing off her dark good looks. Next to the old snapshot of Mariska, it highlighted the striking resemblance between mother and daughter.

Olivia watched her father's face. He went ashen, and sweat gleamed on his forehead. The shock was staggering him, she could tell. Prior to this moment, he had no clue, she was certain of that.

'Her name is Jennifer Anastasia Majesky,'

354

Olivia told her father quietly. 'She was born on March 23, 1978.' The data was easy enough to obtain. Connor had asked the chief of police, Rourke McKnight, who was a friend of his. 'See that necklace she's wearing? You can't make it out in the picture, but there's a pendant on it that matches this.' She handed her father the silver cuff link.

She forced herself to sit quietly as he took it all in.

He slowly lowered his hands, as though forcing himself to face her. 'Are you sure?' he asked.

She knew what he was asking. *Are you sure she's my child?* 'No. That…being sure…is your job.'

He took out a handkerchief and dabbed his face. 'And Mariska?' he asked. 'Is she back in Avalon?'

'No. According to Chief McKnight—the chief of police—she took off when Jenny was three or four and never returned.'

'My God, Mariska,' her father whispered. He lowered his head to his hands, and rested his elbows heavily on his knees. He looked diminished, somehow, as though the revelation had destroyed some vital part of him.

SKY RIVER BAKERY JAM KOLACHES

1/2 cup softened sweet butter
1 small (3-ounce) stick of softened cream cheese
1-1/4 cup flour
a small jar of jam—choose apricot, raspberry or apple
a sprinkle of powdered sugar

Beat the butter and cream cheese until light and fluffy. Add flour, then roll the dough out on a floured surface. With a sharp knife, slice into squares about 2 inches across and place these on a lightly greased cookie sheet. Place a small spoonful of jam on each cookie and loosely fold opposite corners together, pinching at the edge. Bake at 375° for 15 minutes. When cool, sprinkle with powdered sugar. This recipe makes about 2 dozen cookies.

Twenty-Two

September 1977

Camp Kioga was officially closed for the year. Philip Bellamy was among the last of the counselors to depart. His parents had dropped him off at the train station in town and by dinnertime, he'd be in New Haven. He went to wait for the Number Two train headed for New York City. Matthew Alger was on the platform, too, sitting on a bench with his girlfriend, a Barnard student who had worked in the Kioga kitchen all summer.

'Hey, Alger,' Philip said. 'Hey, Shelley. You guys headed back to the city?'

'I am,' said Shelley. 'Matt's staying in Avalon for his internship in city administration.'

Alger shook back his shaggy, Bee Gees–style blond hair. 'I just came to the station to say goodbye to my best girl.' He slid his arm around Shelley.

Philip felt a pang of envy as he watched them. He'd been forced to say goodbye to Mariska in private the night before. Even though he wanted to shout his love for her to the world, she had to remain a secret until he untangled his life and freed himself from Pamela. He'd gone over the plan in his head, again and again. Get through fall registration. Tell Pamela their engagement was off, return to Avalon, propose to Mariska. Simple, he thought. But not easy.

He didn't kid himself. Things were about to change radically for him. Sure, he was supposed to go to law school, but that wasn't what he really wanted to do. What he really wanted was to write. He'd finished two short stories over the summer and was considering submitting them to the *Yale Literary Review*.

He caught a glimpse of his reflection in a big glass-framed poster for that new hit movie, *Annie Hall.* He was wearing a good shirt and school tie because he wouldn't have time to change when he got to campus tonight, and there was an official dinner. As class treasurer, he couldn't miss it.

He stuck his hand in his pants pocket and jingled his change in nervous impatience. His fingers encountered the silver cuff link, and it comforted him to know Mariska had its mate. Pacing up and down, he leaned out over the tracks, as if spotting the train would make it come sooner. He checked his watch, paced some more. Several others arrived, vacationers heading back to the city after Labor Day, people with kids and luggage, sunburns and spots of pink calamine lotion on their mosquito bites.

Amid the growing crowd, he saw a slender woman with dark, shining hair, hurrying toward him. His heart gave a leap. 'Mariska?'

'Philip,' she said, sounding a little breathless.

She looked pale, tired, yet still achingly beautiful. Instantly he cast about to see if anyone was watching. Too risky. He couldn't swing her up into his arms the way he longed to do. Keeping his hands at his sides, he said, 'I didn't know you were coming to the station.'

'I can't put this off any longer,' she said. 'I need to tell you something.'

The expression on her face sent a spike of ice through his heart. He knew already. Before she said a word. 'Mariska—'

'Let's sit down.' She gestured at a bench on one end of the platform, next to the newspaper vending boxes. The *New York Times* headline was about the launch of the second space shuttle orbiter, while the *Avalon Troubadour* proclaimed Camp Kioga Ends Forty-fifth Season.

'What's the matter?' His chest felt funny, as though he'd just swallowed an ice cube whole.

She sat with her knees pointed toward him. 'I think it's time we both faced facts.'

The spike of ice in his heart radiated its cold agony outward. Though the morning sun warmed the train platform, Philip had to fight against an assault of shivering. 'Baby, we spent the whole summer facing facts, and the fact is, we fell in love.'

Her face was a calm mask, the face of a stranger. 'I suppose we did, for a while. We had a good time, Philip, but *we* let things go too far.'

'That's crazy,' he said.

She winced at the loudness of his voice, and cast a quick glance around as if to make sure no one had heard. 'It's not crazy,' she insisted, her voice a half whisper. 'What's crazy is pretending this is going to work out. Pretending we are going to work out.'

'What are you saying? Of course this is going to work out. We have a plan.'

'It's a bad plan, and it was stupid of me to go along with it. We don't belong together, Philip. We never have. It just felt that way for the summer.'

Her words pounded at him. 'I don't believe you.' He reached for her hand, but she snatched it away. 'Something happened,' he said. 'Last night, you—we—' He couldn't find a way to describe how close they'd been without making it sound crude and cheap.

'Last night I was still lying,' she said, her gaze holding his with eerie steadiness. 'To you, and to myself.'

'No. You're lying *now*. You're scared because I'm leaving. But oh, baby, you don't have to worry about me. I made you a promise, and I intend to keep it. Of course I'll be back.'

Her gaze was steady as she looked at him.

360

'That's why I'm asking you—telling you—to respect my wishes and stay away. I don't want to be your girlfriend anymore, Philip. I had fun with you this summer, but things went too far.'

'We fell in love.'

'That was just something I said. Something we both said,' she explained, sounding weirdly older than her years, 'but we were both wrong. It was something that was never meant to last, and now it's over. I have other plans for my life. I'm going to travel, see new places, meet new people—'

'Of course you are, baby. With me. Didn't I say I'd take you anywhere you wanted to go?' Philip could hear the desperation in his own voice. He hated the sound of himself begging her, but he didn't know what else to do.

'You're not listening,' said Mariska. 'I don't want to see the world with you. You're a nice guy, Philip, and this summer was great, but now it's done. I should've had the guts to tell you sooner. Summer is over, and so are we. You need to go back to your life, and I need to get on with mine.'

'I don't have any life without you,' he said, his voice taut with intensity.

'Now you're being dramatic.' She clutched her purse against her stomach. Her thumbs, the nails bitten down, worried the strap as she spoke. 'You have school, and all your friends and any future you want for yourself. And your fiancée, Pamela.'

'I already told you. Pamela and I are done.' He felt sick to his stomach. 'I know what it is—you're mad because we had to sneak around all summer.'

'I'm not mad. You and I are from two completely different worlds, and we need to quit pretending that doesn't matter.' She gave a harsh, humorless laugh. 'Can you picture our families together? My people are Polish immigrants. Yours are Bellamys, for heaven's sake.'

'God, Mariska. Where is this stuff coming from?' A revelation hit him, and he slapped his forehead. 'This is all rehearsed, as if you're reciting it from a script you memorized. None of this is coming from you. Someone put you up to it.'

'Do you see me talking? Do you hear my voice? I'm finally saying what should have been said long ago. The thing I've been lying about all summer is us. I managed to convince myself that I wanted to be with you even though, deep down, I knew it would never work out between us. I'm done now. I don't want to pretend anymore.'

He didn't even know this girl. She was some stranger.

She stood up, holding her purse in front of her like a shield. 'I'm sorry for whatever pain this causes you, but I promise, it's only temporary. Goodbye, Philip.'

'Don't go.' He couldn't help himself. He got up and grabbed her arm, pulled her close. 'I won't let you go. Not now, not ever.'

'Enough,' she said, making a cutting motion with her hand. 'I'm breaking up with you, okay? It happens in every relationship except one. *The* one.'

'This is the one,' he said, growing furious with desperation.

'We both know better than that.' She regarded him with cold, empty eyes. Her expression was one he'd never seen before. 'I don't want this to turn ugly, Philip. I swear, I don't. But if you don't take your hands off me and let me go, I'll call for help.'

He heard the sound of cold steel in her voice. He backed off, dropping his hold on her. 'I'll come back for you.'

'I won't be here.' She turned sharply and walked away from him on the platform.

He hurried after her, reaching out again. 'Come on, Mariska. Don't throw this away.'

She stopped walking, jerked her arm out of reach as her eyes narrowed. 'You know, I was hoping I wouldn't have to be mean about this, but you're getting on my nerves now. We're done, period. I'm leaving now, and if you try to follow me, I'll accuse you of harassment. If you try to contact me, I won't take your calls or read your letters. Nothing, Philip. Swear to God.' Pivoting, she strode

363

with a curious stiff dignity to the concrete exit stairs.

He took a few steps toward her as though propelled by an invisible force. *We're done, period.* Her words rang in his head and he stopped. He couldn't call out to her because his throat was closing up with tears of shock and devastation. He felt himself going numb as she grew smaller and smaller, not hurrying but not looking back, descending the stairs and heading into the pedestrian tunnel that went under Main Street and disappearing without a trace.

The scream of the train's whistle split the air, making him jump. The engine approached with a hiss of steam and a grinding of brakes. With jerky, mechanical movements, Philip picked up his bag and waited for the train to stop. At the other end of the platform, Matthew Alger was kissing the Barnard girl. People picked up their bags and parcels, shuffled toward the edge of the platform. Philip hesitated, poised to flee. He had to go after Mariska, tell her she was making a mistake, convince her they belonged together.

A chic couple emerged from the station lobby and joined the passengers outside.

The Lightseys, Philip realized, with a dull thud of recognition. What completely lousy timing.

Gwen Lightsey spotted him immediately. 'Why, Philip,' she said, 'there you are. Your mother told me you'd be on the train today.'

'Hello, ma'am,' he said with a slight inclination of his head. Manners bubbling up like a thermal spring, he shook hands with Samuel Lightsey. 'How are you, sir?'

'Excellent, Philip.'

The brakes of the train hissed, drowning out all conversation momentarily. Philip stood aside as Mrs. Lightsey boarded, followed by her husband with their bags.

'Join us, dear,' Mrs. Lightsey called through a half-open window of the train. 'I've saved you a seat. We'll have a nice visit on the way back to the city, and we'll be there in no time.'

Mariska's words echoed inside his head. *It's over. I have other plans for my life.*

The conductor's whistle shrilled down the platform.

'Philip, do sit down, son.' Mr. Lightsey frowned. 'Did you forget something?'

My people are Polish immigrants. Yours are Bellamys, for heaven's sake.

The whistle sounded again. He curled his fist around the safety railing. Forcing one foot in front of the other, he went to the banquette seat facing the Lightseys. He stowed his bag overhead and took his seat.

Pamela's parents were the last people he wanted to see. The truth was, he didn't want to see anybody. Like a wounded wild animal, he wanted to curl up in the dark alone

365

somewhere and try to heal.

Instead, he found himself facing his parents' best friends. Mr. and Mrs. Lightsey were earnest and kind, people who had every reason to believe they would become his in-laws one day soon.

He was operating on autopilot, and doing a pretty good job of it, because they didn't seem to notice anything different about him. Apparently, having your heart stomped on and all your hopes and dreams shattered into a million pieces did not necessarily have any physical symptoms.

He heard a stranger talking about Yale, and his plan to work on the paper this year, and his hopes for the future. And then he realized that stranger was himself.

Mrs. Lightsey— 'Do call me Gwen,' she insisted—beamed at him, her trim, elegantly dressed figure swaying with the rhythm of the southbound train. Her jewelry was discreet and tasteful. A slender gold watch. A simple, brilliant diamond ring, a string of pearls, no more. Pamela had once told him that, given the Lightsey jewel fortune, her mother could drape herself in diamonds and gold. But of course, that would be vulgar. Just because you could didn't mean you should.

He leaned back and arranged his face into a pleasant expression as they spoke to him.

'We couldn't be happier with the way things are turning out,' she declared.

'Yes, ma'am.' He didn't know what else to say.

'Pamela is going to be so excited to see you,' Mrs. Lightsey concluded.

Philip smiled because he didn't know what else to do. 'Yes, ma'am,' he said, one final time.

I slept and dreamed that life was beauty.
I awoke—and found that life was duty.
—Ellen Sturgis Hooper, American poet

Twenty-Three

'That was the last I saw of Mariska,' Olivia's dad explained in a tired, distraught voice. 'She walked away from me that day and I never saw her again, never spoke to her.'

'Unbelievable,' Olivia said, trying to picture her father, young and desperate as the girl he loved left him. 'If you loved her that much, why didn't you try getting in touch with her? Why didn't you just miss your train that day?'

He rubbed his forehead as though it ached. 'Shock, I suppose. And something about her...she convinced me that she was done. Of course, once I got back to school, I called her again and again. I wrote letters, sent a telegram, even took the train back to Avalon one weekend. Finally her mother said Mariska was gone, told me to quit trying to get in touch with her.'

'So Mariska's mother knew what was going on?'

'Maybe. I don't know. I suppose I'll never even know if Mariska realized by then that she was pregnant, or if she was really done with me.' He shook his head. 'I should never have believed the things she said to me that day. I should have believed the things she *didn't* say. Her body language, her nervousness, the way she'd chewed off all her fingernails.'

Olivia's head was spinning. She knew he was only giving her the bare bones of the story, glossing over the details. But the fact was, he had been in love with Mariska Majesky.

'So did you keep that engagement with Mother just to hedge your bets?'

'It wasn't like that.' He stared at the sky out the window of his apartment. 'I'm not proud of the way I handled the situation, and being young was no excuse for being stupid.'

'What did you tell Mother when you saw her again?'

'I said we should end the engagement. That I didn't think my heart was still in it.'

'You didn't think?' Olivia demanded, furious now. 'You had the whole summer to think about it. By the time you discussed it with my mother, you should've known.'

'I did know,' he admitted.

She glanced at the photo on the table and winced. What hurt her the most was not that he had been with someone else while engaged to her mother. What hurt the most was how happy he had been with Mariska. Olivia had never, ever seen him that happy.

'Sweetheart,' he said, 'tell me what you're thinking.'

'Believe me, you don't want to know.'

'Let me be the judge of that. There are already too many secrets.'

369

'Fine,' she said. 'If you want to know, it's that when I look at this picture, I feel envious. I wish you could have been this happy with Mom.'

'You're reading too much into a snapshot,' he said. 'Everybody looks that way when they're young, with their whole life in front of them.' He put his hand over hers. 'I tried—your mother and I both tried—for a long time to make it work.'

She drew her hand away. Despite the warmth of the summer day, his fingers felt cold. 'After you told Mother the engagement was off, did she...what? Force you to marry her anyway? I don't get it, Dad. You're leaving something out here.'

He looked out the window again. 'Your mother was not...amenable to ending the engagement. At her request, we went back to school and still acted like a couple. Just for a few days, she told me. But then things changed between us. They got better. I remembered why I started dating your mother in the first place, why I proposed to her. She was—still is—beautiful and intelligent and thoughtful.'

'And she was conveniently available, don't forget,' Olivia said.

'I wasn't much for being alone those days.'

'It's better than being with the wrong person.'

'You're smarter than I was.' He looked her

370

in the eye. 'Listen. I'm sorry those engagements didn't work out. I'm sorry you got hurt. But I'm proud of you, proud that you knew enough to stop things. And that you have the courage to wait for something real, something deep enough to last a lifetime.'

Despite her anger at him, Olivia felt a flash of understanding. The day she and Rand had broken up, her father had spoken with surprising insight: *There's a kind of love that has the power to save you, to get you through life. It's like breathing. You have to do it or you'll die. And when it's over, your soul starts to bleed, Livvy. There's no pain in the world like it, I swear.*

Now, finally, she knew exactly where that insight had come from. Her father had been there. These words were not just platitudes. He was speaking from personal experience. He had once loved like that. Only, the object of that love had been a stranger. Mariska Majesky.

'I wanted to make your mother happy,' he said. 'I wanted to deserve her. I wanted it more than anything. Sometimes if you want something badly enough, you make it happen through sheer force of will.'

'God. Hadn't you learned anything?' she asked in frustration. 'Hadn't Mother? You married in December 1977. Why the rush? You were both so young, you had law school ahead of you—' She broke off, seeing his gaze

371

shift toward the ceiling. 'You have to tell me, Dad. I know too much already.'

He hesitated for a long, searching moment. He looked so old to her then. When had her handsome, vital, man-about-town father turned into a weary old man? Finally he took a deep breath. 'This is your mother's story, too.'

'And it's mine, damn it,' Olivia snapped. 'I deserve to know.' She couldn't imagine what he was protecting her mother from.

'Your mother never thought you should know.'

'Don't make me call her,' Olivia said. 'Don't do that to her.'

He paused, took a breath. 'There was...a baby.'

The words delivered a sucker punch to Olivia. 'What?'

'Your mother and I were trying for a reconciliation. We thought things would work out for us. She was, um, she was pregnant when we got married. No one knew why we moved up the wedding date. The baby would be 'premature,' as people said in those days, but we were happy about the news.' He pressed his fingertips together, staring at the empty space between his hands. 'Then, a couple of weeks after the wedding, Pamela miscarried. It was a sad, hard time for us both.'

Olivia could only imagine. The marriage had been an imperfect structure built on the shakiest of foundations—a guilty, heartsick young man, an ambitious woman determined to make the 'right' match for the wrong reasons. They had probably pinned all their hopes on the baby they'd made, and when the baby ceased to exist, they were left trying to keep their crumbling marriage intact.

'You know, Dad, I'm not big on karma and destiny, but I have to say, you might have interpreted the miscarriage as a sign.'

'A sign of what? That we never should've married in the first place, or that we should work harder to love each other?' He let out a protracted sigh. 'You wanted to know what happened, and I told you. I wish the marriage had turned out better, but I sure as hell don't regret it, because it gave me you.'

Despite her anger and frustration with her father, Olivia felt a twinge. She reminded herself why she was here. 'And your thing with Mariska gave you Jenny Majesky.'

His face looked gray with shock and regret.

'What are you going to do about that?'

'Well, first of all, I'm going to thank you for telling me.'

'Why wouldn't I tell you?'

'You're an only child. My sole heir. The fact that there might be a sibling changes that status.'

She gave a brief laugh. She was feeling so many conflicting emotions—resentment, that both her parents had hidden so much from her. Envy, that her father had been happier with another woman. And yes, fear that the existence of another daughter was shaking her world. But not for the reasons her father thought. 'Believe me, my inheritance is the last thing on my mind. And you still haven't answered my question.'

'There are a lot of things I have to do,' he said. 'I need to check on some things, then come up to Avalon to meet her and verify the fact that I'm her biological father, figure out if she knows about me. Find out where Mariska is. What if Jenny was raised by a man she believes to be her father?'

'From what I've found out, it seems she was raised by her grandparents.'

'Maybe so, but she might believe someone else is her father. What would it do to that family, my just showing up to claim her? I want to do the right thing, but I don't want to hurt any more people than I already have.'

Olivia nodded. 'Why do I feel like I need a drink?'

He stood up and went to the bar. 'It's five o'clock somewhere.'

Twenty-Four

'My dad's going to be a pain in the ass about this,' Daisy muttered to Julian. The two of them had spent the morning raking load after load of pebbles onto the main path leading from the lodge to the dock. When the guests showed up for the celebration, they'd have a brand-new pathway to walk on. She wondered if anyone would appreciate that Julian had deposited at least a dozen wheelbarrows full of pebbles, while she had raked them in place. They had worked fast, wanting to finish before lunch.

'Maybe he'll surprise you,' Julian suggested, tossing his shovel and work gloves into the wheelbarrow. He took a long swig from his water bottle.

His T-shirt was soaked with sweat and his cargo shorts slung low around his hips, the pockets loaded with Lord knew what sort of gear. Guy stuff. When guys got all grubby from hard work, they actually looked good. Not girls, though. She was damp and cranky. 'God,' she said, 'I'm already seventeen. I cannot wait until I can quit asking permission for every damn thing in the world.' She caught a glimpse of Julian's face as he put the cap back on the water bottle. Oh, man. 'I'm sorry, Julian.' She didn't know what else to say.

'Sorry about what?' His eyes narrowed suspiciously. He had beautiful eyes, olive colored, that looked wonderful in contrast to his creamy brown skin.

'Complaining to you about my dad. Olivia told me what happened to your father and…God, I'm really sorry.'

He nodded, his face unreadable. 'Don't worry about it. If my old man was still around, I'd be complaining about him, too.'

She peeled off her work gloves and tossed them into the wheelbarrow. 'You are too good to be true, do you know that?'

He laughed. 'I can honestly say no one has ever said that about me. Not even close.'

'Then no one ever saw you the way I do,' she said, wiping her hands on her jeans. She had an urge to touch him, maybe take his hand or something, but she didn't. She and Julian were in a good place together—just friends without all the craziness of trying to hook up, and she didn't want to mess with that. 'So anyway, if you ever feel like talking about it—or anything—I'm a good listener.'

'That's true,' he said. 'You are.'

'Why do I hear surprise in your voice when you say that?'

He laughed again. 'Well, look at you.'

She knew what he was saying. When most people looked at her, they saw blond hair and big boobs, a girl who liked to party. Very few bothered to look deeper than that. She put the

376

gravel rake and the rest of the tools into the wheelbarrow, and he pushed it up the new path. The gravel made a satisfying crunching sound under their feet.

'Are you sure you want to do this?' she asked as they put everything into the shed.

'What the hell. I might as well see what it's about.'

She studied him, the face that looked like it ought to be on billboards for edgy male fashions, the lanky form, the amazing hair. He was amazing, period. Under different circumstances, she might let herself have a major crush on him, but not now. Not when her family was exploding. Right now, it was all she could do to like herself, much less a boy. 'All right,' she said. 'Let's go ask my dad.'

They found him and Max busily digging and planting a small garden plot between the two biggest cabins. 'Dad,' she called. 'Hey, Dad. Mr. Davis is taking us to Kingston to—What are you guys doing?'

Greg straightened up, took off his baseball cap and wiped the sweat from his brow. He gestured at the freshly turned earth. 'Planting a memorial garden.'

She looked at him, and then at Max. Her brother did his best to emulate their dad, peeling off his own cap, wiping his brow. 'Memorial to what?' she asked.

'Bullwinkle,' Max said simply. 'And Yogi. And all their friends.'

'The trophy heads,' Dad explained.

Daisy felt a twitch of humor. 'You buried the trophy heads. The ones that were in the main hall.'

'Yep. And we're planting photinia and salvia for a memorial,' Max said.

'The heads creeped him out,' Dad explained.

'Hey, me, too,' Julian said, giving Max a high five.

'They creeped everyone out.' Daisy had never liked the dead glass eyes, the bared teeth, the moth-eaten hides. 'Nobody wants to look at a moose trophy head or a stuffed wildcat. But we have about five Dumpsters around here,' she added. 'You could have just thrown them away.'

'We gave them a proper burial. To show respect,' Dad said.

One thing about her dad. He always managed to startle her. She'd spent more time with him this summer than she had in years, but she still hadn't quite figured him out. 'Okaay,' she said. 'So is it all right if we go to Kingston?'

'What's in Kingston?' Dad asked.

Always with the questions. She was so sick of the third degree. 'Dad—'

'Sir,' Julian said, 'Mr. Davis—Connor's father—offered to give us a lift because there's an air force recruiting office in Kingston. I'm looking into signing up for the

378

ROTC. To pay for college.'

Daisy almost laughed at the way her dad's jaw unhinged. He was so used to her slacker guy friends, he wasn't even sure what to do about a boy who showed a little initiative.

'Well,' Dad said. 'Well, that's commendable, I suppose.'

'I give Daisy the credit,' Julian said. 'Never even thought about going to college, but maybe there's a way for that to happen.'

'Good job, Daze,' her dad said. 'Now, how about your own plans for college?'

She glowered at him. 'I knew that was coming.'

'And?'

'And, in case you forgot, you're sending me to a school that makes getting into college a graduation requirement.'

'Really?'

'Well, almost.'

'Good. Then maybe I won't gripe about the tuition bills so much.'

*   *   *

When he went to pick Olivia up later that afternoon, Connor saw that she and her father were waiting for him in the lobby of the building. From a distance, they resembled the usual elegant, WASPy residents of the Upper East Side, successful and self-possessed, confident of their place in the world. Yet when

379

he went to introduce himself, Connor saw that the rich weren't that different after all. Just like anyone else, they made mistakes, hurt each other and hid things.

Philip was tall and slim, wearing expensive-looking shoes, every hair in place. As Olivia made the introductions, Connor had only a flicker of recall. He'd seen Mr. Bellamy once or twice back when they were kids, on Parents' Day at camp.

'I appreciate you driving Olivia to the city,' Philip said.

'Not at all,' Connor replied. He felt awkward, tongue-tied. What the hell did you say to a guy who just learned he had a grown daughter? Congratulations?

Bellamy wasn't exactly passing out the cigars. 'Olivia tells me you're doing a great restoration job up at the camp. I know my parents will be delighted.'

'I hope so.'

'We should go,' Olivia said. 'Try to miss the worst of the traffic.' She lifted up on tiptoe and kissed her father's cheek. 'I'll be in touch, okay?'

'Sure, sweetheart. Thanks for coming.' Then he added, 'I love you.'

'I love you too, Dad.'

Connor helped her into the car and went around to the driver's side. Just watching her in this uptown world of doormen and delivery entrances reminded him of the differences in their lives. She had become the woman she was meant to be, privileged and purposeful. He wondered why she didn't seem to be happier about it. Sure, the meeting with her father had probably been intense, but it wasn't that bad, finding out your parent had a past. People did stupid things all the time, and their loved ones had to endure the fallout. God knew, he was proof of that.

He waited until they crossed into Jersey and headed north until the traffic thinned, and then he started to pry. 'Talk to me.'

She stared straight ahead. 'Not now.'

'You should talk to me.' He knew firsthand that hiding things and keeping secrets never worked.

'If it's all the same to you…'

'All right, new topic.' He balanced his hand at the top of the steering wheel. 'Do you and your dad always say goodbye like that?'

'Like what?'

'By saying you love each other. Or is it because of today?'

'It's habit. Why do you ask?'

'No reason. Just that…it's nice. In my family, people don't really talk like that to each other.'

'You don't tell people that you love them?'

He laughed. 'Honey, that is a foreign concept in my family.'

'Loving each other, or saying it?'

He stared straight ahead, concentrating on

the road. 'I've never said it,' he told her.

'Never said I love you?' she asked.

Shit, he thought. Should have left well enough alone.

'Is that because you've never actually loved someone, or because you haven't said the words?'

'Both, I guess.'

'That's sad.'

'I don't feel sad. It just feels normal.'

'Normal not to love your family?'

'Now you make me sound like a sociopath.' And how the hell did they get on the topic of *his* family?

'I don't mean to. And I think you're full of baloney, too. For someone who claims he doesn't love his family, you've done a lot of loving things.'

He laughed again. 'Yeah, right.' And with that, blessed silence filled the car. He found a station he liked and turned up the radio as it played, appropriately enough, '500 Miles' by the Proclaimers. Connor wanted to kick himself for having let the conversation veer out of control. He never talked with anyone the way he talked with Olivia Bellamy. It seemed to be as true now as it had when he was a kid.

The silence lasted at least a dozen miles and finally, she seemed ready to talk about what had happened. She turned sideways on the seat, drew up one smooth, bare leg and propped her elbow on the seat back. 'Okay, my dad had a sleazy affair while he was engaged to my mother, and he fathered a child he never knew about until today. Then, instead of breaking his engagement with my mother, he got her pregnant and had to marry her after all, and then she had a miscarriage. I just found that out, so forgive me if I'm not bubbling over with news for you.'

Connor cautioned himself not to be distracted by the bare leg, which put him in danger of driving off the road. He forced himself to focus on what she was saying, without showing any sort of surprise or judgment. He used to think people like his mother made terrible life choices because they lacked education and opportunity. Philip Bellamy was proof that stupid choices could cross barriers of wealth, education, class. When it came to matters of the heart, even a genius like Louis Gastineaux could blow it.

'I'm sorry,' he told Olivia. None of this was her fault, yet she was the one who'd gotten hurt. 'I want you to know, I do care, and if there's some way for me to help, then I'm all ears.'

'You drove me to the city today when I could have taken the train. I'd hardly call that nothing.'

'I was glad to do it,' he told her.

'I sure hope I did the right thing. I mean, Mariska never once contacted my father.

Never said a word about Jenny to him. Maybe she had a reason for that.'

'You did what you did. Now the ball is in your dad's court—his problem, not yours,' Connor said philosophically. He turned off the main road. 'Executive decision. We're going to make a stop in Phoenicia.' With a boardwalk lined with antique and curio shops and cafés, the small, picturesque town attracted tourists and collectors.

'I know you're trying to distract me, to make me feel better,' Olivia said.

'So sue me.' He parked and got out of the car, went around and opened the door for her.

'Thanks, but your plan is not going to work.'

'It will if you let it.'

She grabbed her bag, smiling with an obvious effort. 'Why are you really doing this?'

'You said the dining room looked bare and you wanted new chairs for the reception area.' He placed his hand at the small of her back and guided her to the Artisan and Antique Warehouse, which was an old red barn with an ancient ad for Mail Pouch Tobacco still visible on the side.

'I didn't say I needed them today, but—' She broke off and looked around the co-op of craftspeople and collectors, whose open booths shared the huge, airy space. 'This is incredible,' she said, examining a collection of

384

vintage lamps. 'It's exactly what I need. There, I said it. I'm shallow and horrible. I just found out my dad has another daughter, and yet the prospect of buying a wrought-iron lamp has managed to make me feel better.'

'Quit being so hard on yourself. That isn't good for anything or anybody. Your dad made his share of mistakes in the past but he's still your dad. He said he'd be here next week. Sitting around and wringing your hands isn't going to help anyone.'

She took a deep breath as though bracing herself for something painful. 'I might as well go for it, then.'

They found everything from old spinning wheels to yard gnomes. There was a booth entirely devoted to salvaged architectural items. A twisted wrought-iron stairway led to an open loft with a display of vintage Catskills travel posters.

Olivia quickly bought several of them, and that was only the beginning. Connor finally got a glimpse of Olivia Bellamy, founder of her own firm, in full-on work mode. She introduced herself to a salesperson. She was decisive and made swift choices. In a remarkably short time, she acquired some major treasures—the posters for the dining hall, lamps and light fixtures, an antique table made of peeled pine logs for the reception area. She ordered bent-willow porch furniture, including a traditional hanging bed, for the lodge she was preparing for her grandparents. She even found a tall, leather-bound hotel register which had only a few entries on the first page, the last one dated 1929, which she wanted to use as a guest book. The saleswoman tallied everything up and arranged for delivery.

'You're sexy when you're like this,' Connor said.

'Nothing like a little retail therapy when you find out about your father's secret life.' She was trying to be flip, but he could see her vulnerability in the almost imperceptible trembling of her lip. Sometimes, he thought, it was easy enough to forget she had endured so much heartbreak, but he'd always been able to see her, even when others couldn't.

'So it happened,' he said, wishing he could take away her hurt. 'You and your family will survive this.'

'Why do you keep trying to make me feel better?'

'Because it sucks for you, the things you found out today, and there's no fixing any of them. And because I like you.'

'You like me,' she repeated.

'That's what I said.'

'How?'

'What?'

'How do you like me? As a person you feel sorry for because I just found out some really bad news? As someone you've been working

386

with this summer? As an ex-girlfriend you still have old feelings for?'

'Close. As an ex-girlfriend I have new feelings for.' There. He'd said it. Probably not the best timing in the world, but he wanted to put the concept out there.

'*Feelings.* That is such a broad term,' she said, visibly bristling with mistrust.

'That's why guys like it. Lots of ways to interpret or misinterpret.'

'I see. So later, when you break my heart, I'll say, I thought you said you loved me and you'll say, no, I said I had *feelings* for you, and we'll argue about that, about what you said and what you meant.'

'You're assuming I'm going to break your heart.'

'You're assuming you won't.'

'Nice attitude, Lolly.' He thought about her three failed engagements. She was gun-shy for sure.

'You never did say what you meant by feelings, and I'm not supposed to notice that. Well, guess what? I noticed.'

Connor swore softly and shoved a splayed hand through his hair. 'When I say I have feelings for you,' he told her with exaggerated patience, 'it means exactly what you think it means.'

She did a quick scan of the barn, and he knew she was checking to see if anyone had heard. Sure enough, two women looking at fruit-crate labels had their heads together as they whispered something to each other. There were three more women examining old table linens a few booths away. An older man scurried away as though to avoid being tagged as a witness.

Olivia flushed red. 'We'll talk about this later.'

Connor didn't give a shit who was listening. 'We'll talk about this now,' he said. 'They're my feelings. I'll choose when to talk about them.'

'Maybe we could discuss this in the car—'

'Maybe we can discuss this right now.' He felt himself getting pissed. This was what had ruined them before, her insistence that other people's opinions mattered. 'It's simple. When I said I have feelings for you, I meant that I think about you all the time. I wonder what it would feel like to hold you in my arms again. I start to think every sad breakup song on the radio is about us. Just a whiff of your perfume makes me horny, and I can't stop thinking about—'

'Stop,' she said, her voice an urgent hiss. 'I can't believe you're talking like this in...in public. You have to stop.'

'For God's sake,' murmured one of the shoppers in the linen booth, 'don't stop.'

Connor tried not to grin. He was enjoying this way too much.

Olivia wasn't; her face turned even redder.

'What's it going to take to shut you up?' she asked.

He spread his arms, palms out, and surrendered. 'Give me something else to do with my mouth.'

She surprised him—and probably herself—when she took his head between her hands and kissed him full on the mouth. She tasted like heaven, but he could feel her pulling back way too soon. He slid his arms around her and held her in place, taking control of the kiss, deepening it until he felt her resistance soften and then dissolve. He would have stood there all day in the dimly lit barn, kissing her, but after a while, she pulled back, staring up at him. She seemed to have forgotten where they were, what people might think.

'Anyway,' he said, continuing the conversation as though he'd never been interrupted, 'I guess you got your answer.'

'What answer?'

'That's pretty much what I mean when I say I have feelings for you.'

Twenty-Five

Olivia's head was spinning as she followed him out of the antiques barn. She felt herself being swept away, the way she'd been swept away by their kiss. She couldn't believe she'd done that in a public place, just grabbed him and started kissing him. It wasn't the sort of thing she did or even thought about doing—until a few minutes ago.

As they headed to Avalon, she kept quiet, though she was replaying his entire too-loud speech in her head. Though she hadn't trusted herself to say anything, she knew she had feelings for him, too. But she hadn't figured out what those feelings were, beyond raw lust.

'I'm hungry,' Connor said. 'Let's get dinner.'

'We really should be getting back,' she said.

'We're going to dinner,' he stated.

'Fine,' she said. If he wanted to stop somewhere for a burger, she was okay with that. She sensed that resistance was futile. And she admitted to herself that it was a relief to surrender, just for today. She, the queen of all control freaks, was going to surrender to Connor Davis. It felt good, relinquishing control. Because it also absolved her of responsibility.

He took her to a place called the Apple Tree Inn, an historic converted farmhouse in the middle of an orchard, with the river on one side and the road on the other. A small red neon sign in the window said, Dinner and Dancing Nightly. Inside were comfortable chairs and candlelit tables with views of an apple orchard and the river. There were warm wooden floors and deep golden lighting. The hostess led them to a table in a corner that was washed by the colors of the setting sun streaming through the windows.

Okay, Olivia thought, so he had something more in mind than a burger and fries. She eyed Connor suspiciously. This was a date restaurant. Were they on a date?

'Enjoy your meal, Mr. Davis,' said the hostess as Connor held out a chair for Olivia.

'She just called you Mr. Davis.'

A date restaurant where they knew Connor's name. Olivia said, 'Did you do construction work here? Is that how they know you?' The moment the words were out of her mouth, she knew she'd done it again. 'Oh, God,' she said. 'I didn't mean...I meant...'

'That you can't conceive of me actually being a guest at this place?' he suggested.

Yes. That had been exactly what she meant, and he clearly knew it. Mercifully, he didn't seem insulted at all. Instead, he gave her a smile that caused her heart to speed up.

The sommelier stopped by the table. 'Will you be having wine tonight?' he asked.

'Definitely,' Connor said. 'Do you have a preference?' he asked Olivia.

'White, please,' she said automatically.

'A bottle of the Hamilton Russell Chardonnay.'

391

Olivia was surprised. Most of the men she dated had fancied themselves wine aficionados, but they were always clueless, covering it up by ordering according to the menu price. Connor, on the other hand, had chosen a genuinely excellent bottle of wine from South Africa. Maybe that was a coincidence, but maybe not. Maybe he knew what he was doing. Every time she turned around, this man surprised her.

The food was perfection, beautifully arranged on thick white china plates. They had buttered filets of rainbow trout, locally grown produce, cups of huckleberries for dessert. While they ate, darkness fell and the moon came up, and a trio arrived to perform on drums, piano and clarinet. Olivia let the soothing sounds of the ensemble flow over her as she sipped the last of her wine.

'Thank you,' she said quietly to Connor.

'You're welcome.'

'I'm not sure what I would've done without you today.'

'You've done fine without me for years.' He held out his hand, palm up. 'Dance with me.'

The three little words should not have had the power to make her heart flip over in her chest. And yet that was her reaction, that and a flustered intake of breath.

Rather than waiting for her to answer, he took her hand, drew her to her feet and out onto the dance floor. 'Do I make you nervous?'

'Do I seem nervous?'

'Yeah.'

'This is sort of…unexpected.'

'What's unexpected?'

'That we seem to be attracted to one another, that this project has turned into…more than a job. I didn't expect that. Did you?'

'Hell, yeah, I did.' He seemed incredulous that she would question it. 'So now you're starting to feel a little bit turned on by me, right?'

She swallowed past a sudden dryness in her throat and said, 'I'm not starting to feel that way.' She had to swallow again before she could tell him the rest. 'I started a long time ago.'

The couples around them, regardless of age, were all doing their own version of old-fashioned couples dancing. Olivia lost sight of everything except Connor. Under her left hand, she could feel the muscles of his arm. The brush of his hand against her was a wicked temptation. He led smoothly and with confidence. He even hummed along with the music, and initiated some risky turns and dips. He still had a nice voice, still had perfect pitch the way he had as a kid, the first summer she'd met him.

It was tempting to stay here with him and

dance all night, but at the end of the number, she said, 'We really should be going.'

'Why? Do you have a curfew?'

'Worse. I have a cousin. Nosiest cousin in the world, and I'm sharing a cabin with her.'

'Not to worry,' Connor said. 'She's on a date with Freddy tonight.'

'How do you know that?'

'I told them about the Jerry Lewis film festival at the drive-in movie in Coxsackie. Free Bobble Heads and everything.'

He made her laugh. She could not remember the last time she'd been on a date with a guy who made her laugh. One thing she did remember was how sexy that could be.

They danced through one more number, and then Connor said, 'All right, Cinderella. Let's roll.'

Against all expectations, she was feeling more relaxed and hopeful after the wine, the dancing, the laughter. 'All right,' she said, tilting back her head to look up at him. 'Let's roll.'

She buckled herself into the seat beside him, her purse in her lap. Olivia took a deep breath, shut her eyes, leaned her head against the headrest.

'You all right?' Connor asked.

'I'm all right,' she said softly. She smiled, surprising herself because it was a genuine smile. She tried to figure out what she was feeling. Safety. That was it. She was with a man who made her laugh and made her feel safe. What a concept.

Then she opened her eyes and glanced over at him. Out here on the country road, there were no streetlights, so she could barely make out his profile in the glow from the console. The road at night was alarmingly busy with wildlife. Deer, raccoon, opossum and badger seemed to haunt the verges, often wandering out onto the pavement. 'Careful,' she said.

'I'm always careful.'

They entered the city limits, lumbering over the railroad tracks. The train station and town square were artfully illuminated by floodlights. The bed-and-breakfast inns beckoned, warm and inviting, with lights in the windows, and Vacancy signs glowing softly.

'This place rolls up its sidewalks early,' Olivia observed.

'Seems to.'

'That shouldn't bother me. Most weeknights, I make an early night of it.' Rand used to bug her about that. He loved to stay out late, trolling from club to club, feeling the reverberations of a deep bass beat, sighting people he knew and engaging in shouted, pointless conversations with them over pricey drinks delivered by beautiful waitresses. The next day, he rarely remembered whom he'd run into. He could never recall what was said during those lengthy, earnest discussions.

In Avalon's town square, they passed the shop front of the Sky River Bakery. The hanging sign had a small spotlight shining on it. Through the display window, she could see the shadowy hulks of display cases and coffee equipment, and a security light blinking steadily in conjunction with the alarm system.

'A burglar alarm at a bakery,' she said. 'I don't get it. Especially since they're just a few doors down from Palmquist Jewelry. If I was a thief, I'd go for the jewels, not the doughnuts.'

'You've obviously never had a maple bar from Majesky's.'

'That good, huh?'

He glanced over at her. 'Like a small orgasm.'

Yikes, she thought. This was flirting. They'd gone on a date and now they were flirting.

The lights of Avalon fell away as they headed up the mountain. En route, they passed a few farmhouses with lights glimmering in their windows. Then, after a long stretch of darkness, they came to the turnoff for Connor's place, marked by reflective numbers on his mailbox. 'Home, sweet home,' he murmured.

'Do you miss it?' she asked.

'Nope. I like staying at the camp. What about you? Do you miss your place in the city?'

'I thought I would, but I don't,' she

admitted. 'Not one bit.' She was trying to figure out the reason for that. Was it because she knew the summer was speeding by, and she'd soon be home? Or because she'd found something better?

The truck whispered past the turnoff.

'I've never seen your place,' she commented. *God, Olivia. Could you be any more obvious?*

'Would you like to?'

'I've never even seen the inside of an Airstream.'

'Then I have no choice.' He stopped right in the middle of the road and put the car in Reverse. 'It's a matter of honor.'

'Good point,' she said, and smiled into the darkness.

Her pulse sped up as he turned down the gravel road, although she pretended as hard as she could that this was strictly about satisfying her curiosity about the Airstream. Connor parked the car and cut the engine. She thought it was significant that he cut the engine.

Before she could let herself out, he was there, opening the door and giving her a hand. His touch felt so good. Solid and strong. And the mellow warmth of the wine still lingered. She felt so at ease with this man, as though nothing bad could happen to her as long as she was with him.

He opened the door and turned on a light. She stepped inside and saw that everything was neat and stowed. There was a diner-style booth and cupboards in the kitchen area, a two-burner range top and small fridge. The sitting area comprised a banquette with a low table in front of it and a TV and stereo anchored on a shelf. Then there was a narrow passageway with more cupboards, which she assumed led to the bedroom in the back.

Olivia was struck by the Spartan neatness of the place. She felt him watching her and realized she was staring. She smiled. 'I was psychoanalyzing you based on the way you've organized everything.'

'Yeah?' He turned and took something from the fridge. 'So am I a serial killer? A cross-dresser?'

'Neither,' she said. 'My degree is in psychology. I can tell.'

'Then what?'

'At first I thought obsessive-compulsive, but it's not that. Ex-military?'

He didn't say anything.

That wasn't it. She wondered if he was inclined to be so meticulous because of his chaotic childhood. Perhaps, out of a sense of self-preservation, he had been a very organized child, as careful with his belongings as he had been reserved with his emotions. Connor never said much about his life, and lately, she felt something more than nosiness. She wanted to know him, period. Not as a kid or a high-school crush, but as an adult. 'Is it because you moved around a lot? Maybe you developed a habit of being neat in order to keep track of everything?'

'Never thought about it. If everything is where it belongs, then you never have to think.'

She suspected there was more to it. Maybe it was the only way to deal with the chaos of his mother's life—the emotional roller coaster she seemed addicted to, her self-absorbed hunger for attention and approval, her disregard for her sons. 'That's not a very revealing answer,' she said.

'Neither is saying you were a psychology major. This is the purpose of dating, Lolly. To get to know each other.'

'Wait a minute. Dating? Who says we're dating?'

'This feels like a date,' he said simply. 'Dinner, dancing, a nightcap at my place.' He took out two slender, stemmed glasses. 'To me, that spells date.'

'We skipped over the asking out and primping and getting nervous beforehand.'

'Yeah, who needs that?' He popped the cork on a bottle of Moscato and poured two glasses.

She sipped her wine and focused on four framed photographs, lined up on a narrow shelf above the built-in table. In one, Connor stood with his arm draped around his father's shoulders as they stood side by side in front of

399

a rock wall, with gardens and angular brick buildings behind them. Terry Davis appeared thin and haggard, with pale skin and dark circles under his eyes. Connor looked heartbreakingly young, like the boy she'd known years ago.

'Where was it taken?'

'That's at a treatment center. The last one he attended.'

'I'm really happy for you and your dad,' she said. 'You must be proud of him.'

'Yeah. I am.' For a moment, he looked as though he might tell her more, but then seemed to change his mind.

Olivia forbade herself to dig deeper, knowing he'd suffered horribly, growing up with a father who was an alcoholic. Not now, she thought. Connor was calling this a date. Bringing up old wounds would only spoil it. She thought about how different their lives had been, how sharply their paths had diverged. She'd always blamed the rift on the way he'd treated her, their last summer together, but that wasn't it. Their directions had changed. She had entered the granite halls and tree-shaded quadrangles of Columbia, while he had been obliged to look after a man who was supposed to take care of him.

'You like the Moscato?' he asked.

She took a sip of the effervescent wine. 'It's delicious.' She studied a picture of a

400

woman she'd never seen, whose gorgeous face was oddly mesmerizing. 'Your mother?' she asked.

'That's her.'

'She does look like Sharon Stone. You told me once that she did, and you're right.'

Connor didn't reply. In addition to being beautiful, she looked enigmatic, her eyes hard to read. Olivia wanted to know more about this woman, about Connor's fractured family, but she didn't know how to ask and yes, yet again, she didn't trust herself to know what to say. Chicken, she thought, then indicated a long paper tube tucked into the shelf. Maybe this was safer territory. 'Are those blueprints?'

He hesitated, then nodded. 'You can check them out if you want.'

Curious, she unrolled the bundle, weighing down the corners with salt and pepper shakers, a napkin holder. 'House plans,' she said.

'I'm going to break ground this fall,' he said, 'and be done by next fall.'

Finally, she understood. The Airstream was only temporary. He was going to build this house, right here on this lot. From the elevation drawings, she could picture the finished place, situated in the brow of the hill, with a wraparound porch overlooking the river. The stone-and-timber construction had a subtly old-fashioned tone that would harmonize perfectly with the landscape. 'This

401

looks absolutely beautiful,' she said, studying the kitchen layout, the great room and fireplace.

'Thanks.'

'What's this?' She pointed to the plans.

'I think the current trend is to call it a garden room. Like a sunroom. With library shelves.'

She could even make out the small, irregular shape of a baby grand. 'You're still musical,' she said.

'Aren't you?'

'Not as much as I'd like.' She was going to explain that her tiny apartment had no room for a piano, but it was more than that. Her days were so busy, she had no time to give to playing the piano, even though she loved it. For some reason, seeing the house he wanted to build for himself made her feel a strange tug of...yearning? Recognition, maybe. Creating the place where you wanted to live your life was something she could relate to. Returning her attention to the floor plan, she asked, 'Four bedrooms?'

'You never know,' he said.

She bit her lip, stopping herself from asking what she really wanted to know. *Why isn't there someone special in your life to share this with?* There were a number of things that astonished her about Connor's plans. But the thing that surprised her the most, the thing that maybe even scared her, was that these plans reflected things she'd wanted for herself. All right, so maybe her dreams were not unique, but still, it was strangely thrilling that he had unknowingly designed her dream house.

'You have a talented architect,' she said inanely.

'No, I don't. These are my original plans.'

They looked every bit as precisely engineered as the plans made by a degreed architect, one with a special gift for design.

He laughed. 'Don't look so shocked, Lolly. There's a local engineering firm that lets me use their blueline machine. Is it so unbelievable that I could be self-taught?'

She had done it again. She had completely underestimated this man. She'd let surface appearances dictate what she thought of him. He had grown up poor, the product of a broken home, the son of a drunk and a difficult woman. She hadn't let herself see beyond that. Now she realized there was so much more to him. Life hadn't given him very many breaks, yet he'd made good, with an equity fund, a viable company and this God-given talent most architects had to study for years in order to achieve. She felt vaguely ashamed. Even knowing what she knew about him, she'd still thought of him as a biker who lived in a trailer. She hadn't bothered to look any deeper.

'Well,' she said.' Well. I'm intrigued.'

'Good,' he replied. 'Take off your clothes.'

'What?' Her cheeks flamed.

He laughed. 'Just checking.'

'Checking for what?'

'To see if being intrigued is enough.'

'Not funny,' she snapped.

'But you're still intrigued.'

'I might be.'

'Good,' he said. 'That's a start, then.'

'A start for what?'

'For this.' He kissed her, his movements slow and deliberate, completely in control.

Her response was anything but. The instant he touched his mouth to hers, it felt like a match touching dry kindling. She half expected to hear a whoosh as her hair ignited. He tasted of wine, and she parted her lips, wordlessly begging him to deepen his kiss. His hands cupped her shoulders and then slid down her arms and behind her back. She clung to him with a physical need she'd never felt before. What was it about this man, what made her so desperate to feel every inch of him against her? This, she thought, half-afraid, half in wonder, this was what had eluded her through far too many dates, through three failed romances. This sense that one man could obliterate the rest of the world. His kiss, the touch of his hands, took her somewhere far away, to a place of dreams.

He walked her backward a few steps through a narrow passageway. The room was dark, the louvered windows letting in a pine-scented breeze. She sank backward on the bed, keeping her arms around him.

'Damn,' he whispered, 'I think you're sexy as hell, Lolly.'

Oh, she wanted him, she wanted to be as sexy as he thought she was. It occurred to her that when she was with him, she was no longer Olivia, the three-time loser, Olivia, the unlucky in love. She was on fire with a heat that came from a hidden source inside her. She felt his hand on her bare leg, warm and searching, and she discovered to her complete amazement that she was about to lose it. And he hadn't even...all it would take was... She started to move, pressing herself toward that tender, questing hand, wishing he would hurry.

'Connor.' She managed to breathe his name. 'Please—'

He pulled away then, swiftly getting up and turning on a small wall sconce. 'Yeah,' he said, his voice tinged with regret. 'Er, sorry.'

Oh, God. He'd misunderstood. And for the life of her, she couldn't move a muscle. She was still under his spell, paralyzed by desire. She must look like a floozy, lying there, skirt hiked up to her thighs. 'You're sorry?' she managed to whisper.

'I got carried away,' he said. 'I kind of forgot...' He shook his head, offered a self-deprecating grin. He took her hand and helped her to her feet. 'This isn't right. I don't

405

want to take advantage of you. Sorry,' he repeated.

Melting. Her knees were melting. She slumped against him in a stupor from his kisses. Sorry? *Sorry?* She was the one who'd been carried away, and she wanted to scream in frustration.

He held her briefly, one of his hands cupping her head to his chest. His heart was racing. She wished he would kiss her some more, because those first kisses were wearing off and she wanted to be completely under his spell again.

Just as she was trying to figure out how to tell him, he let her go, turning away. Wait, she wanted to say. The bed is here, and I'm here, and—oh, God. Instead, she sat there in a fog, trying to figure out what went wrong, why he'd pushed her away. Maybe, she thought, maybe while they were kissing, Connor had forgotten who it was he held in his arms. Maybe he'd forgotten that she was Lolly Bellamy, the girl everyone laughed at. The girl he himself had turned into a joke. Maybe there was something about the way she tasted or moved or the way her breathing felt against him that reminded him of the past and warned him off. And a part of her—a big part—was still stuck in the past, in a place from where she had never moved on.

'Hey,' she whispered. 'I'm getting some really mixed signals from you.'

'Yeah, I apologize, Olivia. It won't happen again.'

She started to ask him what had made him change his mind, why he'd gone from zero to sixty...and back to zero, all in under a minute. Then she realized she didn't actually want to hear it. Between the previous three, she'd heard it all. You're a nice girl, Olivia, but...after the 'buts,' they found any number of creative ways to fill in the blank there, and when it came to making excuses, men were nothing if not creative.

Twenty-Six

The August heat wave hit Camp Kioga like a wall of fire. Daisy, Max and their father hadn't gotten any better at fishing over the weeks of summer, but at least when they were out on the lake in the canoe, the water-cooled breeze offered soothing relief. Their paddling had improved, and when it was time to head back after a couple of hours of casting their lines, they glided swiftly and smoothly to the dock. Max expertly wrapped a line around a cleat and they got out while Dad held the boat steady. Daisy's shoulders ached from paddling and from casting her line so many times.

Fishing had to be one of the most pointless activities known to man, she decided. Why it was called a sport was beyond her.

Frustrated and sweaty, she grabbed her water bottle. 'I'm going for a swim, Dad. Do you want to—' She broke off, her voice failing her when she saw the expression on her father's face. Somehow, she knew without even turning around what she would see at the end of the dock.

'Mom!' Max burst out, and raced at top speed into his mother's waiting arms.

Daisy cast a panicked look at her father.

'It's okay,' he said. 'Go say hi to your mother.'

Daisy approached her mother slowly, trying painfully to hold in sudden tears. Max was clinging to her like a limpet, his face buried against her. Mom looked totally out of place in the woods. She wore creased slacks and a crisply ironed white shirt that didn't dare to wilt, even in this heat. Her hair was sleekly combed back, makeup applied with precision. The executive camper.

Except that Mom had tears in her eyes, too, and, Daisy knew what was about to happen.

'You came, Mommy,' Max said, oblivious to the warning signs. 'Isn't it nice here? Come on, I'll show you around. We've been working, all of us—'

'I want to see everything, Max,' Mom told him. 'Let me say hi to Daisy, too.'

They hugged, and to Daisy it felt awkward,

and she hated that. When she was little, she used to melt into her mother's arms, and feel surrounded and protected by a sensation of pure comfort. This was different. Everything was different. Even her mom's hair. It was really short. Earlier in the year, she had cut off her hair and given it to Locks of Love, in order to support a friend who was battling breast cancer. How could she be such a good friend and such an unhappy wife?

'Hi, baby,' Mom said to her, pulling back. 'I missed you so much.'

'Me, too.' Daisy stepped out of the embrace. That wasn't exactly right. What she missed was the way her family used to be. She looked at these people, these familiar faces, and tried to remember how they used to laugh together, to feel safe and happy, all under one roof. Where had that family gone? It was like they were frozen in some other dimension, leaving these others in their place, these people with frown lines and trembling lips and eyes that swam in tears but never let them flow.

Dad looked both defensive and scared. Only moments ago, he'd been laughing and splashing in the boat, teaching them silly camp songs. 'Sophie,' he said, and the greeting sounded weary, a breath of defeat.

'Come on, Mom, let me show you everything.' Max seemed determined to be cheerful, to act as if nothing was wrong. He took her by the hand and played tour guide, showing her around the camp, pointing out all the projects they had done to get the place ready for Nana and Granddad's celebration. Dinner was strained, although everyone acted thrilled that Mom had come. Dare served watermelon and cold cuts, but Daisy could only pick at her food. Afterward, there were card games and Ping-Pong in the rec room, but Daisy didn't feel much like playing. Max didn't, either. She saw him standing in the doorway of the dining hall, looking out at the deck, where their parents were talking in low, strained voices. Mom stood with her arms folded across her middle as if she had a stomachache. Dad hung his head in defeat.

Daisy went over to Max and put her hand on his shoulder. He looked up at her, his eyes huge and frightened. Aw, Max, she thought, wishing she could take away his fear, knowing she couldn't.

'It's going to be okay,' she said, giving his shoulder a squeeze. It was probably a lie, but she couldn't think of anything else to say. She squared her shoulders, cleared her throat and opened the door to the deck. 'Come on.'

Mom and Dad tried to smile when Max and Daisy joined them, but it didn't work, and all four of them knew it. Mom put her arms around both of them and held them close. 'I'm sorry,' she said. 'I'm so, so sorry. I love the two of you to pieces, but I can't do this

410

anymore.' Then she stepped back, and glanced from Daisy to Max and back again. 'Your father and I have been discussing this for a long time,' she said. 'We have to make a change in our family.'

*　　*　　*

Later that night, Daisy's parents made coffee in the main hall and sat together, going through official-looking papers in a thick manila folder her mother had brought. Not only was her mom ditching her dad—she was going to be living overseas half the time, in The Hague, practicing international law. 'It's what I've trained for all my life,' Mom explained. 'I can't pass up this opportunity.'

Sure you can, Daisy wanted to say. Women with families pass up opportunities all the time. Or they wait until their kids don't need them anymore. She bit the inside of her lip and told herself not to say it. There was enough bitterness already.

Max asked where The Hague was. Daisy took him to the camp library and showed him in an atlas. Then she took Max to their cabin. Her brother barely spoke a word as he went through the motions of brushing his teeth and washing up. One thing about being at camp— he never complained about bedtime, and tonight was no exception. Daisy lay down beside him on the bunk and switched on the

411

reading light. 'What are you reading now?'

'Treasure Island,' he said in a small voice. 'Dad's been reading it to me.'

'Cool.' She opened the book to the marked page and began to read. Despite the heat, Max snuggled against her as she read about the marooned Ben Gunn, and by the time Jim Hawkins was drawing closer to the treasure, Daisy's brother was nearly asleep.

A soft knock sounded at the door. Olivia and Barkis came in. The dog skittered across the floor and leaped onto the bed, immediately burrowing next to Max. 'Hey, boy,' Max said, smiling a little. 'He can stay if he wants,' he told Olivia.

'I think he wants to,' she said, pulling a chair over by the bunk. 'Keep reading, Daisy.'

'Sure.' She picked up where she'd left off, her mouth saying the words while her mind wandered a million miles away. After a while, both Max and the little dog were asleep. Daisy eased off the bed, marked the page and turned off the reading lamp. She and Olivia sat together on the stoop of the cabin, looking across the meadow to the lake. The stars came out, and fireflies glimmered in the underbrush. A welcome breeze rippled across the compound.

'I was about Max's age when my parents split up,' Olivia said. 'Maybe a little older. I was pretty sure the world was going to come to an end. I got really, really lost for a long time.'

'What do you mean, lost?'

'I never quite knew what to think or feel, and I made some mistakes, like wishing and hoping and praying they'd get back together. I mean, it's so totally normal for a kid to wish that, but if you let it consume you, there's no room in your life for anything else, and you're bound to be disappointed. I didn't let myself see that certain things actually felt better after the breakup.'

'Like what?' Daisy plucked at a blade of grass. She wanted a cigarette but knew Olivia hated smoking.

'You know how the air feels in the house when your mom and dad are together, trying really hard to get along, for your sake?'

That nailed it. The air in an unhappy house. Daisy had felt it like a knot in her gut, and she nodded. She knew that cold, heavy feeling, the unbearable terror that one misstep would upset the balance and everything would shatter beyond recognition.

'I used to actually tiptoe,' Olivia said. 'You know the expression, walking on eggshells? I would tiptoe around, hoping I wouldn't break anything. But that's the thing. Our family was already broken. None of it was my fault, but I had to deal with the broken pieces. I did a bad job for a while.'

'How?'

'I comforted myself with food and I got

413

fat.'

'You? No way.'

'I was a little chubbette, from the age of about twelve right up through my first year of college.'

'I don't remember that. I always thought you were beautiful,' Daisy said. 'You are.'

'And you're a doll,' Olivia said. 'But no, I really was overweight. It was pretty unhealthy, but nobody stopped me, and I didn't get better until I realized I was punishing myself and trying to wall myself off from feeling anything, and that was wrong.'

Like my smoking, thought Daisy. Like the cigarettes and the weed.

'I got better when I went to college, started liking myself and went to a nutritionist and took up swimming.' She paused. 'This isn't helping, is it?'

'I don't know.' Daisy shrugged.

Olivia smoothed her hand over Daisy's hair. 'You and Max are just beginning this journey. I wish I could spare you the pain and confusion you're bound to feel, but that isn't how divorce works. Every family is on its own path, and there aren't any shortcuts. One thing I can promise you is that there'll be surprises. Good ones. Your parents are giving themselves a second chance at happiness, and that's not such a bad thing.' Olivia lowered her hand, gave Daisy a pat on the knee. 'I just hope you and Max don't take as long as I did to adjust to all these changes.'

'I will always, always hate this and I know Max will, too.'

'Fair enough. But, Daisy, try not to cut yourself off or blame yourself. Don't blame anybody. There is simply no point. Tonight you feel horrible, and so does Max, but you have a new opportunity here, a new way to look at your family and your life. A new way to be happy. You have a mom and dad who love you. That's more than lots of kids have, ever. And believe me, it's all you need.'

Twenty-Seven

As he stayed busy on the job the next few days, Connor kept pausing every now and then to take a deep breath and remind himself that he was okay. He hadn't let things get out of hand with Olivia the night they'd gone to his trailer. He'd stopped before they reached the point of no return.

It was damn close, though. That was for sure. If he had let that kissing go on ten seconds longer, he would've been a goner. A total goner. It wasn't that he hadn't wanted to keep her in his arms. Just the opposite. He'd wanted to hold her there forever. But given her state of mind that night, it was a bad idea on many levels. Olivia was probably thinking the same thing, now that the heat of the moment had cooled. She was sophisticated these days, experienced. She got it. She knew as well as he did that you didn't take advantage of someone in emotional distress.

He buried himself in work on the winter lodge, taking refuge in the private wooded glade surrounding the structure, which had once been the camp founder's residence. According to Olivia and Dare, this was actually the most important renovation they were doing, because their grandparents would be staying here. A load of new plumbing and electrical fixtures had arrived, and the installation would begin today.

Just when he started to hope he wasn't going to spend the day thinking about Olivia, she came hiking up the path. She carried a big crate in her arms, and Barkis trotted at her heels. Just the sight of her made his body tense up. She was so damn clean and fresh, like a flower, still moist with early-morning dew. Her face was scrubbed, her blond hair shining. She was dressed for work in jeans and a tank top, but oh, man. Lolly in a tank top. Now his tool belt served a new function—to hide his reaction.

'Hey,' he said, hoping he sounded nonchalant.

There must have been something in his gaze, because she stopped and rested the crate on the porch railing. 'What's the matter?'

'Nothing.' He took out a folding rule and tried desperately to find something to measure. The doorjamb? The distance between him and Lolly? The length of his erection, the depth of his desire?

'You're staring,' she pointed out.

'Sorry. I, uh, I like your outfit. You look like...' Damn. He had no idea what to say.

'Like what?'

'Like you should have your own home-improvement show.' He paused. 'That's a compliment.' If she watched HGTV, she would know that for a fact. The women on those shows always had good hair and toned little bodies in tight jeans and clingy shirts that showed some skin.

'Oh,' she said. 'Thanks, I guess.'

When she bent to set down the crate, the skimpy top rode up a few inches, and that was when he saw it. On her lower back, just above the waistband of her jeans.

She had a tattoo. Lolly Bellamy had a tattoo. It was his favorite kind, too—a tiny butterfly in his favorite spot—the small of her back, right where his hands rested when he danced with her. Right where he wanted to touch her this very minute, maybe even kiss her there. Definitely kiss her there.

A tattoo. Connor was in trouble. If he'd known about it the other night, he would've kept her in his trailer, probably chained to the bed.

417

'Are you sure you're all right?' She straightened up, hooked her thumbs into her back pockets and blew a wisp of hair out of her eyes.

He wondered if women understood that this particular posture made their boobs stand out. She had to know. She was doing this on purpose.

'I'm sure.' He cleared his throat. He heard the sound of an engine in the distance, coming closer. The work crew would be here soon. 'Listen, Lolly. About that night—'

She held up a hand to silence him. 'We don't need to talk about it.'

Well. There was a switch. Usually a woman wanted to parse every waking second of a date, as if they were forensic investigators. Yet Olivia seemed perfectly willing to let the matter drop.

'All right,' he said. 'I just want to make sure you know why we didn't—why I—'

'I know. Believe me, I understand.'

The truck engine crescendoed as the vehicle made its way up the logging road leading to the clearing. All right, thought Connor. He wouldn't press the issue. Olivia had always been uncannily smart and intuitive. She was a psychology major, too. She got it, then.

Good. She understood why he had pushed her away, even when she'd been willing to stay. It would've been a huge mistake, and they both knew it. She was raw and vulnerable, her emotions exposed and unprotected after the revelations about her father. She was in no position to sleep with a guy. If he'd taken advantage of her that night, she'd probably always wonder if she'd slept with him for the right reasons, or because she'd suffered a series of emotional shocks and needed someone to cling to. In her state of mind, she would associate him with trauma and crisis, secrets and betrayal.

That was no way to start a relationship with a woman.

And there—he was now admitting that what he wanted with Olivia Bellamy was a relationship.

Maybe he even wanted to fall in love with her—all over again. But this time as a man who knew where his life was going, not as a confused and scared boy.

It was enough to scare his hard-on into submission.

Not a moment too soon, his foreman and crew arrived, pouring out of the truck—the guys, the radio, the water station, the tools and equipment. Connor greeted them with a wave, indicating the work order posted by the main doorway of the structure. 'Excuse me,' he said to Olivia, and went to talk briefly to the crew. He spent more time than he needed to going over the list with the foreman. They knew each other's rhythm, and the experienced crew didn't need a lot of supervision. Connor lingered, helping one of the guys fix a saw motor. He felt Olivia watching him the whole time and eventually, he ran out of ways to avoid her.

While he used a rag to wipe the grease from his hands, she narrowed her eyes, hooked her thumbs into her pockets again. 'Good job fixing that motor. You've got a lot of hidden talents.'

He checked her out again. She was making no secret of *her* talents. 'You think?' he said.

'Yes, I do.'

'There's a lot more where that came from.' Like, he thought, I bet I can make you scream when you come. He tossed the rag aside. 'I'm lucky to have them.' He gestured at the crate she'd brought. 'So what have you got?'

She was all business as she took out a series of sketches she and Freddy called design sheets and handed them over. 'We've got the bent-willow furniture and the hanging bed for the front porch,' she said, nudging the glider with her foot. 'Freddy's bringing over more of the stuff we bought in Phoenicia.' She stepped inside. The kitchen and living room adjoined each other, with the oversize fireplace at one end and a Vermont Castings woodstove at the other. Light flooded in through picture windows oriented toward the lake, and through the half-round windows that illuminated the sleeping loft above.

In the master bath, there was a claw-foot tub, which was currently strung with cobwebs and furred by sawdust. The adjacent bedroom was nearly bare, except for an old double bed frame of peeled logs. A new mattress and box spring leaned against a wall. 'I want this to turn out really well,' Olivia said. 'I want it to be luxurious for them.'

'The honeymoon suite,' he said.

She smacked him with her steno pad. 'Don't make my mind go there.'

'Come on,' he teased her. 'They've been lovebirds for fifty years. You think any couple can go that long without having the hots for each other?'

'It's much more complicated than that, I'm sure.'

'Are you sure? How do you know it takes anything besides sexual chemistry for a marriage to succeed long-term?'

'Don't be ridiculous. Any couple can conjure up a bit of sexual chemistry.'

Yeah, he thought. Like that night at his place. He should have taken what she'd offered, no more Mr. Nice Guy. She would have slept with him.

'It takes a lot more than that to hold a marriage together for half a century,' she insisted.

'Nope,' he said bluntly. 'You're wrong. You're overcomplicating the situation. If they can seriously ring each other's chimes all night

421

long for all those years, then they've got everything they need.'

'That's just plain silly.'

'Yep, that's me. Silly,' he said, 'but I'm not the one turning this place into a palace of lust for a couple of geezers.'

'Screw you, Connor.'

She'd always been easy to tease. 'Don't you worry, Lolly. We'll get this fixed up just the way you want it.'

'I don't know how you're going to deal with this door,' she said. The door to the dressing room looked as though it had been kicked in.

'Not a problem,' he said. 'I'm taking it out. You don't need it.'

'That's nuts.'

'The hell it is.' He could show her more easily than telling her. 'See, let's say your grandmother—er, the bride—is in here, primping and doing all that stuff women do.' He took Olivia by the shoulders and walked her to the old, pitted mirror above the sink, which was set into an old-fashioned marble-topped washstand.

'And then,' he went on, 'the dude gets impatient because she's taking too long—'

'Wait a minute.' She met his gaze in the mirror. 'What is she doing that's taking so long, brushing her teeth?'

'No clue. I just know she's taking too long. Chicks always do.'

Her lips twitched a little. 'Right.'

'So the dude figures he can start whining and complaining, which is not a turn-on—'

'Finally you got something right,' she said.

'Or he can just grab her and carry her off to bed.' And with that, he scooped Olivia up in his arms.

She gasped in surprise and clung to his neck.

'See, with a wide doorway,' he explained, angling her through, 'this would be a snap.' And damn, he thought, standing by the bed, what I wouldn't give for this to be real. It was the lack of a mattress, and nothing else, that saved her virtue now.

At that moment, Freddy walked in, barely giving them a glance. By now, he seemed resigned to catching them off guard, with lust thick as smoke in the air. 'Working hard again, I see. Never seen anyone work as hard as you kids do,' he deadpanned, brushing past them.

The spell broken, Connor set her down.

'Wise guy,' Olivia muttered.

Twenty-Eight

The heat wave continued unabated, shimmering like quicksilver on the roadways and turning the fields and meadows to seas of buff-colored grass. Around Avalon, the fire department set up fire-advisory signs, banning outdoor burning and fireworks. The hardware store sold out of box fans, and vacationers poured into the area from the city, seeking relief in the cool green wilderness of the mountains.

Olivia stood with her father on the porch of a small, clapboard house on Maple Street in Avalon. She thought her father looked pale and tense, though she didn't know if that was due to the trip he'd made to get here, or the stress of meeting Jenny Majesky for the first time.

He caught her staring at him. 'You don't have to stay, you know,' he said. 'I mean, if you'd rather not be here, I can do this alone.'

'Of course I want to be here.' Although she hadn't created this situation, Olivia had brought it to light. On the way over here, her father insisted that it was his mistake to address, not hers. Yet she was a part of this, and Lord knew, she understood about making mistakes. She punctuated her conviction by knocking smartly on the door.

'Just a sec,' called a voice. The door opened, and there stood Jenny.

There was a moment, just a subtle beat, in which Olivia saw the young woman's soft brown eyes lock with her father's. With *their* father's. It was so obvious, now that she saw them together. Although Jenny was the image of her mother, the resemblance to Philip

424

Bellamy was there, too, in the innately patrician tilt of her face as she looked up at him, in the subtle press of the dimple in her chin and the elegant shape of her hand on the doorknob.

'I'm Philip Bellamy,' her father said. 'Thank you for seeing us.'

'You're welcome,' said Jenny. 'I confess, I was a bit mystified by your phone call. If it's about the wedding cake, I can assure you—'

'It's not strictly about that,' he said. 'May we come in?'

'Of course. How are you, Olivia?' Jenny stepped aside and held the screen door wide open.

'Fine, thank you.' Olivia tried to decide if the two of them looked like sisters, but the thought was so overwhelming that she couldn't see Jenny as anything but a pleasant-looking, unsuspecting woman.

A box fan in the window blew fresh air into a room that was crowded with knickknacks and outdated furniture. In a wheelchair sat an old woman wearing a housedress and pink scuffs. Her hair had been carefully done, and a touch of lipstick colored her mouth. On the phone, Jenny had explained that her grandmother, a widow for ten years, was disabled from a stroke and could neither walk nor speak. Olivia's heart constricted as she thought of her own grandparents—both the Bellamys and the

425

Lightseys—still so vital and happy together. She tried to remember Mrs. Majesky from years past, but could only ever picture the boxy white truck with its hand-painted logo. She wished she'd paid more attention back then. It was sort of eerie to think that, in years past, she and Jenny might have crossed paths, never knowing about their connection.

'Grandma, this is Philip and his daughter, Olivia Bellamy,' Jenny said. 'You remember the Bellamys from Camp Kioga.'

The woman's mouth twisted and she made an inarticulate sound.

'Mrs. Majesky, it's good to see you,' Philip said.

The old woman's dark eyes seemed to clear with comprehension, as though she was trapped behind soundproof glass. 'My grandmother will want to pay you a visit when she comes up next week,' Olivia said, taking Mrs. Majesky's hand. Her thin skin was dry and cool despite the heat.

'I thought we'd go out on the back porch,' Jenny said. 'That's where we get the best shade this time of day. Grandma, would you like to join us?'

Mrs. Majesky made a sound that Jenny took as a no. Olivia glanced at her father, saw his shoulders ease with relief. Explaining the situation to Jenny would be difficult enough. Doing so in front of her grandmother would be that much more awkward.

426

'All right.' Jenny picked up a remote control and turned up the volume on *Oprah*. Then she led the way into an old-fashioned kitchen with Formica countertops and glass-front cabinets stacked with china. She fixed three tall glasses of iced tea and set them on a tray with a platter of cookies. 'Lemon bars,' she said. 'I brought them from the main bakery in Kingston today.'

A laptop computer and stacks of paper littered the kitchen table. 'We must have interrupted your work,' Philip said.

'Oh, it's not work. Not paying work, anyway.' She ducked her head, as though bashful. 'I've been doing some writing.'

'You're a writer?' Philip asked.

'I'm writing a...I'm not sure what it's called.' She seemed flustered, but in a charming way. 'I suppose you'd call it a collection of stories about growing up in my grandparents' bakery. And recipes. Some of them are so old, they're written on school paper my grandmother brought from Poland.' She showed them a collection of brittle, yellowed pages covered in a foreign schoolgirl scrawl. 'Grandma helped me translate a lot of them, but after the stroke...' Jenny carefully set the handwritten stack aside. 'Anyway, it's one of those projects I'll probably never finish.'

For no reason she could fathom, Olivia felt a wave of melancholy. Maybe it was the thought of Jenny, this nice, unassuming girl, growing up without a father and then losing her grandfather at such a young age. No wonder she was working to preserve old family memories and recipes.

Olivia watched her father's face, and she realized there was another reason she felt so unsettled. He had always wanted to be a writer, too, but had chosen a career in law because it was a more practical, stable profession, the sort of thing that was expected of a Bellamy. Now that she knew the real reason he'd married her mother, she understood why he had left his dream behind. And—all right, this was horrible—she felt a subtle sting of resentment, that Jenny unknowingly shared this commonality with their father.

They went to a screened-in porch that was favored by a light breeze, and sat in wicker chairs around a low table. Olivia's father took a nervous sip of tea and set down his glass. 'Thanks,' he said. 'I apologize for seeming so mysterious when I asked to pay you a visit. I just didn't know how to broach the subject. There's no easy way to say this, Miss Majesky. Jenny.'

Something in his tone must have tipped her off, because she gripped the arms of her chair and gave him her full attention, her head tilted to one side. By now, she had to know perfectly well this meeting had nothing to do with a wedding cake. 'Yes?'

'I have no idea how much you know about this situation,' he continued. 'I understand your mother, Mariska, has been away.'

Jenny nodded, a frown appearing on her brow. 'Since I was about four years old. I barely remember her.'

Oh, God, thought Olivia. 'And she's never been in touch? Never called or written you a letter?'

Jenny shook her head, her eyes immeasurably dark and sad. 'I assume there's a point to these questions.'

'I used to know her,' he said. 'Mariska and I were… She was my girlfriend the summer of 1977. Did your grandmother ever tell you that?'

A single bead of sweat trickled down Jenny's temple. The sadness left her eyes as they narrowed in suspicion. 'No. Should she have?'

'I can't answer that.' He clenched and unclenched his hands, and he was sweating, too. Olivia couldn't take her eyes off their faces.

'I…some things have come to light, lately,' Philip continued, 'and I—well, I was wondering if anyone's ever spoken to you about your father. Your biological father.'

The breeze stopped. At least, to Olivia, that was how it felt. Everything stood still—the wind, time, the beating of their hearts.

Jenny seemed frozen rather than flustered. Her face turned visibly paler while the suspicion never quite left her eyes. And though she was a stranger, Olivia was seized by an urge to touch Jenny, to take her hand or perhaps pat her on the shoulder. *I have a sister,* Olivia thought. *I have a sister.*

Philip said, 'I'm sorry to show up like this, out of the blue, and say these things. I didn't see any other way to introduce myself.'

Jenny set down her glass of tea. She studied Philip, and seemed to be taking inventory, seeking all the ways they resembled each other. 'Are you telling me you're...' The words trickled away, as though Jenny couldn't bring herself to utter them. 'This is absurd. I have no idea why you're telling me this.'

Philip handed her the photograph of himself and Mariska. 'This was recently found among my old camp things. It was taken at the end of summer 1977. That whole summer, we were as happy as it's possible to be, or so I believed. I loved your mother very much, and planned to marry her.'

Jenny studied the picture, and a look of raw pain shadowed her face. Olivia suspected she'd swiftly done the math in her head. 'You didn't, though,' she pointed out. 'You didn't marry her.'

'No. Just after Labor Day weekend, Mariska broke off with me. Said she wanted to see the world, go find a life for herself—alone.

I tried to talk her out of it, but I never saw her again, never spoke to her. I wrote dozens of letters, and they all came back marked Return To Sender. Her mother—your grandmother—told me not to call anymore, so I came here by train.' He paused, his eyes clouded with distant memories. 'She was gone. Someone at the jewelry shop where she worked told me she'd left town. Off to see the world, something like that.' He steepled his fingers together and looked at Jenny, but she didn't look at him. 'That was when I gave up on Mariska. I figured she meant what she said when she broke up with me, so I finally accepted it. Then that winter, I married Olivia's mother, Pamela Lightsey.' Mercifully, he didn't go into detail about the circumstances of the engagement and hasty wedding. 'Pamela and I have been divorced for seventeen years, and I never remarried.'

They never even had a chance, Olivia realized. As a child, she'd searched endlessly and fruitlessly for the reason her parents had split up, never knowing that the reason existed long before she was born.

Jenny said nothing. She held the photograph, absently skimming her thumb over the image of her mother.

'When I came to the bakery that day,' Olivia told Jenny, 'I noticed that you have the same picture hanging on the wall, but it's been cropped.'

431

'Probably by my grandmother.'

Olivia realized, with a jolt, that Jenny's mother had been pregnant when the snapshot was taken. Jenny kept staring at the picture. Absently, her hand stole up and she fingered the silver pendant on her necklace.

'I also noticed that pendant you're wearing,' Olivia added. 'Remember, I asked you about it?'

Jenny nodded. 'It was my mother's. My grandparents gave it to me for my sixteenth birthday.'

Philip took out its mate and put it on the table. 'It's from a pair of cuff links I owned. I gave one to Mariska and kept the other.'

A soft gasp escaped from Jenny. Throughout the whole conversation, her reactions had been measured and controlled, but now she seemed to be on the verge of losing it. Her fingers trembled as she picked up the cuff link. 'I never knew if there was a story behind this, or behind anything my mother left me. But are you sure this is not some huge coincidence, or—'

'I'm almost positive,' he told her. 'Of course, we can do a blood test if you choose, but I'm sure it would only confirm what we've found out. I took the liberty of hiring a private investigator to verify dates and certain other details.'

Jenny swallowed hard. Her dark eyes held a hunted look. 'A private investigator? But

432

that's so… It's intrusive.'

'You're right, but I didn't know what else to do. Mr. Rasmussen—he does a lot of work for my law firm—only searched public records. I'm sorry, Jenny. I didn't want to approach you, only to find it's a huge mistake. I didn't want to upset you for no reason. God. For all I knew, you believed someone else was your father.'

With excruciating care, she set down the cuff link. 'I used to ask all the time, but my grandparents swore she never told them. The father's name is blank on my birth certificate.' A terrible hope lit her face when she finally looked at him. 'So did he—your investigator— did he find out anything about my mother?'

Yes, thought Olivia. Like why she ditched her daughter.

Philip took out a printed copy of an e-mail message. 'Probably nothing you haven't already heard. In late 1977, Mariska Majesky left Avalon. She obtained a passport, traveled frequently, though she had no visible means of support. While in Boca Raton in March 1978, she had a baby, naming her Jennifer Anastasia. In 1982, she and her daughter returned to Avalon to stay with her parents. Mariska continued to travel frequently, though she never took her daughter with her.' He checked the printed page. 'In 1983, Mariska left Avalon. This time, she never came back, and there are no further records of her. Her passport expired in 1988 and was never renewed.' He set down the report and looked at Jenny, studying her face with an intense curiosity. 'If you want, I can have Rasmussen keep looking.'

'No, thank you,' she said softly, and studied the brief report.

Everyone was so quiet and still that Olivia could hear the ice melting and shifting in the now-forgotten glasses. Finally, Jenny cleared her throat and regarded Philip and then Olivia with cautious curiosity. 'I don't know what to say.'

'None of us does,' Olivia said. 'I'm glad we found you and that you were willing to hear us out. I hope after the shock of this wears off, you'll be glad, too.'

'You don't have to say anything or feel a certain way,' Philip said.

'Good, because I have no idea what I'm feeling.'

She was feeling something, though. Olivia could see that. Her eyes, those soft honest eyes Olivia had liked immediately, now sparkled with unshed tears.

'Well, I'm happy to meet you,' Olivia whispered. 'I always wanted a sister.' Feeling a bit overwhelmed, she found herself studying Jenny's face again. Were their noses similar? Did they look anything alike? Olivia couldn't tell. 'I hope we'll have plenty of time to, uh, catch up,' she added. 'That is, if you want to.'

'Um, sure.' Jenny blinked as though waking from a dream. 'I never thought I'd meet you,' she said to Philip. 'I never thought I'd learn who you were.'

Philip touched her hand. 'I'm so sorry.'

Olivia's heart sank. She could scarcely imagine what Jenny must be going through, or what an incredible cruelty it must feel like, growing up abandoned by her mother, having never known her father.

Jenny looked down at their hands. 'After a lifetime of being in the dark about this, I appreciate the honesty. I always wondered who you were,' she said. 'What you were like, if I'd ever meet you.'

'I hope I don't disappoint you.'

Finally, one single tear escaped, slipping down Jenny's cheek. She wiped it away with the back of her hand. Olivia couldn't tell if Jenny was elated or sad or simply overwhelmed. Olivia herself was a wreck. She was thrilled to have discovered her half sister, but at the same time, she felt unexpectedly defensive. Sure, she wanted her father to get to know Jenny, but...Olivia, you petty wretch, she told herself. Don't you dare start with the sibling rivalry.

'This is going to take some time,' she said to Jenny. 'I hope you're willing to spend some time with...Dad and me.'

'I suppose so, yes.'

'Are you free for dinner tonight?' Dad

asked.

Jenny looked taken aback. Then she nodded. 'It will have to be after nine. My grandmother goes to bed early.'

'Works for me,' he said. 'Olivia?'

Share and share alike, Olivia thought. She put on a bright smile and said, 'The two of you should go. Maybe I'll join you another time.'

'Olivia—'

'It's fine, Dad. Really. In fact, I know a really great place. The Apple Tree Inn, out on Route 47.' She turned to Jenny, smiling brightly. 'Have you been there?'

'Only once,' Jenny confessed. 'It's sort of a…special-occasion place for us locals.'

'Well, if this isn't a special occasion,' Dad said, 'I don't know what is.'

Twenty-Nine

There were few things, Olivia reflected, that were quite so relaxing as paddling a kayak on a placid lake, especially in the midst of a heat wave. She went out at sundown, dipping her paddle beneath the glassy surface of the motionless water, watching it stir outward. It was hard to believe that soon she would be leaving this place. Summer had sped by so swiftly, each day busy and rich and filled with purpose. Finally, as an adult, Olivia

436

understood why her grandparents loved Camp Kioga so much.

With a troubling sense of surprise, she realized she would miss this place, the placid water and fresh green smells, the sound of the wind in the trees and birdsong every morning. But the crush and hurry of the city awaited. Clients were calling. Each time she checked her messages or e-mail, there they were, asking when she'd be back, needing her to help them out with their property, their plans, their lives. Needing Transformations. That was Olivia—the fluffer. She could sweep through someone's house and within minutes, make it nicer, brighter, more appealing.

It wasn't such a tricky thing to do for other people. As for herself....

Among today's messages, there was even one from Rand. He called to say he was thinking about her, which was probably code for saying he needed to get laid. Rand Whitney. God, had he really been the repository of all her hopes and dreams just a few months before? It seemed like a lifetime ago. She'd been so naive. Her mother's daughter, really. Believing that if your life looked perfect—the husband, the home, the friends, the kids—then surely it must be perfect. And of course, Olivia had built her entire career on that principle. She ought to know better. She ought to know that you could take anything from a crappy downtown

437

walk-up to a run-down rustic summer camp and make it look like the sort of place people would want to be. But dig a little beneath the surface, and the lie was exposed.

The sunset paddle wasn't as relaxing as she'd hoped. She was consumed by thoughts of Jenny Majesky. A few months ago, she didn't even know Jenny existed. Now, suddenly, she had a sister. All it took was one small act, like a stone dropped into still water, to see its significance radiating outward in all directions. Lives were affected, futures, plans by a decision made that long-ago summer. It was impossible to see where the ripples would end.

Though all of this had started before Olivia was born, she still had a role to play—daughter, supporter, friend. Sister.

I have a sister. The knowledge sang inside her, a mingling of elation and fear and trepidation.

She paddled along the edge of the lake, where willows and maples reached down to dip their branches in the water, and families of wood duck glided amid the cattails. From the perspective of the water, Kioga looked exactly the way it should at twilight, with a few lights glowing in the windows of the main lodge and outbuildings, and a cookfire flickering in the river-rock barbecue pit on the shore. Uncle Greg was fixing hamburgers and hot dogs tonight because those were Max's favorites.

The little boy had discovered that one of the very few perks of divorce was that people tried to indulge the kids. Olivia hoped they wouldn't fall into a pattern of *over*indulging, something her own family had done. It was hard, watching her cousins struggle through the same issues she had faced as a child, and bittersweet, watching her uncle become a better dad and a better person—at the cost of his marriage.

Darkness fell, but she didn't turn on her flashlight. The moon would be up soon, and there was just enough light to find the dock at Spruce Island. Which was, after all, where she was headed all along. Connor was still working out here, and she wanted to find him alone.

Yes, she was looking for Connor. Maybe, as Freddy sometimes told her, she really was a glutton for punishment. Here she was, freaked out about Jenny, but also still so frustrated— no, furious—with Connor she couldn't see straight, yet she needed to see him.

If she closed her eyes, she could still feel his kisses and the fiery burn of wanting him, the way she had the night she'd all but thrown herself at him. He'd put a stop to that swiftly enough, but like a fool, she'd given him another chance at the winter lodge, flirting shamelessly—to no avail. Nothing, she thought—*but nothing*—feels quite like sexual rejection.

And really, what better place to have it out with him than here, on this tiny private island in the middle of the lake?

She tied up and got out at the small, floating dock.

'Hello,' she called out.

'Over here.'

Her heart tripped, then sped up as she followed the sound of his voice.

'Hey,' she said, her tone carefully neutral.

'Hey.' He was working by the light of a lantern. He unfastened a wood clamp, stepped back to regard his work. 'I wasn't expecting anyone.'

'You didn't show up for dinner. I came out to make sure everything is all right.'

'You paddled all the way out here just for that?'

'Sure.'

'Liar.' He used a bandanna to wipe his hands. 'What are you doing here, Lolly?'

She couldn't bring herself to reply. Besides, she was pretty sure he knew, anyway. He seemed to call her Lolly—not Olivia—when he saw right through her. It occurred to her to tell him how the meeting with Jenny Majesky had gone, but she wasn't ready to talk about that, not yet. She'd come here—in part, at least—to avoid that situation. She didn't want to think about her father and Jenny at the Apple Tree Inn.

Connor didn't press for an answer, but

busied himself stowing away the clamps and tools. Then he flipped a switch, and strings of fairy lights glimmered in the rafters of the restored gazebo.

Olivia turned slowly in a circle, and for a moment, she forgot her worry and frustration. She forgot everything except the fact that this man had been working long hours to re-create this place for her grandparents. The thought melted every bit of her annoyance at Connor. 'It's exactly the way I wanted it to turn out.'

'Glad you like it.' He looked sexy in this light. In any light, she admitted.

'I'm lucky I found you,' she said, then grew flustered. 'I mean, as a contractor. But then I was worried that it wouldn't work out, that we wouldn't work well together, you know, because…you know.' Oh, she was babbling. They both knew it.

He seemed unruffled as he opened two cans of beer without asking whether or not she wanted one. 'Cheers,' he said.

Olivia wasn't much of a beer drinker, but sometimes, like right now, on the hottest night of the year, it was just the thing. The cold, crisp effervescence soothed her throat.

Connor turned off the strings of lights and picked up a lantern. 'Let's sit over here,' he said, lighting the way down to the water's edge. 'I'd make you a fire, but it's too hot as it is.'

She tilted her head back and touched the

cold beer can to her throat, closed her eyes and let out a sigh. 'It's still so hot out, I almost can't see straight,' she said.

'There's a remedy for that.'

'Hmm. Skinny-dipping.' She kicked off her flip-flops and sat down, bracing one arm behind her.

'Of course. One of Kioga's most secret traditions.'

'Except everyone knew about it.' She cringed, shying away from unwanted memories. Her thoughts careened and ricocheted. Was she going to let him do this? Was she prepared? Was he?

'Let me tell you about my day,' she said. It was only fair to let him know about the invisible baggage she was dragging around. 'I went with my father to introduce him to Jenny. It was horrible and awkward and sad, and tonight he's taking her to the Apple Tree Inn so they can get acquainted. And it's all my fault for opening the whole can of worms but how could I not?'

'Hey. None of this is your fault. Not one damn bit.'

Olivia had a terrible urge to lean against him, as though seeking shelter. Every breath she took seemed to deepen her emotional pain. 'It was so hard,' she said. 'Don't get me wrong, Jenny was terrific. But also...careful. She didn't embrace us as her long-lost family. She didn't push us away, either. The whole

442

time, I couldn't stop thinking about everything we missed out on, all the things we never had. All my life I've had a sister. A big sister. And I never knew. I keep wondering about how different my life would have been if we'd known each other, growing up.'

He slipped his arm around her, and the simple human warmth of the contact brought her to the brink of tears. He didn't say anything, she supposed, because there was nothing to say. Finally, he asked a question. 'What can I do?'

She swallowed a couple of times, hardly trusting herself to speak. 'Maybe I need mind-blowing sex and a shoulder to cry on.'

He tightened his hold on her, and she could hear a rumble of humor in his chest. 'I guess you came to the right place.'

The thing was, Olivia didn't know if she should take what he was offering. She had a perfectly good best friend—Freddy—and a cousin she adored—Dare—who could be the shoulder. The mind-blowing sex, well, that would take a specialist.

She and Connor had tried sex before. It had been a disaster. Just how big a disaster, she was still discovering. She'd thought it was a simple teenage-humiliation-and-rejection scenario, but she'd never left it behind, not really. Instead, she had let that moment define her and govern choices she made years later.

'So what do you say, Lolly?' he whispered,

443

his lips very close to hers, not kissing her but leaning close enough so that she felt as though he was.

God, she was falling for him. All over again, though she should have learned her lesson a long time ago. She wanted him so much, though, that even knowing this could be a mistake couldn't dissuade her.

Maybe, as bona fide adults, they'd do better this time around. God knew, they couldn't do much worse.

CAMP KIOGA SONGBOOK

Taps (Day Is Done)

Day is done, gone the sun,
From the lake, from the hills, from the sky;
All is well, safely rest, God is nigh.

Thirty

Happy but exhausted campers swarmed the main yard on pickup day. Some took the camp bus down the mountain to the train station. Others were collected by gleeful parents in station wagons and SUVs. After ten weeks away, even the most obnoxious child was generally missed. A final sweep of the bunkhouses had been made and the kids milled around, toting their gear, sporting suntans and bug bites and—as Lolly's grandparents said in their farewell talk at breakfast—memories to last a lifetime.

Lolly spotted Connor talking with Julian. The little boy was hopping from one foot to the other, still the most energetic kid at camp. Her heart jumped as it always did when she saw Connor, or even thought about him. Against all expectations, something amazing had happened this summer. He had become her boyfriend, her very first, and she was so dizzy in love with him that she had all but lost the ability to eat or sleep or think. She walked over to him and handed Julian the Fledgling sign to hold. 'Make sure you keep it up in the air so everyone can see it. That'll help parents find their kids.'

445

'My dad's coming. He's coming all the way from Italy to get me.'

'That's what I hear, kiddo. I think that's totally cool,' Lolly said.

Marching around in self-importance, Julian waved his sign and scanned the incoming cars and vans.

'Good move,' Connor said to her. 'Giving him a job to do will keep him busy for a whole minute, maybe.'

'I can't believe he made it through the summer in one piece,' she said. Bungee jumping had been only the beginning. Fortunately for Julian, he had a big brother who was smart and caring. Rather than fighting against the boy's fascination with height and speed, Connor found ways to channel it. He took Julian and some of the other campers to explore the steep white cliffs and ice caves of the Shawangunk's Ridge, hung a rope swing from a tree by the lake and took a group to the top of the highest ranger lookout tower. At yesterday's farewell celebration, there had been a mountain bike descent. Lolly knew she'd never forget the sound of Julian's screams of joy as he'd ridden down, nor would she forget the proud, affectionate grin on Connor's face as he watched.

A wave of love came over her and she moved close to him, her hand brushing his. 'This is the first time in my life I'm sorry to see

446

camp end,' she said.

'I never liked seeing it end.'

Ramona Fisher came running over. 'There you are, Lolly. I told my mom I wasn't leaving until I said goodbye.'

Lolly opened her arms to the little girl for a hug. It had taken lots of time and attention, but she had managed to get Ramona through the crippling homesickness that had paralyzed her at the beginning of summer. She'd convinced the girl that it was only human to miss the people you love, but that their absence didn't have to make you miserable.

Sneaking a glance at Connor, Lolly wondered if she would be able to take her own advice, once she went away to college. The very thought of going for days or weeks or even months without seeing him sent a cold spike of dread clean through her.

'This is for you,' Ramona said, 'to remember me by.' She offered up a friendship bracelet, made of bright threads and beads. Painstakingly woven into the narrow strap were the initials RF and LB.

'That's awesome, Ramona.' Lolly held out her hand so the girl could tie it on. 'I'll wear it with pride.'

'And I'm going to do it,' Ramona said as she carefully knotted the bracelet. 'I'm going to sign up for swim team at the Y in Nyack.'

'They'll be lucky to get you,' Lolly said.

Whistles shrieked and car horns honked,

and everyone got busy sorting kids into car pools and herding them onto the bus. But between Lolly and Connor there was an invisible thread. Over the weeks of summer, the bond had grown and deepened, and now he felt like her whole world. She had admitted to him that he had been the first boy to kiss her. 'That makes me glad,' he'd said. 'I like being your first.'

Tonight would be another first, and they both knew it. She thought about their plans and felt a tug of that invisible thread. He must have felt it, too, because surrounded by boys at the bus circle, helping with luggage, he stopped what he was doing, turned and looked at her. They shared a fleeting, private smile of conspiracy, then went back to their duties.

'Papa! It's Papa!' Julian went into a frenzy, waving the Fledglings sign like a white flag of surrender. 'Connor, my papa's here!' the kid practically screamed. He ditched the banner and went speeding through the crowd.

'It's the Nutty Professor,' Connor said to Lolly as they went to greet Louis Gastineaux.

He was heavyset and jovial, with thick glasses and ill-fitting pants pulled up high over his waist, and a short-sleeved shirt in a very strange shade of yellow. Julian was so excited he ricocheted everywhere, tugging his father along as he showed him around.

'You're going to miss Julian, aren't you?' Lolly said.

'I've been missing him since I was eleven years old,' Connor admitted. 'Weird little guy.'

'Then I'm glad you had this summer. Maybe next year, you'll both come back.'

He grinned at her. 'Maybe. Assuming your grandparents—crap.' His grin disappeared.

'What's the matter?' she asked, but she didn't need to hear his answer. His own father, Terry Davis, came driving up in the maintenance truck. Julian, who genuinely liked Mr. Davis, pulled Louis over to meet him.

'Excuse me,' Connor said, and went to join his father.

Lolly watched them from a distance, two fathers and two sons, each of them broken in some way. She understood that Connor loved his father, but that his pain and shame over Terry's drinking had taken a toll on both of them.

'That's the boy you've been seeing all summer?' asked a voice behind Lolly.

Oh, cripes. Lolly turned with slow reluctance. 'Hi ya, Mom. When did you get here?'

'An hour ago, but you didn't notice.' Lolly's mother had flawlessly styled hair and makeup, and she wore a perfect outfit—a crisp cotton dress and low-heeled sandals, designer shades and a beige Chanel tote bag. Beside her, Lolly felt grubby and unkempt.

She gave her mother a brief hug. 'Come

and meet Connor.'

Her mother stiffened, radiating resistance from every fiber of her being. 'I don't think that's necessary.'

Lolly gave a little snort of disbelief. 'My first real boyfriend, and you don't want to meet him?'

'Sweetie, there's really no point. We're all going our separate ways tomorrow, anyway.'

'I know what you're really thinking,' she said, affecting a snobbish, boarding-school accent. 'You don't consider it appropriate for your daughter to associate with the likes of Connor Davis.'

'Don't be snide.'

'Then come and meet him. Mom, he's so great, I know you're going to like him.' Lolly stopped when she saw her mother watching Connor, with his long hair and slightly punked-out look, standing next to his father, who was wearing a work coverall and smoking a cigarette. Nearby were the Nutty Professor and his biracial kid. Noting the expression on her mother's face, Lolly decided to give up. Her mother was never going to like Connor, no matter what, so she might as well not subject him to the awkward introduction.

'I have to go,' she said. 'I promised to help with the appetizers for tonight. The kitchen has too many eggs left over, so we're making a zillion deviled eggs.'

As she headed for the main lodge, she

forced herself to shrug off her mother's skepticism and focus on the coming evening. She was intercepted by Jazzy Simmons, who scuttled over, her posture conspiratorial. 'Don't forget,' she said, 'leave the ice machine on, at least until we fill the keg barrels.'

'I said I would,' Lolly told her. Tonight was the traditional farewell dance for the staff and counselors. There would be a bonfire down on the lakeshore. And a ton of contraband beer, of course. Lolly didn't mind providing the ice. She and Connor were counting on everyone to be caught up in the celebration, because they planned to steal away. With no kids to look after, no bed-check duty to perform, they would finally have some privacy. The two of them had a plan. Tonight, finally, they were going to make love for the first time.

*　　　*　　　*

The party wasn't excruciating. That was something, at least. One thing getting a boyfriend had done for Lolly was that it had given her more confidence in herself. She didn't stand around at a party as if she were stuck to the wall, unable to get out on the floor and dance. She learned that it was possible to laugh and have a good time and stop worrying about what people thought. She wished her cousins were here, but Dare and

Frankie had left the day before because they were going all the way to California for college.

Fortunately, Lolly's mother wasn't around. She was spending the night in town at the Turning Maple, a luxury B and B. Tomorrow, she would drive Lolly back to the city. Lolly already knew that no more would be said about Connor Davis. That was her mother's way. If you didn't talk about something, it didn't exist.

That was okay with Lolly, though. She wasn't really sure she had the words to tell her mother or anyone how she felt about Connor. She called it love, but it felt so much bigger than that. It felt like a tornado inside her, a forest fire. They danced together, and she felt as if she was going to be swept up into the sky by the sheer force of her emotions. At the end of the song, Connor went to get something to drink, and Lolly just stood there in a daze.

Jazzy Simmons showed up, wearing low-slung combat fatigues and a top that exposed her bra straps. Her headlamp boobs preceded her wherever she went. Never one to mince words, Jazzy took one look at Lolly and said, 'Omigod, you're totally going to do it, aren't you?'

'Shut up, Jazzy.' There was no venom in Lolly. She was still floating.

'Lolly Bellamy, you wicked hussy. You're going to hook up with Connor Davis.' Jazzy's

452

nose had been out of joint all summer long because Connor had chosen Lolly instead of her. 'Lolly and Connor,' she said, slinging her arm around a boy named Kirk. 'That's something I'd like to see.'

'We all would,' Kirk said, and snickered.

Lolly couldn't care less. The knowledge that she and Connor were going to steal away was both delicious and terrifying. As people headed down to the lakeshore to light the bonfire, a raft of thin clouds moved in to shroud the moon. She felt a little thrill of apprehension, and an even stronger thrill of anticipation, and went to meet Connor at the appointed spot. They had a favorite place near the waterfall, where a deep pool had been carved out by the cascade. Moonlight spilled through an opening in the forest canopy, and the low roar of the falls battering the rocks created a strange but soothing music. She found Connor there already, and just for a moment, he looked forbidding, his features in shadow and his tall silhouette outlined by moonlight and the mist of the falls in the background.

'I wasn't sure you'd come,' he said when she reached him, a little breathless from the climb.

'Of course I came.' She felt shy and uncertain, though. 'Did you, um, bring everything?'

'Right here.' He spread out a thick woolen

army blanket and set down two cans of beer and a small, oblong box. The condoms. Oh, God, she thought. We're really going to do this.

'Have a seat,' he said mildly. 'There's no rush.' He opened a can of beer and handed it to her.

'Where did you get this?' she asked, sitting cross-legged on the blanket.

'Where do you think?' He gave a brief laugh. 'My dad's got an unending supply.'

She nodded and took a sip, grimacing a little. She didn't really like the taste of beer, but she felt a sudden need to delay this just a little longer. 'So, what were you talking about earlier today, you and your father and Professor Gastineaux?'

'I don't know. Louis was thanking my dad. And my dad, as usual, was all bowing and scraping, saying it was the least he can do.' There was an edge of annoyance in his voice.

'It *was* nice of your dad.'

'Yeah, he'll probably really tie one on tonight to celebrate how nice he is. We had this big argument tonight because he wanted to go shoot pool at Hilltop Tavern.'

Lolly didn't know what do say. She realized shooting pool was not the issue. It was that Mr. Davis was bound to drink too much, and then try to drive. 'I'm sorry,' was all she could think of to say.

'It's okay. It's not like I'm his keeper.' He

454

took a desultory gulp of his beer. 'That was your mom I saw you with earlier today,' he said.

She was startled that he'd noticed. 'She drove up from the city this morning.'

'You look like her.'

Lolly snorted. 'Yeah, right.'

'How do you think I figured out it was your mom?' He took another glug of beer. 'Why didn't you introduce us?'

Uh-oh. Her cheeks started to burn. 'My mom's not exactly the friendly type.'

'You know damn well that's not the reason. Listen, if you're ashamed to be seen with me—'

'You couldn't be more wrong,' she said in a rush. 'Ashamed of you? Cripes, Connor, every morning I wake up and pinch myself to make sure I didn't dream you. I swear, I'm not ashamed of you, but...'

'But what?'

'Of my mom. Of the way she's so judgmental about people. I didn't want you to be subjected to that, so I didn't force her on you. Okay? And anyway, it's you who should be ashamed to be seen with me.'

'What the hell do you mean by that?'

'Come on, Connor. You think I haven't heard the guys ribbing you about dating the fat chick?'

'They're full of shit,' he said.

'And so is my mom.' She sighed. 'I wish...'

She wasn't sure what she wished. That she had a different mother? That Terry Davis had been a better dad to him? She fell silent, and they sat quietly for a few minutes and let the tension of the previous moments dissolve. She drank a little more of her beer. It didn't take much for her to start feeling the subtle warmth of its effects. 'You know the scariest thing to me about going to college?' she said. 'Being away from you.'

'We'll see each other.'

'We, uh, we never really talked about how.' They hadn't discussed the details of the way this relationship would work, once they were away from camp. She wished time would stop and the world would go away, leaving her and Connor alone forever, like Adam and Eve. Then she fantasized about what life would be like in the city. She would go to classes, and Connor would get work and they'd see each other every night. It would be perfect.

He shrugged. 'People tend to do the things that are important to them.'

'You're important to me,' she told him. 'You're everything to me. I love you, Connor.' A pause. Oh, man. She'd gone and said it. Now if he said it back, it wouldn't mean anything except that she'd put him on the spot.

But he didn't say it back. He said something that was, if possible, even better. 'I never did anything to deserve you,' he said. 'I

456

want to, though. The thing about you, Lolly, is that you've got all these expectations of me. I'm not used to that. Nobody in the world ever expected anything of me, except to get out of their hair. And now here you are, wanting me in your life. That's huge to me. You have no idea how huge.'

'I don't mean to pressure you,' she said.

'You don't get it. This kind of pressure…it's okay. The way I see it, in order for someone to have expectations of you, they have to believe in you. And all my life, only one person has ever done that—you, Lolly.'

He kissed her hard and searchingly, and she was on fire, on the verge of exploding. All summer long, they had been building to this inevitable, planned-for and dreamed-of moment, and she was terrified. She told herself not to be. This was Connor, after all, and it was time, past time. Everybody always said to save yourself for the one you love. Well, if what she felt for Connor wasn't love, she didn't know what was.

Still, even feeling the burn of that in her heart didn't make things easier and somehow, he could sense that. He stopped kissing her and leaned back. 'Look, if you don't—'

'I do. I swear it. Just…give me a minute.' She slid her arms around his neck and took a deep breath. His hair smelled clean and fresh, like the night air. A warm breeze swept through the forest, parting the treetops. She could just make out the glow of the bonfire on the lakeshore below, and felt a flicker of unease. What if someone noticed she and Connor were gone?

He pulled back again. 'Now you're even more tense,' he said. 'If you changed your mind, I'll understand.'

'It's not that,' she said. 'I'm, um…bashful, a little. A lot, actually.' It was the best she could do. It was impossible to explain precisely how self-conscious she truly felt.

'You know what I think?' he said, a funny grin on his face. 'I think we should go swimming.'

'You mean skinny-dipping.' She gulped. 'Right here? Right now?'

'Sure.'

Skinny-dipping at Camp Kioga was an unwritten tradition, performed under dark of night in a hail of giggles. 'I never took part,' Lolly admitted. 'Too self-conscious.' He ought to know, she thought. Hadn't he heard the teasing? She used to lie there alone in the sticky heat, smoldering with yearning as she imagined what it must feel like, swimming naked, with the water flowing over her.

He took a gulp of beer, shook his head. 'Believe me, we weren't checking each other out. It was all about speed and stealth and getting away with something. So what do you say?' His voice was soft and low, almost a whisper. 'How about now?'

458

'What about now?' She knew what he was asking, though. She knew exactly what he was asking.

'Would you feel self-conscious now?' He sat up, set down his can of beer.

'I don't think a person ever gets over that.'

Without taking his eyes off her, he reached over and undid the top button of her blouse. 'It's dark, Lolly. There's nobody here but us.'

She couldn't move. Forgot to breathe for a second. He went on to the next button.

Her heart was pounding so hard, it was about to leap right out of her. Yet when she looked down at his hand, everything looked normal. Well, as normal as it could look, the first time a boy took off your shirt and then your bra. Don't panic, she told herself. Just feel. Lolly felt protected by the darkness and by Connor, and she knew that as long as she was in his arms, nothing bad could happen to her. She was safe with him, and she knew everything would be all right, even though there were moments of tremendous awkwardness and embarrassment. She wanted to die when he whispered, 'Stand up, Lolly, so I can get these off,' and he peeled away her shorts. These moments were tempered by an intensity that stole her breath, and a feeling that made her forget to be embarrassed or bashful. She forgot everything except that she loved Connor Davis with every bit of her heart.

The crazy thing was, standing naked before him didn't quite push her over the edge of panic. No, what caused that was when Connor started to undress. She'd seen him with his shirt off a million times, but when he undid his fly, the panic kicked in.

He must have sensed that, because he got in the water fast and slipped under the surface, then came up, the water spraying around him like stars. All right, thought Lolly, my turn. But before she could make a move, she saw a confusing flash, like a stroke of heat lightning. Connor looked around, as though he'd expected some interruption.

Almost as though it had been planned.

Seconds later, a drunk and rowdy gang of counselors burst from the woods, yodeling war whoops and aiming their flashlight beams with blinding accuracy, right at Lolly. Everything unfolded in a blur after that. She remembered screaming, scrambling for something, anything, with which to cover herself. Somehow a scratchy blanket appeared, swept around her shoulders. The laughter was deafening. She lost track of Connor, or maybe he didn't want to be found. It didn't matter now. She didn't want to see him, or anyone, ever again. She was so mortified that she simply ran, barefoot, over the rocky ground.

Camp Kioga To Close Its Gates Forever

Camp Kioga, an Avalon landmark since 1932, is about to close its gates permanently. Originally founded by Angus Neil Gordon as a rustic nature camp for city families, Kioga earned a reputation for providing challenging and rewarding outdoor experiences for generations of campers. The property is famous for its unparalleled beauty, which encompasses a pristine lake, a waterfall and forested mountains.

The hundred-acre wilderness property has been under the stewardship of Jane Gordon Bellamy and husband Charles Bellamy. When asked about future plans for the property, Mrs. Bellamy was quoted as saying, 'We hope to keep it in the family, if that's possible.'

Thirty-One

Misgivings poured over Olivia. She shouldn't have come here tonight, looking for him, looking for... what? Closure to the past or a new beginning? Or maybe just answers to a fresh set of questions.

'You know, the last time we tried this, things didn't work out so well for us,' she reminded him.

'And here we are, getting a second chance.' He leaned forward and kissed her sweetly, almost chastely.

Except that her response was anything but chaste. 'Lucky us.'

He kept going and the blouse fell open, exposing her to the warm night air and to his frankly tender gaze. She wondered if he could tell her heart was racing. Wondered if he could see the single trickle of sweat that slipped down her throat, into the cleft between her breasts. He could. He reached over and traced its path with his finger.

'Hot night,' he said as he undid the front hook of her bra.

'Yes,' she agreed, making absolutely no move to stop him. If there was one thing she had learned from all her dating mishaps of the past, it was that you didn't mess with something that felt this good. You just let it happen. The time for thinking and analyzing and rationalizing was past. Now was a time to simply feel.

'You should never, ever wear clothes,' he said. 'Ever.'

'Excuse me?'

'Why would you cover this up?'

'I didn't think you wanted to do this, Connor.'

'Why the hell would you think that?'

She couldn't believe he had to ask. The night after their trip to the city, he'd practically had her begging for sex, then stopped without explanation, leaving her to fill in the blanks. She had filled them in with nothing good—doubt and suspicion, mistrust, unsettling memories. But it was all eclipsed by a piercing need, not just for closeness and intimacy, but for him—his strong embrace and the press of his lips against hers. She wondered what he remembered of that night, if he thought of it at all. One thing she had figured out this summer was that memory was a tenuous thing, easily shaped by perception.

'The day we went to New York,' she reminded him. 'That night—I practically threw myself at you, and you ended up showing me the door.'

He laughed at that. *Laughed.*

'I don't believe you,' she said, tugging her blouse around her. 'You think this is funny?'

'Hell, yeah, it's funny. I bet I set a camp

463

record that night, for time spent in a cold shower. I didn't want to back off. Are you kidding?'

'Then why—'

'You were in a tough place that day, after dealing with your father. I didn't want to take advantage of you.'

Oh. She tried to figure out if he really meant it. He couldn't be serious. Could he?

'Looking a little skeptical there, Miss Bellamy,' he said.

'I'm trying to figure out if that's a line, or if you're for real.'

'Let's get something straight. That night at my place, I wanted you so bad it hurt. When we stopped, it was all I could do not to cry like a baby. No guy in his right mind would subject himself to that kind of torture. So I guess what I'm saying is, I'm not in my right mind when it comes to you, Lolly. You're too important to me. Even if it drives me crazy, I'm not going to let anything happen until I know it's right for both of us. And if that's your idea of a line, so be it.'

She was speechless, staring at him, her mouth open. She'd certainly had expectations when she'd come here tonight, but she hadn't expected *that.*

He leaned forward and kissed her with startling delicacy, cupping her head between his hands and touching his mouth to hers, gradually deepening the contact with gentle

464

pressure. She arched her body toward him, yet he didn't seem to be in much of a hurry. He had just stripped her bare to the waist and she was all but throwing herself at him, and still he seemed interested only in kissing, his tongue delicately tracing her lips and then dipping inside in a slow, compelling rhythm that completely mesmerized her.

Finally he lifted his mouth from hers. 'Let's go swimming,' he said.

No. Even as she let him help her to her feet, she protested with every cell in her body. She was dying for him to make love to her—right here, right now—and he wanted to go swimming? Maybe he'd changed his mind about making love. Maybe the kiss had convinced him that he wasn't so attracted to her after all.

Using one arm in a swift motion, he pulled his shirt off over his head. 'Well?' he prompted.

'Do you really want to, or is that just a ploy to get me naked?'

He touched his finger to her bare belly, moving it delicately along the waistband of her shorts. 'Mission is not quite accomplished.' He undid the top snap of her shorts, inched the zipper down, watching her face the whole time. 'See, the reason we should go swimming,' he said, 'is that if we just go for it right now, it will be over too...quick.' He traced his finger around to the small of her back. 'That's, um, a compliment, by the way.' And with that, he stepped back, finished undressing and dived into the water.

Olivia followed seconds later, jumping off the end of the dock. The cool, clean water rushing over her was glorious as they chased each other and swam around aimlessly, splashing and ducking and then coming up for air. The moon on the water drew ripples of pure silver across the surface, and when she tilted her head back, the stars seemed to spin in slow motion. She swam over to him and they held hands, staying afloat with easy fluttering kicks.

'I needed to slow things down,' he said.

'Is it working?' She slipped through the water, closer, until he caught her by the shoulders.

'Not very well.' Then he kissed her again with swift intensity, and she felt a shock of reaction and a sharp, sweet yearning so intense that it hurt.

She pulled back only far enough to whisper, 'Let's get out of the water.'

It was wonderful and terrible, standing there in front of him, dripping wet and wanting him so badly she couldn't see straight. It was strange and awkward and compelling, and when he finally kissed her, she didn't care about any of that. All she cared about was that she was here with him at last, and that she could touch him, all of him, feeling the shape of his muscles, the cool smoothness of his skin.

It crossed her mind that everything was about to change for them as they sank down onto the beach towels they'd spread out. With a meticulousness that was almost comical, he produced a fanfold of condom packets.

'Ambitious, aren't you?' she murmured.

'There's no way I'm only going to want you once tonight, Olivia,' he said, propping himself above her on one elbow.

She lay on her back looking up at him and at the stars, and she felt completely vulnerable. Yet she trusted him, she wanted this and whatever happened after this night, well, they would deal with that later. And finally, she understood what she hadn't realized before—that her previous failures with men had failed for a reason, and that reason was right here in her arms.

With those others, she had clung to some desperate, hopeful illusion that it would work out, but each time something had happened to shatter that illusion. Love wasn't love if she had to try too hard to feel it. With Connor, everything was totally different. She wasn't trying at all now.

Thirty-Two

Connor had certainly intended to seduce Olivia, but he hadn't anticipated that it would happen tonight, out in the wilderness, after a long day of work. He had been telling himself to wait until the time was right, when she was not in the midst of some emotional crisis. Now he realized that if he waited for the perfect time, when they were both in the exact right place, that moment might never come.

Ordinarily, he was very good at maintaining control. With Olivia, he was not quite able to contain himself. Feelings escaped his heart like a pot boiling over, and he had no desire to stop them. There was simply no resisting the hot summer night, the cool inviting water, and Olivia, just showing up like that, willing and beautiful, a reminder of things he'd left behind but still dreamed about. He made love to her at last, the way he'd thought about more often than he wanted to admit, and it was nothing like the fantasies he had in his mind about her. It was better. She was as genuine as she'd always been, and funny and emotional, and somehow he found that sexier than a lap dance.

The cool water of the lake barely did the trick. He bombarded himself with reminders to slow down. Easy. Take it easy. He wasn't exactly a gentleman, but one thing he knew was that you saw to the lady's pleasure first. Always, no exceptions. The good news was, Olivia was incredibly responsive, offering herself up to him, her sounds of pleasure reverberating through him. He kissed her, tasted her, drew long, searching, mindless caresses over her smooth bare skin, and finally—good God, finally—sank down into her with the sort of timing that was too perfect to be planned. He wondered if she experienced the same burning rush as he did. Judging by the sounds coming from her and the way she twined her long, smooth legs around him—well, for once they seemed to be on the same page.

For several minutes after, he couldn't bring himself to move, but then, with a reluctant groan, he untangled his limbs from her. Neither of them said anything and Connor figured that was a good sign. Babbling was a sign of nerves, or of regret. Silence was...well, hopeful. Besides, he was still coasting on a rush so intense it made him feel high.

Olivia let out a sigh and tucked herself against him. She was soft everywhere, her skin, her hair, her body. Her hair was still damp, and held the fresh smell of the water. He felt something in his heart, something rare and tender and wholly unfamiliar. She moved him, and not because she was sweet and emotional and sexy as hell, but also because she was someone he'd known more than half his life, even if it was only in the summer.

There was a good chance that this was all she needed from him. Mind-blowing sex and a shoulder to cry on, wasn't that what she'd said, maybe only half joking? He tried to figure out if that would be enough for him, and if it was, how long it would last.

This summer, he cautioned himself, could turn out like other summers long ago. When the season ended, they would go their separate ways. That was always how it happened.

Correction, he thought. That was how it had happened in the past. The future was another story. Their story. Maybe they'd get it right this time.

They stayed at the island long enough to watch the moon rise and set again. She moved to her side, her head pillowed on her arm, watching him with an expression of such blissfully sated desire that he couldn't help smiling.

'What's funny?' she asked.

'Nothing. I'm happy, that's all.'

She stretched luxuriously, ran her hand up his arm, over his chest. 'Really?'

'It wouldn't take much for me to get happy again,' he said, detaching another condom.

'What?' she whispered. 'What would it take?'

They skipped the preliminaries this time, and Connor knew it was still there between them, the explosive sensuality they'd discovered as teenagers. But back then it had been too intense, too confusing and—predictably—had ended badly. Neither of them had the emotional hardware to support a passion like that. Now it was exactly what he wanted, maybe even what they both wanted.

'I guess,' she said, sinking down to kiss him, 'I have my answer.'

He could have stayed there forever, alternating between making love and resting and dreaming, rousing himself to make love to her yet again. When they were together like this, it didn't matter who they were or where they'd come from. For some reason, they clicked. He had no idea why, or if this was something that would last, or if their need for each other would ever end.

'Is it just me,' she asked, 'or was that…incredible?'

He chuckled. 'It's not just you. I figured we'd be good together.'

'You figured? You *figured?*' She pushed herself up on one elbow. Though her face was in shadow, he could hear the glare in her voice.

'What, now you're mad about this?'

'I'm just wondering why you waited all summer to…for us to…'

'Me, too.' Determined to win back her

471

good humor, he pressed her back onto the beach towel and smiled down into her face. In the moonlight, she looked pale and soft, full lipped and vulnerable. 'Olivia, believe me, this was definitely in my plans. Not tonight, specifically, but I had it on the agenda.'

'Why?' She studied him through slitted eyes.

He realized he was bracing himself for the obvious question, the one women always seemed to ask—*Did you make love to me just now because you love me?*

She didn't ask it, although she sat up and pulled on her shorts. Connor tried not to groan aloud in disappointment. He traced the tattoo in the small of her back. 'This is sexy,' he said.

'Freddy and I got them together to celebrate graduation,' she said.

'Is his a pink butterfly, too?'

'I'm sure he'll let you see it if you ask nicely.'

'I'm never nice to Freddy.'

'I've noticed. Everyone noticed.'

'It's because I'm jealous of him.'

She laughed, tugging her bra into place. 'Of Freddy? Why?'

'Because you love him,' Connor said simply. 'Because he's been a part of your life.'

She froze in the middle of buttoning her shirt, and stared at him.

He'd said too much, exposed too much of

his heart. He got up swiftly and pulled on his jeans. He was an idiot. He should have waited, given himself time to figure out what—besides the obvious—was going on between him and Olivia. She was quiet now, probably freaking, wishing he hadn't blurted that out.

'I can't be completely certain,' she said, 'but I think that's the best thing you've ever said to me.'

'It wasn't that good.' Then he grinned. All right, so maybe he was wrong. Maybe it wasn't such a crazy thing, leveling with her.

'You know what really bugged me about you, at the beginning of summer?'

He chuckled. 'Everything.'

'Huh.' She sniffed. 'But the thing that bugged me the most is that the first time you saw me again, you didn't recognize me.'

'Maybe I was only playing dumb, ever think of that?'

'God, Connor. If that's the case, then it's even worse.'

'Listen,' he said, holding her by the waist, drawing her near so their hips were touching intimately. 'You weren't playing fair that day, changing everything on me, including your name.'

'Maybe that's always been our problem,' she whispered. 'Not playing fair.'

He couldn't help himself; he leaned down and kissed her again, and just the taste of her made him want her all over again. He traced the outline of her jaw, her neck, lower, until she slipped her hands between them and stepped back.

'We should go,' she said softly.

'Why?' he asked.

'Because…I have no idea.' She laughed and took another step back. 'Because it's nearly dawn.'

Oh, she'd gotten sophisticated on him, Connor thought, still tasting that kiss. She'd learned to be cagey with her emotions. She'd learned to surround herself with brittle armor. She knew now that some guys were only good for getting laid.

He should have been gratified by her reply. Instead, it made him feel hollow. Expendable, maybe. For the first time in his life, he wanted to be more to a woman than a good lay.

Kioga Couple To Celebrate Golden Anniversary

Charles Langston Bellamy and Jane Gordon Bellamy, longtime owners of the legendary Camp Kioga on Willow Lake, will return to the camp next week to celebrate their fiftieth wedding anniversary. The couple was married there on August 26, 1956, and spent the next four decades running the camp, which was founded by Mrs. Bellamy's grandfather, Angus Gordon, in 1932. The camp ceased operating in 1997, though the property remains in the possession of the Bellamy family. Over the past summer, the camp has undergone a renovation in preparation for the festivities. Next Saturday, friends and relatives of Mr. and Mrs. Bellamy will step back in time as they celebrate the couple's milestone. The gala affair will feature a catered gourmet meal, live music and a replica of the original wedding cake from Sky River Bakery.

Over the summer, there has been keen speculation regarding the future of Camp

475

Kioga, which encompasses a parcel of pristine wilderness. The Bellamys could not be reached for comment.

Thirty-Three

As Julian walked across the camp compound, he noticed how the place had been transformed. Kioga now looked like something out of a picture book or brochure, with its neat cottages and newly mown grass and fields. The grounds had been pruned, the walkways covered with a new layer of gravel. Bright red geraniums and deep purple lobelia spilled from the window boxes. By now, he knew the names of all the plants they'd put in because he'd busted his ass working on the gardens. He didn't care if he never saw a flat of marigolds again, as long as he lived.

There was a lift in his step as he headed for breakfast. He'd risen at the crack of dawn so he could finish work early and head to New Paltz to go rock climbing in the Shawangunks, something he'd been wanting to do all summer. On his back was a knapsack clanking with gear from the sports-storage shed—open-fingered gloves, carabiners and quickdraws, climbing shoes, helmet, harness and chalk. He wore low-slung cargo shorts and one of his father's ancient T-shirts. After Louis Gastineaux died, Julian's aunts had tried to give away all his dorky old T-shirts, mostly freebies given out at engineering conferences. Julian had rescued a few, and he liked wearing them. They felt lucky. Today's shirt bore the slogan It *Is* Rocket Science.

He found Connor hitching the backhoe trailer to the truck. With most of the work done, it was time to move the heavy equipment out of the way.

'Hey,' said Julian.

Connor connected the wiring between the truck and trailer and straightened up. 'Hey, Julian.'

'I was wondering if I could borrow the truck. But, um, looks like you're going to be using it.'

'I need to get the backhoe down to the river-road property. I'm planning on breaking ground soon.'

Julian nodded. His brother had this whole elaborate plan to build himself a house.

'What do you need the truck for?' Connor asked.

'I was planning to go rock climbing this afternoon.'

'By yourself?'

'Not if I can talk Daisy into going with me.'

Connor leaned against the side of the truck. 'I don't think it'll take much talking.'

Julian suppressed a grin. 'Hope not.'

Connor held out a set of keys. 'Park the trailer on the flat at the top of the driveway,' he said. 'Don't back in, just unhitch it and go. You know how to unhitch it, right?'

'Sure. You only showed me about a million

times. And thanks, Connor. I didn't know if you'd let me.'

'Try not to look too surprised,' Connor said as Julian loaded his gear into the back of the truck. 'I had my doubts at the beginning of summer, but I'm glad you came.'

The funny thing was, Julian was glad he'd come, too. Sure, he'd busted his ass, working here. It wasn't so bad, though. Connor paid him a decent wage. Everything about Connor was decent. He still made Julian feel like a screwup sometimes.

They headed to the dining hall together. The others would probably be getting ready for lunch. 'So... you and Olivia,' Julian said.

'What about me and Olivia?'

Julian flashed him a grin. 'You worked late last night. Really late. Like, all night long.' He almost laughed aloud when he saw Connor's ears turn red.

'Do me a favor and don't say anything to her,' Connor muttered. 'Or anyone.'

Julian wouldn't commit to that. He wanted to say it was about damn time, but he restrained himself. 'She's totally into you,' he said, giving his brother a slug on the arm.

Connor slugged him back. 'Yeah, well, I'm totally into her.'

'What are you going to do about it?'

'Be into her for a while. I guess I could probably propose to her, get turned down.'

'Nice attitude, Con.'

479

'I usually prepare for the worst, and then I'm surprised by the best.'

'Why not expect the best? Reach beyond your grasp and all that?'

'You've been reading those air force recruiting brochures.'

*   *   *

As Julian had hoped, Daisy was in the dining hall. Over the summer, he'd thought often and intensely of hooking up with her. She was sophisticated and was clearly experienced, but he got a weird vibe from her. And she was dealing with a lot of crap with her family, which made him reluctant to hook up with her for laughs. That just didn't seem right.

He fixed himself a sandwich. 'So are you up for some rock climbing?' he asked her.

'I told Dare I'd help her with the centerpieces for the big celebration. She's making them out of birdhouses,' Daisy said.

Great, he thought. She wasn't even going to pretend to be interested. 'Oh, that's important,' he said. Sometimes girls were such a drag.

'I was totally planning on going with you,' she said airily.

'Really.' He couldn't keep the grin off his face.

'Are you sure, Daisy?' asked Greg. 'Rock climbing is incredibly hard, not to mention dangerous.'

A dad who worried about you, thought Julian. What a concept. 'She'll be fine,' he said. 'I've done tons of climbs at Joshua Tree in California, honest. We've got all the gear we need, and I'll only pick easy climbs—no more than a five-point-one, max. And we'll use a top rope and belay from the top.'

'Cool,' Max piped up, handing a crust of his sandwich to the dog. 'Can I come?'

'*No.*' Both Daisy and her father spoke emphatically, at the same time.

'But I can, right, Dad?' she said.

Greg leaned back, arms folded, and considered for a moment. 'I'll make you a deal. You can take the afternoon off and go rock climbing. But only if you promise to go fishing with Max and me one more time.'

To her credit, she didn't roll her eyes or pout. 'Deal,' she said, and headed for the door.

*　　　*　　　*

They parked inside the Mohonk Preserve and hiked along a marked trail to the cliffs.

'Okay, now *this* is disturbing,' Daisy said. She bent back and shaded her eyes to look up at the pebbled rock face, seamed by fissures and shadowed by overhangs, with little tufts of vegetation growing out of the cracks. There were a few climbers out, their routes marked

481

by rock-colored slings at rappel stations.

'Dude,' Julian said, already picking his route as he followed her gaze.

'It's not quite what I pictured.'

'We could find another ascent if you like,' Julian said. 'The climbing guidebook lists a bunch that are a lot more challenging.'

'You're not challenged enough by this?'

'It's a rock.'

'A vertical one.'

He laughed. 'That's what makes it fun.' He demonstrated the basic techniques of climbing, which she was familiar with from the indoor climbing walls she'd done. He chalked his hands and took a quick side route to the top, where he secured a rope to an anchor and then rappelled back down. 'Not too heinous,' he commented, already exhilarated from the rhythm and balance of the climb. He showed her a simple opening move, pointing out the way to the crux and then to the top. 'The main thing is to take your time. Don't grab the wrong thing because you're scared or in a hurry.'

'How do I know which choice is the right one?'

'Because it leads to the next right choice.'

'Jeez, Julian.'

'And don't be afraid. You can always stretch a little farther than you think.'

She laughed. 'Now you're sounding like a graduation commencement speaker.'

482

'I don't think we have those at my school. Come on, let's give it a try.'

She took a deep breath, squared her shoulders. 'All right.'

He helped her with her gear, which led to a couple of strangely intimate moments, especially when she stepped into the swami harness and he drew the webbing snug against her crotch. 'Sorry,' he said. 'I just need to make sure you're safe.'

'It's all right. This is the closest I've had to a date all summer.'

She was a beginner but not clueless. He demonstrated the climb and it felt good, reaching and stretching, conquering the rock face hold by hold while she spotted him.

'I'm going to fall,' he said when he was about halfway up.

'You look fine to me,' she said. 'A regular Spider-Man.'

'I mean on purpose. So you can see how the sling works. I'm going to fall, and you're going to catch me, just like I showed you.'

'Don't—'

'I trust you.' He let go with his hands. There was a moment of weightlessness and an even shorter moment of free fall; then the apparatus kicked in and caught him.

'You're insane,' she scolded.

'Nah. I just like the rush.' He reprised the climb, showing her again. Hold by hold, always looking ahead to the next move.

'What if you can't see what your next move is going to be?' she asked.

'Then you grab for something and hope for the best.'

They did a relatively short climb, no overhangs or anything too hazardous. She was a bit shaky but did all right, shrieking a little here and there. He spotted her while she made the climb. She went slowly and cautiously, but she was strong and didn't make many mistakes. When she did, she was smart about correcting them. Ultimately, they both reached the summit, covered in sweat. Daisy did a little dance of triumph. 'I feel like Frodo at the top of Mount Doom.'

They toasted each other with their water bottles. Then she took out a pack of cigarettes. He scowled at her. 'Those'll kill you before climbing will.'

She hunkered down and flicked her lighter. Ignoring him, she dumped the cigarettes onto a rock and set fire to them, one by one, adding twigs to keep it burning. As the small heap smoldered and turned to ashes, she sat back on her heels and said, 'I've been wanting to do that all summer.'

'Then why didn't you?'

She stood up, stubbed out the smoke with her heel. 'It turned into this thing between me and my dad. I kept expecting him to put his foot down, but he never did. So I realized waiting for my parents to tell me to stop might have taken years and by then, I'd be a hopeless addict. Might as well quit now on my own, without being told.'

'Good plan.' On impulse, he leaned down and kissed her, briefly and sweetly, on the mouth. 'I've been wanting to do that all summer.'

'Then why didn't you?'

'I wasn't sure you wanted me to.' His heart was beating erratically. 'Let's try rappelling.' He backed off, bouncing expertly off the surface and measuring the rope with his gloved hands. When he touched down, she leaned over the ledge and gave him a little round of applause.

'Are you ready to give it a shot, or do you want another demo?'

'Hmm. I don't know. What does your Spidey sense tell you?'

'That you're going to be great.'

She was hesitant at first, testing the gear, and then finally letting herself down. Her descent was none too smooth, but she was flushed with victory when she touched down. 'That was awesome,' she yelled, and her voice bounced off the walls of the cliffs.

'You're a good coach,' she said. 'Do you do this a lot?'

'You're my first student.'

'Yeah? Then you're a natural. That'll come in handy if you decide to go for that ROTC scholarship.'

They had stayed up late many a night, discussing the pros and cons. By now, Julian understood the process. It was, like, ten times more involved than applying for college because there was a physical-fitness component and a health exam in addition to the usual stuff.

'I'm not going to go for it,' he said glumly, considering the long road ahead.

'Why not?'

'They take your freedom away, monitor your every move. Your life is totally regulated. How is that different from going to juvenile detention?'

'It's not that different,' she admitted.

'I came here this summer just to avoid incarceration. Why would I sign up for four years of it?' He shook his head. 'Besides, it'd just be a waste of time.'

'Why do you say that?'

'My grades suck. My school sucks. I got nothing going for me.'

'Nice attitude, Gastineaux. And what was it you were just saying about stretching farther than you think you can?'

'I was just bullshitting you so you'd do the climb.'

'Were not.' She adjusted her helmet. 'I'm ready to try another climb now.'

Her exuberance as she bounced down the rock wall made him laugh. *She* made him laugh. More than that, she made him think

486

outside the box. Just because he lived in a crappy town and went to a crappy school didn't mean he had to have a crappy life. If he took a chance, and he made it, he might be sent all over the globe. He might learn to fly.

'Maybe you're right,' he said. 'So you think I should go for it?'

She took off her helmet and brushed the hair off her sweaty brow. 'What does your Spidey sense tell you?'

Thirty-Four

Daisy's fishing expeditions with her father and brother had become a joke around the camp. Not once, all summer long, had they come home with a trout. Daisy didn't really care, though. She and Max had finally learned that the whole point of fishing was not to catch a fish. The act was more about learning to be patient. Be still inside your head and relaxed in your body and be in the moment. Simple as that.

Still, hope sprang eternal and they went out yet again, probably for the last time of the summer. At least it gave her plenty of time to daydream about Julian. He was like no other guy she'd ever met. Inhumanly good-looking, but that wasn't what was so special about him. It was the way he made her look at things like her life, her family. A few months ago, she figured her life was in the toilet, what with her parents splitting up. Julian made her see that there were all kinds of definitions of a family, and it didn't only have to be people who were related, who lived under the same roof. He also made her see that there was no such thing as a perfect family, but that didn't mean giving up on the whole idea. Here he was, this guy who had lost his father, whose mother sounded like a loser, coming all the way across the country just to be with the one person he could count on—a brother he barely knew.

'What're you looking at?' Max said. 'You're looking at me funny.'

'Just appreciating the fact that I have a brother,' she said.

He snorted. 'Yeah, right.'

She shook her head, knowing she'd never convince him she was sincere. Then the unthinkable happened. The bobber on Max's line dipped. Daisy thought she was seeing things, but there it went again. It trembled and dipped down.

'Are you watching, Max?' she whispered.

'Yeah,' he said. 'Dad, check it out. I'm getting a bite.'

'You sure are, son. You want some help?'

'Nope, I got it.'

'Remember to give a quick tug. You have to time it just—'

'Got it.' As if he'd been doing it all his life,

Max whipped his pole back. Then he started cranking the reel. The fish put up a fight, jumping clear out of the water, spraying diamond droplets across the surface. Max dropped down on his knees in the bottom of the canoe, his face a mask of total absorption. Smoothly, with a patience hard learned over the course of the summer, he reeled in the fish. Dad scooped it into the net and it flopped down in the boat, lying on its side as if in exhaustion.

The fish had been neatly hooked through the lip, a clean catch. It was a good size, too. Definitely big enough to keep. 'Finally,' Max said, gently lifting the nylon line and holding up the prize.

Dad snapped a picture. 'How about that?' he said. 'Fresh trout for supper. Or maybe we should have it stuffed and mounted.'

Three concentric circles outlined the trout's eye. The fish was strangely beautiful, definitely worthy of its name: rainbow trout. Along its slender length were all the colors of the spectrum, shimmering in the sunlight.

Within moments, the fish started to die. It was drowning in air, its gills fanning out with what looked to Daisy like desperation. She could see the delicate structure of the gills, a series of bright red petals, working hard to find water to breathe.

The trout's mouth worked in a silent plea: Oh. Oh. Oh.

'Throw it back, Max,' Daisy said with sudden urgency.

'What? No way. I've been trying all summer to catch a fish.'

'And now you have. But you should throw the thing back before it dies.'

Max looked at their father. 'What should I do, Dad?'

'Up to you, buddy.'

No, it wasn't. God, just once she'd like to see her father step up and make a decision. Instead, he retreated behind his usual, 'Up to you.'

Gritting her teeth, Daisy picked up the fish. It was shiny and writhing in her hands, almost impossible to hold on to. She tried to be gentle as she carefully extracted the hook, wincing as she pulled the sharp barb through.

'Say goodbye to the fish, Max,' she said.

He didn't protest. He touched the fish with a grubby index finger and said, 'It's okay to let it go now.'

She leaned down and put it in the water. To her horror, the trout didn't go anywhere but instead floated crookedly, its mouth still gasping. 'It's too late,' she said. 'We killed it.'

It was just a stupid fish. She wondered why its death felt like such a tragedy.

'We did,' Max said despondently. 'We killed him.'

Dad didn't say anything, but leaned down and gently took the fish between his hands.

He didn't pick it up out of the lake, though. He ran the trout through the water, nose first in long strokes, and then released it. The tail swayed and propelled it slowly forward, and then the fish glided away.

Daisy felt a welling of emotion. Max gaped at his father.

'You have to get the water flowing through their gills to revive them sometimes,' Dad said.

'Cool,' said Max. 'You saved it.'

'No, Daisy did.' Dad dried his hands on his shorts.

Daisy felt limp with relief. 'Sorry about that, Max,' she said. 'I just figured we should let it go.' She couldn't explain the compulsion, not without digging into the pain she had endured over the coming divorce, a pain that was out of her control.

'I don't mind,' Max said amiably enough. 'I wouldn't have wanted to eat it, anyway. And we got a picture, so there's proof.'

'You guys are two amazing kids,' Dad said. 'Good job on the fish.'

Daisy laughed. 'It only took us all summer.'

'There was never any hurry.'

Dad picked up his paddle. 'Ready to call it a day?'

'Yes,' said Max. 'I'm starving for a peanut butter and baloney sandwich.'

They paddled back in tandem, their

rhythm in sync now, with strong, assured strokes. 'We might suck at fishing,' Daisy said, 'but we sure can paddle a canoe.'

Their dad, who had a good memory for lyrics, sang every fish song he could think of, from 'Jeremiah Was a Bullfrog' to 'Octopus's Garden.' Max and Daisy joined in, no longer required to be quiet, because they didn't care how many fish they scared. Their voices carried across the flat, beautiful water and seemed to float upward, and in that moment, Daisy felt more buoyant and hopeful than she had in months.

It was kind of dumb, of course, because nothing different had happened except that Max had caught a fish and they'd let it go. What was so uplifting about that?

Then she looked at the laughing faces of her father and brother and realized the reason didn't matter. Sometimes it was enough just to be happy, for no reason at all.

Thirty-Five

The excitement in the air was palpable. Guests had been arriving all week, some of them people Olivia hadn't seen since she was a child. As visitors arrived and settled in, the camp came to life once more, reflecting the glory days of a more innocent time. Olivia watched families falling into their old patterns as life took on a different, slower rhythm. The younger generation, unfamiliar with camp life, took delight in discovering a whole new world. In the days leading up to the celebration, there were footraces and water sports, pranks and late-night kitchen raids, all imbued with a sense of nostalgia.

The day of the anniversary was favored by perfect weather, just as everyone had hoped. Guests emerged from their bunkhouses and cabins, dressed to the nines. Others drove up from the city for the day. The town of Avalon was represented by the mayor, who presented the Bellamys with a special citation in their honor.

Olivia was moved by the number of people who showed up. That her grandparents had so many loyal friends was a testament to the way they'd lived their lives. There were moments of poignancy as well, when they reflected on the people they had lost.

In the midst of all the preparations, she had no time to indulge in daydreams about Connor Davis, although she yearned to do just that. It was probably for the best. Her daydreams usually turned into worry and sometimes full-blown paranoia. Had it been a one-night stand? Would they part ways now that summer was over? The misgivings were already starting, so when the Sky River Bakery truck backed up to the kitchen, she welcomed the distraction. Jenny Majesky and her assistant, the blond teenager named Zach Alger, brought the cake in sections to assemble on the center table.

'It's going to be beautiful,' Olivia said.

'Thanks.' Jenny smiled at her. She was dressed with discreet professionalism, in a sleeveless black A-line dress and low-heeled pumps, and no jewelry except a pair of small gold earrings. Over the dress, she wore a fitted caterer's jacket and her dark hair was pulled back in a sleek ponytail.

Looking around the dining hall, Jenny said, 'You've made it really beautiful, Olivia.'

'Thanks. I had a lot of help.' She hesitated, wanting to say more. She and Jenny were still so new to each other, still cautious. She heard the low growl of an engine and craned her neck to look past Jenny. It wasn't Connor, but Rourke McKnight, the chief of police.

Jenny was watching her. 'You look as if you were expecting someone else.'

Olivia conceded with a nod. 'Connor Davis.'

Jenny opened a box of small white roses in tiny glass bulbs and started arranging them around the base of the cake. 'Is he your date for the party?'

Olivia stepped up to help with the roses. 'I'm not sure what he is,' she admitted. To her horror, her throat suddenly felt thick, as if she was on the verge of tears. 'We're just…not

494

good together.' She swallowed hard, took a deep breath. 'No, that's not right. *I'm* not good in a relationship, not even with Connor.'

Jenny took out an antique silver cake server and tied a satin ribbon around its handle. 'I don't know much about Connor,' she said. 'A little, though. In a town this size, everybody knows a little of everything. He's always seemed lonely to me.'

Olivia thought about the big piece of property on the river, the tiny Airstream trailer. 'Maybe he likes being a bachelor.'

Jenny set the server on a bone china plate and stepped back, eyeing the arrangement critically. 'He's planning to build a place he designed himself, did you know that?'

'I saw the plans.'

'Then you saw that he's building a four-bedroom house. Guys who like their bachelorhood don't build four-bedroom houses.' She adjusted the groom on top of the cake.

There was something calm and reasonable about Jenny, and somehow it quieted the flurry of butterflies in Olivia's stomach. Maybe she was going to like having a sister.

She looked out the window again as a limousine pulled up and recognized the tall, silver-haired man who emerged. 'Is Senator McKnight any relation to Police Chief McKnight?' she asked.

'They're father and son.'

Wow. Now there was a puzzle. The senator was one of the wealthiest, most powerful men in the state. The chief lived in an apartment in an old brick building in the town's historic district, and when he was off duty, drove an El Camino that had seen better days. The two men passed each other on the walkway, barely acknowledging one another. Olivia noticed the way Jenny was watching Rourke McKnight, with his golden hair, full lips and brooding eyes that was not such a puzzle. A sharp perception tingled through her. 'Are the two of you...?'

'God, no,' Jenny was quick to say. 'I mean... God.' She shuddered.

'Is there something wrong with him?' Olivia offered an ironic smile. 'Doesn't he look enough like Ryan Philippe for you?'

'There's nothing wrong, except he's...Rourke. He dates women who look like lingerie models and have the IQ of a zucchini.'

'Oh. Not good.'

'No.' She grinned. 'Do you really think he looks like Ryan Philippe?'

'I'm guessing there's a reason half the women in town park illegally. Probably hoping he'll handcuff himself to them.' Catching Jenny's look, she added, 'Other than his taste in women, he seems like a good guy.'

'I suppose.' There was a world of wistfulness in her sigh.

They left the dining hall and headed

outside. 'He helped me figure out that you...that we're related,' Olivia said.

'Rourke did?' Jenny looked amazed.

As they stepped out into the sunlight, Olivia heard a car door slam, and there was something in the sound that made her turn. Suddenly, a more immediate dilemma presented itself. 'Okay,' she said, taking Jenny by the elbow and steering her to the side, 'don't freak out.'

'What?'

'My mother Pamela just arrived. She's with her parents—my grandparents—Gwen and Samuel Lightsey.'

As awkward moments went, this one was bound to make family history. 'Do they know about me?' asked Jenny.

'I told Dad it was up to him to explain it. He's a lawyer, Jenny. He's good with words. It'll be all right.'

Jenny squared her shoulders. 'Then I'll let him introduce me.'

Olivia felt an unexpected sense of solidarity with Jenny, yet she couldn't deny a flood of relief that she wouldn't have to be the one to make the introductions. Jenny had gone back inside by the time Olivia's mother and grandparents approached. 'Hello, Mom,' Olivia said. 'Grandma and Grandpa.' She kissed each of them. Then she noticed her grandmother's complexion resembled the dull white of chalk. 'Grandma?' she said, taking her arm.

Gwen Lightsey practically slumped against her husband. They helped her to a bench.

'I'll get a doctor,' Olivia's mother said.

'Pamela, no,' Gwen said. 'It's not...I'll be all right.' She fanned her face. 'It's just a rather unpleasant surprise to see her, looking so much like that woman....'

Pamela frowned, looked at Olivia and back at her mother. 'You've seen that girl's mother?'

Samuel waved a dismissive hand. 'It was ages ago.'

'You never told me you'd seen her,' Pamela said.

'There was nothing to tell.' Some of Gwen's color began to return. 'She was a horrid woman of low morals, and Philip was well rid of her.'

'Here's an idea,' Olivia said, forcing a bright smile. 'Let's let today be about Nana and Granddad, all right? That's what we're here for, right?'

'Of course.' Pamela completely surprised her by giving her a hug. 'You're absolutely right.' She pulled back and studied Olivia. 'And you're absolutely glowing. What's going on, Olivia?'

Olivia laughed. 'It's a long story, Mom.'

Her mother pulled her aside. 'Just make it short.'

'Let's see. I discovered I have a half sister,

restored an entire wilderness camp, and oh, yes, I fell in love with Connor Davis for the second time in my life.' She laughed again at the expression on her mother's face.

'Connor Davis? You mean Terry Davis's boy?'

'He's not a boy anymore.'

'He's not right for you, Olivia. He wasn't years ago, and he isn't now.'

'You don't know anything about him, Mom.'

'I know about you. Don't do anything foolish, Olivia.'

'Oh, believe me,' she said. 'I already have.'

*　　*　　*

'What a dumb ass,' Julian said to Connor. 'You are, like, this close to missing the ceremony.' Julian was in charge of ferrying guests back and forth on the pontoon boat, its railings festooned with swags of flowers and greenery. He hastened to push off the dock. The small trolling engine sputtered to life, and Julian steered expertly toward the island, where the guests were gathering for the renewal of the vows. The only other passengers were an elderly couple who had arrived a few minutes ago.

'Watch your mouth,' Connor warned his brother. 'Show a little respect.'

The old man and his wife were either hard

of hearing or they weren't listening. They sat at the rail of the boat, looking across the water, their hands touching. There was something about a long-married couple, Connor thought. They knew each other's rhythms and they seemed to fit together naturally, like trees that had grown side by side for so long their branches intertwined.

He straightened his bow tie. 'Do I look okay?'

Julian studied him with a critical eye, then gave a thumbs-up. 'What took you so long?'

'I had to go into town to pick something up.'

'Huh. Like what?'

Connor tapped his breast pocket, feeling the small rounded box from Palmquist Jewelry. 'I'll show you later.'

Julian raised his eyebrows. *'Dude.'*

'If you say one word to anyone, I'll—'

'Man, you don't need to worry. Anyway, it's not like anybody's going to be surprised, except maybe Olivia.' Julian paused. 'It's all good, Con. She's great.'

Understatement of the year, Connor thought. She was better than great. She was adorable and affectionate and funny, and he loved her with every cell in his body. She was the one he wanted to grow old with, twining his life with hers. All this time, she was what he had been missing without even realizing he was missing her. He grinned at his brother. 'So you think she'll be surprised?'

'Who knows how a girl thinks?'

That made Connor laugh. 'Maybe you can study that in college.'

'Maybe,' he said. 'So do you think it's crazy, me trying to get into the air force ROTC?'

'Nah. You're just what they're looking for.' Connor hoped his brother would go through with the process. If the kid could hack the discipline, it could be a good match for him— a place where he could put both his brains and his fearlessness to use.

Julian flicked a dreadlock out of his eyes. 'I guess I could use a haircut anyway.'

* * *

'You're late,' Olivia said without looking at Connor as he slid into the folding chair next to hers. She felt a fundamental change when he was near. The air took on a certain quality, an intensity, though she seemed to be the only one who noticed that.

'Sorry.'

Like most guys, Connor didn't seem to care much for weddings. She relented and glanced his way. Oh, my. He looked like something out of a dream, in a flawless tux, perfectly shaved, his hair recognizably styled. He smelled delicious. If Connor Davis was the sexiest man she'd ever known, Connor Davis in a tux was something beyond that. It was possible that he was *too* good-looking, to the point of being intimidating, like someone in a BBC production.

'Something the matter?' he asked, his breath warm as he leaned down to whisper in her ear.

She realized then she'd gasped aloud at his appearance. 'You clean up real well,' she said.

'Ha ha.'

'Dearly beloved,' said the pastor. 'On August 26, 1956, in this very spot, my father performed the ceremony that bound these two hearts as one. Now, half a century later, our dear friends Charles Bellamy and Jane Gordon Bellamy have come back to celebrate their love and to renew their lifelong bond in the presence of those they hold most dear. My own father has passed on to his reward, but today, on this glorious summer day, I feel his pleasure. Surely this pleases the Almighty as well, this glorious celebration of the enduring grace of love.'

Olivia knew it wouldn't take long for the tears to start. There was no question there would be crying. She and her cousins and aunts had all lacquered on the waterproof mascara. However, they felt duty bound to lay some ground rules. No audible sobs, no visible shaking. Dark glasses would be required for those who were most at risk. The women had made a pact that when the vows began, they

502

wouldn't look at each other, because eye contact under these circumstances tended to set off a chain reaction.

Still, nothing could have prepared Olivia for the huge wave of sentiment that came over her the very second her grandfather turned to her grandmother and took her hands in his as gently as if they were two shy birds about to fly away.

There was something so holy in the way they looked at one another, with love shining from their faces, brighter than the sun. Nana was beyond gorgeous in a dress of cream silk charmeuse with a lace collar, her silver hair swept into a graceful coil. Granddad, tall and distinguished in his tux, cleared his throat and began to speak the vows he had prepared.

'When I was a young man,' he said, 'it was drummed into me that a person's great ambition in life should be to marry well. In the Bellamy family, that meant I should find a certain type of girl, from a certain type of family. But that's not what I found, here in this small mountain town, so far from everything I knew. One summer when I least expected it, I met the most beautiful girl in the world. She wasn't that certain type I was supposed to be looking for. She was the one I was supposed to be with. Now, fifty years later, I can honestly say that I have married well. So here's to you, my love, my beautiful Janie. It's been a grand adventure.'

'I, too, have married well,' Nana replied, beaming at him. 'I married my best friend, the love of my life, the one who has walked by my side on our life's journey, the father of my four wonderful, beloved children. I'm proud to marry you all over again. I feel so blessed to have shared these years with you, Charles, and I vow to share all the years to come, to love you every single day with every bit of my heart.'

Daisy and her mother Sophie played a soft duet on flute and clarinet, a Brahms air. With ritual solemnity, Charles and Jane exchanged the new rings that had been forged especially for the occasion by a goldsmith of Lightsey Gold & Gem. His open hands hovering over a missal, the pastor read a prayer.

Olivia felt an eruption of emotion inside her, and knew she was about to violate every ground rule they'd laid out for themselves. She had already committed an audible sniffle. She was trembling, blinking fast. If she opened her mouth, she knew a loud sob would escape.

'Code red.' Beside her, Dare murmured a warning to Freddy. 'Olivia's about to go into meltdown. Quick, say something to distract her.'

Freddy was useless. He was staring at the ground, the tears pouring down his face.

'You barely know these people,' Dare hissed at him, and then she nearly lost it as well, crushing a Kleenex to her face.

504

'Hold on, Lolly,' Connor whispered in her ear. 'You're doing fine.'

*   *   *

In contrast to the solemnity of the ceremony, the celebration afterward was a frenzy of food, drink, music and good wishes. Dare had created a beautiful setting with crisp white tablecloths and colorful centerpieces, and rented crystal and silver that caught the deep light of sunset as it streamed through the windows. The champagne flowed freely, toasts were raised to the Bellamys and there was a tangible air of happiness in the dining hall and on the adjacent deck.

'Not too shabby,' Freddy said, giving Olivia a nudge as the dance floor filled.

'Not at all,' she agreed. 'Thanks for everything this summer.'

'Are you kidding? It's one of the best gigs I've ever had.'

She smiled, watching his gaze devour Dare, who was drawing a reluctant but good-natured Max out onto the floor for a dance. Everyone, it seemed, was dancing, even the most frail of wedding guests, who needed the aid of a walker. The entire space was filled with laughter and movement. This summer, Olivia thought, had been an amazing ride.

'Are you all right?' Freddy asked her.

'Sure.'

505

'What's going on with you and Mr. Wonderful?'

Between the emotional ceremony and getting the party under way, she'd barely had time to talk to Connor. Even if she did, she wasn't sure what she'd say. *I fell in love with you all over again? Can we make it work this time?* The questions were so new and so raw, she couldn't even answer them for herself, let alone for him.

'I don't know,' she said to Freddy.

'Sure you do. I can see it on your face.' He led her onto the dance floor as 'Somewhere Beyond the Sea' played.

She bit her lip, fought for control, because she felt like crying. She'd felt that way all day long. 'There's the small matter of my track record,' she reminded him. 'Three strikes and you're out, isn't that how most things work?'

'Not this, you idiot,' Freddy said. 'Listen, the last three are history for a reason. And okay, I admit it, I thought maybe I could be that reason, but that was just wishful thinking.'

'Aw, Freddy.'

'Think about the story your granddad told earlier, about his family threatening to boycott his wedding, his father cutting him out of the family fortune. What if he'd caved to that?' Freddy let go of her hand and gestured around the room. 'If he had, none of this would have happened. This is the kind of thing you stay and fight for.'

506

'I have a life in the city, my business—'

'Details, details,' he said impatiently. 'For every problem you bring up, I'll hand you a solution, and you know it. I'll sublet your apartment. Take care of the business.'

'It's my job.'

'But this,' he said, 'this could be your life if you'd quit resisting it.'

She kissed his cheek. 'I'll keep that in mind.' She'd thought of nothing else lately, her heart pounding in terror, yet she had no idea what she was afraid of. The only thing scarier than imagining a future with Connor was imagining a future without him.

'Do better than that,' he said, bringing her to the edge of the dance floor and smoothly trading her for Dare. Before Olivia could respond, the two of them were off, laughing and lost in each other, making love seem like such a simple proposition.

'You said you wouldn't cry during the ceremony,' said a stern, familiar voice behind her. 'You nearly made *me* lose it, and think what a disaster that would have been.'

Olivia turned and gave her grandmother a hug. 'I'm sorry, Nana. It was all so lovely. I couldn't stifle myself.'

Nana slipped her arm through Olivia's and the two of them strolled out through the French doors to the deck overlooking the lake. The last colors of sunset glazed the water and imbued the camp with a deep, rich glow.

The sounds of music, laughter and clinking glasses melded beautifully with the quieter sounds of the summer breeze and the birds of evening. Nana sighed happily. 'You did this, Olivia,' she said. 'You made the camp look even more beautiful than I remember. It's everything I'd hoped for and more.'

'I loved doing it, Nana.'

When they'd first arrived, her grandparents had been like children again, scurrying from place to place, oohing and aahing over the camp's transformation.

'I'm glad you agreed to do it,' Nana said. 'I did so want you to come back here.' A sly look flickered in her eyes. 'You had unfinished business.'

'Connor Davis,' Olivia said. 'I take it Dare's filled you in.' She pressed her hands against the deck railing. 'It's...complicated. I'm not lucky like you, Nan—'

'Luck.' Nana made a tsking sound. 'That kind of thinking is naive. A monumental love and a great marriage don't simply happen, like winning the lottery. You have to build it and nurture it, and quite often, it's hard work. It's not like checking into a spa, being pampered into a state of bliss.'

'I know. I'm not naive,' Olivia said. 'Just...risk averse.'

Another tsk. 'If you're going to take a risk on something, why not love?'

Because I suck at love, okay? Olivia

508

thought, but she held her tongue.

A passing waiter offered them champagne, and they toasted each other, easing the tension of the moment. Nana took a sip and sighed again. 'Charles and I have a decision to make about Camp Kioga,' she said. 'We've been putting it off too long as it is.'

'What are you going to do?'

'We were hoping to see it reopened, not just for children, but for families. It's quite the thing these days, you know, for families to seek a summer haven together. People's lives have gotten too busy. Families drift apart. This is a place that can bring them together—private cabins, communal meals, planned activities. Of course, people would only stay for a week or two, but there would be all the traditions and then some, like wine tastings in the evening for adults. There's been quite a movement afoot these days, the revival of family camp.' She finished her champagne and set down the glass. 'Anyway, it's a lovely notion but we've hit a snag.'

'What's that?'

'Earlier this year, we talked to Greg and Sophie about the project, and they seemed very interested. Unfortunately, that plan fell through, for obvious reasons. Greg will have enough going on in his life without taking on the camp.' Disappointment seemed to weight her shoulders.

'We'll figure something out,' Olivia said,

509

slipping her arm through her grandmother's. 'Don't worry.'

'You sound exactly like Charles. I think he's got something up his sleeve.'

They headed inside together and joined her father, who was with Granddad and Jenny Majesky. Philip had made the introductions in private the day before. Jenny looked lovely, but seemed a little lost. Her large, dark eyes devoured Nana and Granddad as well as all the undiscovered relatives on the dance floor and lining the buffet tables.

'I was just telling Jenny that we've known her grandparents even longer than we've been married,' Granddad said.

'That's true,' Nana said. 'I bought a sweet cheese kolache from Sky River Bakery on opening day—the Fourth of July, 1952.'

Jenny looked amazed. 'You remember that?'

Nana beamed. 'Helen's kolaches are quite unforgettable. I hope we can pay her a visit tomorrow.'

'Of course,' Jenny said, and Olivia realized she was on the verge of tears.

'Do you dance, Jenny?' Their father stepped in with an air of gallantry. He'd probably seen what Olivia had seen, that Jenny was getting overwhelmed. Olivia couldn't imagine what it must be like, discovering so many new connections, practically overnight.

'Not very well,' Jenny confessed.

'Me neither, but I would love to dance with my daughter.'

'I was going to help serve the cake,' Jenny said, hesitating.

'I'll take care of it,' Olivia said. 'Go and dance with Dad.'

Jenny put her hand in his and they came together awkwardly, laughing a little. Olivia stood and watched them, feeling a funny catch in her throat. This, she realized, was going to take some time—getting acquainted with the sister she'd never known. She saw her mother's parents, Gwen and Samuel, watching from their table.

'If looks could kill,' Dare said under her breath as she came to help with the cake.

'I'll go talk to them.' Olivia took two plates over to the Lightseys' table. 'Enjoying the party?' she asked brightly.

'Oh, indeed,' her grandfather said.

'Where's Mom?' Olivia looked around for her mother.

'Unfortunately, Pamela wasn't feeling well, so she went back to the hotel.'

The knot in Olivia's stomach tightened. 'I know it's awkward,' she said, 'but I hope you'll be happy for us. Jenny is wonderful.'

'She seems perfectly lovely,' Grandma Gwen agreed, pushing aside her slice of cake without tasting it. 'And we understand that none of this is her fault. Still, you have to

511

consider what this means to you, Olivia.'

Olivia caught the implication. As her sibling, Jenny would share in their father's affections—and in other aspects of his life, including his fortune. 'I'm fine with this,' she said firmly. 'Dad and I talked about it at length. She's as much his daughter as I am.'

Grandma Gwen sniffed. 'You must be certain to look out for your own interests, shouldn't she, Samuel?'

'Indeed,' he said again, which seemed to be his standard reply to everything since he'd grown hard of hearing.

Olivia escaped, not wanting to continue the conversation. She understood their loyalty to her mother, but now was not the time to discuss the matter. Suddenly she felt every bit of the heat and the crowd and all the champagne she'd drunk, and she stepped outside to get some air. It was quiet here. The sun was gone, and the deep purple night seemed to breathe mystery.

She was hoping—praying—that Connor had seen her head outside. They still hadn't had a minute together, and she felt lost without him. This was a first for Olivia; she wasn't used to this desire to share every aspect of herself with someone.

As she was pacing back and forth, pondering this new development, a car's lights washed across the parking lot, then stopped and went dark. A few moments later, a shadow stirred on the path from the parking area and she saw the outline of a tall, big-shouldered man. The orange spark of a cigarette end made an arc through the air, then disappeared as the man approached.

'Mr. Davis?' Olivia said. 'Please, come inside. My grandparents were hoping you'd stop in.'

Terry Davis was dressed in dark pants and a shirt that still bore creases of newness. 'I can't stay long,' he told her. 'I just stopped by to pay my respects.'

'You know they'd love to see you,' she assured him.

He shrugged, looked at the ground. He was a large man, tall and broad. Studying him, Olivia could see where Connor got his striking good looks, but in Terry, that deferential air diminished him, somehow. 'To tell you the truth, I really came here to have a word with you, Miss Bellamy. That is, if you don't mind.'

'I don't mind a bit, but please, call me Olivia.'

'Yes, ma'am. The fact is, ma'am, I'm working on step nine.'

'I don't understand.'

'Of my twelve-step program. It's the one about redressing people I've hurt in the past. There are a lot of them, you included.'

'Me?' Olivia couldn't fathom what he'd ever done to cause her harm. 'But I don't—'

He held up a hand. 'I need to try to make

amends if I can.'

'Oh. Um, so this is something I can help you with?'

'All you have to do is listen.'

She hesitated, then had a seat on the bottom stair of the main entrance. 'I can do that.'

He sat down beside her. 'It's about that night nine years ago. You know the night I mean.'

*   *   *

'Why didn't you tell me?' Olivia asked Connor. The evening had slipped away and it was nearly midnight by the time she found him.

Connor pushed away from the bar, where he'd been talking—with seeming civility—to Freddy. When Olivia saw Connor, she nearly forgot what she meant to say. It was really the first chance she'd had all night to get a good look at him and, for a few moments, it was impossible to stare and think at the same time.

'Tell you what?' he asked.

She flushed, feeling several pairs of eyes on them, and led him out to the relative privacy of the deck, now lit with twinkling lights. 'Your father found me earlier. He told me some things about that last night back when we were kids. Things you never bothered to explain.'

514

'Like what?' His posture turned defensive, stiff and unyielding.

'He said he drank too much that night.'

'My father drank too much every night.'

'But that night, he told me he chose to do it at Hilltop Tavern, and afterward, he ended up with his car in a ditch. He said you showed up just before the state patrol, and that you got behind the wheel and claimed you were the one driving, so your father wouldn't get a DUI charge.'

'Yeah. So?'

'So you never told me any of this, Connor.'

'It's not mine to tell. There's that pesky anonymity thing—'

'You let me think…' She was starting to sputter, all the old hurt flaring to life inside her.

'That it was all about you?'

Ouch. 'It was a simple enough explanation. You should have told me,' she said.

'Christ, do you think it was easy, talking about the fact that my father was a drunk? What would telling you accomplish?'

The memory of that night still had the power to burn. 'You were my first boyfriend. That night—what we were going to do—it meant everything to me. *Everything*. And then to have it turn into some kind of joke, and you disappear—'

'Lolly.' His voice was quiet, anguished. 'You were the one who walked away that night.'

Oh, God. He was right. She'd always blamed Connor but she'd made a choice that night, and she'd never bothered to find out what really happened. She'd spent nine years believing Connor had walked away from her that night, and now she had to face the fact that it simply hadn't happened that way. She had fled from the pool at the waterfall and never looked back. Now she realized that if she had, she would have seen Connor ignoring the jeering, drunk counselors, throwing on his clothes, going after her.

Finally, just moments ago, Terry Davis explained why Connor had never made it to her cabin that night. Someone tipped him off that his father was in trouble. What followed sounded like a nightmare—Connor insisting to the state patrol that he was the driver.

'Your father said you were sent to the county jail over in Kingston.'

'That's right.'

His face was unreadable, but she knew it concealed a world of pain. He'd been a scared kid, alone, trying to save his father from a DUI charge and jail time. She could picture him all too vividly, caught in the glare of the harsh lights, tossed in among the other Saturday-night guests, shouted at, 'roughed up,' as his father had put it.

'I wish you'd told me. Called me or—'

A very small smile flickered on his lips.

'Lolly. It didn't work like that. And then, trying to explain everything to you, well, it would have been harder on us both.'

She nodded, aching for the boy he'd been, the one who hid so much pain, even from her. She'd been afraid of his intensity and of the complexity of his life. And that, she realized, was the fundamental difference between her and Connor. Her childhood had not been ideal, but at least she'd *had* a childhood. When they were together at camp, it was too easy to forget how different their lives were. But the reality was that Connor had grown up fending for himself and watching over his own father, just as he'd done that night.

According to Terry, seeing his son sent to jail in his place was the bottom he needed to hit in order to make the decision to get sober, and he went into a ninety-day rehab program.

And Olivia, knowing none of this, went back in New York, moved into her college dorm and tried to pretend the whole summer had never happened.

'What could be harder than losing you without explanation?' she asked, remembering the agony she'd suffered.

'Losing you now,' he said simply, and finally his smile warmed. 'That would be harder.' He bent down and kissed her, briefly but firmly, on the mouth. 'The implication being that we're together now.'

Olivia felt dizzy from his kiss and wished

he'd do it again. She paused, letting the cool ripple of a breeze off the lake clear her head. 'I'm not going to contradict you.' She wanted him to throw her on the back of his motorcycle and ride off into the hills, never to return. She wanted their lives to fit together the way their hearts seemed to. 'I just want...' She paused. It was so hard to put into words. 'I want to know I'm not making a mistake this time. I've been wrong so many times, I don't trust myself anymore.'

He chuckled. 'I can't save you from making mistakes, Lolly. No one can, not even you. And why would you want that anyway?'

So simple, she thought. That was his gift, that clarity, whereas she tended to think things through to their most absurd degree. 'But—'

'Sometimes you just have to take a leap of faith.'

She couldn't believe he was smiling at her, as though he was enjoying this. 'We've built separate lives, Connor. I just don't see how this can work.'

'You move to Avalon and we build the house together. And you tell your grandparents you'll oversee the reopening of the camp.' He was almost infuriatingly matter-of-fact.

'You've been talking to Granddad and Greg.'

'At length,' he admitted.

Olivia bit her lip and gazed up at him. She pressed the palms of her hands against the impossibly fine fabric of his tuxedo jacket, feeling the solid warmth of him. Her heart leaped, but another part of her reared back. Connor was asking her the same thing Rand Whitney had asked her—to walk away from the life she'd built, the business she'd struggled with and nurtured.

'Their idea about the camp—I think they're having trouble letting go. It's a great idea, creating a retreat for families, but it's just...a dream,' she said.

He gestured out across the lake. 'This whole place started as a dream. I never told you this, but my dreams started here, too. The first time I came to this place, I was able to imagine some sort of life for myself that didn't completely suck. That was huge for me. I can't tell you how huge.'

She remembered that angry, blue-eyed boy, with the hip-hop clothes and duct tape on his sneakers, and she wished she could somehow reach back in time, put her arms around him and embrace him, tell him everything was going to be all right. She'd had that chance, though. Years ago. And she hadn't taken it.

'I'm so glad...' she began, then laughed a bit nervously. 'I don't know what I'm glad about. That we had this summer. That maybe we...'

'Maybe we what?' He slid his hands under hers and laced their fingers together. 'Listen, I can be flexible. If you don't like the idea of staying around here, we'll live where you want.'

Again, so simple. 'You'd move to the city for me?'

'Hell, I'd move to Tierra del Fuego for you if that's what you wanted.'

She looked at their hands, the palms pressed together, fingers entwined. She'd held on to him like this the last time they'd made love. 'I'm not sure what you want me to say,' she admitted.

'Then just listen. I love you, Lolly. I've loved you since we were kids, and that's never, ever changed, even though I never told you. Instead, I hurt you and let you go. I'm not doing that again, honey. Ever. We're grown-ups now. We know how to do this. You follow me?'

She felt dazed, her heart filling up with a cautious but undeniable joy. 'I'm sort of stuck on the part where you said you love me.'

'That's a good place to be stuck. I love you and I always will, every single day of my life. We're from two completely different worlds, and we live completely different lives, but there's this thing between us. It's always been there. Tell me I'm not imagining it, Lolly.'

Her throat felt thick with tears, and it hurt

to swallow. She refused to let herself cry, though. Refused to ruin this perfect, perfect moment with tears. 'I love you, too, Connor,' she whispered. The words came from a place inside her that welled up like a hidden spring. 'I always have, too, even when I was hating you.'

He smiled, touched her cheek. 'I know, honey. I know.'

As she tilted her head back to study his face, she felt the tears melt away, replaced by pure joy. He made her smile, and he made her feel safe. Could love really be that simple?

He let go of her briefly, checked his watch.

'Is something the matter?' she asked.

'I'm in a slight hurry here.' He grinned again, perhaps with a flash of nervousness. 'I need to do this before midnight.'

'Do what?'

'I just think it would be good luck to propose to you on your grandparents' fiftieth wedding anniversary.'

Her heart sped up. She panicked, yet at the same time she knew that this was exactly what she wanted. In a crazy way, it made sense. 'You're proposing to me?'

'I haven't done it yet. I'm still getting up my nerve.'

She laughed aloud with a joy that was no longer cautious, but boundless. 'Do it now,' she said. 'Ask me now.'

'Right this minute?'

'Right this minute,' she agreed, flinging her arms around his neck. 'Because I can't wait to say yes to you.'

Epilogue

THE AVALON TROUBADOUR
SEPTEMBER 2, 2006

Mr. Philip Bellamy of Manhattan and Ms. Pamela Lightsey Bellamy, also of Manhattan, announce the engagement of their daughter, Olivia Jane, to Connor Davis, son of Terence Davis of Avalon, New York. Ms. Bellamy graduated summa cum laude from Columbia University, and is relocating to Avalon following the wedding. Mr. Davis is the owner of Davis Contracting and Construction in Avalon, and this fall, will be building a new home on the river road. An August wedding is planned. The couple will take over the management of Camp Kioga, which is scheduled to reopen as a family resort next summer.

Afterword

Dear Reader,

There is something timeless and magical about summer camp. Set apart from the rush and care of everyday life, camp can take the heart places it doesn't ordinarily go. The quiet lapping of the lake at the shore, the flicker of birds through the trees, the night sky filled with stars—these are the images that inspired the creation of Camp Kioga on Willow Lake.

There are more stories to tell about the Bellamy family, their friends and rivals and the people who come unexpectedly—and uninvited—into their lives. Coming in February 2007, *The Winter Lodge* is a brand-new story filled with love and laughter, secrets and surprises. Please visit my Web site at www.susanwiggs.com to sign up for updates and to learn more about the Lakeshore Chronicles.

Happy reading,
Susan Wiggs
Rollingbay, Washington